AMERICA IS IN THE HEART

AMERICA IS IN THE HEART

A Personal History

CARLOS BULOSAN

With a new introduction by
Marilyn C. Alquizola and Lane Ryo Hirabayashi

UNIVERSITY OF WASHINGTON PRESS

Seattle & London

Originally published by Harcourt, Brace and Company, Inc., 1946
Introduction by Carey McWilliams © 1973 by the University of Washington Press
Introduction to the 2014 edition © 2014 by Marilyn C. Alquizola and
Lane Ryo Hirabayashi
Printed and bound in the United States of America
17 16 15   5 4 3 2

University of Washington Press
www.washington.edu/uwpress

Library of Congress Cataloging-in-Publication Data
Bulosan, Carlos.
   America is in the heart : a personal history / Carlos Bulosan ; with a new intro-
duction by Marilyn C. Alquizola and Lane Ryo Hirabayashi. — New 2014 edition.
      pages   cm. — (Classics of Asian American Literature)
   Includes bibliographical references.
ISBN 978-0-295-99353-9 (paperback)
1. Bulosan, Carlos.   2. Filipino Americans—Biography.   3. Filipino American
migrant agricultural laborers—Biography.   4. Philippines—Social life and customs.
I. Title.
PR9550.9.B8A8 2014
818'.5209—dc23
[B]

                                                                    2013044470

The paper used in this publication is acid-free and meets the minimum requirements of American National Standard for Information Sciences—Permanence of
Paper for Printed Library Materials, ANSI z39.48–1984.∞

TO GRACE FUNK

AND

JOHN WOODBURN

Because I would like to thank you for accepting
me into your world, I dedicate this book of my
life in the years past: let it be the testament of
one who longed to become a part of America.

INTRODUCTION

IT IS hard to be a Filipino in California," a countryman sadly warned Carlos Bulosan shortly after his arrival in Seattle from the Philippines. But Carlos, of course, had to find this out for himself. "I came to know afterwards," he wrote, "that in many ways it was a crime to be a Filipino in California" (p. 121). That says it about as succinctly and accurately as it can be said. *America Is in the Heart* is a deeply moving account of what it is like to be treated as a criminal in a strange and alien society—one to which the immigrant has been drawn precisely because of the attraction of its ideals. "I know deep down in my heart," he wrote, "that I am an exile in America . . . I feel like a criminal running away from a crime I did not commit. And this crime is that I am a Filipino in America."

One may doubt that Bulosan personally experienced each and every one of the manifold brutalities and indecencies so vividly described in this book, but it can fairly be said—making allowances for occasional minor histrionics—that some Filipino was indeed the victim of each of these or similar incidents. For this reason alone, *America Is in the Heart* is a social classic. It reflects the collective life experience of thousands of Filipino immigrants who were attracted to this country by its legendary promises of a better life or who were recruited for employment here. It is the first and best account in English of just what it was like to be a Filipino in California and its sister states in the period, say, from 1930 to 1941. But it is more than that. "Of the Filipino writers in English," writes E. San Juan, Jr. (*Carlos Bulosan and the Imagination of the Class Struggle*, 1972, p. 125), "who began their careers before World War II, Bulosan remains the most viable, startling and contemporary." Paradoxical as it may sound, one may well argue that it was the shock, the traumatic impact, of his experience as a Filipino immigrant that invested his writing with precisely these qualities.

A great deal has happened around the rim of the Pacific in the wake of World War II, the Korean War, and the war in Vietnam, that is, in the period immediately subsequent to publication of this book. Once thought to be a vanishing ethnic element, the number of Filipinos in this country has sharply increased and is likely to continue to increase in the immediate future. Some discriminations against Filipinos have been lifted and a few of the harsher folkways have been modified. At the same time, relations between the Philippines and the United States have radically changed. Against the background of what has happened since 1941, it is not surprising that a younger generation in the Philippines should see in Bulosan's writings a reflection, even a foreshadowing, of their own experience. The first third of the book gives a fine account of life in a peasant village in the Philippines; the remaining pages reflect the reaction of an imaginative and talented young Filipino, from one of these peasant villages, to life in the United States. If a new generation in the Philippines finds Bulosan illuminating so, too, should a new generation in this country. For what he had to say should serve to remind us of aspects of the American experience we are always in danger of forgetting. Excellent documentation is provided in these pages for the proposition that America is, and always has been, at any point in time, the sum of the tensions between its older and newer immigrants, whether they came from Europe or south of the border or across the Pacific. If it were not for this on-going experience, American ideals would long since have lost much of their relevance.

About the Pinoy

In 1920 there were only about 5,603 Filipinos in the United States. Most of these were students or "fountain pen boys," as they were called, some of whom had elected to stay in this country after a period of enlistment as "messboys" in the Navy. But with adoption of the Gentlemen's Agreement of 1907, and other developments, the Hawaiian sugar planters began to fear a shortage of field labor, a role then largely filled by Japanese immigrants. From 1907 to 1926 the number of Filipinos in the islands increased to around 100,000 and some of these, in small numbers, began to come to the West Coast states. The Immigration Act of 1924, which barred further Japanese immigration to Hawaii, stimulated the recruitment of more Filipinos. Between 1925 and 1929, an additional 45,000 (approximately) came to Hawaii. The exclusion of Japanese—and the threatened exclusion of Mexican labor —through immigration restrictions, gave an impetus to the employment of Filipinos on the mainland. In all, between 1907 and 1926 about 150,000 Filipinos had left the Philippines, and of these, 52,810 were to be found in Hawaii, some 45,263 in the states.

A majority of the Filipinos who came to the mainland eventually landed in California. They were mostly young unmarried males with limited education and few skills. Most of them did not come to this country as immigrants, that is, to become citizens and permanent residents. Most of them thought they would reside here for a limited period and then return to the Philippines and so made little effort to assimilate in the conventional sense. Their education had been limited and badly mangled. Fifty years after English had in theory (i.e., officially) supplanted Spanish as the language of instruction in the Philippines, the natives still spoke some forty languages divided into eighty-seven dialects and were still largely illiterate. Culturally the petty bourgeoisie villagers of the Philippines had been reared and suckled by "Mother Spain and unfortunately castrated by the United States" (see San Juan, p. 121). Most of the Filipinos on the West Coast came from villages not unlike the one so vividly described in this volume.

Regarded as immigrants, Filipinos—the third Oriental invasion —were even less prepared to cope with the hurly-burly of American life than immigrants of the same period who crossed the Atlantic. The West Coast was still frontier terrain and the xenophobia that afflicts all "outposts of empire" was widely prevalent. The older white residents felt that they were "holding a line" against possible tidal waves of Asiatics who were neither white-skinned nor Christian. Anti-Oriental agitation had a long history in the region before local residents began to be agitated about Filipinos. The Chinese had been welcomed with open arms initially, but after the completion of the Central Pacific—the western section was largely built by Chinese immigrants—sentiment turned sharply and savagely against them. Long before the Southern states began to experiment with Jim Crow legislation after the collapse of Reconstruction, the Californians had enacted a series of ingenious legislative measures to curb, restrict, harass, and humiliate Chinese residents. Baiting the Chinese became, of course, a favorite political pastime, particularly for politicians who catered to the white labor vote. And behind the Chinese came the Japanese who, caught in the same Oriental stereotype, quickly became victims of a similar agitation which continued even after the Gentlemen's Agreement, the enactment of Alien Land Acts aimed at the Japanese, and the exclusionary Immigration Act of 1924.

Naturally, Filipinos were victimized by the same anti-Oriental stereotype, but with added difficulties. Filipinos had no governmental authority willing to speak for them as Imperial Japan had been prepared to speak for the resident Japanese. Their status was ambiguous. They were "wards" or "nationals" who could not be deported because they had not entered as immigrants, nor could they be excluded. Yet they were not eligible for citizenship. But when they traveled abroad, they used United States passports. In brief, they were neither fish nor fowl. The Chinese and Japanese were notably thrifty, law abiding, and hard working. Both exhibited strong family and community ties and settled their own problems. The age and sex imbalance of Filipinos, by contrast, precipitated them into sharp conflicts with the dominant white majority when they attempted to date white girls or gambled or fought among themselves (see H. Brett Melendy, *Racism in California,* 1972, p. 141). And let it be admitted that these young men, without social contacts or family ties, often liked to gamble, drink, and "chase around" and had a talent, which the young of all races share, for getting into trouble. However, so-called Filipino taxi-dance halls, gambling spots, and bordellos acquired a notoriety which they really did not deserve in the sense that many of them were not operated by Filipinos.

Bulosan was aware of all this and gives a vivid account of the ways Filipinos were exploited because of their special social status. They were exploited by the older and better-established Chinese and Japanese communities, but their worst exploiters, perhaps, were Filipino labor contractors, whom the growers used to recruit, transport, train, house, and feed Filipino field workers. The contractors—in the field and in the fish canneries—overcharged, underpaid, and in other ways ingeniously exploited Filipino imigrants. At four o'clock in the morning, I have seen Filipino field workers wearing lighted miners' caps and bending low in the fields, moving up the rows to cut asparagus that had to be transported to San Francisco and other markets before noon. The labor contractors often brought high-priced prostitutes to labor camps in the asparagus fields near Stockton in auto trailers.

And it was not only Filipino labor contractors who exploited Filipinos with loaded dice, rigged cock fights, phoney raffles, tickets for "sweetheart" contests, and other artful devices. At the height of the harvest season, Filipino field workers poured a huge weekly payroll into Stockton—the "Fat City" of the movie—only to be fleeced of most of it by the complex of interests that controlled "skid row"—Chinese, Japanese, Filipinos, and others. I have visited dance halls in Stockton in which a Filipino buying dime-a-dance tickets could spend the equivalent of a night at the Mark Hopkins Hotel in San Francisco in the course of an evening, so rapidly did the big, red, overhead rotating lights signal the end of a dance. Estimates have been made that as much as two million dollars a year was skimmed off the earnings of Filipinos and other field workers in Stockton in the way of services, gambling, prostitution, and the like.

For a variety of reasons it was my good fortune to know many Filipinos in California. My first contact with them, as a group, came in the late twenties and early thirties, when, as part of a group then engaged in a quixotic attempt to repeal the state's criminal syndicalism law, I had occasion to speak at a number of Filipino meetings up and down the state. The Pinoy could not vote but they listened well and applauded vociferously. In this way I got to know some of their leaders and, in later years, was occasionally asked to speak at Filipino banquets which usually involved presentation of awards to the winners in "sweetheart contests"! Then too I became interested in migratory farm labor —an interest which led to the publication of *Factories in the Field* in the spring of 1939. Research on the book brought me in touch with various minorities that had participated in the farm labor saga and a variety of labor leaders, mostly of a left-wing orientation, who had tried at one time or another to organize farm workers. From 1938 to 1942 I served as chief of the Division of Immigration and Housing in California, during the administration of Governor Culbert L. Olson, and thus had occasion to investigate farm labor camps and to work with various minority groups including Filipinos. During this period, I inspected hundreds of farm labor camps including many Filipino camps near Stockton, Nipomo, Pismo Beach, the beautiful little "oriental" town of Guadalupe, Salinas, Santa Maria, Watsonville, and other areas. It was in these days that I came to know a fair sample of Filipinos, including 'Carlos Bulosan. These friends were, in a manner of speaking, my tutors on many aspects of the experience of Filipino immigrants.

Regarded as immigrants, although not many regarded themselves in this light, the Pinoy were innocent, credulous, and wide-eyed. Numerically they were not a threat nor did they present an economic threat real or imagined; they lacked the business sense of the Chinese and the agricultural and other skills of the Japanese. They were without resources, family ties, or a fixed abode. As immigrants they encountered a previously erected wall of discrimination: they were barred from hotels, cafes, swimming pools, many pool halls, barber shops, apartments, and other facilities. The result was that they had to "gang up" and often live ten or twelve to an apartment. Their mode of living naturlly fostered the appearance if not the reality of clannishness; they seemed to move in packs or gangs. As I wrote in *Brothers under the Skin,* "To be a Filipino in California is to belong to blood brotherhood, a freemasonry of the ostracized." The mobility which was forced upon them made it impossible for all but a few to put down roots or to establish firm community ties. Consider, for example, the place names, just in California alone, that figure in this book: Marysville, Stockton, Niles, San Jose, San Luis Obispo, Los Angeles, Lompoc, Santa Maria, Delano, San Diego, Calipatria, Brawley, El Centro, Holtville, Bakersfield, Calexico, Fresno, Pismo Beach, Nipomo, Guadalupe, Arroyo Grande, Goleta, Solvang, Santa Barbara, Walnut Grove, Oxnard, Monterey, Salinas, Las Cruces, San Fernando, Oakland. Just to list these names is to suggest the mobility of Filipinos, always on the move, never staying long in one place. It baffles belief that the dominant white majority could have regarded the Pinoy as a threat or menace of any kind but it did.

In part the innocence of the immigrants was part of their problem. They came here with high expectations. As wards, as almost citizens, they thought they would be received if not with open arms then in a friendly way, the more so since they had not come to stay or to acquire permanent residence. It was their eager initial reaching out for acceptance that seemed to stimulate the reaction against them. They took too much for granted; they assumed that as wards or nationals they had rights which were denied to other immigrants. Bulosan states the dilemma Filipinos faced as well as it has ever been stated (quoted by Melendy, p. 141):

> Western people are brought up to regard Orientals or colored peoples as inferior, but the mockery of it all is that Filipinos are taught to regard Americans as our equals. Adhering to American ideals, living American lives, these are contributory to our feeling of equality. The terrible truth in America shatters the Filipinos' dream of fraternity. I was completely disillusioned when I came to know this American attitude. If I had not been born in a lyrical world, grown up with honest people and studied about American institutions and racial equality in the Philippines I should never have minded so much the horrible impact of white chauvinism.

A disillusionment of this depth can breed antisocial attitudes. "Do you know what a Filipino feels in America?" asked Bulosan (quoted by San Juan p. 114). "I mean one who is aware of the intricate forces of chaos? He is the loneliest thing on earth. There is much to be appreciated all about him, beauty, wealth, power, grandeur. But is he a part of these luxuries? He looks, poor man, through the fingers of his eyes. He is enchained, damnably to his race, his heritage. He is betrayed."

So it is not surprising that the initial encounter between Filipinos and mainland residents was brief (1924-34) and seemed to end in disaster. The depression merely accelerated the agitation, which had begun in Yakima, Washington, on September 19, 1928, to "kick the Filipinos out." The drive got under way in Exeter, California, on October 24, 1929, and soon spread to other communities. Filipinos were then largely defenseless; they lacked defense organizations or any solid basis of opposition. The pogrom-like movement culminated in the passage on March 24, 1934, of the Tydings-McDuffie Act (ratified by the Philippine legislature on May 1, 1935), which, for all practical purposes, barred further immigration (it established a quota of fifty a year). In the wake of this legislation—the so-called Philippine Island Independence Act —President Roosevelt signed the "Repatriation Act" under the terms of which Filipinos were offered free transportation back to their homeland; the act, however, did not apply to those in Hawaii. But Filipinos who took avantage of the offer could not again re-enter, so, in effect, the Repatriation Act was a deportation act, or was intended as such. The same intention was expressed in amendments to maritime legislation requiring that 90 percent of the crews of American merchant vessels had to be citizens; the effect, of course, was to force many Filipinos out of work. Even so, not many Filipinos took advantage of the Repatriation Act; on the contrary, angered by the move to drive them out of the country, they began to organize and stage a resistance. By the end of the 1930s, however, it did seem as though the brief Filipino chapter in the immigration saga had been concluded.

But then came World War II and a new chapter began. At first the disillusionment among Filipinos was such that they were not eager to support the war effort. But a speech by Carlos Romulo in Salinas, in which he urged them to help drive Japanese "imperialist" from the Philippines, was one of several factors that brought about a change in attitude. The First and Second Filipino Regiments were formed, trained in Lompoc, and later played a role in the liberation of the Philippines. When the First Regiment paraded up Broadway in Los Angeles on November 15, 1943, Carlos and his friend, Stanley B. Garibay, were observers. Garibay tells me that as he was taking a snapshot of the parade, he noticed that Carlos was crying. Pride or pity? or both? For a time, this country was quite Philippine-conscious; the word "Bataan" enjoyed a splendid resonance. And when the Independence of the Philippines was proclaimed on July 4, 1946, it seemed to many Filipinos, and to the rest of us, that a new day had dawned. Most Americans seemed to be touched by the loyalty of the Filipinos who, in turn, seemed to be grateful to us for helping them compel the Japanese to withdraw. During the war years some of the discriminatory bars were lifted or modified and resident Filipinos were able to get better paying jobs in shipyards and other defense facilities. Those who served in the armed services were also eligible for citizenship.

In the postwar period, the Philippines were given a quota and subsequent enactments made it possible for more Filipinos to enter as immigrants. Those who enter legally may now become citizens. The Census of 1970 indicated that some 343,060 Filipinos were residing in the United States, most of them in California, Oregon, and Washington. This new "wave" of immigration has been made up of better educated, more highly skilled Filipinos, including many women so that the sexes are now more nearly in balance. Under the new immigration laws, the Philippines and Italy have replaced Canada and Great Britain at the top of the list. So now there is no reason to believe that the resident Filipino population is "vanishing"; on the contrary, it is growing and will continue to increase. In 1970, Filipinos made up 12 percent of the scientists and engineers and 24 percent of the physicians entering this country as immigrants. In 1972 alone 782 physicians from the Philippines were listed as immigrants. (See *Scientist, Engineers, and Physicians from Abroad,* National Science Foundation, June, 1972.) Many of those entering as nurses and physicians show little interest in returning to the Philippines. So much, then, for the background of Filipino immigration.

Remembering Carlos

Carlos Bulosan was born on November 24, 1913, in Binalonan, Pangasinan, in Luzon, in the central Philippines, the son of a small farmer. His boyhood, the village in which he lived, and the tribulations of his family are vividly described in this book. In the familiar pattern of the Pinoy, he managed to accumulate enough money to buy steerage passage to Seattle, where he arrived on July 22, 1930, at the age of seventeen. He had completed only three years of schooling and spoke little if any English. He never returned to the Philippines, and he never became a U.S. citizen.

In Seattle, Carlos was told, and correctly, by one of his countrymen that for Filipinos "all roads go to California and all travelers wind up in Los Angeles." Shortly after his arrival there, he and my friend Chris Mensalvas, and other Filipinos, were caught up in the effort, stimulated by left-wing political groups, to organize independent unions. The campaign, if you could call it that, was a reaction against the consequences of the depression—wage cuts, unemployment, vile working conditions—but more immediately a protest against the drive to exclude Filipinos which was in full swing from 1930 to 1934. This independent organizing effort, 1934 to 1938, culminated in the formtion of a new international union (CIO) known as UCAPAWA—United Cannery and Packing House Workers of America—which had been spearheaded by the organization of fish cannery workers in Seattle and packing house workers in Salinas, California. The present-day Local 37, affiliated with the International Longshoremen and Warehousemen's Union, based in Seattle, is the outcome of these efforts.

For a time Carlos lived in Los Angeles with Chris. Fortunately each had an older brother and the two brothers managed to get enough work to keep the four of them alive. Carlos was not well and Chris had lost part of a leg trying to catch a freight train out of Bakersfield, an accident described in this book. Chris, with his wooden leg, and Carlos, with his limp, were able to get a little work now and then, mostly as dishwashers. For long periods, Chris tells me, they lived on pig head (fifteen cents) and free mackerel from San Pedro, along with seven-cent coffee and doughnuts. In 1936, Carlos was taken to the Los Angeles County Hospital where he underwent three operations for a lesion in his right lung. In all he spent two years in the hospital, most of the time in the convalescent ward. When he finally emerged, on June 7, 1938, his doctor said to him: "You have no more ribs on your right side, young man. But you will live for a while. *Mabuhay!*"

In a way, this long confinement in the hospital was a boon to Carlos. So far as I know he had never written anything until he arrived in this country; his first story was sold while he was working in a fish cannery in San Pedro. "Writing is a pleasure and a passion to me," he once wrote (quoted by San Juan, p. 6). "I seem to be babbling with multitudinous ideas, but my body is weak and tired." But once he started to write he kept at it. He was an omnivorous reader. During his stay in the hospital, he read a book a day "including Sundays." When he was not in the hospital, he spent long hours at the Los Angeles Public Library, particularly during periods when he was not well enough to work or was unable to find a job. "I am trying to write every day in the midst of utter misery and starvation," he wrote in 1949 (quoted by San Juan, p. 61.) "I locked myself in the room, plugged the phone, pulled down the shades and shut out the whole damned world. I knew enough of it to carry me for a lifetime of writing"—and indeed he did. Most of his writing seems to have been crowded into the 1936-46 decade.

In 1944, Bulosan published a story, "The End of the War," in the *New Yorker*. Publication of this story prompted a charge of plagiarism by Guido D'Agostino, author of a story entitled "The Dream of Angelo Zara." Mr. San Juan refers to a letter he received from the editor of the *New Yorker*, dated August 27, 1970, in which he dismisses the charge as being without merit and vindicates Bulosan's originality (San Juan, p. 56). Recently legal counsel for the *New Yorker* gave me the following information. The D'Agostino manuscript appeared originally in *Story* magazine and was included in *The Best American Short Stories of 1945*, edited by Martha Foley. Shortly before the plagiarism suit came on for trial it was settled for a nominal sum and the *New Yorker* never assigned copyright on the story. Whatever the merits of the controversy may have been, the claim of plagiarism and the publicity it aroused were damaging and were acutely embarrassing to Carlos, a most sensitive person.

The emergence of the Asian writer in America, as William Saroyan reminded me recently, is an immensely interesting story which demands thorough investigation. Once the story is finally put together, if it ever is, Carlos will occupy an important niche. There had been journalists—Manuel Buaken for one—reporters, and editors of numerous Filipino publications, and poets galore, but Bulosan was one of the first Filipino writers of any consequence to write in English in this country. "It was only when I began to write about the life and people I have known," he once explained, "that a certain measure of confidence began to form as my periscope for future writing." As I see it, it was his traumatic experience in this country, notaby his California experience—so sharply in contrast with that peasant village in the Philippines—with the fear, terror, stimulation, exaltation, and excitement it engendered, and the discovery that he could write in English, that provided the motive-force for his writing. "It did not make me conceited," he wrote, "that out of the slums and kitchens of California, out of the fear and hatred, the terror and hunger, the utter loneliness and death, I came out alive spiritually and intellectually! Instead it made me humble and serious in my relations with my fellow men . . ." (quoted by San Juan, p. 48).

What was Carlos like? I'll let my friend, John Fante, the novelist and screen writer, give his impressions:

> A tiny person with a limp, with an exquisite face, almost facially beautiful, with gleaming teeth and lovely brown eyes, shy, generous, terribly poor, terribly exiled in California, adoring Caucasian women, sartorially exquisite, always laughing through a face that masked tragedy, a Filipino patriot, a touch of the melodramatic about him, given to telling wildly improbable stories about himself, disappearing from Southern California for months at a time, probably to work in a Seattle or Alaska cannery, showing up finally at my home with some touching gift, a book of poems, a box of Filipino candy. . . . If I were a good Christian I think I might label him a saint, for he radiated kindness and gentleness.

Professor Dolores S. Feria conveys much the same impression: "An astounding child-man of acute artistic sensibilities thrust full-blown into a world of the cruelly insensitive." Hypersensitive, gentle, wildly imaginative, he had the bright eyes, ready smile, and innocent laughter of a precocious child. Incidentally, those "Caucasian women" were always as interested in him as he undoubtedly was in them. Most of them were large enough to have held him in their laps with ease but they adored him as much as he adored them.

Perhaps because he had suffered so much, Carlos could not endure the thought of suffering in others. But he resolutely refused to succumb to self-pity; he tried, he said, to choke "the sudden tears of regret." "I have," he wrote, "a tremendous passion to make others happy. So daily I have to fortify my heart against assaults, abuses, inconsiderations of people around me, close to me, dear to me." He tried to understand and interpret chaos and cruelty "from a collective point of view, because it was pervasive and universal." It was, he insisted, this "narrowing of our life into an island, into a filthy segment of American society, that had driven Filipinos . . . inward, hating everyone and despising all positive urgencies toward freedom." He loved all living things and was determined to maintain a generous view of the species. No doubt his immigrant experience helped him to see what it is that shapes and distorts class and social relationships but he was by nature gentle, loving, as Fante says, something of a poet-saint. "I knew, even then," he writes in this book (p. 184) of his early life here, "that it was not natural for a man to hate himself, or to be afraid of himself. It was not natural, indeed, to run from goodness and beauty, which I had done so many times. It was not natural for him to be cruel and without compassion."

Stanley P. Garibay, who knew Carlos well (he used to edit a journal of Filipino poetry), once wrote that he and Carlos had "many laughters together" but that when Carlos had a little to drink "his poetical self babbles." Indeed it did. He was never robust and, during the years I knew him, he was never really well. He would get a bit tight on a glass of wine or a highball, but he dearly loved a good time and liked to drink.

John Fante and I, and some of our friends, saw a lot of Carlos. He came often to our homes and we visited Filipino night clubs, bars, and restaurants with him. Once Carlos threw a party for Fante in a night club near Temple and Figueroa streets in Los Angeles, on the edge of Bunker Hill, a place much frequented by Filipinos. I was invited. On this memorable evening, at the height of the festivities, Carlos presented John with a gift: a glossy white rat. Fante, like Carlos a lover of all living things including snakes, was instantly enchanted with the rat. But his wife Joyce, while amazingly tolerant of highly sexed, ferocious dogs, cats, lascivious king snakes, and other strange pets, drew the line at the thought of a rat in the house and stalked out of the place in high dudgeon. I drove her home and, en route, managed as tactfully as possible to get in a few kind words for John and the white rat. Later, much

later, when John returned, the rat promptly escaped into the
stuffing of a divan and it was a day or more before the Fantes
could extricate him. In the end, of course, Joyce prevailed: the
white rat went and John was left desolate, briefly. (I am grateful
to Bill Saroyan for reminding me that Fante was the first or at
least one of the first to write earnestly and decently about the Filipinos, as in his story "Helen, Thy Beauty." Saroyan himself once
wrote a story "The Filipino and the Drunkard" which was anthol-
ogized and even made into a movie in Moscow.)

In the early 1940s, the war years, I saw Carlos often; in fact he
was, in those years, part of a circle of friends with whom we
usually observed Christmas, New Year's Eve, and other ceremo-
nial occasions. My diary notes indicate that Carlos went with us
to a New Year's party at the Fantes in 1950, along with other
friends, and spent Christmas that year with the same group, again
at the Fantes. This was, I think, the last time I saw him before I
left Los Angeles in the spring of 1951 to join the staff of the *Nation*
in New York. In 1952 Chris Mensalvas, who was president of
UCAPAWA from 1949 to 1959, arranged to have Carlos come to
Seattle to edit the union's *Yearbook*. From then until his death on
September 13, 1956, he lived with the Mensalvas family.

The Underview

One of the best ways to view and understand a society is to see
it from the bottom looking up. To be sure, the underview is in-
complete. Bottom dogs see, know, and learn a lot but their
perspective is limited. But they see more, I have come to believe,
than those who occupy the middle and upper reaches; their view
is less inhibited, less circumscribed. The view from down under
exposes the deceits, self-deceptions, distortions, apostasies; it is
likely to be bitterly realistic. It offers a good, if limited, guide to
what the society is really like, not what it professes to be. The traditional values sound fine but what happens to them when put to
the test? A good test is the extent to which the society is willing to
extend to outsiders, lesser breeds, strangers, the same rights and
protections it extends to those who inhabit the upper zones. In

this sense, the view of a sensitive, idealistic, imaginative Filipino
provides an excellent corrective to the view that leading West
Coast institutions projected in the period, say, from 1930 to 1941.
For the Filipino was the bottom dog; he occupied the lowest rung
on the ladder. Within its limitations, his view was accurate. Although the scene has changed for the better and hopefully it will
continue to change, this book will stand as a graphic, historical
reminder of what it was like to be a Filipino in California in the
years it embraces.

It is my conviction that there are always two nations in every
nation: the dominant on-going nation, enchanted with its self-
proclaimed virtues, values, and glorious traditions, and another
nation that exists on sufferance, half-buried, seldom surfacing,
struggling to survive. Disraeli projected such a vision. Daniel
Corkery wrote perceptively of "The Hidden Ireland" and Michael
Harrington has written with honesty and insight of "The Other
America." Oddly enough the enduring historical values of the
nation—the values it celebrates but does not always observe—are
kept alive by this half-suppressed, half-buried sector. Again and
again, despised, outcast groups in this country, by struggling for
"equal enforcement of the law," "due process," and "equal opportunity," have kept such values alive. Many of these struggles have
been forgotten even by groups whose parents and grandparents
were involved in them.

A case in point—one of many—is that of the Irish in Boston. The
stereotype of the Irish that prevailed in the years immediately following the first waves of immigration was indistinguishable from
the stereotype of the Negro or, for that matter, of the Okies and
Arkies when these predominantly Anglo-Saxon–White–Protestant
groups first surged into California and thereby set in motion the
always latent prejudice against the stranger, the outsider, the possible competitor. Abundant documentation can be cited for the
proposition that the struggle of Blacks, in recent years, for full citizenship, has enlarged and provided new procedural and other
safeguards for the rights of all Americans. The struggles of Okies
and Arkies for "a place in the sun" was brief—they proved to be a
godsend once we had entered World War II—but significant all
the same. Several key court decisions upheld their right to enter

the "sovereign" state of California, and to acquire legal residence, and they even won the right to vote while living in labor camps.

When Filipinos first entered California, the law prohibited marriages between white persons and Negroes, Mongolians, or mulattoes; and local officials had no difficulty in ruling that Filipinos were Mongolians. So marriage licenses were refused until it was ruled in *Roldan* vs. *Los Angeles County* in 1931 that a Filipino was not a Mongolian. This did not faze the legislators: the statute was promptly amended by adding the phrase "or member of the Malay race" but the struggle continued; today these statutes have been repealed or set aside. In brief, the struggles and pressures from down under have kept this country a bit more true to its ideals than it would have been without them.

In this context, the Filipinos were, and are, a special case. Mark Twain was right (see "To the Person Sitting in Darkness," which first appeared in *North American Review,* 1901). The Philippines were our first real temptation—the temptation, that is, to play the role of the imperialist power asserting dominance over a place and a people far removed from these shores. The Teller Amendment ruled out annexation of Cuba; the Puerto Ricans regarded us as liberators; and special circumstances were presented in the case of Hawaii. But Admiral Dewey had permitted Aguinaldo to proclaim a republic before United States forces landed in the Philippines and it took us three years and cost as much in life and effort as the whole war with Spain to suppress this rebellion, which was never completely extinguished. The Tydings-McDuffie Act of 1934 did not invest the Philippines with real independence nor did the proclamation of 1946. From colonialism we shifted to neocolonialsm and the economic exploitation of the Philippines continued. In these circumstances, the experience of Filipinos in this country has come to have a considerable psychological and political impact in the islands. Slight wonder, then, that there is an active and growing interest in Bulosan's writings in the Philippines.

Today the American investment is larger than ever. Thousands of Americans live and work in the Philippines. Our military bases there have acquired a new significance in the wake of the disastrous war in Vietnam. Thousands of Filipinos, male and female,

have come to the United States in recent years and many more
would come if they could. The fact is that we have made such a
mess of the economy of the Philippines that only about 40 percent
of Filipino college and university graduates can find useful employment there. On August 8, 1972, the *Los Angeles Times* reported from Manila that each week some two thousand Filipinos
apply at the United States Embassy for tourist visas. Applicants
are supposed to offer proof that they will return but the authori-
ties have learned that they will often violate a pledge to return if
once given a visa. The embassy has, in fact, become the "biggest
overseas American visa-issue mill in the world." Under present
United States immigration laws, which became operative in 1968,
Filipinos can emigrate in greater numbers than before and about
twenty thousand are admitted into this country each year. Even
so there are one hundred sixty-eight thousand Filipino names on
the waiting list. Canada and other Western nations are getting
some of this immigration but "because of historic ties," the United
States remains first preference for most immigrants.

The fact that a new phase in what Mark Twain called "the Philippine temptation" has now begun invests this book with new
meaning and relevance. As Twain pointed out in his superb sat-
ire, referring to "the Business of Extending the Blessings of Civilization to Our Brother Who Sits in Darkness," the time was
bound to come when this brother would say: "There is something
curious about this—curious and unacceptable. There must be two
Americas: one that sets the captive free, and the one that takes a
once-captive's new freedom away from him and picks a quarrel
with him with nothing to found it on, then kills him to get his
land." It was curious and unacceptable then, if more brutal and
obvious. It is less curious now but no less unacceptable. Hopefully we may yet summon the resources to reject "the Philippine
temptation" in its current form and, with the aid of the Filipinos
in the islands and here, discover that America really is in the
heart. For all its somewhat overblown rhetoric, what Bulosan
wrote has enduring significance:

> America is not a land of one race or one class of men. We are all
> Americans that have toiled and suffered and known oppression

and defeat, from the first Indian that offered peace in Manhattan to the last Filipino peapickers. America is not bound by geographical latitudes. America is not merely a land or an institution. America is in the hearts of men that died for freedom; it is also in the eyes of men that are building a new world. America is a prophecy of a new society of men: of a system that knows no sorrow or strife or suffering. America is a warning to those who would try to falsify the ideals of free men.

America is also the nameless foreigner, the homeless refugee, the hungry boy begging for a job and the black body dangling from a tree. America is the illiterate immigrant who is ashamed that the world of books and intellectual opportunities is closed to him. We are all that nameless foreigner, that homeless refugee, that hungry boy, that illiterate immigrant and that lynched black body. All of us, from the first Adams to the last Filipino, native born or alien, educated or illiterate—*We are America!*

CAREY McWILLIAMS

New York
February 20, 1973

INTRODUCTION
TO THE 2014 EDITION
Marilyn C. Alquizola and Lane Ryo Hirabayashi

O N OCTOBER 2, 2013, Governor Jerry Brown signed Assembly
Bill 123, a bill that will require public school instruction featuring Filipino Americans' contributions to the farm labor movement in California. Assembly member Rob Bonta, who sponsored
the bill, explained:

> The goal of AB 123 is to supplement California's rich farm worker history
> with the contributions of the Filipino American community. The Filipino
> American population composes the largest Asian population in California and
> it continues to grow, yet the story of Filipinos and their official efforts in the
> farm labor movement is an untold part of California history.[1]

Sadly, as is thoroughly documented in publications such as the
Southern Poverty Law Center's *Close to Slavery: Guestworker Programs in the United States* (2013), the plight of farm laborers—not
from the Philippines, for the most part, but now mainly men, wom-
en, and children from Mexico and Central American countries—is
as horrific and unsettling in the new millennium as ever. Perhaps
public awareness of today's exploitation of field-workers will be
heightened by AB 123, as well as by the continuing circulation of
Filipino American author Carlos Bulosan's masterpiece of labor
history, *America Is in the Heart*.

Since its original publication in 1943, *America Is in the Heart* has
appealed to a wide variety of audiences that continue to have dif-
fering interpretations of the book's conclusion. The responses of a
1940s postwar readership reflected a relative innocence bordering
on naiveté with regard to American foreign policies. The paranoia
of the subsequent McCarthy era may have generated receptions
that were less open to Bulosan's socialist underpinnings. With its
republication in 1973 by the University of Washington Press in the
midst of anti–Vietnam War protests and progressive student movements, Bulosan's work was taught in many ethnic studies and other

politically progressive classes that utilized *America Is in the Heart* as a vehicle to reveal social injustices. From the 1970s onward, the classroom use of the book in college courses was diverse, running the gamut from literature to sociology to history to psychology.

America Is in the Heart stands apart from the body of American literature in its form as well as in its content. In its noncompliance with traditional novelistic form, *America*, which was written about Filipino immigrant experiences of the 1930s, defies inclusion in the traditional Anglo-American canon. With Bulosan's disregard—perhaps tacit defiance—of novelistic conventions, *America* stands as a de facto redefinition of aesthetic principles. Moreover, the protagonist's geographic and emotional journey forces readers to redefine the spatial parameters of the United States, a place in which geography is written on the historical map of imperialism and etched into the hearts of immigrants of color who sought a life framed by falsely sold ideals.

In its accessibility and the seeming simplicity of its narrative style, *America* can be read as an expression of hope and belief in the United States' ideals, in spite of the terrible struggles that had to be endured by the protagonist and his compatriots. To gain an appreciation of the narrative's actual complexity, we suggest that readers adapt a simple reading strategy: be aware of the different voices or vantage points that Bulosan has woven into the book's narrative. Two distinct narrative voices should be readily apparent to the mindful reader. One is that of an analytical Carlos Bulosan, who has grown wise and politically savvy with hard experience, while the younger voice, Allos (presumably a nickname for Carlos), is bewildered, naive, and prone to questioning the reason for the hardships that befall him and his fellows.[2] With this heuristic device in mind, we will summarize the four parts that make up *America* and then revisit and reassess in a global context what Allos might have meant by America's "final fulfillment."

Part 1 of *America* delineates the effect of the Spanish-American War of the late 1890s, when in the aftermath of the defeat of the Filipino independence movement, the United States was able to consolidate its colonial rule in the Philippines. The narrative presents a macro-level analysis of the dislocation—at once economic, political, and cultural—that the United States' imperialist design wreaked on the peasantry in the northern provinces of Luzon, the region in which Bulosan was born and raised. If Bulosan, as the author, recounts this bloody, tragic upheaval as would a historian, Allos, his alter ego, endures it, and suffers at a very immediate and personal level the poverty, alienation, and exploitation that a land-poor peasant family might well have suffered at the turn of the century in the rural hinterlands of Pangasinan.

The narrator establishes even from the beginning that the Philippines has had a history of interlinking economic and political dependency on the United States. Bulosan the narrator expresses a characteristic Filipino gratitude toward Americans that is rooted in the history of US occupation and false benevolence, and he disparages the outgoing oppression of the former Spanish regime. Although Filipinos like Bulosan may have held a favorable attitude toward the educational opportunities that US annexation afforded some individuals, the negative effects of this connection very shortly come to surface, as Allos's traditional family unit is disrupted, both physically (in a geographical sense) and psychologically.

Allos, filled with hopes and aspirations, spurred in part by his elder brother's emigration to the United States, and seeing no future in the Philippines, resolves to leave his family and home in search of opportunity. Thus does the misleading optimism of false promises prevent the prescience of harder times that would follow in the new land; the naive protagonist is momentarily seen to occupy what has been characterized as the ambiguous space of the colonial subject.[3]

Part 2 begins with Allos's journey by ship and arrival in Seattle, followed by all the new and bewildering experiences that so many Asian immigrants from agricultural backgrounds in China, Japan, Korea, the Philippines, and South Asia endured before the war. The varied and sometimes violent events experienced by Bulosan's generation of Pinoys densely comprise this section of *America*, especially in terms of the intensity of racist viciousness meted upon Filipinos.

Note here that Allos, as the foil to the wiser Bulosan, is also a composite figure who embodies all of the hurt from the cruel experiences and fractured lives of his compatriots, Filipino and non-Filipino alike, male and female. He is a composite because Bulosan writes of him as enduring the experiences that befell the members of Bulosan's working-class community. Keeping in mind that fictive does not mean untruthful, one can allow that Allos's narrative is fictive, not because the experiences recounted were invented but because the narrative sequence is constructed rather than drawn from a strict historical chronology of any single Filipino American life. Thus although *America* principally represents the tenor of the times, it does so in a personalized fashion, since Allos, as the central character, bears the brunt of collective sufferings, both in the Philippines and abroad. With this literary convention in mind, even if Bulosan's work is regarded as something other than strictly autobiographical, it is imperative that it be read as a personal history as well. The process of eliciting emotional identification, peculiar to the arts as a genre, enables Bulosan to vivify the experiences of the Pinoys. In fact, the reader's empathy with Allos's hardships gives *America* the effect of personal identification, and it conveys emotion in a way that historical narratives cannot, do not, or should not if they are to remain "objective."

Finally, it is also worth noting that in part 2, in the context of his peripatetic experiences, Allos has his first ambivalent encounters with women. Given that his generation of Filipino immigrant laborers was largely made up of men, it is not surprising that Allos's world is populated first by prostitutes, taxi dancers, and faithless girlfriends and wives and then by an intense Euro-American socialist and a strike breaker.

Part 3 is the most literally autobiographical part of the book. Bulosan's biographers indicate that he was born after the first decade of the 1900s (some accounts say 1911, others 1913) in the Philippines and came from a rather materially impoverished background. Bulosan probably received at least some high school education in his home province of Pangasinan before he arrived in the United States in 1930. After a short period of adjustment, which included wage-labor jobs, Bulosan began to write. He published some poems and was also attracted by and drawn into the American labor movement. Throughout the rest of his short but productive life,

Bulosan periodically wrote pieces revolving around labor and politics, encompassing both the domestic and the international scenes, particularly his native Philippines.

Bulosan, perhaps exacerbated by poverty and the nomadic nature of his livelihood, became seriously ill with tuberculosis in the mid-1930s and required various surgeries. As recounted in part 3 of *America*, Bulosan read widely while he recuperated in a hospital setting. During an extended period of convalescence, Bulosan crafted a new identity for himself as an author, and passages in *America* express his delight at his self-discovered prowess as an intellectual and author, conveying his tremendous intellectual growth during this period. Upon his release, Bulosan was able to achieve considerable success for a relatively young writer; he published poems, articles, and stories during the late 1930s and early 1940s and, by the mid-1940s, a number of books, including *America Is in the Heart*.

Notably, it is during this period of illness and recuperation that Bulosan records his experiences with Euro-American women in the United States of a different tenor than those women he met while on the road. Angels of mercy, women appear in Bulosan's life who seemingly seek only to protect and nurture him. Intelligent and beautiful, these women also appear when he is in the hospital and encourage him to read and grow intellectually, bringing him new books as well as offering succor.[4]

Part 4 of *America* has generated considerable controversy over the years. In this concluding section of the novel, Bulosan's penchant for socialism as a possible solution to exploitation finds its clearest expression. At the same time, Bulosan's ostensible faith in the ideals touted by the United States is also clearly and undeniably expressed in the climactic conclusion to the book, a trust not so inimical to socialist leanings as it would be during the subsequent McCarthy era. For any reader who views this as a fundamental contradiction in political stance, the separation of the naive and the politically astute voices is a critically important device.

From today's vantage point, we can see that the complexities of meaning in *America*, its historical changes, vicissitudes in socioeconomic conditions, and restructuring of political alliances—all of which affect personal politics—have allowed and still allow its readership to extrapolate contradictory interpretations from the text. This becomes apparent when one examines the critical response that the text received after it was republished by the University of Washington Press in 1973. Unlike its reception directly after the war years, later critical work and reader reception indicated that Bulosan's work was read as a critique of American ideology as well as of US foreign policies in Asia. Due to the domestic friction generated by US participation in the Vietnam War in the wake of the civil rights movement, and the more politically radical point of view of an ethnic studies university readership, critical interpretation focused primarily on the text as a subversion rather than an affirmation of the United States' domestic and international practices. The general reception of *America* after its republication focused on the inverse of the prodemocratic, pro-American 1940s-era reception of the text. Quite in contrast to the Filipino immigrant's notion of the United States as a land of equal opportunity are a plethora of textual events that exemplify racism in America, situations that far outnumber their positive counterparts. Nonetheless, the protagonist's final utterance is an undying belief in the America of his dreams. His resounding statement is the final word, in spite of everything he had withstood.

In *A Theory of Literary Production*, critic Pierre Macherey observed that "to know the work, we must move outside it."[5] The difficulties that Bulosan faced in his own time inform the psychological nature of his narrative design, which, for him and for others like him, may also have served as a survival strategy. Allos's idealistic Americanism functions as a survival mechanism for the protagonist, as it does for those who identify with him. Perhaps the sustenance of hope, in spite of all else, is a viable defense against cynicism. For the idealistic immigrant who is impoverished and stranded in the United States, the survival mechanism of hope could act against the despair that felled many of Bulosan's compatriots as well as his characters within the narrative of *America*. Certainly, Bulosan's strategic use of the naive narrator allowed him to report on, document, and validate the psychological history of survival and adaptation used by many of his compatriots.

Pragmatically speaking, the novel's conclusion may have also served as a political strategy allowing for its publication and insertion into American readership. Had the text been received as less hopeful or less affirming of the United States, it may have slipped the attention of a mainstream publishing company, or may even have been regarded as inappropriate or anti-American.

Initially heralded by some as a poignant autobiography, expressing the dreams of downtrodden immigrants of color, *America* still stands today as both an indictment of twentieth-century American imperialist designs overseas and a testament condemning a pre–World War II domestic regime of racialized class warfare. At its most explicit and compelling level, the book documents how Filipino immigrants suffered brutal treatment in the Anglo-oriented west of the United States before the war, evolving a specifically race- and class-oriented consciousness as a response. However, their evolution of an awareness from a racialized "class in itself" to a "class for itself" was not a linear, orderly, or clear-cut process.[6] It is amazing that Bulosan was able to conjecture both the transnational and global dimensions of the larger working-class Filipino immigrants' trajectories in terms of conditions at home and conditions abroad. And, as the Southern Poverty Law Center reminds us, for farmworkers these conditions remain as material and compelling today as they have been in the past. Beyond this, *America* endures because Bulosan was wise enough to know that the path of racialized class consciousness may be a necessary route, but it may also be a provisional one, if we are to truly grapple with the miasmas of global capitalism.

NOTES

Our names appear in alphabetical order, indicating our shared responsibility in writing this text. We would like to thank Tim Zimmermann and Eloisa Borah for their comments on an earlier draft, Kerrie Maynes for her copy editing, and Jacqueline Volin for taking the book through production. We alone, however, are responsible for the introduction.

1   Assemblyperson Bonta's quote appears on his official website, asmdc.org/members/a18 (accessed July 26, 2013).

2   We draw here from two previous essays by Marilyn C. Alquizola: "The Fictive
    Narrator of *America Is in the Heart*," pp. 211–17 in *Frontiers of Asian American
    Studies: Writing, Research, and Commentary*, ed. Gail M. Nomura et al. (Pullman:
    Washington State University Press, 1989), and "Subversion or Affirmation: The
    Text and Subtext of *America Is in the Heart*," pp. 199–209 in *Asian Americans:
    Comparative and Global Perspectives*, ed. Shirley Hune et al. (Pullman: Washington
    State University Press, 1991).

3   The sense of this idea can be found in Homi Bhabha's article "Of Mimicry and Men:
    The Ambivalence of Colonial Discourse," *Psychoanalysis* 28 (Spring 1984): 125–33.

4   In terms of Bulosan's biography, visits to the hospital in Los Angeles by writer
    Dorothy Babb and her sister Sonora, among others, were probably very much like
    the somewhat fictionalized visits by Euro-American women friends described in
    America.

5   Pierre Macherey, *A Theory of Literary Production* (London: Routledge and Kegan
    Paul, 1978), 90.

6   The distinction between a "class in itself" and a "class for itself" (that is, between a
    group that can be seen as holding a similar relationship to the means of production
    and a group that is self-consciously aware of itself as holding similar class interests)
    has been a conceptual tool that sociologists, political scientists, and historians have
    all drawn from and found useful in their analyses. Although attributed to Karl Marx,
    some scholars dispute that claim; e.g., Edward Anrew, "Class in Itself and Class
    against Capital: Karl Marx and His Classifiers," *Canadian Journal of Political Science*
    16, no. 3 (1983): 577–84.

FOR FURTHER READING

Encountering *America Is in the Heart* will generate an interest in
further reading. These notes suggest how much related literature
there actually is, including Bulosan's other publications, criticism
revolving around Bulosan's work, and pieces on Bulosan himself.

There are now a good many biographies of Carlos Bulosan.
Short overviews by McWilliams (in this volume), San Juan Jr.
(e.g., 1994), Campomanes (1998), Cordova (1999), and Evangelista (2005) are good places to begin. An interesting full-length
biography of Bulosan, by a contemporary and friend, is available
in Morantte (1984).

For readers who are interested in Bulosan's other publications,
a logical next step is to tackle Bulosan's short stories, both his own
compilations (e.g., *The Laughter of My Father*) and those compiled

by others (posthumous publications such as *The Philippines Is in the Heart*, edited by San Juan Jr.). There are also a number of books featuring Bulosan's essays and prose (e.g., *If You Want to Know What We Are*), as well as collections of his personal correspondence (Feria's *The Sound of Falling Light*). Readers can also peruse chapbooks of Bulosan's published poetry (e.g., *Letter from America*) as well as analysis of his poetic sensibilities as a whole, especially as they have affected his writing overall (Evangelista's *Carlos Bulosan and His Poetry*). Yet other authors have taken a more biographic perspective on Bulosan the writer (e.g., Campomanes and Gernes 1988), and then there is Bulosan, just before he passed away, on Bulosan himself (1955).

A key theme in *America* that has attracted a great deal of criticism has to do with Bulosan's approach to class analysis. The major proponent of this perspective is undoubtedly the Filipino/American literary critic E. San Juan Jr. In numerous books and essays, San Juan Jr., was the first to highlight how central class inequities were to the oppression faced by Allos/Carlos and his countrymen in the Philippines, in the United States, and particularly in the fields, towns, cities, and canneries of the West and Pacific Northwest. More recently, San Juan Jr. has extended his use of Bulosan's class analysis to generate a wide-ranging critique of contemporary capitalism and the ravages of neocolonial domination as far as US-Philippines relations are concerned in the twenty-first century (San Juan Jr., 2008).

Extending San Juan Jr.'s seminal analysis, Tim Libretti links the largely historical treatment of the Philippines in *America* to the postwar revolutionary politics of the Hukbalahups in the northern island of Luzon (1998, 2001). This is a subject treated by Bulosan in his posthumously published novel, *The Cry and the Dedication*. The political vision Libretti finds in *The Cry* posits that there cannot, and will not, be liberation for Filipinos in overseas destinations such as the United States unless there is a concomitant liberation of Filipinos from neocolonialism in the Islands.

The activist legacy of Bulosan's corpus—represented by Bulosan's editorial charge over the 1952 *Yearbook: Cannery Workers Local 37*—has been taken up by a younger generation of scholars in creative but solidly consistent ways. Journalist Ron Chew (2012) ties Bulosan's legacy directly to the 1970s union building efforts of Silme Domingo and Gene Viernes, two Filipino American organizers who were so successful that then-president Ferdinand Marcos orchestrated their assassination in broad daylight in Seattle's Pioneer Square. In a pair of related articles he published in *Kritika Kultura*, Jeffrey Arellano Cabusao made connections between Bulosan's generation and the Occupy movement (Cabusao 2012). In his "Decolonizing Knowledges" (2011) Cabusao links the development of the Critical Filipino Studies Collective with Bulosan's vision for radical change, suggesting three areas of "Bulosan Studies" that warrant further exploration. That contemporary activist/scholars still turn to the old master is surely an indication that Bulosan's analysis has something to offer proponents of newer movements for social justice.

Yet another angle of Bulosan's vision, as presented in *America*, has to do with the way that critics, deploying feminist and queer theories, unpack Bulosan's perspectives on gender and sexuality. Despite the fact that Filipina women were few in number before the war, critics working from a feminist standpoint have raised issues with Bulosan's supposedly stereotypical portrayals of women in *America*: that is, as either the virgin/pure or whore/compromised types (see Ma 1997; Lee 1999). Moreover, some critics express suspicion that in the search for solidarity the fraternal bonds between men in *America*, as well as their ethnic solidarity, overdetermine any subtle or nuanced possibilities that women, Filipina or otherwise, might receive in Bulosan's accounts (note, however, that there is debate between authors Lee [1999] and Higashida [2006] on this matter, and Alquizola and Hirabayashi [2011] question whether Bulosan's representations of women can be fully and adequately deduced from a reading of *America* only).

More radically, with the application of queer theory to the reinterpretation of Bulosan generally, and to America specifically, we have holistically distinctive interpretations of the way that sublimated erotics might color the entire text related to the Pinoys and their feelings of love and ethnic solidarity (de Jesus 2002). Here, readings of *America*, along with psychosexual readings of Bulosan's conscious and subconscious desires, are taken by some critics to a different plane altogether (Ponce 2012).

Noteworthy, as well, is an intriguing interpretation that reads Bulosan and *America* in terms of cultural and literary traditions deeply rooted in the Islands. The historian Augusto Fauni Espritu (2003) proposes that Bulosan's narrative is informed, in its structure, by practices of clientelism and reciprocity, as well as by the tradition of *pasyon* in the Philippines. Espiritu proposes that understanding the latter cues readers to expressions of grief and grieving that must be recognized in order to fully appreciate Bulosan's aesthetics in *America* and their intended emotional effect.

Finally, ongoing historiography offers fascinating accounts of the domestic and international contexts that frame *America*. If *America* offers a critique of imperialism's effect on the Philippines, recent studies by historians Rafael (2000) and McCoy (2009) provide more detailed and nuanced discussions of the United States' role in the Islands. Historian Dorothy Fujita-Rony (2003) provides a detailed study of labor in Seattle that will be of interest to readers who want to learn more about the evolution of the Filipino American community in the context of the Pacific Northwest. Historian Micah Ellison (2005) documents the rise of the Local 7/Local 37 cannery union that Bulosan worked for back in his day, and scholar Arleen De Vera (1994) details how legislation such as the Smith Act, originally developed in order to deport labor leader Harry Bridges, was subsequently utilized to prosecute a number of Filipino labor organizers in Local 7, some of whom were close colleagues and friends of Bulosan. As far as we can determine (Alquizola and Hirabayashi 2012) the hope of the Federal Bureau of Investigation, in surveilling Bulosan toward the end of his life, was gathering information on him such that the US immigration officials would be able to deport him as well. Future work may unveil, in detail, the intersection of domestic and international intelligence work as it eddied about the life and literary career of perhaps the most famous Filipino writer of the prewar generation of Pinoys.

WORKS CITED

Alquizola, Marilyn C. 1989. "The Fictive Narrator of American Is in the Heart." In *Frontiers of Asian American Studies: Writing, Research, and Commentary*, ed. Gail M. Nomura et al., 211–17. Pullman: Washington State University Press.

———. 1991. "Subversion or Affirmation: The Text and Subtext of *America Is in the Heart*." In *Asian Americans: Comparative and Global Perspectives*, ed. Shirley Hune et al., 199–209. Pullman: Washington State University Press.

Alquizola, Marilyn, and Lane Ryo Hirabayashi. 2011. "Carlos Bulosan's *Laughter of My Father*: Adding Feminist and Class Perspectives to the 'Casebook of Resistance.'" *Frontiers: A Journal of Women Studies* 32 (3): 64–91.

———. 2012. "Carlos Bulosan's Final Defiant Acts: Achievements during the McCarthy Era." *Amerasia Journal* 38 (3): 29–50.

Anrew, Edward. 1983. "Class in Itself and Class against Capital: Karl Marx and His Classifiers." *Canadian Journal of Political Science* 16 (3): 577–84.

Bhabha, Homi. 1984. "Of Mimicry and Men: The Ambivalence of Colonial Discourse." *Psychoanalysis* 28 (Spring): 125–33.

Bulosan, Carlos. 1942. *Letter from America*. Prairie City, IL: J. A. Decker.

———. 1944. *The Laughter of My Father*. New York: Bantam Books.

———, ed. 1952. *1952 Yearbook: Cannery Workers Local 37*. Seattle: Local 7, ILWU.

———. 1955. "Bulosan, Carlos." In *Twentieth Century Authors, First Supplement*, ed. Stanley J. Kunitz, 144–45. New York: H. W. Wilson Company.

———. 1973. *America Is in the Heart: A Personal History*. Seattle: University of Washington Press. (Originally published in 1943.)

———. 1978. *The Philippines Is in the Heart: A Collection of Short Stories*, ed. E. San Juan Jr. Quezon City, Philippines: New Day Publishers.

———. 1983. *If You Want to Know What We Are: A Carlos Bulosan Reader*, ed. E. San Juan Jr. New York: West End Press.

———. 1995. *The Cry and the Dedication*. Philadelphia: Temple University Press.

Cabusao, Jeffrey Arellano. 2011. "Decolonializing Knowledges: Asian American Studies, Carlos Bulosan, and the Insurgent Filipino Diasporic Critical Imagination." *Kritika Kultura* 16: 122–44.

———. 2012. "Toward a Renewal of Critical Practice: Reflections on the Occupy Movement and Filipino Self-Determination." *Kritika Kultura* 18: 220–43.

Campomanes, Oscar V. 1998. "Bulosan, Carlos." In *Encyclopedia of the American Left*, ed. Mari Jo Buhle et al., 113–14. 2nd ed. New York: Oxford University Press.

Campomanes, Oscar V., and Todd S. Gernes. 1988. "Two Letters from America: Carlos Bulosan and the Act of Writing." *MELUS* 15 (3): 15–46.

Chew, Ron. 2012. *Remembering Silme Domingo and Gene Viernes: The Legacy of Filipino American Labor Activism*. Seattle: ILWU, Local 37; University of Washington Press.

Cordova, Dorothy. 1999. "Carlos Bulosan." In *Distinguished Asian Americans*, ed. Hyung-Chan Kim, 34–36. Westport, CT: Greenwood Press.

de Jesus, Melinda Lisa Maria. 2002. "Rereading History/Rewriting Desire: Reclaiming Queerness in Carlos Bulosan's *America Is in the Heart* and Bienvenido Santos's *Scent of Apples*." *Journal of Asian American Studies* 5 (2): 91-111.

De Vera, Arleen. 1994. "Without Parallel: The Local 7 Deportation Cases, 1949–1955." *Amerasia Journal* 20 (2): 1–25.

Ellison, Micah. 2005. "The Local 7/Local 37 Story: Filipino American Cannery Unionism in Seattle, 1940–1959." Available at depts.washington.edu/civilr/local_7.htm (accessed July 26, 2013).

Espiritu, Augusto Fauni. 2003. "Beyond Eve and Mary: Filipino American Intellectual Heroes and the Transnational Performance of Gender and Reciprocity." *Diaspora* 12 (3): 361–86.

———. 2005. *Five Faces of Exile: The Nation and Filipino American Intellectuals*. Stanford, CA: Stanford University Press.

Evangelista, Susan. 1985. *Carlos Bulosan and His Poetry: A Biography and Anthology*. Seattle: University of Washington Press.

———. 2005. "Carlos Bulosan." In *Asian American Writers*, ed. Deborah L. Madsen, 10–18. Farmington Hills, MI: Thomson Gale.

Feria, Dolores S., ed. 1960. *The Sound of Falling Light: Letters in Exile*. Quezon City, Philippines: N.p.

Fujita-Rony, Dorothy B. 2003. *American Workers, Colonial Power: Philippine Seattle and the Transpacific West*. Berkeley: University of California Press.

Higashida, Cheryl. 2006. "Re-Signed Subjects: Women, Work, and World in the Fiction of Carlos Bulosan and Hisaye Yamamoto." In *Transnational Asian American Literature: Sites and Transits*, ed. Shirley Geok-Lin Lim et al., 29–54. Philadelphia: Temple University Press.

Lee, Rachael. 1999. *The Americas of Asian American Literature: Gendered Fiction of Nation and Transnation*. Princeton, NJ: Princeton University Press.

Libretti, Tim. 1998. "First and Third Worlds in U.S. Literature: Rethinking Carlos Bulosan." *MELUS* 23 (4): 135–55.

———. 2001. "*America Is in the Heart* by Carlos Bulosan." In *A Resource Guide to Asian American Literature*, ed. Sau-ling Cynthia Wong and Stephen H. Sumida, 21–31. New York: The Modern Language Association of America.

Ma, Sheng-Mei. 1997. "Postcolonial Feminizing of America in Carlos Bulosan." In *Ideas of Home: Literature of Asian Migration*, ed. Geoffrey Kain, 129–39. East Lansing: Michigan State University Press.

Macherey, Pierre. 1978. *A Theory of Literary Production*. London: Routledge and Kegan Paul.

McCoy, Alfred W. 2009. *Policing America's Empire: The United States, the Philippines, and the Rise of the Surveillance State*. Madison: University of Wisconsin Press.

McWilliams, Carey. 2000. *Factories in the Field: The Story of Migratory Farm Labor in California*. Berkeley: University of California Press. (Originally published in 1939.)

Morantte, P. C. 1984. *Remembering Carlos Bulosan (His Heart Affair with America)*. Quezon City: Philippines: New Day Publishers.

Ponce, Martin Joseph. 2012. *Beyond the Nation: Diasporic Filipino Literature and Queer Reading*. New York: New York University Press.

Rafael, Vicente. 2000. *White Love and Other Essays in Filipino History*. Durham, NC: Duke University Press.

San Juan Jr., E. 1972. *Carlos Bulosan and the Imagination of the Class Struggle*. Quezon City, Philippines: University of the Philippines Press.

———. 1994. "Carlos Bulosan." In *The American Radical*, ed. Mari Jo Buhle et al., 253–59. New York: Routledge.

———. 2008. "An Introduction to Carlos Bulosan." E. San Juan Jr., Archives. Available at http://rizalarchive.blogspot.com/2008/01/introduction-to-carlos-bulosan.html (accessed July 26, 2013).

Southern Poverty Law Center. 2013. *Close to Slavery: Guestworker Programs in the United States*. Montgomery, AL: Southern Poverty Law Center.

PART ONE

CHAPTER I

I WAS the first to see him coming slowly through the tall grass in the dry bottom of the river. He walked with measured steps and when he reached the spreading mango tree that separated our land from my grandfather's, he put his bundle on the ground and sat on it, looking toward our house with the anxiety of a man who had been away from home for a long time. He was as yet unrecognizable in the early morning light, but it was evident from the way he walked that he had come a long distance. Apparently he was not a stranger in our *barrio* or village, for he seemed to know where he was going and to be unhurried.

I rushed out of the house and ran across the pasture where some of our animals were grazing. I headed for the rich piece of land my father was plowing. It was the season for corn and my father, like the other farmers in our *barrio*, had gone to our land at early dawn to start the spring plowing. I could smell the fresh upturned earth in the air and the bitter smoke of burning grass. The fields were dotted with men plowing and harrowing and raking weeds into the river.

My father halted the *carabao*, or water buffalo, and bit the rope. He put his wet hands on his hips and waited patiently for me. When I reached him, I leaned against the *carabao* and gasped for breath. The kind animal turned his head toward me and switched the flies off his back with his long tail.

"What is it, son?" asked my father, taking the rope from his mouth and tying it to the plow handle. "Why are you running like a hound so early in the morning?"

"I think I saw brother Leon," I said, hoping that I was right about the stranger who resembled my oldest brother. "I saw him coming toward our house."

Father kicked the dirt off his feet and said: "Your brother

3

Leon is still fighting in Europe. Maybe he is dead now. I have not heard from him." He took the rope again and flipped it gently and suggestively across the *carabao's* back, and the two of them, the patient animal and my father, walked slowly and industriously away, the sharp plow blade breaking smoothly through the rich soil between them.

I ran to the tamarind at the other end of the farm and climbed quickly to its top. I looked toward the mango tree, but the stranger was no longer there. I looked around as far as my eyes could see. Then I saw him coming toward our land with slow, firm steps, stopping now and then to look at the surrounding landscape. He was coming from the direction of our house.

When the *carabao* had reached the ditch and was trying to snatch a tuft of grass, I shouted to father to stop and look toward the stranger. He put the rope between his teeth, but when he saw the stranger and recognized him, his mouth opened in surprise and the rope fell to the wet ground. I climbed down the tree hurriedly and ran as fast as I could across the plowed earth. My father was already talking with the stranger.

I stopped suddenly when I saw my brother Leon. I had seen only his picture on the large table in our house in town. I did not know what to say now that I was seeing him for the first time. My father looked at me and his face broke into sudden gentleness.

"It is your brother, son," he said, picking up the rope. "He is home now, from the war."

"Welcome home, soldier," I said.

Leon grabbed my shoulders and swung me swiftly above his head; then he put me back on the ground and looked blank for a moment. Suddenly, with an affectionate glance at the animal, he took the rope from my father and started plowing the common earth that had fed our family for generations.

That was how I met my brother who had gone to fight a strange war in Europe. The sudden, sweeping years that later came to my life and pushed me into the unknown, the vital, negative years of hard work and bitter trials oftentimes resurrected his face for me with great vividness. And at other times I was to go back again and again to this moment for an assurance of righteous anger against the crushing terror that filled my life in a land far away. . . .

It was springtime when my brother Leon came back to our *barrio*, in the little farming town of Binalonan, on the island of Luzon. I must have been five years old at the time, but I remember vividly those first days when he stayed with us. He immediately discarded his khaki army uniform and opened the small trunk where he had put his old clothes before he went away. He followed the plow again and worked patiently with us, hoping, as the weeks passed into months, and the corn grew tall and ripened, that we would have a good crop.

But the Philippines was undergoing a radical social change; all over the archipelago the younger generation was stirring and adapting new attitudes. And although for years the agitation for national independence had been growing, the government was actually in the hands of powerful native leaders. It was such a juicy issue that obscure men with ample education exploited it to their own advantage, thus slowly but inevitably plunging the nation into a great economic catastrophe that tore the islands from their roots, and obfuscated the people's resurgence toward a broad national unity.

For a time it seemed that the younger generation, influenced by false American ideals and modes of living, had become total strangers to the older generation. In the provinces where the poor peasants lived and toiled for the rich *hacienderos*, or landlords, the young men were stirring and rebelling against their heritage. Those who could no longer tolerate existing conditions adventured into the new land, for the opening of the United States to them was one of the gratifying provisions of the peace treaty that culminated the Spanish-American War.

At this time we had four hectares of land, which were barely sufficient to keep our family from starving. We had crop rotation as an insurance against starvation, and the generosity of the soil was miraculous. In the spring we planted corn and beans and a few rows of tobacco; we harvested our crops toward the rainy season and stored them in the granary. Then we planted rice and fattened our animals in the grassy forest at the edge of the *barrio;* and sometimes, when the rice was growing rapidly under the warm rains, we would go to a wedding or a christening party.

Then my brother Leon met the girl who became his wife. She came from a poor family in the north, in the province of Ilocos Sur, where the peasants were overcrowded in a narrow barren land. She came to our *barrio* and hired herself to one of the farmers who had more hectares of land than the others. Because she came from a thrifty and industrious people, the villagers liked her and they tried wisely, before my brother Leon returned from the war, to bring their eligible sons to her attention. Fortunately my brother came back before she was betrothed, and in no time they became engaged to be married.

I do not remember the exact details of my brother's marriage, but I remember my father's immediate approval and great joy. I remember how I sat on a bamboo chair in the dancing pavilion, between the bride and the groom, watching the peasant boys and girls dancing in bare feet. It must have been the third day of the wedding, because the women in the kitchen were already putting away the plates and the large wooden bowls used as rice receptacles on the long dining table. The men were moving away the chairs, piling them into oxcarts and sleds, and giving them back to the people from whom they had been borrowed. The merrymakers, who had sat at the tables earlier that day eating rice with their bare hands and washing their mouths in a large bowl that was passed around the tables, were scattering in the yard and waiting for the momentous hour of the wedding.

It was the time for the groom to carry his bride to the new house which had been built especially for them in the yard, near the little grass hut where my father and I lived. He would then find out if his wife were virginal. When I was growing up in the *barrio* of Mangusmana this primitive custom was still prevalent, although in the town of Binalonan itself, of which our *barrio* was merely a part, it had never existed. The custom had come down to the peasants in the valleys from the hill people who had intermarried with the villagers and had imposed their own traditions.

The ritual was very simple. But it was also the most dramatic of the series of colorful wedding events. My brother Leon carried his wife across the harvested fields to their new home. We followed, shouting with joy and throwing rice upon them. We stopped in the yard when they entered the house. Then we waited silently, anxious to see the black smoke come out of the house, for it would mean that the bride was a virgin. If no smoke showed, we would know that the groom had been deceived, and we would justify his action if he returned the girl to her people. It was a cruel custom, because the women could no longer marry when they were returned to their parents, and would be looked upon with abhorrence and would be ostracized. But it was a fast-dying custom, in line with other backward customs in the Philippines, yielding to the new ways of the younger generation that were shaping out sharply from the growing industrialism.

I do not think the smoke came out of the house where my brother and his bride were alone, because I remember the crowd milling around my father and rushing into the house. The men brought the girl out and tied her to a guava tree. The angry women spat in her eyes and tore off her clothes, calling her obscene names. When one of the men rushed out of the toolshed with a horsewhip, my father frantically fought his way through the crowd. He had hardly reached the girl when a man knocked him down, and he was trampled upon by angry feet.

The men must also have knocked down my brother Leon in the house. I saw him staggering toward his bride with blood on his face. He flung himself upon her, covering her bleeding body with his, and the stones and sticks fell upon him mercilessly. Then they tied him to the tree, beside his bride, and the angry peasants, who had been his good friends and neighbors a moment ago, began throwing stones at them.

My father crawled on his knees and flung himself upon my brother and his bride.

"Stop, you devils!" he shouted helplessly. "She is a good, industrious woman, and my son wants to live with her!"

But the whips began falling upon him. A deep gash was cut across his face and blood came out of his mouth. I could no longer hear what he was saying. The shouting became deafening and the cries of the girl were drowned by that horrible human sound. Then the crowd went away, still angry but spent.

I fumbled in the dark with the *bolo* or butcher knife, cutting the ropes that bound them to the guava tree. It was now far into the night, and the stars were few and faraway. The sky was like a field of dying fire trees, vast and remote in the night. The girl flung her bleeding arms about my brother and wept silently. I saw my father's face searching for an answer in the earth to the unanswerable question in my brother's eyes.

I will never forget how my brother lifted the girl in his arms, as ceremoniously and gently as he had done that afternoon, and carried her tenderly into their house to begin a new life.

Not long afterward my brother Leon, who had already sold one hectare of our land, which was his share of the family property, left the *barrio* with his wife to live in another part of Luzon. I saw him again on my way to America, but he was then a mature man with children of his own. I had written him that I would pass through his town on my way to Manila, and had asked him, if he would, to stand in front of his house and wait for my bus. In those days there was only one bus a day from Binalonan to the train station, in the town of Dagupan. I could at least look through the window of my bus and wave good-bye to him.

When my bus came to the white saltbeds, I knew that I was nearing the place where my brother Leon lived. I saw the mango grove and the shining fish ponds beyond it, near the mouth of the Agno River that opens lazily into Lingayen gulf. At the edge of the shimmering plain, standing like a huge mushroom by the highway, was my brother's grass house. My heart began to beat faster as I drew nearer; eagerly I leaned out of the window.

Then I saw him, then his small wife, and then his children. They were standing in front of their house—the father first, then the mother, and then the children. They waved good-bye to me, all of them; and I leaned far out the window, waving to them. It was good-bye to my brother Leon and to the war that he had fought in a strange land; good-bye to his silent wife and all that was magnificent in her. It was only several hours afterward that I tried to recall how many children were beside my brother.

CHAPTER II

W HEN my brother Leon left the *barrio* immediately after the tragedy, my father went to town and came back with my brother Amado, who was attending grade school there and living with my mother and a baby sister. Amado was the youngest of my four brothers. He was a few years older than I, and we were the only ones left to help my father on the farm. My other brothers had already gone to other towns, striking into the dark unknown for the sound of life; and if there was an echo there— if only for a brief moment—they came back to share it with our family. It was inspiring to sit with them, to listen to them talk of other times and lands; and I knew that if there was one redeeming quality in our poverty, it was this boundless affinity for each other, this humanity that grew in each of us, as boundless as this green earth.

Luciano, who was next to my brother Leon, was in Camp Stotsenburg completing his three-year service in the Philippine Scouts, a native detachment of the United States army. Macario, who was next to him, was a student at the high school in Lingayen, the capital of the province of Pangasinan. It was for Macario that we were all working so hard, so that he could come back to Binalonan to teach school and, perhaps, to help us support our large family. . . .

But now it was Amado's job, when plowing time came, to follow my father with a bamboo harrow until the land was cleared, leveled, and ready for planting. I did the cooking and other simple chores in the house. The work on the farm was heavy and every hand was needed until the harvest was over. But there were gratifying compensations in the depth of my childhood.

At sundown my father told me to take our animals into the

corral. It was a clear evening and he wanted to work with my brother into the night. I pulled our *carabaos* and goats from their pegs in the pasture and drove them to our house. I hitched a little bamboo sled to the largest goat and went to the village well with three empty petroleum cans. Many people were waiting to fill their earthen drinking jars or to water their working animals. When my turn came, I lowered the wooden bucket into the deep well and tied the end of the rope to a papaya tree; then I pulled it up slowly and laboriously to the mouth of the well and poured the water carefully into the cans. Before the cans were full many people had arrived and were waiting for their turn.

I walked ahead of the docile goat, and it followed me obediently to our house. I filled the water trough in the corral and the animals stopped chewing the dry rice stalks. They came anxiously to the trough and plunged their muzzles into the water, their throats making gulping noises as the cold water thundered into their stomachs. I carried the remaining can of water into the house and filled the earthen drinking jars on the makeshift stand by the wall.

The night came at last and darkness filled the house; except for the tiny needles of light that filtered through the walls from the sky, there was no other illumination. I found the small oil lamp where my father kept it in the bamboo rack under the homemade pillows. I lighted it and went to the kitchen. There was no food left. I went to the rice bin and filled the cooking pot. I prepared string beans and mixed them with small slices of beef. When the pot began to bubble on the roaring stove, I heard my father and brother coming noisily through the gate with their implements. They went to the water trough to wash their feet and hands; then they came into the house and asked me if dinner was ready.

We sat on the floor and ate in the twilight with our bare hands. We spread the salted fish on the steaming rice and soaked it with the broth from the vegetable pot. When we finished eating my father started washing the polished coconut shells which had been our plates and drinking cups for many generations. I went outside the house to feed our dog with cold rice.

Amado followed and watched me, out of habit. Then my father came out also and sat on a long log under the eaves, and we talked about our farm for hours, centering our thoughts around my brother Macario, who was our pride and the star of all our hope. When midnight came we went to bed because we would have to be up early in the morning.

The sun shone generously and the corn grew tall and ripened fast as the spring passed into the rainy season. My father hitched the cart to the *carabao* and drove through the stony village road to our land. Amado, who had gone there before sunrise, was waiting with a huge pile of corn he had harvested.

After I had driven our animals into the pasture, I followed them with a bamboo tube of drinking water. A slight rain had begun to fall upon the corn, and far in the eastern horizon, above the Cordilleras Mountains, was a gigantic rainbow whose brilliance leaped across the sky for hundreds of kilometers. But as long as it was there to prevent the heavy rain from coming to our land, from soaking and destroying the ripe corn, we knew that we would have time enough to harvest it.

My father cupped his hands and put them on his mouth, and the voice that called for me was disturbed and sounded far away. I was still a kilometer from our land, but I could hear his voice rolling down the valley. It was familiar and unforgettable, like the trees that whispered as I ran eagerly toward them. Then I saw them working furiously between the long rows, running from one end to the other with large ears of unhusked corn, and making a pile near the empty cart.

I put my straw hat on the horns of the *carabao* and rushed to their aid. Then the three of us worked furiously, looking now and then toward the east to see if the rainbow were still there; but in our hearts we knew that it was only a matter of hours before the heavy rain would come. My father had rolled up his cotton pants to his thighs. Amado was hatless and bare to the waist; he threw the ears of corn between the rows, ripping the long stalks like a wild animal. I could see his black head appearing and disappearing in the sunlight.

There were three hectares of corn, and we could not afford to lose any of it. In the early afternoon, working on the last hectare, my father looked toward the east only to discover that the rainbow had vanished. There was a thin trace of color in the sky. We knew that the heavy, dangerous rain was on its way to our village, so we worked desperately with a hope that we might save everything. Amado jumped into the cart, which I had filled with harvested corn, and went flying down the road to our house. He came back and, calling me to help him, looked unhappily toward the east where a dark rain was approaching.

We tried to save every ear of corn, but the first cold rain came while we were working on the last row. Amado came back again with the empty cart. The corn was already wet and spoiled, but my father thought we could give it to the animals. The rain was so thick and heavy that we could scarcely see what we were doing. The irrigation ditch broke loose and the water thundered toward the cornlands. We jumped into the cart and watched the green stalks falling into the water.

My brother expertly jerked the rope that was attached to the nose of the *carabao*, and the animal, familiar with the routine, shook his short legs and moved slowly toward our house. Then we could hear the banks of the river falling, dragging down boulders and dead trunks of trees.

"Binalonan will be flooded tonight," my father said. "The rice in Binalonan will be destroyed tonight."

"Do you think so, Father?" Amado said.

But he knew that my father had spoken wisely. Amado was only making conversation. In the morning news came to the village that the rice fields in Binalonan were flooded. My mother and the rest of our family were living there, but we had no property in Binalonan except a little wooden house.

The sun came out again in the month of September, and we put the strung ears of corn in the yard. The rice was now nearly a foot high above the water and our animals were fattening in the grazing land. It was the beginning of another school year, and my brother Macario, who was in Binalonan for a month's vacation, was ready to return. He needed money to continue his studies, but we had nothing to give him. He stayed on for two more weeks, losing that time in his studies. My father began to worry; then one day he went to town with the deed to our land.

Popular education was spreading throughout the archipelago and this opened up new opportunities. It was a new and democratic system brought by the American government into the Philippines, and a nation hitherto illiterate and backward was beginning to awaken. In Spanish times education was something that belonged exclusively to the rulers and to some fortunate natives affluent enough to go to Europe. But the poor people, the peasants, were denied even the most elementary schooling. When the free education that the United States had introduced spread throughout the islands, every family who had a son pooled its resources and sent him to school.

My father and mother, who could not read or write, were willing to sacrifice anything and everything to put my brother Macario through high school. We had free education, but the school was in Lingayen, the only high school in the large province of Pangasinan at this time. Going to school in Lingayen, in those predatory years, took plenty of money. The students paid for their room and board; and sometimes, unless they washed their clothes themselves, they paid for their laundry.

My father sold one hectare of our land and gave the money to my brother Macario. Then we worked even harder on the farm, and sometimes we planted beans between the rows to make use of time and space. My mother also worked harder, going around the villages with a large earthen jar of salted fish and a bamboo tube of salt. The peasants had no money but they gave my mother chickens, eggs, and beans, and these she sold in the public market for a few centavos.

We had deprived ourselves of any form of leisure and simple luxury so that my brother could finish high school. But even then he kept asking for more money, threatening that he would stop if we did not send him enough. The thought that he would really stop terrified us.

My father went to town once more and found the money-lender who had given him two hundred pesos some months before for one hectare of farm land. He gave my father more money and got the deed to another hectare. The stipulation was that after a certain period of time we would pay back the money and thus retrieve the land; but in the event that we could not pay the moneylender, we automatically lost ownership of our land. Oddly enough, we were not bothered by this usurious arrangement. We were waiting for the day when my brother Macario would teach school and pay back the moneylender.

All this time my brother Amado was working industriously with us on the farm. He worked seriously because he, too, wanted Macario to go through high school. Amado had gone as far as the fifth grade, but although he was eager to go farther, my father stopped him. We could afford only my brother Macario's education.

Now we had only one hectare of land left, not enough to maintain our family. Not far from us was a wide piece of church land which had not been touched for years. The soil was rich and the vegetation that grew in it thick and lusty. My father went to the men in the church and asked them to let him clear away five hectares. His request was granted, and he came back to the village with a new hope.

We started working when the slight rain came. We let the roots and logs float down the river. We set fire to the land and watched the flames eat the bushes. When the heavy rains came, in the last days of April, we started digging out the huge roots of fallen trees. Sometimes we put a sturdy pole under the roots and heaved them slowly out of the hole; then we put down the pole and used our *bolos* and axes, cutting wildly here and there until we were ready to pull the whole cluster of roots away.

Then we were ready for the biggest roots. We put a sturdier pole under them and hitched it to the *carabao*. It was slow and painful work. The heavy rains kept beating upon us and the lightning flashed incessantly in the sky. The thunder rolled and broke like a huge drum near us. The *carabao* stopped pulling the pole and quivered with fright. But we worked on, rain or shine, until the work was almost done.

There was now only a narrow section of the land where the big, stubborn roots were firmly embedded. The other section was already as level and clean as our other land, spreading out like a rainbow toward the river. My father was plowing it, hoping that we could plant highland rice when the water receded and the soil became firm.

My brother Amado and I were pulling out the remaining huge roots with our *carabao*. It was during these last days of our backbreaking work that Amado entered my consciousness and stayed there like a firebrand for years. We were working under a heavy rain. It was getting dark and our bodies were aching with pain. The *carabao* we had been using stopped suddenly and refused to move. My brother jumped out of the hole and urged the animal with his mud-caked, trembling hands, shouting with controlled anger as he pushed him. Then he shouted at me to jump into the hole and to push the pole while he slapped the *carabao* a little harder. But the animal did not move; he sank slowly into the mud.

Suddenly my brother began beating the *carabao* with a stick. I stopped pushing the pole and jumped quickly out of the hole. The animal's hind legs collapsed weakly in the water, and he sank deeper into the mud. Then my father came running toward us and, seeing the helpless animal, leaped at my brother and slapped him sharply across the face.

"What are you doing to the *carabao?*" shouted my father, striking my brother again.

Amado stepped back and for a moment I thought the hand with the stick would strike my father. My brother raised his hand and stopped, shaking with blind fury; then he flung the stick angrily upon the *carabao* and started running furiously in the direction of Binalonan. When he had gone a hundred yards, he stopped and looked back at me; then he came running back to where I was standing near the huge roots and touched my head. Then he ran away again and halted almost on the same spot where he had first stopped. He raised his dirty right hand and waved lovingly at me.

"Good-bye, Allos!" he shouted.

I watched him disappear behind the tall grass in the river, his bare feet pounding in the mud as the rain swallowed him. I did not know then that he was running away from the cruelty of our hard peasant life. There were tears in my eyes, but the rain washed them away. My father heard me sniffling and saw my lips quivering in anguish.

"What are you crying about?" he said, rubbing the back of the *carabao* affectionately with his palms.

I saw my brother Amado again not long afterward in Binalonan, where I had gone to live with my mother. He was then a janitor at the *presidencia*, or town hall, and helping us support my brother Macario who was still in high school. I went from house to house in the neighborhood, climbing coconut trees out of which, if I picked five of the fruit, I could have one nut for myself. Toward the end of the day *compradores* or buyers would come to the grove and buy all the coconuts, including my share. I would run home and give the money to my mother; she in turn would give it to Macario.

But one day when it was raining, I fell from a coconut tree. I lay on my grass mat for a long time waiting for the broken bones to heal. My mother was away most of the time. My sister Irene was still a baby; she crawled on the floor when we were alone in the house. My brother Amado came home every lunch time and prepared something for us to eat; then he went back to work, running home again in the evening before my mother arrived. He brought home old stamps and magazines that he had picked up while sweeping the floor of the *presidencia*.

A year passed slowly by. In July, when school again opened, I was well enough to walk around the house. Amado came home with a big book filled with pictures and large letters.

"If you learn to read this book," he said kindly, "I will take you to school with me."

"I will learn to read it in one day," I said boastfully.

"I know you will, Allos," he said.

There was something moving in the way he talked to me; his words seized my mind and nourished my life to the edge of the day. I was greatly fascinated with the idea of going to school, but did not know why, since there was no hope of my going beyond the third grade.

I remember Amado putting a frayed cap on my head one morning and taking me to school, along with the other children in our neighborhood who were accompanied by their parents. He had stopped going to school when my father took him to the village to help us. But he had always had a passionate desire for education; and even later, in a distant land, where he was thrown to make his world, it never completely died.

CHAPTER III

IT WAS now the end of my brother Macario's school year. We gave a sigh of relief. We knew that our burden would end at last. God willing, he would shoulder the responsibility of buying back our land.

There was a national election that year, and the peasants went to the *presidencia* to cast their ballots. My father was not a political man, but he had always considered his right to vote a great privilege. One morning he told me to tie a rope around the neck of the white kid in the pasture. My brother Macario would be home for a few days, and we had an occasion to celebrate. It was my first opportunity to see him. I had been born in the *barrio* and when I had gone to town he had always been away.

My father filled a large sack with eggplants and tomatoes and told me to take the kid. The animal followed me obediently. When we were nearing the town, my father saw a pond with many snails in it. We took off our clothes and went into the water, gathering the slow-moving snails from the bottom of the pond. We filled our hats, which the kid carried to town, stopping now and then to kick the burden off its back.

When we got home my mother was still in the public market. We put the snails in a large earthen jar. I tied the kid to the ladder so that my mother could see it when she came home.

"Let's go to town and wait for your brother, son," said my father.

"Is he coming home today?" I asked.

"Sometime this afternoon," he said.

"I hope he will bring some books with him," I said.

The street was filled with voters on their way to the *presidencia* to cast their ballots. They carried little jugs of *basi*, which is a homemade drink extracted from sugar cane and seasoned with herbs and leaves; and some of them brought their food and blankets with them.

My father and I stopped in the public market to see my mother. She was selling salted fish and an indescribable aggregation of vegetables under an umbrella, while my sister Irene was crawling on a blanket near by. My mother gave me two centavos for *pan*, a kind of bread made from rice flour, which children in my day particularly enjoyed.

Then my father and I went to the plaza and sat in the shade of the kiosk, listening attentively to the band playing our national anthem and other patriotic songs. When the students from Lingayen began to arrive, we ran to the station under the large arbor tree. We sat in the coffee shop and watched every bus that stopped, but my brother Macario did not arrive. After a while my father went to the *presidencia* to cast his ballot; but before he came back a bus full of students came along. A young man in a white cotton suit alighted from the bus and kept turning around, as though he were looking for someone. I knew he was my brother Macario because even at his age his resemblance to my father was unmistakable. The way he carried his head slightly toward the left made me sure.

But I was afraid to go up to him. I could not move from my stool. I kept watching him for fear he might disappear before my father came back. Then he saw my father coming out of the *presidencia* with the old felt hat in his hand. My brother lifted his rattan suitcase and ran to meet him. They shook hands affectionately, which was uncommon because ordinarily Macario would have kissed my father's hand; but he was being educated in the American way. Then my father waved to me.

It was the first time I had seen Macario, surely the most educated man in our family. He looked at me wordlessly for a moment and then passed his hand over my head.

"Is this Allos, Father?" he asked.

"Yes, son," father said.

"Well, let us go home and I will cut your long hair," said Macario to me. "Don't you ever cut your hair, brother?"

I was speechless. I was ashamed to say anything.

"He needs it for protection against vicious mosquitoes and flies," said my father. "It is also his shield from the sun in hot summer."

"I will make a gentleman out of him," Macario said. "Wouldn't you like to be a gentleman, Allos?"

I could not say anything. I walked silently between them: my brother on my left, my father on my right. They were like two strong walls protecting me from the attack of an unseen enemy (moving into my life to give me the warm assurance of their proximity, and guiding me into the future that was waiting with all its ferocity).

We went to the public market, but my mother had already left. We walked eagerly to our house; then we saw the black smoke coming out of the small kitchen window. My mother was preparing an early dinner. My father told me to run ahead and untie the kid under the ladder.

My mother was boiling rice, but she came running to meet my brother at the door, uttered a few words of affection, and returned hastily to the stove. My father carried the kid on his shoulder to the bench in the kitchen and tied its legs. It was very gentle; it did not resist. While my father sharpened the *bolo* on a soft stone, I poured vinegar and uncooked rice into a large wooden bowl. When he struck the jugular vein with the sharp blade, I knelt on the floor and put the bowl in place. The kid jerked convulsively, moaned, stiffened, and died. The warm blood rushed out of its gurgling throat into the bowl.

The night came on quickly. I could hear my father hacking at the meat in the lean-to; once in a while his *bolo* flashed in the faint lamplight. Beyond him, in the backyard, I could see the weird silhouettes of the banana leaves, and above them, in the light of the sky, I caught glimpses of the coconut trees moving in the wind. Then the stars shone brightly in the sky, and my mother opened the windows so that the light would fill the house.

After we had eaten our dinner we went to the living room and sat around the low table.

"How are you getting along with your studies, son?" asked my mother.

"Three months more and I will be through forever," said my brother, moving uneasily in his chair. "But I need two hundred pesos to finish the course. That is why I am here."

"Two hundred pesos?" said my mother, rising slightly from where she sat on the floor. "You might as well ask for two thousand pesos."

"Don't you have it?" asked my brother, looking at my father and then at my mother. "Can't you do anything at all? Can't you sell some more land?"

"We have only one hectare left, son," said my mother, trying desperately to make my brother understand our poverty with futile movements of her hands.

"Can't you sell this house?" asked my brother.

It was then that my father stirred in his seat and said: "We will sell the land. You can go back to school and do not worry at all. We will send you the money and you will finish your studies."

My mother's hands leaped frantically from her lap to her mouth and stayed there, stifling the protest. In one fleeting instant I saw her hands—big-veined, hard, and bleeding in spots. I saw her lips tremble for a moment, and the fear in her eyes.

"You can go back to school and do not worry about anything," said my father again, rising to go to the kitchen for our bundles.

Now, toward midnight, we were on our way to the village to work all the harder because we would have no more land. What words of great conviction were said when my father got up from his seat, I had not heard, and if I had, they were forgotten in the sudden rush of conflicting emotions.

We had no more land except the narrow strip of ground where our hut stood and the lot where my father had built a house for my brother Leon and his wife. We still had the clearing, but it did not really belong to us; most of what we raised still went to the church. According to the verbal agreement we could raise anything but the church would have one third of it, and from the third year on, we would share the crop on equal basis.

The land was not for sale, so there was no hope of possessing it. There were no usury laws and we the peasants were the victims of large corporations and absentee landlords. When the church took part in the corruption, the consequences almost tore the Philippines from its economic roots. It was only years afterward that a definite program was adopted for the peasantry, but even then it was merely a bait tossed by politicians into the restless life of the nation.

Some of my uncles were already dispossessed of their lands, so they went to the provincial government and fought for justice; but they came back to the village puzzled and defeated. It was then that one of my uncles resorted to violence and died violently, and another entered a world of crime and criminals.

But my father believed in the eternal goodness of man, and only once did he almost give up his faith. Even when the usurers were closing in on us, he did not believe that he would be cheated. He was an honest, simple man, who went about his work hoping for an ample reward at the end. He was also a strong man when his deep convictions were at stake. Illiterate as he was, my father had an instinct for the truth. It was this inborn quality, common among peasants, that had kept him going in a country rapidly changing to new conditions and ideals.

One summer day, when the rice lay golden in the sun, startling rumors came to Mangusmana: the peasants in a province to the south of us had revolted against their landlords. There the peasants had been the victims of ruthless exploitation for years, dating back to the eighteenth century when Spanish colonizers instituted severe restrictive measures in order to impoverish the natives. So from then on the peasants became poorer each year and the landlords became richer at every harvest time. And the better part of it was that the landlord was always away, sometimes merely a name on a piece of paper.

The peasants did not know to whom they should present their grievances or whom to fight when the cancer of exploitation became intolerable. They became cynical about the national government and the few powerful Filipinos of foreign extraction who were squeezing a fat livelihood out of it. They began to think for themselves and to take matters into their own hands, and they resorted to anarchistic methods. But there came a time when an intelligent campaign for revolt was started, with the positive influences of peasant revolts in other lands; and the Philippine peasants came out with their demands, ready to destroy every force that had taken from them their inherited lands.

The unorganized revolt in the southern province ended in tragedy; the peasants were shot down and those who survived were thrown into medieval dungeons. But these conditions could not go on for long without disastrously rocking the very foundation of Philippine life. These sporadic revolts and uprisings unquestionably indicated the malignant cancer that was eating away the nation's future security and negatively influencing the growth of the Philippines from a backward and undeveloped agricultural land into a gigantic industrial country. The wealth that was not already in the power of the large corporations, banks, and the church, was beginning to flow into the vaults of new corporations, banks, and other groups. As bloodily as this wealth concentrated into the hands of the new companies, as swiftly did the peasants and workers become poorer.

But some were favored by this sudden upsurge of industry. The sons of the professional classes studied law and went to the provinces, victimizing their own people and enriching themselves at the expense of the nation. In a few years these lawyers were elected to the national government, and once secure in their positions and connections, they also took part in the merciless exploitation of the peasantry and a new class of dispossessed peasants who were working in the factories or on the vast haciendas.

These conditions could not continue forever. In every house and hut in the far-flung *barrios* where the common man or *tao* was dehumanized by absentee landlordism, where a peasant had a son who went to school through the sacrifice of his family and who came back with invigorating ideas of social equality and of equal justice before the law, there grew a great conflict that threatened to plunge the Philippines into one of its bloodiest revolutions.

Such were conditions in the Philippines when my brother Macario graduated from high school and started teaching in Binalonan. Since he was an exceptionally bright student, he was appointed to teach in the sixth grade at a monthly salary of fifty pesos. His salary, which amounted to twenty-five dollars, was the highest in our town and therefore the most enviable.

Now my father began to feel at ease despite the fact that we had no more land of our own. The plow became lighter and he followed it gaily through the water and under the stifling heat of the summer sun. The nights became more peaceful and the days of labor shorter and more promising. The burden was off his shoulders at last and now he could relax for the first time in his life.

I remember this period of my childhood vividly because it was the only time that my father and I went hunting together. It was spring and the grass in the plain was young and as green as the pine trees on the mountains where we were going with our dog and a week's provision of rice. As we walked through the stony village road, I could see the tall *talahib* grass with its crown of white flowers spreading majestically on the ditches and the soft, windswept *cogon* grass parting beautifully as the breeze came blowing, as though it were a wave pushed seaward by a gentle inland wind; the murmuring sound sang through the thin, long blades, stopping our dog in its tracks with a puzzled look in its eyes.

When we reached the stony bottom of the river at the edge of Mangusmana, I saw my face in the clear, cool water that stood like a pool of light between two boulders. My father took off his clothes and plunged in; the dog followed him, whimpering in the sudden cold of the spring water. I took off my clothes also and crept slowly to the edge of the pool, holding onto the boulders as I submerged myself. We sat in the fine sand at the bottom of the pool and played with the little fishes that emerged from the crevices between the stones. It was clear and quiet in the water, and we sat side by side as though we were sitting in the sun.

I will never forget the *kilins*, or mountain bamboo, that we saw on the way up the trail, and how my father made tubes from the young shoots and filled them with shrimps. As soon as we had made a camp, I built a fire between two large stones. My father wrapped the bamboo tubes with banana leaves and put them under the fire.

"This is called *doayen*, son," said my father, pushing the burning coals over the tubes. "It is more delicious than the wild boar."

"How did you learn to make it, Father?" I asked.

"From the Igorots in the mountains of Baguio," he said. "I lived with them when the revolution was broken in southern Luzon. I fought with them, and we were called guerrillas. Someday you will understand, and maybe when you grow up you will see my Igorot friends. . . ."

To this distant day, I know that my father was right about the *doayen*. I remember that we caught one *alingo*, or wild boar, and tried its meat, but it was not as palatable as the *doayen*. I also remember that we caught a little deer and took it back with us to Mangusmana. I tried to feed it with tender tamarind leaves and *marongay* flowers, but it refused to eat anything, and our dog would stand for hours facing the wild animal. Finally, it became too weak to stand. I have forgotten, now, what happened to it.

Some weeks after our hunting trip a man came from nowhere to our house and presented my father with a paper purportedly signed by the church people. Because my father could not read the document and there was no man in the village who could read it, he went to town and let my brother Macario explain it to him.

It was midnight when he came back to Mangusmana. I heard him come into the hut, stopping at the door to locate me in the dark. Then he sat on the bench by the window for a long time. I could not see him in the dark, but knew that he was looking out of the window toward our clearing.

When the moon came out at dawn my father awakened me. We went outside and walked side by side to the clearing. There were crickets everywhere in the fields. I remember their tinny chirping and the fine moonlight that was streaming like a flood of silk as far as the eyes could see. Walking with my father in the moonlight was as peaceful as sitting with him in the bottom of the clear mountain pool. When we arrived at the clearing the quails were singing their mating songs between the growing rows of corn. The long, broad leaves were like human arms upraised to heaven in gentle supplication, moving slowly with the night breeze toward the west, as though they were making the sign of the cross and bowing to the wet earth in reverence.

"We will have a good crop this year, Father," I said.

"It is not our plantation any more, son," said my father, touching the leaves with the gentleness that he showed toward plants and animals. "It belongs to a man in Manila now. We will have to look for another land tomorrow."

I could not understand why. "You mean the land does not belong to us any more?" I asked.

"The land never did belong to us," said my father. "It belonged to the church. But now it belongs to a rich man in Manila."

"What about our corn?" I asked.

"They paid me for the corn, son," said my father. "But it is not enough to cover the seeds we have used. I accepted it because they told me that I had no right to plant corn in a land that did not belong to me."

I did not ask my father again about the agreement between him and the church. It was only fifteen months since we had cleared the land, and we had had a good crop of highland rice; and now we were expecting a good crop of corn. But a strange man appeared from nowhere and claimed that the land belonged to another man in Manila.

This incident was actually the beginning of my father's struggle to hold onto the land he knew so well, fighting to the end and dying on it like a peasant.

When the clearing was finally taken away from us, my father went to town several times and consulted with my brother Macario on how to get it back. There was nothing he could do; even my brother was desperate because we had no more

land left. He had been at his job three months now, but had
saved only about a hundred pesos. It was not enough for a first
payment on what we owed the moneylender.

In the month of August of that year, when the provincial
government was in session, my father filled a sack with rice and
fresh vegetables and walked to Lingayen to fight for the repos-
session of our land. Three weeks later he came back to Binalonan
a defeated man. Lingayen was about fifty kilometers away, and
when he came back on foot, which was the way he had gone,
his feet were bleeding from walking on the rough and stony
road. He walked about in great agony, but he went around asking farmers to lend him some land to cultivate. . . .

CHAPTER IV

THIS family tragedy marked the beginning of my conscious life, when my responses to outward influences grew so acute that I almost wrecked my whole future. I became sensitive in the presence of poverty and degradation, so sensitive that my unexpressed feelings tempered my psychological relation to the world. It was only long afterward in a land far away, long after these conflicts were conquered and forged as a weapon against another chaos that threatened to plunge me into despair and rootlessness, that the full significance of our tragedy burst into a flaming reality and drove me, suddenly and inevitably, into the struggle for the fulfillment of the redeeming qualities which I believed were inherent in me.

It was at this time that my father lost the land we had cleared for the church. Because our own land was still in the possession of the moneylender, there was no longer anything to do in the village. My brother Macario had not yet earned enough money to redeem the four hectares of land, which were all that was left of the original family property. My father could not find a man who would lend him farming land, and could not even hire himself to a farmer. The villagers were all small farmers, and they had only enough hectares to cultivate for themselves.

For a long time it seemed that my father and I could find nothing to do except to go to some farmer's rice field and help in the harvesting. But my father was a farmer, not a hired laborer. It humiliated him to hire himself out to someone. Yet he was willing to swallow his pride and to forget the honor of his ancestors.

It was only when my maternal grandmother died that my father was allowed by my uncles on my mother's side to cultivate the old woman's little piece of land. But it was stony ground and far from the reach of water, and the grass was stunted and yellowish in color. It was not good for anything, not even *camote* or sweet potato, but my father was a stubborn man born to dig in the earth. He even said jokingly, when he saw my interest dying, that he would squeeze enough water from the stones to irrigate the land.

I tried to help him cut the tall grass with a broad cutting knife called a *palang,* but when we started digging a ditch to connect the land with the main waterways, I was shocked to discover that one foot below the surface were large stones and fossils of trees buried by floods many years before. My interest in the project died.

"I think you should go to town and live with your mother," said my father. "Besides it is high time for you to go to school. I will try to farm alone."

"I will come back and help you again," I said.

"I will call you when I need you, son," said my father.

"I will always be ready," I said, looking at the boulders and huge roots of trees in the mouths of the caves that we had dug for the irrigation ditch to pass through, looking beyond this nightmare of my childhood into the future and the dark unknown.

"Good-bye, son," said my father sadly. "Come to the village once in a while, when you feel like helping me."

"I will, Father," I said.

But I knew it was the end of my life in Mangusmana, the end of the bitter days of childhood. It was actually the end of my life with my father, the end of my farming life in the Philippines, the end of blinding heat and heavy rains. I was leaving all of my childhood now, leaving forever to face the demands of sudden manhood, and there was no return journey anywhere. I knew I could not go back to Mangusmana, and my father knew it too because he had witnessed it before, when my other brothers went the way I was going, away from him and his earth forever.

When I arrived in Binalonan the overland highway was under construction and a few people of the town were employed

The new road connected Manila in the south with the beautiful summer city of Baguio in the north. Hundreds of men and women were working on it, pounding the gravel into the sand with flattened pieces of wood. At night when there was a bright moon their pounding was like the distant roar of the sea. There was only one crushing machine in the ten-kilometer stretch under construction, but it was used in the daytime for leveling the ground that had been pounded by the men and women working through the night.

I went to the *capataz*, or foreman, of the construction gang and asked for a job. The work went on for three months; sometimes it rained torrentially and the water washed away the soft shoulders of the road. We wrapped palm raincoats around our bodies and worked furiously to save the road, but the strong rain tore our coverings to shreds. We discarded them and went on working without protection in the total rain. But sometimes it was so extremely hot we could hardly see what we were doing; the heat rose from the sand and stone like steam and hurt our eyes. It made the foreman irritable and angry, so we worked harder only to drop on the road from exhaustion.

But on the moonlit nights the children in the neighborhood came out with rice pestles and helped us without asking for any compensation. It was fun for them to work with us before they went to bed. We worked on toward the river that separates Binalonan and Puzzorobio, until one day the water came rushing upon us. I was swept away into a deep bend of the river and was pasted there against the bank, struggling.

I was told afterward that three men had hung on ropes tied to the huge mango tree near the river and reached for me. When I regained consciousness, I was lying on a soft grass mat in our house. It was two days after the accident, and the road had been finished. The foreman came to our house and gave me my salary, plus a small bonus. I gave it to my mother, and my father took it from her; then putting our earnings together, he went to the moneylender. It was the first payment on our land.

One day my brother Macario came home from school and saw me in bed.

"You should not work too hard at your age, Allos," he said.

"Did you bring home a book with pictures?" I asked.

"Sure," he said. "But you should wait until you are better."

"I would like to look at the pictures now," I said.

He went to the kitchen and came back with the oil lamp. He sat on the floor beside me. He started reading the story of a man named Robinson Crusoe who had been shipwrecked in some unknown sea and drifted to a little island far away. My brother patiently explained the struggle of this ingenious man who had lived alone for years in inclement weathers and had survived loneliness and returned safely to his native land.

I was fascinated by the bearded man, and a strong desire grew in me to see his island.

"You must remember the good example of Robinson Crusoe," my brother said. "Someday you may be left alone somewhere in the world and you will have to depend on your own ingenuity." Then he pointed to the picture of the lonely man and his faithful dog sitting side by side on an unknown shore. "Maybe you will be thrown upon some unknown island someday with nothing to protect you except your hands and your mind. Now read this line after me, Allos. . . ."

It was the beginning of my intellectual life with Macario, the beginning of sharing our thoughts with each other; and although he went away not long afterward to escape a tragedy that was about to crush him, I found him again in another land where we resumed the friendship we had found long ago at my sickbed.

When I was well again I saw that my mother needed help in her small trading business. It was because I wanted to help keep our family together that I had neglected going to school. My older brothers were all away from home, and I knew that they would not come back to Binalonan except for brief visits. Amado, who had left the village two years before, was now in the province of Bulacan working on a sugar plantation. Only Macario and I were left, and I did not want our family to disperse completely. But circumstances stronger than my hands and faster than my feet were inevitably dividing us, and no matter what I did our family was on its way to final dissolution and tragedy.

My mother's trading business was very simple and primitive, yet the effort and time we put on it was incalculable. We awakened in the early morning and filled an earthen jar with *boggoong*, or salted fish, and peddled it in the villages. My mother carried the jar on her head, while I carried a long tube of salt on my shoulder. The villagers had no time to come to town for their supply of salted fish and salt, so we brought it to them once a week, hoping for a little profit.

Boggoong is an essential food to the peasants, for without it their simple fare of rice and leaves of trees is tasteless. They spread it thinly on the rice, if they have nothing else to eat; but most of the time they mix it with vegetables, especially with eggplants and *paria*, or bitter melon, which they like better than any other vegetable. They are always without money, and if they have saved anything at all, it is only a few centavos wrapped tightly in dirty rags.

My mother and I carried on our trade with the peasants by barter. For one cup of salt we would get three cups of rice, or four cups of beans; but for one cup of salted fish, which was more valuable than salt, we would get five cups of rice or six cups of beans. Sometimes the peasants had no rice or beans, so we willingly accepted chickens or eggs. But my mother gave even to those peasants who had nothing to barter in the hope that when we came around again they would be ready to pay. We were not always able to collect everything we had loaned, but my mother kept on giving our products to needy peasants.

It was during this period that I came to understand my mother's heart. We had gone to a village where the women made decorative potteries. Most of the women gave us rice and chickens, but there was one woman who had nothing to give except a beautiful drinking jar that she had made out of the red clay in her backyard. My mother was attracted by it instantly, and she gave the woman more than the pot's value. I had never before known her to appreciate beauty, but perhaps it was because she had had no time to express the finer qualities in her.

It was an unusually successful day. We had sold everything at a good price and our baskets were bulging with rice and beans. My mother carried the basket on her head and the beautiful jar in her left hand. Her right hand was holding the edge of the basket. I walked ahead of her and pushed away the tall grasses, stopping only when the chickens I was carrying made too much noise.

When we reached the Tagamusin River that separates Binalonan and the town of San Manuel, it began to rain and the red clay made the footpath slippery. My mother tucked her skirt between her legs, so that from a distance she looked like a man with short pants. We waded carefully across the murky water with the baskets held high above our heads. But when we reached the rise that led up to the road to town, her feet began to slip. She dug her toes into the mud and held desperately onto the beautiful pot, but she kept slipping back to the water. She was like a woman rolling on a pair of skates, slowly moving downward without losing her balance. Then suddenly she lost her grip on the jar, and it rolled into the water.

My mother wanted to turn her head to see what happened to it, but could not because she would have spilled the rice in the basket. Slowly and carefully she climbed up the rise, holding her head high and straight, digging the toes of one foot after the other into the mud and clutching the bank with her left hand. When she reached the level of the road, she heaved the basket to safety.

The jar was floating down the river. My mother slid down the mud, rushed into the water, and came back to the footpath wiping the undamaged jar with her skirt. When we arrived home I told the story to my brother Macario, who burst into laughter.

"Allos, stop that now!" said my mother.

My mother and I had another experience, a sad one, in a village called Cabolloan, where the poorest peasants lived on a barren land. The women asked for credit, or if refused, paid very little. When Saturday came around and our debtors saw us walking into the village, they started hiding in their empty granaries or pretended to be sick.

One woman came down from her grass hut trembling and looking very hungry and ill.

"I have not tasted *boggoong* for a long time," she told my mother.

"You can taste it now," said my mother, pretending not to know that the woman wanted credit.

Finally the peasant said, "I have nothing to barter because I am all alone and I am sick."

My mother did not say anything. She was thinking of the next payment on our land.

Then the woman said pathetically, "Cannot I even dip my hands into it?"

"What good will it do you, old woman?" I said, noticing that her hands were cracked in places. "You know that the *boggoong* will hurt your hands the moment you touch it."

The woman looked at me blankly; then she ran into her house and came back with a small earthen bowl half-filled with water. Quickly she put her hands into my mother's can of salted fish, and taking them out as quickly, she washed them in her bowl of clean water. There was agony in her face. When the water had reached the deepest recesses of the cracks in her hands, the woman looked at me with forgiving eyes. Suddenly she lifted the bowl to her mouth and drank hungrily of the water where she had washed her hands that had been smeared with salted fish. When it was empty she scraped the sediment in the bottom of the bowl with her forefinger; then she rushed into her hut to look for rice.

I wanted to laugh because it was so comical, but my mother looked at me with angry eyes.

"Someday you will understand these things," she said, looking up at the house. Then she knelt on the ground, lifted the basket, and put it expertly on her head.

I followed her slowly down the road.

CHAPTER V

I HAD come upon another world that was to become a fore-taste of my later struggles for a place in the sun. Selling *bog-goong* and salt with my mother gave me an opportunity to meet many people and to become a part of their lives. I became inti-mate with the obsession for food, and this, too, was to become a part of my life. Many of the peasants were starving, but like my family they were full of pride. They promised to pay their debts at a certain time when they knew well enough that they could not afford to pay. But my mother was a patient and trusting woman; even when our profit for a day's work was only twenty centavos, or ten cents, her interest in our business never diminished.

I do not know now why we began going to the town of Puzzorobio. Early one morning my mother woke me up and told me that we would go there to sell beans. The town was much nearer than Binalonan to Dagupan, where salted fish was the principal product, so my mother figured that beans would bring us more profits there than at our public market. Like my father, she could not read or write, but her practical sense was sharper than most of those who had learned to read. Her common sense had kept our family going for many desperate years.

It was five in the morning when we started with big baskets of beans on our heads. The overland highway had just been finished on our side of the Kataklan River, but beyond it and on to Puzzorobio it was still muddy. We waded through this dangerous road, holding onto each other firmly to keep from falling; and sometimes in our intimate grasp we communicated a rare and lovely understanding. Maybe it would be only the sudden tightening of my mother's thumb or forefinger on my arm, but the delicate message would be transmitted and it would

36

linger in my memory. Sometimes it was the frantic trembling of her arm, when her foot would slip and the basket almost fall from her head, and she would stifle a cry of sudden fear. And I would feel it, the unmistakable cry for help between two suffering people.

When we arrived at our destination we knew at once that we would have a good day. It was always raining there, a warm, gentle rain. While my mother sat in the booth, behind her two baskets of beans, I stood on the cement pavement and watched the buyers going by. They were more elegant there than in our town. The marketers were dressed in immaculate white dresses. The women were agile in their leather slippers. Sometimes they came by *caromata*, or horse-drawn, flimsy cab, and leaped upon the pavement as expertly as trained dogs.

My mother brightened up when the more well-to-do citizens came with their servants. When she dished out the beans with a polished coconut shell her hands trembled and the beans spilled over the pavement. She did not pay too much attention to her work, but was admiring the delicately embroidered dresses of the rich women, their smooth, silk handkerchiefs, and the way they carried themselves in the market. For the first time I realized that mother, always in rags, noticed how people wore elegant clothes and walked royally in the crowded place.

A young girl who came into the market with two women servants attracted general attention. I knew immediately that she had not come to buy anything, but to display her elegant dress and obedient servants. She walked like a queen between the long rows of cloth dealers, poking at the merchandise with her tiny silk umbrella. Then, having poked every roll of finery, she turned and came to our side of the market; and the traders of beans and rice looked up from their baskets, trembling with envy and admiration for the beautiful creature. She was walking very fast and her servants were hurrying to catch up with her. She was like a fawn dancing before the doe when taken for the first time to the bright meadow at the edge of the forest.

My mother looked up enraptured, not believing that all loveliness and wealth could be so bestowed upon one person. Her hands lingered absently in the basket of beans. The wonderful creature with the dainty agility approached our booth and noticed my mother's shining curiosity and envy. She stopped abruptly in front of my mother, her lips trembling with contempt.

"What are you looking at, poor woman?" she asked, raising the silk umbrella in her hand.

My mother was dumfounded by her elegance. Suddenly the girl struck the basket of beans and dashed off, leaving my mother with startled eyes. The basket toppled over on the pavement and the beans were scattered. My mother crawled on her knees scooping up the beans into the basket.

"It is all right," she kept saying. "It is all right."

I knelt on the wet cement picking out the dirt and pebbles from the beans. It was another discovery: my first clash with the middle classes in the Philippines. Afterward I came to know their social attitude, their stand on the peasant problem. I knew where they stood regarding national issues. I hated their arrogance and their contempt for the peasantry.

I was one peasant who did not crawl on my knees and say: "It is all right. It is all right. . . ."

Our trips to Puzzorobio were always successful. We were inspired to awaken earlier on weekdays. We went to the peasants in the villages and traded with them. We piled the beans and rice in our house, but when Saturday came we went to Puzzorobio.

Then a great misfortune came upon us. It had been raining all day, and the better customers would not come to the market because it was too wet for their beautiful clothes. Only the poor people came with a few centavos to buy a pinch of salt. Toward five o'clock our baskets of beans were still untouched, and we started the long journey homeward.

When we came to the river it was beginning to flood. I stood at the edge of the embankment wondering if we would be able to cross it. It was the same river which had swept me away some months before when I had been working on the highway. I kept thinking of our basket of beans.

My mother started for the water, holding the basket on her head with both hands. She no longer cared about her skirt. I followed close behind. It was easy for the first few yards; the water was still shallow and slow. But when we came to midstream it reached my mother's neck. Suddenly she stopped and ordered me to go ahead. I raised the basket as high as my hands would go and circled around. I looked like a floating mushroom. My head was completely submerged, but I reached the other side of the river safely.

Then my mother proceeded to cross: she had gone past the danger zone when her foot caught on a stone in the bottom of the river. I saw the basket of beans disappear into the water and then, in a little while, it came up and floated down the river. My mother turned about and dove into the water, trying to scoop up the beans that were being swiftly carried away by the strong current. When she realized that it was impossible to save anything, she swam after the basket and came back with a handful of beans. She stood on the river bank for a long time watching the rising water.

This incident ended our trips to Puzzorobio.

My father had taken back our farm, but he still had several more payments to make. He had finally given up the stony ground which belonged to my grandmother. Sometimes he came to town with a sack of vegetables, and after picking out the choicest tomatoes and eggplants, my mother sold the rest in the public market. Sometimes my father came with a sack of peanuts, which I would roast in a pile of heated sand. My mother would also sell the roasted peanuts. After a while we had saved enough money to pay for the next installment on our land.

It was during this period that my mother and I began going to San Manuel, noted for *mongoes* or yellow beans. Harvest season came in the middle of summer, long after the rice was put away. We went to San Manuel on Mondays and picked *mongoes*, returning to Binalonan on Saturdays with our share. We left my sister Irene in the care of my brother Macario, who took her to school with him.

In San Manuel we worked in the *mongo* fields on shares. Out of every five pounds of *mongo* seeds we harvested and threshed, we got one pound. I helped my mother pick the black pods and put them into the baskets we used for carrying beans and rice.

On one occasion we were unusually successful. We had worked fast, had made more money, and my mother was very happy. She did not want to go back to Binalonan right away. She told me that we would go to the public market of San Manuel. We walked slowly in the muddy road and, when we reached the town, I was surprised to see the plaza covered with tall grass. There were pigs and goats in the yard of the *presidencia*, and *carabaos* feeding in the school yard.

There were many Igorots in the market place, come down from the mountains to trade with the lowlanders. They walked among the people in their G-strings with their poisoned arrows and dogs. They had long black hair like mine, but while they knotted theirs and stuck brightly polished sticks through the knots, I tangled my hair like a bird's nest and put a straw hat on it to keep it from falling over my face. The lowland people did not even bother to look at them or at their dogs, when they went around offering their wild honey, rattan, and medicinal herbs.

I had never before seen the Igorots. They were a peaceful people, bent only on hard work, and religious in their own way. They came to the lowland villages once a year to trade their products, sometimes staying over for one season to help the farmers with their plowing and harvesting. Then they would leave for their tree houses in the mountain villages, dragging their dogs with them and raising the dust as they passed from view.

When my mother had bought what she wanted for my sister Irene—a piece of cotton cloth with polka dots—we started for Binalonan. She had paid more than one peso for it, she said, but it would make a beautiful dress for my sister.

"And if I have a little left," said my mother, "I will make you a handkerchief."

One peso was an exorbitant sum to my mother, but she had

been planning on it for a long time. She had also a plan for me.

"What is it, Mother?" I asked.

"You can go to school now, son," she said.

School! The stars gleamed brightly. There was a gentle breeze in the trees. The moon was rising out of the east, and it shone in my head. Everywhere in the fields the crickets were chirping melodiously. Why not? The prospect of going to school made the whole night enchanted. My bleeding hands were forgotten. The long and weary road to Binalonan was as nothing. Yes, even the hard work with my father in the village was also forgotten.

"I would like to be a doctor," I said, thinking of our relatives and friends who would have lived if there had been a doctor to take care of them.

"Doctor, son?" said my mother, and stopped suddenly, considering. "I thought you would like to be a lawyer. The lawyers and politicians at the *presidencia* have nice offices and soft chairs. Wouldn't you like to be with them?"

"Maybe I will change my mind," I said.

My mother put her hand on my neck affectionately. I pushed aside the tall grass that rose in our way. When we arrived at our house it was already twilight and the shadows of the trees in the yard were long and bizarre. My sister Irene was sick in bed, very quiet and uncomplaining. She lay quietly on her grass mat, following my mother with her eyes. She smiled when my mother showed her the polka dot cloth; then she held it weakly in her hands and went to sleep.

Toward midnight Irene began to cry. My mother took the oil lamp and prepared some herbs, while my brother Macario and I stood near, trying to assist her. Irene was calm for a while, weakly fingering the cloth and asking my mother what she would do with it. Suddenly she screamed with pain, rolling over on her stomach and beating the floor with her fists. My mother pressed Irene's stomach with a little bag of hot ashes. Irene screamed again, jerking her knees up to her chin, then relaxed, her face white as paper.

Then blood began to pour from her nose, choking her. My mother ran frantically for cloths, but the blood kept coming.

Afterward it started pouring from her mouth and ears. There was nothing we could do for her. In a few minutes she died like an animal that has been strangled with a rope. My mother looked at us helplessly. Then she knelt beside Irene, holding the polka dot cotton cloth.

For a long time I heard my mother weeping softly on her mat. I decided I would work hard and become a doctor.

CHAPTER VI

AFTER the death of my sister Irene one misfortune after another fell upon our family.

We were eating lunch one day when a young girl came to our house and sat in the living room waiting for my brother Macario. She had brought a large trunk with her, which I helped my mother carry into the house. I rushed to the schoolhouse and told my brother.

He commanded me to wait. When classes were over we ran to our house. The girl was still waiting. My mother and I went to the kitchen and pretended to be washing clothes. My brother and the girl were arguing in English. After dinner, while my mother was busy washing the dishes, they began arguing again and kept it up far into the night. My mother blew out the oil lamp and lay on her mat.

I sat in the darkness watching my brother and the strange girl moving in the room. Then I went to sleep quietly, but was awakened by the girl's soft weeping. My brother accompanied her down from the house and out to the gate. I went to the window and saw them waiting for a *caromata* to take the girl away.

But it was not long before the girl came back. She brought all her possessions with her: a large trunk of clothes, a green lamp, two pairs of shoes, and a little cat.

"Why did you come back when we had already agreed that you should wait for another year?" asked my brother Macario, casting furtive glances at my mother.

"I like this house," said the girl. "I shall never leave it again."

And it was true. She stayed on. One day my brother threatened to throw her out, and she defied him. When he struck her, she struck back. My brother was furious. The next day he moved

43

to the house of a cousin. Then the girl went to the school principal, and before we knew it my brother was asked to resign his job. There was only one alternative for him: to marry the girl. But he did not want to marry her. He went to the *presidencia* every day and played dominoes or checkers with the policemen and other men who had no work.

Macario had one important reason for not marrying the girl. He knew that if he married he would have to give up helping us pay the installments on our land. He took the civil service examinations hoping to get a place in the tax department, but there was no opening for him. My father was becoming desperate. He came to town and stayed on for weeks, neglecting his growing corn and other farm duties.

Then my mother began to grow big in the belly again. She could hardly walk about any more. I could not go alone to the public market. It was then that my brother Amado came back from the sugar cane plantation in Bulacan and got a job in the public market. It was an easy job, collecting tickets from the traders. He was helping toward the next installment.

It was also at this time that the copra industry came to Binalonan. Several agents of the copra companies in Manila came to the provinces, and one of them came to our town. I began climbing the coconut trees for other people, cutting the nuts with a *compay*, or sickle, so that they fell to the ground with a solid thud. One out of every five that I cut was my share. It was a very dangerous job, climbing the tall coconut trees. Sometimes they were one hundred feet high; sometimes their trunks were too big for my short arms.

A nut sold for five centavos, so I usually made one peso a day climbing the tall trees from six to six. I would give the money to my mother, who was now recuperating in bed with the new baby.

"What is her name?" I asked.

"Francisca, son," said my mother.

I had a sister again.

✦

At last the day for paying the installment was drawing near. I tried to climb the coconut trees faster, hoping to have a greater share. I was naked to the waist. But one afternoon, when I was working unusually late, I fell from the top of a tree.

I was carried off to our house. When I woke up my mother was crying. One leg and one arm were broken.

"Be brave, Allos," said my mother.

A week afterward my father came to town with the cart filled with straw. He put me on the warm straw and drove to an *albolario*, or chiropractor, on the other side of town. The man was a primitive doctor, little better than a witch doctor. He burned many leaves of trees and rubbed the ashes mixed with oil over my body, uttering unintelligible incantations and dancing mysteriously around me. His face was deeply stained with some kind of juice. His hands were rough working hands, but gentle and kind to my body. They crept over my leg smoothly and soothingly, pressing and rubbing gently.

"There you are, son," he said when he was through. "Come and see me when you can walk again."

"Yes, sir," I said.

He patted my legs with his gentle hands. My father gave him three chickens and a sack of fresh tomatoes. They carried me back to the cart.

"Good-bye and good luck," said the *albolario*.

I knew that I would get well and walk back to his house. There was something about him that made me feel sure. My bones began to knit together and in two months I was able to move my arm and leg. I looked forward to the day when I could visit the old man.

One day my brother Macario told me that when I got well he would take me to school. He sat with me near the lamplight and read the Old Testament. He read the story of a man named Moses who delivered his persecuted people to safety in another land.

"When did this tragedy happen?" I asked.

"A long time ago," he said.

"Who was Moses?"

"He was a wise Jew. His moral code was obeyed by his people for centuries."

"Do we have a man like him in our country?"

"Yes, Allos," he said. "His name is José Rizal."

"What happened to him?"

"The cruel Spanish rulers killed him."

"Why?"

"Because he was the leader of our people."

"I would like to know more about Rizal," I said.

"You don't realize what it is to be like Rizal," Macario said, looking curiously at me.

"I would like to fight for you, our parents, my brothers and sister."

"You will suffer," Macario said.

"I am not afraid," I said.

"You will know more about him someday," said my brother, going back to the Old Testament and reading solemnly.

It filled me with wonder as he explained the significance of the great men who had died for their persecuted peoples centuries ago. But now he had to go away. We could not read any more in the lamplight, could not travel through history into other lands and times.

Macario would be allowed to teach again without marrying the strange girl provided he would go to Mindanao.

"Where is Mindanao?" I asked.

"It is in the south, but not so far away," said my brother.

"Are you afraid to go?" I asked.

"I will be brave like you, Allos," he said. "And maybe when you grow up, I will ask you to visit me."

"I will come," I said.

"Good-bye, little brother," he said.

Mindanao was a dangerous land because the native Moros still resented the presence of Christians. They were Mohammedans, although their religion was already fast disintegrating. The faith had been brought by the mercenary Moors from Spain through

India during the eleventh century. The Moors at that time were at the height of their power and glory, having conquered all the Christian lands in Europe and Asia. They had ransacked and pillaged all the civilized countries of the world as far as the Euphrates River, following the trail of another insatiable conquerer and vandal before them, Alexander the Great, who was alleged to have reached Mindanao in search of fine horses and gold.

When the Spaniards discovered the Philippines in the later part of the fourteenth century, war with the Moros began and continued for centuries. It was both a religious and an economic war, for in those early days of global vandalism the sword and the cross went together. But foreign aggression only made the Mohammedan Moros more ardent defenders of their faith and their land, and even the Christian Filipinos became their enemies when they attempted to impose their customs and laws.

When Macario went to teach in Mindanao, the Moros had not been entirely pacified. But some of their young men and women were already absorbing Christian ideals and modes of living. In fact, the better families were sending their children to America for a liberal education. The sudden contact of the Moros with Christianity and with American ideals was actually the liberation of their potentialities as a people and the discovery of the natural wealth of their land.

My brother Macario sent his monthly earnings from Mindanao to my mother so that we could pay the installment on our land. Then suddenly he stopped writing and sending money. We had one more payment to make.

That year a new *presidente*, or mayor, was elected and all the employees in the *presidencia* and public market were thrown out of office. It was always like that in Binalonan. When a new *presidente* was elected all the old employees, unless they supported him, were dismissed, and immediately his own family, relatives, and supporters were employed.

My brother Amado, who was a ticket collector at the public market, was also dismissed. He tried to look for a job in the local dance hall, where the businessmen and teachers found pleasure. But there was no opening for him, so he worked his way on a ship to America.

It was the last time that I saw Amado in the Philippines. Immediately afterward Macario wrote from Manila that he had not been teaching for some time. The strange girl had followed him to Mindanao, and he had escaped to Manila. Now he too was contemplating going to America.

My father knew then that it was the end of our family. He was not sure where to get the last payment for our land, because the rice was only a foot high and it would be at least five months before it could be harvested. The last payment was only two months off and none of our family was earning any money. And my mother was big with child again.

I limped to school every day carrying my boiled rice and salted fish. I walked three miles to the schoolhouse. When I went home in the afternoon people looked out of their houses and pointed at me.

"Look at that Igorot boy," they said. "He is going to school with his long hair. Hey, Igorot!"

I did not listen to them. I was too absorbed with my book. The other children taunted me in the school yard and threw stones at me, laughing at my long hair and bare feet. I sat attentively in the classroom, listening eagerly to my teacher. I knew that my schooldays would not last long. I tried to learn everything I could in a short time, because I knew I would soon have to stop and go back to work.

CHAPTER VII

THEN the heavy rains came and my legs began to swell, preventing me from going to school. I stayed in the house wondering what would happen to me. But when I began to recover, Francisca played with me. Like my baby sister, I crawled on the floor to the window and watched the boys and girls of my age going to school. Sometimes a boy on his way home would stop beneath the window and read aloud to me. Sometimes a girl would come to the house and teach me how to sing.

One afternoon my mother came home from the public market and found me crying silently.

"What is it, Allos?" she asked.

"I would like to continue going to school," I said.

There was a puzzled look in her eyes. "You will go as soon as your sister is big enough to be alone in the house," she said.

I showed my teeth and smiled. "I will wait, Mother," I said.

"That is a good boy," she said.

But I did not get well for a long time. There were days when my legs were reduced to normal size, but there were also days when they were abnormally large. I thought I would never walk on my feet again.

My father no longer came to town because the last installment on our land was past due. Although he felt that the moneylender would not be too drastic with us, he had hired himself out to some farmers in the village. He earned fifty centavos a day, digging in the muddy fields with antiquated implements. But it was the only work he knew, the only work available, and he could earn a little money on which to hang his hope.

At this time my brother Luciano, the soldier, came home to live with us. He had just completed his three-year service in the Philippine Scouts, and was honorably discharged. He had

49

contracted a serious lung disease while he was in service. The army sent him home with the idea that in a few months he would receive some kind of monthly pension from the United States government.

Luciano was twenty years old, but he looked younger because of his pale face. He had joined the army at seventeen, but before that he had been an agent for one of the large sugar companies in Manila. He had recruited workers from the dispossessed peasant provinces in northern Luzon, passing through Binalonan with truckloads of men and women on their way to the great sugar cane plantations in the south. He had stopped now and then at our house, but I was then living with my father on the farm. I first saw Luciano when he came home from the army, sick and tired and disillusioned.

He bought a small soldier's cap and gave it to me, but it was stolen by one of the boys in the neighborhood. My brother carried me in his arms and we went from house to house, asking about my cap. He was in uniform and when the peasants saw him, they whipped their boys mercilessly until they revealed who had stolen my cap.

Luciano was a young man of wide experience. He was one of two men in the town who could operate a typewriter, and so was needed at the *presidencia*. He was also the first to know about machines—automobiles and motorcycles—when these first came to Binalonan. There were many important things he could do that few of the townspeople knew.

While I was still unable to walk out of the house, Luciano used to go to the grassy river with horsehair snares. He would entwine two thick strands together and loop them to about the size of a peso; attaching the twines to the sturdy *talahib* stem, he would plant them under the bushes in the river bottom.

"The birds will go to the river at noon for a drink of water," he would explain to me, "so I put the snares in their *sibbang*, or trail, and they will go through the loops without knowing it. Their eyes are very weak in the sunlight."

"I would like to see you plant the snares," I said.

"You must get well and I will show you how to catch birds without hurting them," he said.

One afternoon Luciano brought a *sibbed*, or crying bird, and tied it to the table in the living room. It was a beautiful bird, but it cried all the time. My sister Francisca played with it, but the bird would not eat anything.

"It is dying of starvation," I said.

"It is your bird, Allos," said my brother. "You must keep it alive."

I hobbled about the *sibbed* and tried to feed it with corn. It looked me straight in the eye and cried, filling the house with its mournful nocturnal noise. I caught it in my arms and held it in the light.

"Why is it crying, brother?" I asked.

"It has lost something precious, I guess," said my brother, stroking the bird gently, his eyes far away. "Maybe a wife and some little *sibbed*. Wouldn't you cry if you had lost something dear to you?"

"I would," I said. "I would cry until I died."

Francisca started laughing and pushing the bird toward the wall. She could not understand why it would not eat. The bird crouched in a corner and looked at my sister, crying and bowing to the floor as though it were a human being in mourning.

"It is about to die," I said.

"You must try to make it live, Allos," said my brother. "The bird is healthy and strong outside, but something is eating it inside. Its heart is bleeding, Allos."

I tried to make the bird live. I blew my breath into its delicate throat, cooing soft words to it. But nothing helped.

When the bird died no word could console me. My brother carried me in his arms to the river and let me watch him contrive the snares under the bushes. I would hang on his neck and watch his hands expertly push the thin blades of grass, putting the snares in place and patting the soft sand under them.

After we had planted all the snares we would go to the shade of a *camatchile* tree. My brother would climb the tree and throw the choicest fruits to me. The taste was bitter, but we liked it. Sometimes we went farther up the river and bathed in the deep pool. Luciano would place me on the edge of the pool and rub my legs slowly with red clay; then holding me gently in his arms, he would dive into the water and spring up for air when he knew that I needed it.

At sundown we rounded up our snares. Some birds struggled violently and the snares tightened sharply around their necks and they died. Some stood placidly and waited for us to catch them. My brother held them with one hand and I with the other. I put my arms around his neck and hung on his back. Then we went home slowly, shouting at the village dogs that tried to leap at our birds.

While it was customary among the peasants to eat birds, my brother never allowed us to eat the ones we caught. We never thought of killing them, but considered them part of our family. They became tame, and ate with us like children. They walked freely in the house, running to safety when a stranger came to visit us.

I remember this was the most pleasant period of my life. My father had taught me to be kind to animals because they were useful on the farm, and from him I had learned to deal with our *carabaos* as though they were human beings. I used to sleep on the back of our favorite *carabao* when I was a herd boy in the village; when I fell on the ground the animal would crop the grass around me until I awakened. My brother Leon had taught me to be few of words and to stick to my convictions. He had also taught me to love the earth. Amado, because he had had no chance to go further, had taught me how important it was for a man to study. He who had so little education knew how necessary it was to go into the world with a good education. And Macario, who was torn by inner conflicts, had widened my mental horizon by telling me about the lives of other men in faraway lands.

But Luciano did not have to go away to show me the beauty of the world. We went to the river and snared birds and brought them home. We did not catch them for their usefulness, but for the esthetic pleasure we found in observing them. I had the rare opportunity of watching them in their various moods. My education with Luciano was very useful to me when I was thrown into the world of men, when all that I held beautiful was to be touched with ugliness. Perhaps it was this wonderful interlude with my brother that finally led me to an appreciation of beauty—that drove me with a burning desire to find beauty and goodness in the world.

The rarest bird in our part of the Philippines was the parrot. It was a small, gray and red-breasted bird, with a melodious voice. It was Luciano who introduced tamed parrots to our town. He built a small cage and covered it with horsehair snares. He put a quail in the cage and hung it on the highest branch of the *santol* tree in our yard. The cage was connected to one of the windows of our house with a long string that we had made from *maguey* fibers.

The quail was not the best decoy for a parrot, but it was the smallest bird we had in the house. A parrot appeared and when it noticed the quail, it flew from one limb to another until it was close to the cage. It stopped and peeked around the tiny bars, singing rapturously to the quail. It jumped on the roof of the cage, where the snares were thick. Its neck was caught by several loops. It struggled violently only to be caught by the legs. My brother lowered the cage to the ground, and we rushed outside to look at the parrot.

"It is our first parrot, Allos," said my brother. "But we will catch others when they come to the tree."

"I like it," I said. "It is a very brave bird."

"It is in love with the quail," said my brother. "When you are in love you are brave. You are not afraid of death."

"Do you think it knew that there was danger in the cage?" I asked.

"Maybe," said my brother. "Birds are like human beings. They have a strong sense of death. And of life. Now let us go to the house and feed it with bananas."

We tamed the parrot and put it in another cage, but it looked sullenly at us. After a while we hung the cage outside one of our windows and it began to sing; then we put it in a strong cage and used it for a decoy. We caught many parrots after that and sold them. When we had saved enough to start a little store, Luciano went to town and borrowed some building implements. He found a suitable spot by the overland highway that had become popular with American and European tourists. They passed through Binalonan on their way to Baguio, stopping only for water and food and to take pictures of the natives.

My mother was in bed again with another baby sister, and my father was very happy to have two daughters. When the store was finished Luciano bought some bananas and mangoes from the people in the neighborhood. All day we sat on the bamboo bench in front of the store waiting for customers. The women in the neighborhood came with their few centavos, but mainly they wanted petroleum for their lamps. My brother wanted to sell petroleum, but he did not have enough money to buy a whole can. When a tourist car would break down near the store he would repair it and earn a little money. We watched the automobiles pass by hoping the tires would blow out.

When the moon was out in full my brother would call the boys in the neighborhood and persuade them to wrestle in the empty lot at the back of the store. The ground was softer there than on the highway, where we usually wrestled in the daytime. But when there was no moon he would bring out the oil lamp and watch us wrestle in the faint light. I was not strong enough to be shaken, but my brother told the smallest boy to wrestle with me. It was a good practice, and it taught us to be fair and decent.

Then Luciano began to worry about his pension from the United States government. He lost interest in the store and wanted to go into politics. He was thinner now. He coughed at night, and there was a sad shine in his eyes. I sat in the store waiting for customers, but nobody came. The vegetables and fruits began to rot. Finally we closed the store and sat on the bench waiting for some miracle to happen.

One morning my father came running to my brother.

"The moneylender has taken my land, son," he said.

"How much more do you owe him, Father?" asked Luciano.

"It is one hundred pesos," said my father. "I promised to pay in three weeks, but he won't listen to me. I'd thought that by that time the rice would be harvested and I could sell some of it; then I would be able to pay him. He sent two policemen to Mangusmana to see that I do not touch the rice. It is my *own* rice and land. Is it possible, son?" My father stopped and looked eagerly into my brother's eyes. "Can a stranger take away what we have molded with our hands?"

"Yes, Father," said Luciano. "It is possible under the present government. There are no laws to protect the *tao* against the unscrupulous practices of wealthy men in our country. I am afraid you will have to give up your land."

My father could not believe it. Sadly he glanced at his ugly, dark hands, then looked into my brother's eyes, his face dim with broken hope.

"There is something wrong in our country when a man can take away something that belongs to you and your family," he said, looking at his hands again and standing silently for a long time.

After a while he noticed me. He put his hand on my head and said, "This is the end, son." He turned around and walked slowly toward our house.

When he was gone Luciano coughed violently and tears filled his eyes. He went to the store and came out with a handful of sharp nails and threw them into the road. An automobile appeared and burst a tire. My brother ran out with his tools, knelt by the damaged tire, and began fixing it. When it was repaired the man at the wheel gave him ten centavos, and Luciano laughed guiltily when he put it in his pocket.

We used to sit on the bench in front of the store waiting for automobiles. My brother was always ready with the tools. Now and then an automobile came, but we did not earn enough to help my father. Then we gave up waiting for automobiles. My brother went to Mangusmana and planted tobacco, while I stayed in town looking for a job. When his pension finally came he sold his tobacco to a farmer and came back to Binalonan.

"Now I can go into politics," he said.

"Is it profitable?" I asked.

"Yes, if you care to make a business of it," he said. "I don't know what to do yet, but there is fun and glory in it."

"I like practical results," I said.

"I am a different person," he said. "Watch me turn this town into something else."

Not long afterward he became mayor of Binalonan. But even then he knew that he was dying. I would go to visit him when I was in town, and he would take me to his house to show me his books. I would be coming home from another town where I had found some kind of work, and when I would arrive in Binalonan Luciano would discuss politics with me. It seemed to me then that he was a man of great convictions, that he had great potentialities, and that he hated his narrow environment. It was the only world he knew, and he realized it. But he was determined to use every opportunity he had in that limited place.

"You must never stop reading good books, Allos," he said.

"My eyes are not good for reading," I said.

"Go to Manila someday and buy a pair of good glasses," he said. "Reading is food for the mind. Healthy ideas are food for the mind. Maybe someday you will be a journalist. . . ."

Journalist! What did it mean?

Years afterward I remembered Luciano's hope. I was in a hospital when the letter came telling me that he had died of tuberculosis. I crept out of the bed and cried in the bathroom, holding my chest for fear the blood would burst out of my own perforated lungs.

It was midnight and the hospital was in total darkness. Far away in the city the lights were flickering like a string of pearls strung on the huge neck of a dark woman. And far away also, in the workers' republic of Spain, a civil war was going on that a democracy might live. I remembered all my years in the Philippines, my father fighting for his inherited land, my mother selling *boggoong* to the impoverished peasants. I remembered all my brothers and their bitter fight for a place in the sun, their tragic fear that they might not live long enough to contribute something vital to the world. I remembered my own swift and dangerous life in America. And I cried, recalling all the years that had come and gone, but my remembrance gave me a strange courage and the vision of a better life.

"Yes, I will be a writer and make all of you live again in my words," I sobbed.

CHAPTER VIII

THE LAND question in Luzon was becoming more acute, and there were rumors of uprisings in the provinces where absentee landlordism was crippling the peasant economy. Rice was the main staple and the peasants could not exist without it, but the rich rice lands were owned by men who never saw them. Each year the landlords demanded a larger share, until it became impossible for the peasants to live.

It was at this time that my father's land was taken away from him. A stubborn peasant like his ancestors before him, my father had always believed that life should be rooted in the soil. He sold our animals and came to town, and after a day of secret deliberation with my mother he went to Lingayen to fight in the provincial court for the restoration of our farm.

After three weeks my father returned, defeated and broken in spirit. He had walked to the capital of Pangasinan carrying his sack of provisions and when he arrived there had had great difficulty in locating the proper court in which to present his case. When he found the court he could not locate the right people. He went from one clerk to another and from one room to another, pleading in his dialect and cursing his illiteracy, until he had ransacked the entire provincial capital.

He had no money and the wise men at the court spoke to him in Spanish and English. What could a poor and ignorant peasant like my father do in an organization such as the provincial government of Pangasinan? He came back and stayed on in town, sitting around in the house until he was driven to drunkenness.

My mother and I went to the town of Tayug, a rich rice land, and helped in the harvest. Tayug and two other neighboring towns belonged to one family. One could see the flowing expanse of gold in the month of October; but in November and far into the month of January there was a continuous procession of carts hauling harvested rice to the granaries of the landlord. There it was threshed and sold to the rice companies in Manila.

Then my mother went to Binalonan and returned with my sisters. Francisca was now nearly four years old, but Marcela was only a baby. They sat in the shade of the umbrella at the end of the long rows, away from the strong sun. My mother stopped now and then to feed Marcela, undoing her rough cotton blouse to her waist and putting her dark, pointed nipple into the baby's hungry mouth. Then she would put her in a makeshift hammock and go back to work.

Francisca was already beginning to be aware of what we were doing. She stayed in the shade watching Marcela, but she came now and then to where we were working to bring us a jar of cool drinking water. Then she would watch over the baby until the day's work was done, singing when Marcela became restless and hungry.

In the middle of the season strange men began coming to the rice fields. They distributed leaflets and talked to us. My mother and I were so deeply absorbed in our work that we were not aware of what was going on. A rugged peasant boy made impassioned speeches to the harvesters, but as he was only a simple peasant like themselves they paid no attention to him.

I remember this fanatical peasant boy because years afterward I met him again in America. His name was Felix Razon. One day he came to the field where we were working with several men wearing black armbands. They told us to leave, but we did not understand.

At night we slept in the field. The stars were so near it seemed we could touch them with our hands. Sometimes when I awakened between the tall rice stalks, I could feel the soft breathing of the earth. The sun came like gold, throwing its first beams downward into the immense plain. It lighted a new day of activity for us, and we cooked our breakfast on an improvised stove.

Working with my mother was pleasant, and it gave me an

impetus to strive for a better place. It was actually like working with my father in Mangusmana, with only one difference: I was a little older and more experienced. In the village, life was a simple peasant lullaby; we had our animals and our house. In Tayug the work was harder and harsher, and the people were more varied. And I had two little sisters who interrupted our work with delight.

A few days later Felix and the other men came to the rice fields again to persuade us to sell our shares of rice and to leave. Most of the harvesters sold theirs, but my mother sold only a part of ours. We were some distance from the highway when we saw hundreds of men with black armbands walking excitedly toward the town. They were members of the Colorum Party, a fanatical organization of dispossessed peasants that terrorized Luzon. It professed to be semi-religious, but it was actually a vengeful sect of anarchistic men led by a college-bred peasant who had become embittered in the United States.

As soon as Felix came to our part of the field and told us of the impending revolt, my mother tied our share of rice with a rope and carried some of the rice bundles on her head. I carried some of it, too. But she also carried the baby Marcela. Francisca, however, refused to be carried. When we reached the plaza we saw many of the Colorum at the kiosk, falling in line and preparing their attack. The policemen were running excitedly about the *presidencia*, piling bricks and sandbags outside the windows and doors. They were waiting, ready with their guns.

Then from beyond the *presidencia*, climbing up the river bank like a stream of black beetles, the Colorum came rushing upon the building, dispersing the few guards who were waiting outside with their antiquated pistols. They fired into the air and leaped behind trees when the police challenged them from behind the barricaded windows.

The *caromata* ponies at the station started running away in all directions. The bus that was discharging passengers near the schoolhouse turned around and sped toward Binalonan. The attacking band of the Colorum increased; they appeared from everywhere with their black flag and fired upon the men in the *presidencia*.

My mother grabbed Francisca, and we ran to the tall bushes by the roadside.

"Why are they fighting, Mother?" I asked.

"Why, son?" she said, her ignorant face searching for the words to answer me. "Why? I don't know, son."

"Are we not coming back to cut some more rice?" I asked.

"No, son," she said.

Francisca started to cry, hanging on my mother's skirt.

"Hush," said my mother.

We looked toward the *presidencia*. A policeman came out bravely, but he had not gone far when he was shot in the back. He fell under a flagpole. Another policeman arrived, then another; but five of the Colorum ran after them, shooting as they emerged from the tall acacia trees around the *presidencia*. They engaged in hand-to-hand fighting behind the coffee shop at the station. The Colorum rushed into the *presidencia* and after a while their flag appeared at the window. Then there was a respite; except for the jubilant rebels who were pouring into the town hall, the town was deserted. The dead were scattered on the lawn and in the street.

When it began to get dark my mother told us to follow her. We crept through the bushes, dragging the bundles of rice. We came to a wooded place west of town, away from the rice fields. We stopped and looked back. Then the guns began again, sputtering like a speeding motorcycle. The black flag was no longer atop the *presidencia*.

I saw a mass of men scattering at random, running into the bushes in the plaza and firing. Then the Philippine and American flags appeared on the poles in front of the town hall. The night came on and there was silence.

We walked to Binalonan silently, looking up when a *caromata* came by. I carried Francisca on my shoulders; sometimes my mother gave the baby to me, and she carried Francisca. We met a detachment of the Philippine constabulary rushing toward Tayug.

When we arrived in Binalonan the news of the uprising was already there, and our neighbors assailed us with many questions; but we could not explain the incident. Eagerly we awaited developments: during four days of unrest the local government of Tayug had changed hands several times a day. Finally, the constabulary conquered the rebels and restored law and order.

But the revolt in Tayug made me aware of the circumscribed life of the peasants through my brother Luciano, who explained its significance to me. I was determined to leave that environment and all its crushing forces, and if I were successful in escaping unscathed, I would go back someday to understand what it meant to be born of the peasantry. I would go back because I was a part of it, because I could not really escape from it no matter where I went or what became of me. I would go back to give significance to all that was starved and thwarted in my life.

CHAPTER IX

Now my father was a pathetic little figure in the house, and he went out only when it was absolutely necessary. He was now a landless farmer; local politics no longer interested him. He was completely broken in spirit. He had none of his animals; even the store by the highway that had been given to him by my brother Luciano was gone. The new *presidente* had closed it for reasons never clear to any of us. The court had threatened to put my father in jail, so he finally gave it up and sat in the house all day.

Luciano was getting deeper in local politics. He was receiving twenty-four pesos from the United States government, but he spent most of it on his doctor because his lungs were becoming worse. With what he had left he bought cigars and cigarettes for the loafers in the *presidencia*. He was looking ahead, he informed me. He looked so far ahead that the scavengers had him stripped to his shirt before he finally became mayor of Binalonan.

I was getting restless and fearful of the uncertainty that pervaded our household. I felt like running away—anywhere. I wanted to cast off the sudden gloom that shadowed our family, and I thought the only way to do that was to escape from it. I would also be escaping from my family, and from the bitter memories of childhood.

"I am leaving now, Father," I said one day.

My father said nothing. He simply looked at me. He was trying hard to hold back the tears that were gathering in his eyes. He was remembering and looking through me into the uncertain future and the dark fate that awaited me there, and his mouth trembled a little because he knew what it was I was forsaking, what I was plunging into so desperately, because he, too, had been young once and broken by a wall that stood between him and the future.

My mother wept silently. She was a woman who had shed few tears for anyone; but now that her last son was leaving, the reserve that had kept her composed for so long broke down in one disturbing maternal agony. Like my father, she was afraid to foresee what would happen to me now that I was leaving them and would be alone in the world.

My sister Francisca came to the door and touched my bundle. But the baby Marcela was on the floor, pushing my bundle and saying "*Manong*"—which means "brother" in our dialect. This was almost the only word she knew, and she expressed her grief with it.

I started down the ladder. Francisca put her face on the door and started to cry aloud.

"Allos!" my mother cried. "You are too young to go out into the world."

I was thirteen years old. Maybe my mother was right, although she believed that it was reasonable for me to work like a man in Binalonan, near them. But to live alone in some unknown place? No! She did not know that doing the work of a full-grown man had matured me beyond my age, that I had outgrown my narrow environment.

My father lifted my bundle and put it on his back. I walked after him without looking back at the house that was my childhood, because that time of my life was gone forever and there was no return. There were fears in that house of childhood, and I was leaving them forever. I was fleeing into manhood, into another struggle against other fears.

We stopped in the *presidencia* and Luciano came out with a bunch of newspapers and magazines under his arm.

"Where are you going, Allos?" he asked.

"I am going to Baguio," I said.

"I thought you would wait another year," he said, putting some money into my pocket.

"It will be easier for me if I go now," I said. "And maybe I will be able to go to America someday."

"Be sure to let me hear from you wherever you are," he said.

"Are you really planning to go to America, son?" asked my father suddenly.

"Yes, Father," I said. "But I will come back to Binalonan before I leave. I hope I shall be able to save enough passage money in two years."

"Your bus is not due for two hours," said my brother. "Let us walk to the schoolhouse and see what the children are doing."

We walked through the tall *talahib* grass in the plaza. It was recess time and the children in the yard were playing and singing. We hung on the pointed bamboo fence and watched them, shifting our weight when the ants bit our legs. The bells on the church tower began to ring, and we looked up to see what it meant. It was not the Mass hour and there was no funeral procession in the street. There was something portentous about the tolling bells. The sound was deep and sad, as though they were mourning the death of an important man.

"What is it, Father?" asked my brother suddenly.

"It is nothing of importance," said my father. "The bells are ringing for the end of a decade." Then he looked at me meaningfully, and there was a sudden surge of affection in his face. "But they are also announcing the birth of another decade."

I did not understand what my father meant. We moved to another corner of the fence and watched the younger children singing and circling an acacia tree. When my bus was ready to leave we rushed through the tall grass again and my father fell into a paddy. He took off his muddy shirt and came running after us to say good-bye. Then my bus started northward, following the road that I had helped build three years before.

It was good-bye to Binalonan and my childhood. I was going away from all of it forever. I looked back through the window and saw my father and Luciano becoming smaller and smaller in the distance. Then it came to me that my life there was too small to float the vessel of my desires. I wanted to cry out to all those who were left behind, but my tears choked me and only a violent fit of trembling shook my body. I knew that even if I went back to them, after many years of loneliness in another land, I would not be able to pick up where I had left off. I was going out into the world to build a new life with untried materials, and I knew that if I succeeded and went back to them, then it was only to drink of the water of our common spring.

At last we came to the river where I had been almost washed away to my death—the same river where my mother had lost her precious beans. Then Puzzorobio and its cement public market, and I remembered the elegant girl who had struck our basket of beans and how my mother had knelt on the pavement picking up the beans saying: "It is all right. It is all right."

When we came to the first hill it began to darken, and the air changed radically. The bus climbed steadily, passing through tall pine trees, skidding and stopping when we came to sharp turns in the road. I looked down into the valley below. It was deep and dark; a few lights twinkled here and there. I sat in position and looked ahead, remembering what my father had said in parting.

Baguio is a small city in the heart of tall mountains where the weather is always temperate. There are no rains nor heavy winds. But in the morning there is a light mist in the air and when you walk through it you feel as though you are walking through silk. The roads are asphalt and the most modern and beautiful in the Philippines. The houses and theaters are built in Western fashion. Tall pine trees cover the mountains and at night one can hear the leaves singing in the slight wind from the deep canyons beyond the city that comes up with the sweet tang of fragrant vegetation from the surrounding valleys. Far down, there are lustrous truck farms where industrious Igorots produce grapes, cabbages, lettuce, and various fruits.

In the center of the city is a lake strung with multicolored light bulbs that sparkle at night. Near the lake is a dancing pavilion, open only on Saturdays. And farther down, within shouting distance of the town hall, is the public market, teeming with European and American tourists. Under the cement awnings are numerous oxcarts owned by the lowland people who come to Baguio periodically to sell rice, corn, and bananas.

It was at this market that I first landed. Europeans of affluence, Americans with big businesses in the islands, and rich Filipinos lived in Baguio. Their beautiful white houses dotted the hills.

I went about asking the store managers if they needed a janitor or a messenger boy. But the stores were fully staffed because it was summer and the students were on vacation from high school. The storekeepers preferred students because they could speak English to the foreigners. I went to the great hotels and asked if there were anything open for me, but they also catered to English-speaking clients. Only the public market remained.

I walked around the lake and watched the lights in the water, yearning for the sight of food and the touch of bed. When twelve o'clock came the lights went out. Once more I retraced my steps to the market and found a place to sleep between the sacks of rice.

In the morning some of the traders from the lowland began cooking on improvised stoves. I hung about and offered whatever services I could, hoping I would be invited to eat with them. Sometimes they would let me eat hot rice, and sometimes they would give me a banana or an egg. I went around the vegetable stalls and picked up what they had thrown away in the gutter.

My clothes began to wear out. I was sick from eating what the traders discarded. One day an American lady tourist asked me to undress before her camera, and gave me ten centavos for doing it. I had found a simple way to make a living. Whenever I saw a white person in the market with a camera, I made myself conspicuously ugly, hoping to earn ten centavos. But what interested the tourists most were the naked Igorot women and their children. Sometimes they took pictures of the old men with G-strings. They were not interested in Christian Filipinos like me. They seemed to take a particular delight in photographing young Igorot girls with large breasts and robust mountain men whose genitals were nearly exposed, their G-strings bulging large and alive.

Then a rice trader from Binalonan took pity on me. He could not afford to hire anyone because he did all his own work, but he had noticed that I was acquiring a cough. He told me to help him carry the large sacks of rice on a wheelbarrow from the cart to the booth. I also wheeled the sacks to the automobiles of the customers. The wheelbarrow was almost too large for me to push, but it was a job and I had to eat.

It was on one of these trips with the wheelbarrow to the houses near the market that I found a better job. An American woman came to the market one day, bought some rice from my employer, and asked me to carry it for her. I followed her with the small sack of rice on my back. She went about the booths and bought pottery and other products from the Igorots. I returned to my employer's booth and, taking the wheelbarrow, put the woman's purchases into the barrow and pushed it down the road to her apartment.

She lived near the library, where she was working. She was really a painter, but working in the library brought her a small income. She had worked for fifteen years in a small-town library in Iowa and had saved her earnings. When she had saved enough, she bought an artist's paraphernalia and sailed for the Philippines, where her father had gone and died in the war that was to link the destiny of those two countries.

I will never forget Miss Mary Strandon on the day I pushed the wheelbarrow to her apartment. When I had carefully piled the vegetables and rice in the kitchen, she opened her purse and offered me five centavos.

"What did you do to your face?" she asked suddenly.

I was ashamed to tell her that I had hoped the white men and women who came to the market with cameras would photograph me for ten centavos. They had always taken pictures of natives with painted faces, and I had hoped that I could fool them with the charcoal marks on my face. I said it must be dirt.

"Wash it off!" she said, giving me a bar of soap.

I filled the bucket in the kitchen and the soapsuds tickled my skin. It was the first time I had ever used soap.

"Go along now and return the wheelbarrow," she said finally. "But come back here if you would like to work for me."

I returned the wheelbarrow to the man from Binalonan. Miss Strandon hired me and I learned to cook the way she wanted me to, and to clean the apartment the way she did. I became adept at general housework.

There was another American woman who lived in the apartment next door. She had an Igorot houseboy whose name was Dalmacio. She was a teacher in one of the city schools, and the boy, who did her washing and cooking, was one of her pupils. When our work was done for the day, Dalmacio and I would go to the lake and sit on the grass.

"I will soon go to America," he said one day. "I am trying to learn English so that I will not get lost over there."

"I am planning to go to America in two years," I said. "If I save enough passage money to take me there."

"You don't need money," Dalmacio said. "You could work on the boat. But English is the best weapon. I will teach you if you will do some work for me now and then."

He put a book in my hand and started reading aloud to me.

"Repeat after me," he said. "Don't swallow your words. Blow them out like the Americans."

I repeated after him, uttering strange words and thinking of America. We were reading the story of a homely man named Abraham Lincoln.

"Who *is* this Abraham Lincoln?" I asked Dalmacio.

"He was a poor boy who became a president of the United States," he said. "He was born in a log cabin and walked miles and miles to borrow a book so that he would know more about his country."

A poor boy became a president of the United States! Deep down in me something was touched, was springing out, demanding to be born, to be given a name. I was fascinated by the story of this boy who was born in a log cabin and became a president of the United States.

That evening I troubled Miss Strandon with questions. "Will you tell me what happened to Abraham Lincoln, ma'am?" I asked.

"Where did you hear about him?" she asked.

"I was reading," I said.

"I didn't know you could read, Allos," she said. "Lincoln was a poor boy who became a president of the United States."

"I know that already," I said. "Tell me what he did when he became president."

"Well, when he became president he said that all men are created equal," Miss Strandon said. "But some men, vicious men, who had Negro slaves, did not like what he said. So a terrible war was fought between the states of the United States, and the slaves were freed and the nation was preserved. But one night he was murdered by an assassin. . . ."

"Why?" I asked.

"*Why?*" she said. "He was a great man."

"What is a Negro?" I asked.

"A Negro is a black person," she said.

"Abraham Lincoln died for a black person?" I asked.

"Yes," she said. "He was a great man."

From that day onward this poor boy who became president filled my thoughts. Miss Strandon began giving me books from the library. It was still hard for me to read and to understand what I was reading. Miss Strandon realized that I had a passion for books, so she made arrangements with the city librarian to let me work with her.

I found great pleasure in the library. I dusted the books and put them in order. When Miss Strandon wanted a book she would tell me. I would put my feather duster in a corner and rush to the rack. I was slowly becoming acquainted with the intricacies of a library. Names of authors flashed in my mind and reverberated in a strange song in my consciousness. A whole new world was opened to me.

A few people came in to the library; they were always elegant and patronizing. Now and then a stranger would come and talk with Miss Strandon about books. But most of the wealthy residents asked that books be delivered to their homes. I used to make the deliveries, hugging the books and running joyfully in the sun. How beautiful their homes were! I would stand outside the door and hand over the books to a white-liveried servant. On my way back, I would remember our grass hut in the village of Mangusmana and compare it with the magnificent mansion I had just left. I would remember many things in my childhood: my father and his land, my mother and her salted fish, my brother Luciano, slowly dying of tuberculosis, and my two other brothers who had gone away. . . .

I was fortunate to find work in a library and to be close to books. In later years I remembered this opportunity when I read that the American Negro writer, Richard Wright, had not been allowed to borrow books from his local library because of his color. I was beginning to understand what was going on around me, and the darkness that had covered my present life was lifting. I was emerging into sunlight, and I was to know, a decade afterward in America, that this light was not too strong for eyes that had known only darkness and gloom.

The months passed quickly and suddenly a year had gone. I stayed in Baguio until another year was nearly completed. I became restless and homesick. I told Miss Strandon that I wanted to go back to Binalonan. I had saved a little money working for her, but I did not know what to do with it. It was not sufficient to ransom our land from the moneylender, so I considered buying a *carabao* for my father. With this plan in my mind, I left Baguio.

I do not remember all that Miss Mary Strandon said to me in parting. But I remember her saying that she would like me to come someday to her home town of Spencer, Iowa. She told me that the trees there were as luxuriant as in Baguio. Fifteen years afterward I went to Spencer, hoping to find her. But she had been dead for more than ten years. I wrote her name on a copy of my first book and donated it to the local library. I think she would have been happy to know that I would someday write a book about her country.

CHAPTER X

I HAD written to Luciano that I was coming home, but he was not at the station in Binalonan when I arrived. I put my suitcase on my back and walked in the darkness, watching the flickering lamps in the houses on both sides of the street. It was a time of religious festival and there were many peasants in the street, on their way to church. They wore homespun clothes and rough wooden sandals, and there were townspeople in the crowd who wore leather slippers and shoes and cotton suits. The more fortunate ones rode in decorated *caromatas* with their perfumed daughters and sleek-haired sons. The peasants moved carefully out of their way. If the man in the *caromata* were an important personage or a government official of rank, the driver would lash at the peasants or spit on them. The important passenger would merely show his face in the window and everything would be forgiven and forgotten.

I was surprised to find our house in total darkness. When I saw that it was empty, I felt desolated. I stood at the gate for a long time trying to decide what to do. Several of our neighbors passed by with their *carabaos* and other beasts of burden and called my name, but I did not answer them because I lacked the courage to say anything.

Slowly I climbed into the house and fumbled under the earthen stove for matches. When I found the little box, I went into the living room and struck a match. The tiny yellow flame flared up and lingered in the small cup of my hand. Mice scampered into their holes and house lizards fell from the roof, turning over and over on their scaly sides. Then I saw the oil lamp on the rack at the edge of the table and lit it.

I took the lighted lamp and went to the kitchen. The pots were all clean and in order. The rice bin in the corner was empty. The plates were clean and the earthen drinking jars were full. There was firewood by the stove, and the salt tube above it, stuck in the grass roof, was full and leaking where the rain had touched it. Hanging on a rope above the stove was a leg of lamb. I was relieved to find something to eat, because I had not eaten since I had left Baguio.

I went to the wall where we kept our sharp *bolos*. The rack was still there, but the *bolos* were gone. I began to wonder what had become of my family. Had they come upon a fortune? Had they recovered the land? Had they gone to the village? I cut a piece of meat and chopped it into little pieces. Spraying vinegar and chopped pepper on the meat, I started to eat the hard rice crinkle I found in the bottom of one of the pots. The food warmed my stomach and my heart. I was in my own house.

I washed my hands and took off my clothes. I spread the grass mat on the bamboo floor and tried to sleep, but the mice kept coming out of their holes and running about the house. I was thinking of going to the village when the bells in the church tower began pealing and people from everywhere started shouting. I could hear the resounding roar of *pagbayoan*, or threshing boxes. When the spreading clamor reached our neighborhood, I could see people rushing into the street and children waving palm leaves and screaming.

I went outside and ran to the street where the crowd was thick and noisy. I rushed into the crowd and mingled with the people milling madly up and down the street. Then I heard them shouting:

"Happy New Year! Happy New Year!"

I pushed my way deeper into the crowd, shouting and laughing aloud when I accidentally ruffled the dignity of a shy village girl.

"Happy New Year!" I shouted at the top of my voice. "Happy New Year!" I pushed and moved slowly with the crowd. I kicked the ground like a little boy again, remembering other years that were not like this one.

"Happy New Year, Allos!" I said to myself.

Suddenly I felt a hand on my neck. I turned around and saw Luciano waving a palm leaf in his hand.

"This is a miracle!" he shouted above the noise. "I did not know you were in town. When did you arrive?"

"A few hours ago," I said, beginning to feel the miracle of the new year. "Since when did you start celebrating like this?"

"This is the first time, Allos," said my brother, putting his arm around me and shouting, "Happy New Year! Happy New Year!"

I cupped my hands to my mouth. "What year is it?" I shouted into my brother's ear.

"It is the year of the Lord," he shouted back. "You must remember this year because it is significant: it is the year of all years. In the United States it is the sad end of another depression year and the beginning of a sadder one. Happy New Year! Happy New Year, Allos!"

When one o'clock came the celebrants circled the plaza and crowded into the *presidencia*. The noise suddenly ceased, and the people started for home. One by one lamps in the houses went out and the policemen barred the door of the *presidencia*. My brother and I walked in the street, suddenly exhausted.

"Where is your suitcase?" he asked.

"I have it in the house," I said.

"House?" he said. "That house was sold months ago."

"I did not know that," I said.

"Father sold it because he had a chance to buy a small piece of land in Mangusmana," said my brother. "Mother and the two girls are there with him. I have heard that mother is doing most of the work. Father is very sick."

"I must see them at once," I said. It was unbearable to think that my mother was now doing the farm work. And my two little sisters—how were they going to grow up now?

We went to our former house and picked up my suitcase. Then we proceeded to Luciano's house where, greatly disturbed by the thought of my mother, I got up from my mat at dawn and walked to Mangusmana through the wet rice fields.

✦

It was only when I was nearing our village that I remembered my brother Leon. He had come back from a war about which he had never spoken, and then had gone away again with his wife to start a new life. I was not coming from a war, but it was my first homecoming—home to the village and our grass hut, home to years of hard labor and bitter memories. And the grass was taller than usual, the water in the ditch was sweeter, the mango trees by the footpath were greener and the meadow larks more melodious. There was a sweet feeling of homecoming in me.

Then I saw my mother's familiar back. She was following the plow, her skirt tucked between her legs. Suddenly I knew what Leon had felt the day he came home, running suddenly to take the plow from my father. I started running across the fields and leaping over ditches, shouting and calling frantically:

"Mother! Mother! Mother!"

My mother stopped the *carabao* and looked toward me. The sun was falling directly upon her face, and she raised her hand to protect her eyes from the strong morning light. When she recognized me, she tied the rope to the handle of the plow, as my father used to do, and waited for me.

"Have you come home, son?" she said. And that was all she could say. Her mouth began to tremble with joy and sorrow, because to her joy and sorrow were always one and the same. Suddenly she grabbed me affectionately and wept, murmuring: "We are poor people, son. We are very poor people, son."

I brushed back the tears from my eyes. I tried to laugh in order not to cry. Gently I pushed my mother out of the way and took the rope from her.

"Go home, Mother," I said. "I will finish this piece for you."

"Don't work. the animal too hard," she said.

"I won't," I said. I watched her go away, a little peasant woman who carried the world on her shoulders. Then I flipped the rope gently across the *carabao's* back, and the animal moved obediently and expertly along the deep furrows.

The sun came slowly up and burnished the upturned earth, felling the sweet dew in the grass and rousing the birds in their nests. I could hear dogs barking in the houses near by and the roar of water rushing through the tall *talahib* grass and rolling over the flat, fine sand in the river. I unhitched the *carabao* and tied it to a peg with a long *maguey* rope, so that it could reach the shade of the tamarind and the water in the ditch. I covered the plow with grass and started for our hut.

My father was lying in a corner in the kitchen, coughing violently and shivering whenever the draft reached him. His body had shrunken and his teeth had fallen out. He ate only soup and *logao*, or soft-boiled rice. He could no longer stand up even to get a cup of water, but my sister Francisca attended to his needs. She was only six years old, but she knew what to do around the house. I knew that she would grow up into a fine peasant girl.

I was home with my family and this alone was a comforting feeling. I had come back to manhood, here in my native village. I had come back to myself and my roots, here in this narrow strip of land. Back to my soil and to my father's faith. I had not forgotten him limping through Mangusmana on his sore feet, going from house to house and asking the farmers if they could lend him a piece of land to cultivate or could hire him. I had not forgotten his love for the earth where his parents and their parents before him had lacerated their lives digging away the stones and trees to make the forest land of our village a fragrant and livable place.

While we were planting rice seedlings one of my cousins came to our house and invited me to go to a dance in a nearby village. We wrapped our clothes with banana leaves and walked through the rain and mud, shouting our manhood into the night.

We found a well near a banana grove where we washed our feet. My cousin was a high school student in Vigan, a large city in the province of Ilocos Sur. He had a good pair of shoes and his alpaca suit was new and smoothly pressed. He wore a red tie and striped silk shirt. My feet were still as bare as when I was born, but Luciano had given me an old khaki suit. I put a bandanna around my neck and the girls thought that it was better than a necktie.

I noticed a girl who had fallen for my cousin. I saw him kiss her on the mouth, a thing which was very daring in those days. The old men looked at them with great anticipation, but the women frowned with scorn. The girls snickered in their corners, sticking out their little yellow tongues behind outspread fans. The little girls and boys around the dance floor drummed on their bloated bellies. Sometimes they danced among themselves and attracted much attention from the crowd with their naked bodies and ugly, spreading toes: spitting as they jumped to the wild music, their spittle falling on their naked loins.

I was too shy to dance, so I hung about the pavilion.

"Approach a girl you like and stand before her if you are afraid to talk," said my cousin.

"Do you think it will work?" I asked.

"It always works with these shy peasant girls," he said. "Watch me do it." He saw a rather good-looking girl in a red dress. He strode across like a peacock and stood in front of her.

I was watching her mouth to see if she would say something to him, but she almost jumped into his arms. My cousin turned around and winked at me. I saw a girl I liked sitting on the bench near the door, at the far end of the dance floor. I circled the people and stood in front of her. The girl flung herself into my arms, and I was taken by surprise, and for a while I could not move my legs. Then we were holding each other innocently and dancing the way it should not have been done in the village. I could see the sensual stare of the men and the anger of the women. The children spread out along the walls, sticking out their tongues and giggling.

When you dance for the first time, the world is like a cradle upon the biggest ocean in the universe. There are no other sounds except the beating of your hearts, and when the wild blaring of the trumpet and the savage boom-boom of the drum bring you back to reality, you get scared and begin to misstep and falter. Your hands weaken their hold on the rapturous being near you, and you want to apologize to her but the words are stuck in your throat. Suddenly you become conscious of the staring people around you, appraising you with obscene eyes and lascivious tongues, and slowly you lead the beauteous creature in your arms back to her seat. Then the orchestra becomes a cymbal of crashing noises, meaningless and riotous, and you return to your corner, trembling with cold and sudden fear. You are pushed back to reality, to the world of puny men and women who are circumscribed by fear. Then you, too, are one among them and one of them, prisoned by their fears and the ugliness of their lives. You go to the window and lean far out, savoring the bitter taste on your tongue. . . .

The next morning my cousin came running to the field where I was planting rice.

"Let us go away at once, Allos," he said.

"I think I will stay until the rice is all planted," I said. "And I would like to help my mother with the crop. I am sorry I cannot go with you."

"You don't understand what I mean," he said. "Remember those two girls we danced with last night? Well, they are sisters. They are in the village now looking for us. I think they would like to force us into marriage."

I laughed, because it seemed incredible.

"It is no laughing matter," my cousin said.

"Well, what have we done?" I asked.

"We danced, that is all," he said. "But you'd better come with me to Lingayen if you don't want to be married to a mud-smelling peasant girl. I will go to school there instead of Vigan, but I am on my way to town now. Hurry, Allos!"

"I will think it over," I said.

My cousin started running toward Binalonan, looking back and shouting to me to follow him. I waved at him innocently and went back to my work. But when I went home in the afternoon, Francisca met me at the door.

"Mother said for you to go away for a while," she said, giving me a bundle and a basket of vegetables.

I thought it was all very foolish, but when I reached the ladder, the heads of the two village girls became visible. They were talking to my mother. My father was coughing violently. I could see Marcela playing with the girl near the stove. I took the bundle from Francisca and ran for the gate. Only when I reached the rice fields did I begin to feel free.

I wanted to stay in town for a week. But ten days afterward, when I returned to Mangusmana, the rice seedlings were already planted. My mother told me that I could go. I went to Binalonan and stayed with Luciano. When my cousin set out for Lingayen in an oxcart, I decided to go with him. I had saved a little money in Baguio, but it was not enough to take me to America. With Lingayen's fishing industry in mind, I went with my cousin. But the cow was very small and lazy, and it was three days before we arrived in Lingayen.

CHAPTER XI

IT WAS the second week of June and the students were coming back to Lingayen. They came by oxcart with their provisions of rice and assorted vegetables, bringing with them members of their families or close relatives to do their cooking and laundry. When they could not make this arrangement, the poorer students did their own cooking after school hours and their washing on Saturdays. They went to church on Sundays. Those who had a little money came by *caromata*, their rough wooden trunks and rattan suitcases piled on top of the flimsy vehicle. The horses looked like fleas about to be thrown into the sky by the weight of their burdens. The students who lived in the neighboring towns consigned their belongings to their more fortunate friends and came on foot. They could be seen on the highway waving their hands eagerly when an automobile or a bus came by.

The students filled the little houses of the fishermen on the shore of Lingayen gulf. Even the three chapels were converted into boarding houses, for while the students were devoted Catholics and went to church regularly, they could not always afford to buy a candle or contribute to the church fund. The chapels depended only on the fishermen who had houses and who took in boarders, but the donations from these frugal men were not enough to sustain the buildings.

As soon as we arrived in Lingayen, my cousin told me to stay at his boarding house. The owner of the building was a fisherman who owned two fishing boats. He was in need of men, and he asked me if I wanted to work with him. I was glad, because I could earn a little money while away from home.

My cousin lived with fourteen boys attending high school, but the house was too small for all of us. The toilet was connected with the house by a narrow bamboo footbridge that hung on two *abaca* ropes. The kitchen was a hive of activities. There was a cook, an elderly peasant woman, and a young girl who did the washing. They were always going in and out of the house, throwing the bucket into the well in the yard and shouting with friendliness to the other women in the neighborhood.

At meal time the girls next door, fifteen of them in a house like ours, came to the long table in our dining room wearing their heavily starched cotton dresses. As soon as we were through eating, some of the more considerate girls stayed to help the cook with the dishes. Sometimes they stayed to discuss their school work with the boys. But the others returned to their rooms to sing or sew. All of them came from peasant families in other towns.

There was a town ordinance forbidding students of opposite sexes to live in the same house. It had been prompted by the birth of illegitimate children some years before. Since only students were specified in the ordinance, I was free to go into the house of the girls. When another student moved into our house, the landlady found a small corner for me in the girls' house.

I used to wake up at dawn to go to work. I walked between small *nipa* houses, and when I arrived at our meeting place, my companions were already waiting for me. When our crew was completed and we were ready to put out to sea, the man on the prow of the boat blew a horn. We climbed into the boat with our meager lunch of rice and salted fish and started rowing seaward.

It was wonderful to work with men who knew the sea. They knew nothing of books, but they could tell what kind of tuna was running a mile away. They stood in the boat and put their hands over their eyes: then they knew whether it was a school of lobster or white fish. They wasted no motion of their sea-browned bodies. When they spoke, it was full of wisdom. And from them I learned the different edible weeds and grasses in the sea.

We cast our end of the long net about three miles away from land and the men in the other boat cast theirs. Then we started rowing slowly away from each other until the net was stretched

taut. Another blast of the horn, deep and challenging and mean-
ingful to men of the sea, and then we started rowing toward the
shore, toward the day's end.

The process was slow because we had to be careful with the
net. It would be about three in the afternoon when our boats
reached the shore. Putting small yokes about our bodies, we
would start pulling in the long nets and singing:

"*Sin-ta! Sin-ta! Sin-ta!*"

Slowly and rhythmically our legs moved in the sand, on and
on, until the children in the grass houses near by came to the
shore and started singing with us:

"*Sin-ta! Sin-ta! Sin-ta!*"

They would begin pulling the rope with us and singing at
the top of their voices. After two long hours of slow pulling the
catch would be drawn to the shore. We could see the fish desperately swimming in circles, crashing against the net and bouncing back into the water. When we were ready to land the catch,
the children would release the rope and run to the center of the
net. The fish would leap tirelessly until they were heavy with
sand.

Then the owner of the boat would see to it that every man
had his due share; even the children who had done a little pulling
had something. The fish buyers were waiting with their carts
to buy our catch. Then I would be on my way home, stopping
at the school ground and watching the students playing and
singing. I would try to single out my cousin, but there were
over ten thousand boys and girls in the yard. I would proceed
to my boarding house, where my landlady was waiting for me.

Not long afterward my cousin asked me to go to school with
him. Since the fishing season was over and there would be no
work for three months, I eagerly consented to his suggestion.
It was an experience to be with my cousin in his classes. But it
was tiresome to sit in one place for forty minutes, the time
allowed for each subject. The boys, thinking me a regular student, would start talking to me in English. I saw some of the
girls glancing at my long hair and bare feet with pitying eyes.

My cousin's English teacher was a man who had been in America. He wore American shoes and clothes, and came to class smoking a large pipe. He sat on a small chair which he tilted backward, putting his feet on the table so that we could see his silk socks. The timid girls in the front seats were embarrassed. But he took an interest in me, and even invited me to his house. There he wrote out a credit card which made it appear that I had been going to school regularly for two years, graduating from one grade to another with excellent marks.

"These fat sons and soft daughters of the sons-of-bitches think they are smart," he used to say to me, referring to the children of the crooked politicians and land grabbers in Pangasinan. "The girls come to my classes to show me their pretty little rumps, as if they could buy me with that! I will show them!"

I did not understand him at times, but I was learning rapidly about the Philippine middle classes. It seemed that he had gone to America as a boy, had worked as houseboy, and in fifteen years had finished his course. His parents were poor peasants; they had died by the time he returned to the Philippines. This misfortune had made him bitter and confused. Instead of using his experience as an inspiring example to other peasant children, he had turned inward and used it as a weapon of revenge. He had turned against the *haciendaros*, or landed gentry, and finally against his own class and heritage.

But he was kind and considerate to me. When a general intelligence test was given to all the students, he gave me a copy of the examination paper in advance. I studied the questions and found the answers in my cousin's books. I took the examination along with the rest, but only for fun.

I was playing baseball with the girls in the vacant lot between our houses when my cousin came running to me. He grabbed the bat from my hand, gasping for breath.

"You have the highest score in the entire school, Allos," he said excitedly. "And you have the highest score throughout the province of Pangasinan. Perhaps you have the highest score in the Philippines. You know, we have the same examination papers throughout the islands."

I felt guilty and ashamed. The girls dropped their gloves and came running to me. Their eyes shone with envy. They trembled with love. When my cousin read them their marks, which he had copied on a slip of paper, they slunk away like cats and did not come out of their rooms for a long time. Those who had fair grades joked with the landlady and the cook, but they refused to talk to me.

There were one hundred thirty questions and I had correctly answered one hundred twenty-seven in thirty minutes. The students had been given one hour, but I had finished my paper thirty minutes ahead of time. It had been so stated by the examiner on my paper. My fame spread far and wide. I saw my teacher regularly and we had fun laughing at the joke that we had played upon the school. Then he urged me to study seriously.

The girls from other houses began coming to my boarding house with their lessons, bringing neatly embroidered handkerchiefs. They came after school and filled the house with the smell of their powder and cheap perfume. They washed my shirts and helped the cook with the dishes. My landlady began to look on me as someone miraculous. I had become a valuable asset to her business.

But my fame had become a nuisance. When the fishing season came again, I felt a great relief. I stayed away until dark hoping that no one would be waiting for me. I noticed that one girl was always in the kitchen with one of the boys when I came home. This girl, Veronica, had evidenced a great dislike for me. I had never paid any attention to her, but I could see that she wanted to hurt me.

One night I had gone to the *presidencia* to send money to my mother. I returned to my boarding house eating peanuts and looking up at the bright stars in the sky. As I drew near the school, I heard the dogs barking excitedly. I stopped and listened. Then I heard the pathetic wail of a baby. I could not believe my ears. I picked up a stone and chased the dogs away.

I found the baby lying on the grass. It was so small. I picked it up carefully and carried it into the house. I woke up my land-lady and showed her the baby.

"Where did you get it?" she asked, trembling with sudden fear.

"I found it on the grass in the schoolyard," I said. "The dogs were barking over it. I was lucky to come along, because they might have killed it."

"In the schoolyard, did you say?" she asked.

"Yes," I said.

The woman collapsed. When she came to, the boys were al-ready awake. They surrounded her, rubbing their eyes and looking at the baby with surprise. My landlady cried out:

"My business is ruined! My business is ruined!"

When I went to my room, I saw a faint light in the kitchen. I walked on tiptoe and peeped through the door. Veronica was burning some clothes in the stove. She became angry when she saw me.

"What are you doing?" I asked, going into the kitchen and looking at the burning clothes.

"Go away!" she screamed. "Go away or I will kill you!"

I saw the blood on her feet and on the floor near the stove. I went into my room and tried to sleep, pushing away the face of the little baby when it came to my mind. I could still hear the excited voices of the boys in the other house. Then the roosters started crowing and the fishermen came out of their houses with their lunch boxes. It was time for me to go with them. I felt my way in the dark and climbed down the ladder.

When I came home in the afternoon there was a large crowd near the house. I saw two policemen at the door and two others in the house. My landlady came running to me with my suitcase.

"Don't go into the house, Allos!" she said, putting the suitcase in my hand. "There is going to be trouble with that girl. Go!"

"I did not do anything," I said weakly.

"Go away from here, son!" she insisted. "Go anywhere! Don't stay another minute in Lingayen. You are a good boy and I'd hate to see you in trouble. Go!"

I walked away from her and took the first bus to Binalonan.

It was foolish of my landlady to think that I had any part in the birth of the baby. I looked at the perfect credit cards that my teacher had given me. I thought of my cousin and sighed. I leaned far out the window and looked at the twinkling stars in the sky. I was nearing the dark land of home.

CHAPTER XII

I T WAS ten o'clock in the morning when I reached Binalonan. I went to the *presidencia* and asked the postmaster if he had seen my brother Luciano. The policemen told me that he had not been around for a long time. I carried my suitcase to his house. I saw a young woman looking out of one of the windows. She was holding a crying baby. Then I saw my brother coming down the ladder with an ax. He put the ax on a pile of firewood and met me.

"When did you arrive, Allos?" he asked.

"I have just arrived," I said. "Do you think mother is still in Mangusmana?"

"I have heard that she has gone to San Manuel with the girls," he said. "They went there to harvest *mongo*. It is the season, you know."

"What about father?" I asked.

"Father went with them," he said.

When my brother noticed that I was looking toward the window, he opened the gate and said: "I am married now and I have a daughter. Come and meet my wife."

I did not want to ask him about his political aspirations. He had been deep in politics when I had left Binalonan. I noticed that his wife was big with child again.

"We are expecting another," he said in apology.

Later he and I went to our old house. A gambler and his wife had bought it. They were in the yard admiring a gamecock. We stood outside the fence looking into the house, but when the man invited us to play cards, we walked around the fence silently and left.

"It is a good house," I said, beginning to feel badly because a professional gambler had bought it.

"We were all born in it," my brother said. "We grew up in it, too. If I had enough money, I would like to buy it for my children."

"I would, too," I said. "Remember the window where we used to hang the parrot cage? And the beautiful pot that mother brought home with her from one of the villages? I had fun in that house. I guess I will never live in it again."

"It is too bad we are all scattered now," he said.

"I will come back someday," I said. "I will come back and buy that house. I will buy it and build a high cement wall around it. I will come back with lots of money and put on a new roof. It must be leaking now. I will put new walls, too. Wait and see!"

"I don't have my health any more, Allos," Luciano said sadly. "If I were you I would never stop moving until I came back with money. When are you leaving again?"

"Tomorrow," I said. "But I would like to go to San Manuel and say good-bye to the family before I leave for Manila. I think I know where to find them. I used to work there with mother, you know."

In the morning I took a *caromata* for San Manuel. The town had not changed. I went directly to the field where mother and I had worked years before. They were all glad to see me, but when I told them that I was leaving for America, they became sad and silent. Then Francisca unwrapped the bit of cloth where she kept her earnings and put the money in my pocket.

"I cannot take your money, Francisca," I said.

She looked at me as though she had something important to say. Then she said: "Take it anyway, brother. When you are in America go to school, and when you come back to Binalonan teach Marcela and me to read. That is all I want from you. We will be working hard with mother while you are gone."

There was a big lump in my throat. A little girl giving me five pesos so that I could go to school in America! It was her whole year's savings.

I took my father's hand and tried to tell him that it was good-bye. He leaned on his walking stick to keep himself from falling.

"Be sure to come back, son," he said weakly. "When you find

it hard and there is no other way, you must come back to Binalonan and stay with us."

"I will come back, Father," I said.

My sisters clung to my hands, looking at me with pleading
eyes. There was a meadow lark somewhere in the sunlit field,
and it was singing rapturously. Not far away a peasant girl was
singing a *kundiman*, or love song, and a young man answered
with a song as sweet and innocent. Near by a little boy was
playing with a quail that he had snared with horsehair in the un-
harvested *mongo* field. In a metallic instant, I remembered how
Luciano and I had snared birds.

I walked on the footpath that led to the driveway. When I
reached the gravel road that finally took me to the highway, I
looked back at my family for the last time. I saw my mother in
bold outline. Raising her dark hands, she wept without moving
her eyes; without moving her lips, she cried, and in the aching
surge of a moment she put her face in her hands and sobbed
loudly between fits of agonized laughter.

I went to Binalonan to say good-bye to Luciano. His wife
had just given birth to another baby. I knew that he would have
a child every year. I knew that in ten years he would be so
burdened with responsibilities that he would want to lie down
and die. I was glad that I was free from the life he was living.
When I had finally settled myself in the bus, I looked down and
saw my brother's pitiful eyes.

"Don't come back to Binalonan, Allos!" he said. "Even if you
have to steal and kill, don't come back to this damned town.
Don't ever come back, please, little brother!" He was running
furiously alongside the bus and waving his hands desperately
with the importance of what he had to say. "Don't come back
as I have done. See what happened to me?" He let my hand go
and suddenly stopped running. He was crying and shaking, as
though a strong wind were bending him from side to side.

On the train to Manila I met a tall university student from
La Union, where he had spent his vacation. He was going back

to the university, but was unhappy at the prospect. He looked at his books contemptuously and glanced quickly out of the window, waving at the peasant girls selling rice cakes and boiled eggs in makeshift stands near the railroad tracks. I saw the engraved name on his leather suitcase: *Juan Cablaan.*

When he noticed my inquisitive eyes, Juan said: "Yes, that is my name. My father is the governor of my province. He is a good lawyer and he wants me to follow his profession. Hell!" He cursed and kicked his suitcase away, looking out of the window and waving at the girls.

But he was very helpful to me. He said: "Don't let the *choceros*, or drivers, cheat you. Don't talk to them in the dialect."

When we arrived at the station in Manila, Juan called for a *caromata.* He instructed the driver to go to a certain address. When we reached the place, we saw many barefoot *provincianos* at the gate. It was evident that they had just arrived in the city from the provinces. They were carrying homemade suitcases.

"These peasants from the provinces are also going to America," Juan said to me, glancing nonchalantly at my rattan suitcase.

"How did you know I am going to America?" I asked.

He did not answer me. When the *caromata* stopped in front of the little house, Juan opened his suitcase and offered me a pair of old shoes.

"Wear these shoes, if you don't want people to know that you are from the provinces and on your way to America," he said. "Some thieves and pickpockets might think that you have money about you. I know you have only a few pesos tied with a cloth belt under your coat."

He was right, and I felt embarrassed. "I have no money to pay for the shoes," I said.

"Forget it," he said.

I entered the gate with the rest of the peasants from the provinces. The house was overflowing with boys, chattering in their dialects and putting away their provisions in the corners of the house. I went to the window and looked out. For nearly a mile around I saw only *nipa* houses.

We were in Tondo, in the slum district of Manila. Every day

there was *panguingue*, a card game, in the house. Some of the peasants were tempted to play and lost. They stayed on in Manila hoping to earn enough money to take them to America. But they never earned enough, so they stayed on and on in the city, and their relatives never heard from them again.

There was a cockpit in the neighborhood, and I went to watch. The bettors were outside the rope enclosure shouting their bets. Only the owners of the cocks and the referee were inside. When the betting had been arranged by three hawkers who went around, the owners of the fighting cocks stepped out of their corners and met in the center of the ring. They held the game-cocks in their arms, the birds glaring at each other challengingly.

The referee came forward with two sharp steel spurs and, showing the dangerous sharp blades to the two men, he attached one to the right leg of one bird with a leather strap and the other to the second rooster. When this was done to the satisfaction of both men, the referee wrapped the bases of the spurs with pieces of thick black cloth. The men allowed the birds to peck at each other, instructively and challengingly. Then they threw them decisively in the center of the ring.

The men and the referee moved back to their corners watching the cocks intently. The birds flung their full weight against each other, and their weapons interlocked. They fluttered about on the ground. The men ran and picked them up. There was no damage: the birds were unharmed. They turned around swiftly and flung themselves upon each other. The bettors screamed at the top of their voices and stamped wildly on the ground.

Suddenly one of the cocks rushed the other, but its opponent was alert to danger, and the first rooster fell to the ground. Then a tragic and pathetic thing happened. The fallen cock had buried its spur in the ground and the other cock turned around and began attacking it viciously. The crowd screamed shrilly, a fanatical screaming. The free bird attacked the helpless one again and again, trying to bury the sharp steel blade, but the armorless cock evaded it miraculously. Suddenly the earth gave way: the bird freed the spur. Stepping backward, it buried its gaft in the neck of the other. The head fell like a stone to the ground. The victor strutted shakily, raised its bloody head and crowed. The maddened screaming stopped.

Then something happened. The men suddenly started pushing each other and milling around the enclosure. I ran toward the gate and jumped over the fence. Someone was following me. I looked back, and to my surprise, I saw Juan Cablaan running behind me.

"What happened?" I asked.

"I don't know," he said. "I come here now and then to see how the slum people live. I also come here for a good time. It is a good experience. I know another interesting place in this district. I will show it to you."

It was evening. I could hear church bells ringing. We walked around awhile, and Juan pointed out interesting antiquities and other relics of the past. When the lights came on in the better districts of Manila, we retraced our steps to Tondo and the slum dwellers. We stopped in front of an inconspicuous *nipa* house. There was a little red light near the door. I could see the dark figure of a man coming slowly down the ladder.

"There is something I would like you to see before you leave for America," Juan said. "Have you ever been with a girl?"

Not fully comprehending what he meant, I followed him quietly into the dark house. A woman stopped us at the door. Juan touched me.

"Do you see her?" he whispered.

I peered through the door and saw a young girl on the bamboo floor with a naked man.

"What are they doing there?" I asked.

"The girl is a prostitute," he said. "And this old witch is her mother. Do you want to try it?"

I groped my way to the ladder and ran to the street, glad to feel the fresh air. Juan was walking rapidly beside me.

"There are many girls like her in Manila," he said sadly. "They came from the provinces, hoping to find work in the city. But look where they have landed!" He laughed bitterly.

I began to run furiously away from him. When I reached my

boarding house the men looked at me. I put my arms around a post and tried to ease the wild beating of my heart. I wanted to cry. Suddenly, I started beating the post with my fists.

In the morning a big truck came to take us to the government detention station. We carried our bundles and suitcases and waited in a wide room. After a while a doctor came and tapped on our chests; then we were taken to our boat. The people began throwing confetti, and suddenly it began to rain. The boat moved slowly out of the harbor, threading the sharp tongue of land that led out into the open sea.

I stood on the deck and watched the fading shores of Manila. Long afterward I found myself standing in the heavy rain, holding my rattan suitcase and looking toward the disappearing Philippines. I knew that I was going away from everything I had loved and known. I knew that if I ever returned the first sight of that horizon would be the most beautiful sight in the world. I waved my hat and went into the vestibule that led to the filthy hold below where the other steerage passengers were waiting for me.

PART TWO

CHAPTER XIII

I FOUND the dark hole of the steerage and lay on my bunk for days without food, seasick and lonely. I was restless at night and many disturbing thoughts came to my mind. Why had I left home? What would I do in America? I looked into the faces of my companions for a comforting answer, but they were as young and bewildered as I, and my only consolation was their proximity and the familiarity of their dialects. It was not until we had left Japan that I began to feel better.

One day in mid-ocean, I climbed through the narrow passageway to the deck where other steerage passengers were sunning themselves. Most of them were Ilocanos, who were fishermen in the northern coastal regions of Luzon. They were talking easily and eating rice with salted fish with their bare hands, and some of them were walking, barefoot and unconcerned, in their homemade cotton shorts. The first-class passengers were annoyed, and an official of the boat came down and drove us back into the dark haven below. The small opening at the top of the iron ladder was shut tight, and we did not see the sun again until we had passed Hawaii.

But before we anchored at Honolulu an epidemic of meningitis spread throughout the boat and concentrated among the steerage passengers. The Chinese waiters stopped coming into our dining room, because so many of us had been attacked by the disease. They pushed the tin plates under the door of the kitchen and ran back to their rooms, afraid of being contaminated. Those hungry enough crawled miserably on their bellies and reached for their plates.

But somewhere in the room a peasant boy was playing a guitar and another was strumming a mandolin. I lay on my bunk listening and wishing I could join them. In the far corner of the dining room, crouched around the dining table, five young students were discussing the coming presidential election in the United States. Not far from them was a dying boy from Pangasinan.

One night when I could no longer stand the heat in the closed room, I screamed aloud and woke up most of the steerage passengers. The boy who had been playing the guitar came to my bed with cold water and rubbed my forehead and back with it. I was relieved of my discomfort a little and told him so.

"My name is Marcelo," he said. "I came from San Manuel, Pangasinan."

"*San Manuel?*" I said. "I used to work there—in the *mongo* fields. I am glad to meet you."

"Go to sleep now," he said. "Call for me if you need my help."

I heard his feet pattering away from me, and I was comforted. It was enough that Marcelo had come from a familiar town. It was a bond that bound us together in our journey. And I was to discover later this same regional friendship, which developed into tribalism, obstructed all efforts toward Filipino unity in America.

There were more than two hundred of us in the steerage. A young doctor and an assistant came now and then to check the number of deaths and to examine those about to die. It was only when we reached Hawaii that the epidemic was checked, and we were allowed to go out again. Some of the stronger passengers carried their sick relatives and friends through the narrow hatch and put them in the sunlight.

I was pleasantly sunning myself one afternoon when Marcelo rolled over on his stomach and touched me. I turned and saw a young white girl wearing a brief bathing suit walking toward us with a young man. They stopped some distance away from us; then as though the girl's moral conscience had been provoked, she put her small hand on her mouth and said in a frightened voice:

"Look at those half-naked savages from the Philippines, Roger! Haven't they any idea of decency?"

"I don't blame them for coming into the sun," the young man said. "I know how it is below."

"Roger!" said the terrified girl. "Don't tell me you have been down in that horrible place? I simply can't believe it!"

The man said something, but they had already turned and the wind carried it away. I was to hear that girl's voice in many ways afterward in the United States. It became no longer her voice, but an angry chorus shouting:

"*Why don't they ship those monkeys back where they came from?*"

We arrived in Seattle on a June day. My first sight of the approaching land was an exhilarating experience. Everything seemed native and promising to me. It was like coming home after a long voyage, although as yet I had no home in this city. Everything seemed familiar and kind—the white faces of the buildings melting in the soft afternoon sun, the gray contours of the surrounding valleys that seemed to vanish in the last periphery of light. With a sudden surge of joy, I knew that I must find a home in this new land.

I had only twenty cents left, not even enough to take me to Chinatown where, I had been informed, a Filipino hotel and two restaurants were located. Fortunately two oldtimers put me in a car with four others, and took us to a hotel on King Street, the heart of Filipino life in Seattle. Marcelo, who was also in the car, had a cousin named Elias who came to our room with another oldtimer. Elias and his unknown friend persuaded my companions to play a strange kind of card game. In a little while Elias got up and touched his friend suggestively; then they disappeared and we never saw them again.

It was only when our two countrymen had left that my companions realized what happened. They had taken all their money. Marcelo asked me if I had any money. I gave him my twenty cents. After collecting a few more cents from the others, he went downstairs and when he came back he told us that he had telegraphed for money to his brother in California.

All night we waited for the money to come, hungry and afraid to go out in the street. Outside we could hear shouting and singing; then a woman screamed lustily in one of the rooms down the hall. Across from our hotel a jazz band was playing noisily; it went on until dawn. But in the morning a telegram came to Marcelo which said:

YOUR BROTHER DIED AUTOMOBILE ACCIDENT LAST WEEK

Marcelo looked at us and began to cry. His anguish stirred an aching fear in me. I knelt on the floor looking for my suitcase under the bed. I knew that I had to go out now—alone. I put the suitcase on my shoulder and walked toward the door, stopping for a moment to look back at my friends who were still standing silently around Marcelo. Suddenly a man came into the room and announced that he was the proprietor.

"Well, boys," he said, looking at our suitcases, "where is the rent?"

"We have no money, sir," I said, trying to impress him with my politeness.

"That is too bad," he said quickly, glancing furtively at our suitcases again. "That is just too bad." He walked outside and went down the hall. He came back with a short, fat Filipino, who looked at us stupidly with his dull, small eyes, and spat his cigar out of the window.

"There they are, Jake," said the proprietor.

Jake looked disappointed. "They are too young," he said.

"You can break them in, Jake," said the proprietor.

"They will be sending babies next," Jake said.

"You can break them in, can't you, Jake?" the proprietor pleaded. "This is not the first time you have broken babies in. You have done it in the sugar plantations in Hawaii, Jake!"

"Hell!" Jake said, striding across the room to the proprietor. He pulled a fat roll of bills from his pocket and gave twenty-five dollars to the proprietor. Then he turned to us and said, "All right, Pinoys, you are working for me now. Get your hats and follow me."

We were too frightened to hesitate. When we lifted our suitcases the proprietor ordered us not to touch them.

"I'll take care of them until you come back from Alaska," he said. "Good fishing, boys!"

In this way we were sold for five dollars each to work in the fish canneries in Alaska, by a Visayan from the island of Leyte to an Ilocano from the province of La Union. Both were old-timers; both were tough. They exploited young immigrants until one of them, the hotel proprietor, was shot dead by an unknown assailant. We were forced to sign a paper which stated that each of us owed the contractor twenty dollars for bedding and another twenty for luxuries. What the luxuries were, I have never found out. The contractor turned out to be a tall, heavy-set, dark Filipino, who came to the small hold of the boat barking at us like a dog. He was drunk and saliva was running down his shirt.

"And get this, you devils!" he shouted at us. "You will never come back alive if you don't do what I say!"

It was the beginning of my life in America, the beginning of a long flight that carried me down the years, fighting desperately to find peace in some corner of life.

I had struck up a friendship with two oldtimers who were not much older than I. One was Conrado Torres, a journalism student at a university in Oregon, who was fired with a dream to unionize the cannery workers. I discovered that he had come from Binalonan, but could hardly remember the names of people there because he had been very young when he had come to America. Conrado was small and dark, with slant eyes and thick eyebrows; but his nose was thin above a wise, sensuous mouth. He introduced me to Paulo Lorca, a gay fellow, who had graduated from law school in Los Angeles. This surreptitious meeting at a cannery in Rose Inlet was the beginning of a friendship that grew simultaneously with the growth of the trade union movement and progressive ideas among the Filipinos in the United States.

In those days labor unions were still unheard of in the canneries, so the contractors rapaciously exploited their workers. They had henchmen in every cannery who saw to it that every attempt at unionization was frustrated and the instigators of the idea punished. The companies also had their share in the exploitation; our bunkhouses were unfit for human habitation. The lighting system was bad and dangerous to our eyes, and those of us who were working in the semi-darkness were severely affected by the strong ammonia from the machinery.

I was working in a section called "wash lye." Actually a certain amount of lye was diluted in the water where I washed the beheaded fish that came down on a small escalator. One afternoon a cutter above me, working in the poor light, slashed off his right arm with the cutting machine. It happened so swiftly he did not cry out. I saw his arm floating down the water among the fish heads.

It was only at night that we felt free, although the sun seemed never to disappear from the sky. It stayed on in the western horizon and its magnificence inflamed the snows on the island, giving us a world of soft, continuous light, until the moon rose at about ten o'clock to take its place. Then trembling shadows began to form on the rise of the brilliant snow in our yard, and we would come out with baseball bats, gloves and balls, and the Indian girls who worked in the cannery would join us, shouting huskily like men.

We played far into the night. Sometimes a Filipino and an Indian girl would run off into the moonlight; we could hear them chasing each other in the snow. Then we would hear the girl giggling and laughing deliciously in the shadows. Paulo was always running off with a girl named La Belle. How she acquired that name in Alaska, I never found out. But hardly had we started our game when off they ran, chasing each other madly and suddenly disappearing out of sight.

Toward the end of the season La Belle gave birth to a baby. We were sure, however, that the father was not in our group. We were sure that she had got it from one of the Italian fishermen on the island. La Belle did not come to work for two days, but when she appeared on the third day with the baby slung on her back, she threw water into Conrado's face.

"Are you going to marry me or not?" she asked him.

Conrado was frightened. He was familiar with the ways of Indians, so he said: "Why should I marry you?"

"We'll see about that!" La Belle shouted, running to the door.

She came back with an official of the company. "That's the one!" she said, pointing to Conrado.

"You'd better come to the office with us," said the official.

Conrado did not know what to do. He looked at me for help. Paulo left his washing machine and nodded to me to follow him. We went with them into the building which was the town hall.

"You are going to marry this Indian girl and stay on the island for seven years as prescribed by law," said the official to Conrado. "And as the father of the baby, you must support both mother and child, and, if you have four more children by the time your turn is up, you will be sent back to the mainland with a bonus."

"But, sir, the baby is not mine," said Conrado weakly.

Paulo stepped up quickly beside him and said: "The baby is mine, sir. I guess I'll have to stay."

La Belle looked at Paulo with surprise. After a moment, however, she began to smile with satisfaction. Paulo was well-educated and spoke good English. But I think what finally drove Conrado from La Belle's primitive mind were Paulo's curly hair, his even, white teeth. Meekly she signed the paper after Paulo.

"I'll stay here for seven years, all right," Paulo said to me. "I'm in a mess in Los Angeles anyway—so I'll stay with this dirty Indian girl."

"Stop talking like that if you know what is good for you," La Belle said, giving him the baby.

"I guess you are right," Paulo said.

"You shouldn't have done it for me," Conrado said.

"It's all right," Paulo laughed. "I'll be in the United States before you know it."

I still do not understand why Paulo interceded for Conrado. When the season was over Paulo came to our bunks in the boat and asked Conrado to send him something to drink. I did not see him again.

CHAPTER XIV

WHEN I landed in Seattle for the second time, I expected a fair amount of money from the company. But the contractor, Max Feuga, came into the play room and handed us slips of paper. I looked at mine and was amazed at the neatly itemized expenditures that I was supposed to have incurred during the season. Twenty-five dollars for withdrawals, one hundred for board and room, twenty for bedding, and another twenty for something I do not now remember. At the bottom was the actual amount I was to receive after all the deductions: *thirteen dollars!*

I could do nothing. I did not even go to the hotel where I had left my suitcase. I went to a Japanese dry goods store on Jackson Street and bought a pair of corduroy pants and a blue shirt. It was already twilight and the cannery workers were in the crowded Chinese gambling houses, losing their season's earnings and drinking bootleg whisky. They became quarrelsome and abusive to their own people when they lost, and subservient to the Chinese gambling lords and marijuana peddlers. They pawed at the semi-nude whores with their dirty hands and made suggestive gestures, running out into the night when they were rebuffed for lack of money.

I was already in America, and I felt good and safe. I did not understand why. The gamblers, prostitutes and Chinese opium smokers did not excite me, but they aroused in me a feeling of flight. I knew that I must run away from them, but it was not that I was afraid of contamination. I wanted to see other aspects of American life, for surely these destitute and vicious people were merely a small part of it. Where would I begin this pilgrimage, this search for a door into America?

I went outside and walked around looking into the faces of

my countrymen, wondering if I would see someone I had known in the Philippines. I came to a building which brightly dressed white women were entering, lifting their diaphanous gowns as they climbed the stairs. I looked up and saw the huge sign:

MANILA DANCE HALL

The orchestra upstairs was playing; Filipinos were entering. I put my hands in my pockets and followed them, beginning to feel lonely for the sound of home.

The dance hall was crowded with Filipino cannery workers and domestic servants. But the girls were very few, and the Filipinos fought over them. When a boy liked a girl he bought a roll of tickets from the hawker on the floor and kept dancing with her. But the other boys who also liked the same girl shouted at him to stop, cursing him in the dialects and sometimes throwing rolled wet papers at him. At the bar the glasses were tinkling, the bottles popping loudly, and the girls in the back room were smoking marijuana. It was almost impossible to breathe.

Then I saw Marcelo's familiar back. He was dancing with a tall blonde in a green dress, a girl so tall that Marcelo looked like a dwarf climbing a tree. But the girl was pretty and her body was nicely curved and graceful, and she had a way of swaying that aroused confused sensations in me. It was evident that many of the boys wanted to dance with her; they were shouting maliciously at Marcelo. The way the blonde waved to them made me think that she knew most of them. They were nearly all oldtimers and strangers to Marcelo. They were probably gamblers and pimps, because they had fat rolls of money and expensive clothing.

But Marcelo was learning very fast. He requested one of his friends to buy another roll of tickets for him. The girl was supposed to tear off one ticket every three minutes, but I noticed that she tore off a ticket for every minute. That was ten cents a minute. Marcelo was unaware of what she was doing; he was spending his whole season's earnings on his first day in America. It was only when one of his friends shouted to him in the dialect that he became angry at the girl. Marcelo was not tough, but his friend was an oldtimer. Marcelo pushed the girl toward the gaping bystanders. His friend opened a knife and gave it to him.

Then something happened that made my heart leap. One of the blonde girl's admirers came from behind and struck Marcelo with a piece of lead pipe. Marcelo's friend whipped out a pistol and fired. Marcelo and the boy with the lead pipe fell on the floor simultaneously, one on top of the other, but the blonde girl ran into the crowd screaming frantically. Several guns banged at once, and the lights went out. I saw Marcelo's friend crumple in the fading light.

At once the crowd seemed to flow out of the windows. I went to a side window and saw three heavy electric wires strung from the top of the building to the ground. I reached for them and slid to the ground. My palms were burning when I came out of the alley. Then I heard the sirens of police cars screaming infernally toward the place. I put my cap in my pocket and ran as fast as I could in the direction of a neon sign two blocks down the street.

It was a small church where Filipino farm workers were packing their suitcases and bundles. I found out later that Filipino immigrants used their churches as rest houses while they were waiting for work. There were two large trucks outside. I went to one of them and sat on the running board, holding my hands over my heart for fear it would beat too fast. The lights in the church went out and the workers came into the street. The driver of the truck in which I was sitting pointed a strong flashlight at me.

"Hey, you, are you looking for a job?" he asked.

"Yes, sir," I said.

"Get in the truck," he said, jumping into the cab. "Let's go, Flo!" he shouted to the other driver.

I was still trembling with excitement. But I was glad to get out of Seattle—to anywhere else in America. I did not care where so long as it was in America. I found a corner and sat down heavily. The drivers shouted to each other. Then we were off to work.

It was already midnight and the lights in the city of Seattle were beginning to fade. I could see the reflections on the bright lake in Bremerton. I was reminded of Baguio. Then some of the men began singing. The driver and two men were arguing over money. A boy in the other truck was playing a violin. We were on the highway to Yakima Valley.

After a day and a night of driving we arrived in a little town called Moxee City. The apple trees were heavy with fruit and the branches drooped to the ground. It was late afternoon when we passed through the town; the hard light of the sun punctuated the ugliness of the buildings. I was struck dumb by its isolation and the dry air that hung oppressively over the place. The heart-shaped valley was walled by high treeless mountains, and the hot breeze that blew in from a distant sea was injurious to the apple trees.

The leader of our crew was called Cornelio Paez; but most of the oldtimers suspected that it was not his real name. There was something shifty about him, and his so-called bookkeeper, a pockmarked man we simply called Pinoy (which is a term generally applied to all Filipino immigrant workers), had a strange trick of squinting sideways when he looked at you. There seemed to be an old animosity between Paez and his bookkeeper.

But we were drawn together because the white people of Yakima Valley were suspicious of us. Years before, in the town of Toppenish, two Filipino apple pickers had been found murdered on the road to Sunnyside. At that time, there was ruthless persecution of the Filipinos throughout the Pacific Coast, instigated by orchardists who feared the unity of white and Filipino workers. A small farmer in Wapato who had tried to protect his Filipino workers had had his house burned. So however much we distrusted each other under Paez, we knew that beyond the walls of our bunkhouse were our real enemies, waiting to drive us out of Yakima Valley.

I had become acquainted with an oldtimer who had had considerable experience in the United States. His name was Julio, and it seemed that he was hiding from some trouble in Chicago. At night, when the men gambled in the kitchen, I would stand silently behind him and watch him cheat the other players. He was very deft, and his eyes were sharp and trained. Sometimes when there was no game, Julio would teach me tricks.

Mr. Malraux, our employer, had three daughters who used to work with us after school hours. He was a Frenchman who had gone to Moxee City when it consisted of only a few houses. At that time the valley was still a haven for Indians, but they had been gradually driven out when farming had been started on a large scale. Malraux had married an American woman in Spokane and begun farming; the girls came one by one, helping him on the farm as they grew. When I arrived in Moxee City they were already in their teens.

The oldest girl was called Estelle; she had just finished high school. She had a delightful disposition and her industry was something that men talked about with approval. The other girls, Maria and Diane, were still too young to be going about so freely; but whenever Estelle came to our bunkhouse they were always with her.

It was now the end of summer and there was a bright moon in the sky. Not far from Moxee City was a wide grassland where cottontails and jack rabbits roamed at night. Estelle used to drive her father's old car and would pick up some of us at the bunk-house; then we would go hunting with their dogs and a few antiquated shotguns.

When we came back from hunting we would go to the Mal-raux house with some of the men who had musical instruments. We would sit on the lawn for hours singing American songs. But when they started singing Philippine songs their voices were so sad, so full of yesterday and the haunting presence of familiar seas, as if they had reached the end of creation, that life seemed ended and no bright spark was left in the world.

But one afternoon toward the end of the season, Paez went to the bank to get our paychecks and did not come back. The pockmarked bookkeeper was furious.

"I'll get him this time!" he said, running up and down the house. "He did that last year in California and I didn't get a cent. I know where to find the bastard!"

Julio grabbed him by the neck. "You'd better tell me where to find him if you know what is good for you," he said angrily, pushing the frightened bookkeeper toward the stove.

"Let me alone!" he shouted.

Julio hit him between the eyes, and the bookkeeper struggled violently. Julio hit him again. The bookkeeper rolled on the floor like a baby. Julio picked him up and threw him outside the house. I thought he was dead, but his legs began to move. Then he opened his eyes and got up quickly, staggering like a drunken stevedore toward the highway. Julio came out of the house with brass knuckles, but the bookkeeper was already disappearing behind the apple orchard. Julio came back and began hitting the door of the kitchen with all his force, in futile anger.

I had not seen this sort of brutality in the Philippines, but my first contact with it in America made me brave. My bravery was still nameless, and waiting to express itself. I was not shocked when I saw that my countrymen had become ruthless toward one another, and this sudden impact of cruelty made me insensate to pain and kindness, so that it took me a long time to wholly trust other men. As time went by I became as ruthless as the worst of them, and I became afraid that I would never feel like a human being again. Yet no matter what bestiality encompassed my life, I felt sure that somewhere, sometime, I would break free. This faith kept me from completely succumbing to the degradation into which many of my countrymen had fallen. It finally paved my way out of our small, harsh life, painfully but cleanly, into a world of strange intellectual adventures and self-fulfillment.

The apples were nearly picked when Paez disappeared with our money. We lost interest in our work. We sat on the lawn of the Malraux's and sang. They came out of the house and joined us. The moonlight shimmered like a large diamond on the land around the farm. The men in the bunkhouse came with

their violins and guitars. Julio grabbed Diane and started dancing with her; then the two younger girls were grabbed by other
men.

It was while Estelle was singing that we heard a gun crack
from the dirt road not far from the house. Malraux saw them
first, saw the clubs and the iron bars in their hands, and yelled
at us in warning. But it was too late. They had taken us by
surprise.

I saw Malraux run into the house for his gun. I jumped to the
nearest apple tree. I wanted a weapon—anything to hit back at
these white men who had leaped upon us from the dark. Three
or four guns banged all at once, and I turned to see Maria falling
to the ground. A streak of red light flashed from the window
into the crowd. Estelle was screaming and shouting to her father.
Diane was already climbing the stairs, her long black hair shining
in the moonlight.

I saw Julio motioning to me to follow him. Run away from
our friends and companions? No! *Goddamn you, Julio!* I
jumped into the thick of fight, dark with fury. Then I felt Julio's
hands pulling me away, screaming into my ears:

"Come on, you crazy punk! Come on before I kill you myself!"

He was hurting me. Blinded with anger and tears, I ran after
him toward our bunkhouse. We stopped behind a pear tree
when we saw that our house was burning. Julio whispered to
me to follow him.

We groped our way through the pear trees and came out,
after what seemed like hours of running, on a wide grass plain
traversed by a roaring irrigation ditch. Once when we thought
we were being followed, we jumped into the water and waited.
The night was silent and the stars in the sky were as far away
as home. Was there peace somewhere in the world? The silence
was broken only by the rushing water and the startled cry of
little birds that stirred in the night.

Julio led the way. We came to a dirt road that led to some
farmhouses. We decided to stay away from it. We turned off
the road and walked silently between the trees. Then we came

to a wide desert land. We followed a narrow footpath and, to our surprise, came to the low, uninhabited, wide desert of the Rattlesnake Mountains. The stars were our only guide.

We walked on and on. Toward dawn, when a strong wind came, we jumped into the dunes and covered our heads with dry bushes until it had passed by. We were no longer afraid of pursuit. We were in another land, on another planet. The desert was wide and flat. There were rabbits in the bushes, and once we came upon a herd of small deer. We ran after them with a burning bush, but they just stood nonchalantly and waited for us. When we were near enough for them to recognize our scent, they turned about and galloped down the sand dunes.

When morning came we were still in the desert. We walked until about noon. Then we came to a narrow grassland. We stood on a rise and looked around to see the edge of the desert. Julio started running crazily and jumping into the air. I ran after him. At last we came to the beginning of a wide plain.

The town of Toppenish was behind us now, and the cool wind from the valley swept the plain. We rested under a tree. Julio was different from other oldtimers; he did not talk much. I felt that he had many stories within him, and I longed to know America through him. His patience and nameless kindness had led me away from Moxee City into a new life.

After a while we crossed the plain again, hiding behind the trees whenever we saw anyone approaching us. I was too exhausted to continue when we reached Zillah, where some children stoned us. We hid in an orange grove and rested. At sunset we started again. When we were nearing the town of Granger, I heard the sudden tumult of the Yakima River. Julio started running again, and I followed him. Suddenly we saw the clear, cool water of the river. We sat in the tall grass, cooling our tired bodies beside the bright stream.

I was the first to enter the water. I washed my shirt and spread it to dry on the grass. Sunnyside was not far off. I could hear the loud whistle of trains running seaward.

"This is the beginning of your life in America," Julio said. "We'll take a freight train from Sunnyside and go to nowhere."

"I would like to go to California," I said. "I have two brothers there—but I don't know if I could find them."

"All roads go to California and all travelers wind up in Los Angeles," Julio said. "But not this traveler. I have lived there too long. I know that state too damn well. . . ."

"What do you mean?" I asked.

Suddenly he became sad and said: "It is hard to be a Filipino in California."

Not comprehending what he meant, I began to dream of going to California. Then we started for Sunnyside, listening eagerly to the train whistle piercing the summer sky. It was nearly ten in the evening when we reached Sunnyside. We circled the town, and then we saw the trains—every car bursting with fruit —screaming fiercely and chugging like beetles up and down the tracks. The voices of the trainmen came clearly through the night.

We stopped in the shadow of a water tower. Julio disappeared for a moment and came back.

"Our train leaves in an hour," he said. "I'll go around for something to eat. Wait for me here."

I waited for him to come back for several hours. The train left. Then I began to worry. I went to town and walked in the shadows, looking into the darkened windows of wooden houses. Julio had disappeared like a wind.

I returned to our rendezvous and waited all night. Early the next morning another train was ready to go; I ran behind the boxcars and climbed inside one. When the train began to move, I opened the door and looked sadly toward Sunnyside. Julio was there somewhere, friendless and alone in a strange town.

"Good-bye, Julio," I said. "And thanks for everything, Julio. I hope I will meet you again somewhere in America."

Then the train screamed and the thought of Julio hurt me. I stood peering outside and listening to the monotonous chugging of the engine. I knew that I could never be unkind to any Filipino, because Julio had left me a token of friendship, a seed of trust, that ached to grow to fruition as I rushed toward another city.

CHAPTER XV

LIKE a thundering river the train rushed toward Pasco, crossing wide, level lands, and passing through badlands, plateaus, and rill-marked hills. At Grandview, a prairie town whose sharp winds cut through the valleys and swept the plains, a dozen men jumped on and several of them came to my car. Two looked like professional hoboes, but the others were young men in search of work. I did not notice that there was a girl among them until we reached Kennewick, when the railroad detectives came to the boxes and scattered us among the trees. When they were gone and we had run back to the car, I learned that she was with her brother, who was younger than she. They were on their way to California where an uncle was waiting for them.

The sun went down slowly and sudden darkness came over the land. I sat back in my corner and tried to sleep, brushing off the obscene conversations of the men around me. Then in the middle of the night, isolated in a corner of the box, I was awakened by the young girl's whimpering. She was desperately struggling with someone in the dark, breathing as though she were being choked to death. Then I heard her fall heavily on the floor, and she began to sob hopelessly. Her assailant dragged her to my corner. I could hear the man fumbling at her. He was tearing hungrily at her clothes. I strained my eyes in the dark to see what was happening. After a while the girl did not struggle any more. She turned lifelessly toward me, and in the dark I could hear her agony.

With a sudden revulsion, I got up and felt for the man. But someone struck me on the head, and I rolled on the floor. There was silence for a long time; then as I returned to consciousness, I heard the stifled sobbing of the girl again. Another man approached her. . . .

When the train stopped many of the men in our car jumped out. The girl crawled about in the dark searching for her brother. "Bill—Bill, honey, where are you?" she whispered.

But the boy had disappeared in the night. Afraid and alone, she leaned against the wall and cried brokenly. I got up from my corner and looked out. We were in Hood, on the Columbia River. It was still dark, but I could hear the rushing water and, somewhere on the other side of the town, the sharp whistle of another train. The girl spread some newspapers on the floor and lay down to sleep. I struck a match and watched her face affectionately. She looked a little like my older sister, Francisca. There was a sudden rush of warm feeling in me, yearning to comfort her with the words I knew. This ravished girl and this lonely night, in a freight train bound for an unknown city. . . . I could not hold back the tears that came to my eyes.

When we reached Portland it was already after midnight. The girl walked with me in the streets.

"Where are you going?" she asked me.

"I am looking for an address," I said, trying to make her understand my broken English. "But the houses are too dark."

"Do you have a friend here?" But she did not wait for an answer. "Let's go back to the station," she suggested.

We found a train about ready to leave for California. A few men came into the car where the girl and I were sitting. Then a woman came in with her husband, who was carrying a baby. There was a Negro boy with a harmonica; he kept playing for hours, stopping only to say "Salem!" "Eugene!" "Klamath Falls!" when we passed through those places.

The girl leaned on me and went to sleep, her breath warming my face. I dozed off and did not waken until the following morning. The girl was gone, but the newspapers on which she had lain were still warm. Everybody was gone except the Negro boy with the harmonica. He was still playing. I kept staring at him because it was the first time I had ever seen a black person.

"Where are you going, boy?" he asked.

"California, sir," I said.

He laughed, "*Sir?*"

"Yes, sir," I said again.

"Boy, you are far from California!" He laughed aloud, taking up the harmonica again.

I opened the door and looked out. The train was still moving. When the train stopped at the station, the Negro began to laugh again.

"Boy, boy, boy!" he screamed. "This is Reno, Nevada!"

I went to the door again and looked out. Then I saw the startling sign:

RENO, THE BIGGEST SMALL CITY IN THE WORLD!

The girl had left three strands of her brown hair on my shoulder. I picked them up and wrapped them in a piece of newspaper. I do not know why I did it, but felt somehow that I would meet her again. Innocent-looking she was, and forlorn, and I felt that there was a bond between us, a bond of fear and a common loneliness.

When the Negro told me what train to take to California, I thanked him and left, hoping I would encounter him again. The cars were full of hoboes and drifting men, who sat on the floor eating stale bread and drinking cold coffee. The wide desert land was shimmering with heat, and except for a bit of brush here and there, it reminded me of my escape with Julio across the Rattlesnake Mountains.

At last we came to some mountains, tall frowning mountains, and deep, narrow rivers rushing down the canyons. I counted thirteen short tunnels before we came out to the border of California, rolling across a wide land of luxuriant vegetation and busy towns. Then there was a river, and not far off the town of Marysville loomed above a valley of grapes and sugar beets, all green and ready for the summer harvest.

I wanted to stop and walk around town, but some of the hoboes told me that there were thousands of Filipinos in Stockton. I remained on the same train until it got to Sacramento, where I boarded another that took me to Stockton. It was twilight when the train pulled into the yards. I asked some of the hoboes where I could find Chinatown, for there I would be sure to find my countrymen.

"El Dorado Street," they said.

It was like a song, for the words actually mean "the land of gold." I did not know that I wanted gold in the new land, but the name was like a song. I walked slowly in the streets, avoiding the business district and the lights. Then familiar signs glowed in the coming night, and I began to walk faster. I saw many Filipinos in magnificent suits standing in front of poolrooms and gambling houses. There must have been hundreds in the street somewhere, waiting for the night.

I walked eagerly among them, looking into every face and hoping to see a familiar one. The asparagus season was over and most of the Filipino farmhands were in town, bent on spending their earnings because they had no other place to go. They were sitting in the bars and poolrooms, in the dance halls and gambling dens; and when they had lost or spent all their money, they went to the whorehouses and pawed at the prostitutes.

I entered a big gambling house on El Dorado and Lafayette Streets, where ten prostitutes circulated, obscenely clutching at some of the gamblers. I went to a stove in the middle of the room where a pot of tea was boiling. I filled a cup and then another, and the liquid warmed my empty stomach. This was to save me in harsher times, in the hungry years of my life in America. Drinking tea in Chinese gambling houses was something tangible, and gratifying, and perhaps it was because of this that most of the Filipino unemployed frequented these places.

I was still drinking when a Chinese came out of a back room with a gun and shot a Filipino who was standing by a table. When the bullet hit the Filipino, he turned toward the Chinese with a stupid look of surprise. I saw his eyes and I knew that the philosophers lied when they said death was easy and beautiful. I knew that there was nothing better than life, even a hard life, even a frustrated life. Yes, even a broken-down gambler's life. And I wanted to live.

I ran to the door without looking back. I ran furiously down the street. A block away, I stopped in a doorway and stood, shivering, afraid, and wanting to spit out the tea that I had drunk in the gambling house. When my heart ceased pounding, I walked blindly up a side street. I had not gone far when I saw a building ablaze.

"What is it?" I asked a Filipino near me.

"It is the Filipino Federation Building," he said. "I don't agree with this organization, but I know why the building is burning. I know the Chinese gambling lords control this town."

I did not know what he meant. I looked at him with eager eyes.

"I don't know what you mean," I said. "I've just arrived in the United States."

"My name is Claro," he said, extending a long, thin hand, and coughing behind the other. "I came from Luna, in the province of La Union. Let us go to my restaurant and I will explain everything to you. Are you hungry, boy?"

He was not much older than I, and he spoke my dialect.

"I have not eaten for two days," I said. "You see, I took the freight train in Sunnyside, Washington."

Claro hugged me. When he entered the restaurant, he locked the door and put down the shades.

"I don't want the swine in the street to see us," he said, going to the stove. "They disgust me with their filthy interest in money. That is why I am always behind in my bills. I like good people, so I am keeping this restaurant for them."

I watched him prepare vegetable soup and fry a piece of chicken. When the pot started to boil, Claro put a record on a portable phonograph at the other end of the counter; then there was a sudden softness in his face, and his eyes shone. He had put on a Strauss waltz. Going back to the stove, Claro raised his hands expertly above his head in the manner of boleros and started to dance, swaying gracefully in the narrow space between the stove and the counter. He was smiling blissfully, and when someone knocked on the door he stopped suddenly and shouted:

"Go away! The place is closed for tonight!"

When he had placed everything on the counter, Claro took a chair and sat near me.

"Listen, my friend," he said. "The Chinese syndicates, the gambling lords, are sucking the blood of our people. The Pinoys work every day in the fields but when the season is over their money is in the Chinese vaults! And what do the Chinese do? Nothing! I see them only at night in their filthy gambling dens waiting for the Filipinos to throw their hard-earned money on the tables. Why, the Chinese control this town! The local banks can't do business without them, and the farmers, who badly need the health and interest of their Filipino workers, don't want to do anything because they borrow money from the banks. See!"

I was too hungry to listen. But I was also beginning to understand what he was trying to say.

"Perhaps in another year I will be able to understand what you are saying, Claro," I said.

"Stay away from Stockton," he warned me. "Stay away from the Chinese gambling houses, and the dance halls and the whorehouses operated by Americans. Don't come back to this corrupt town until you are ready to fight for our people!"

I thanked him and walked hastily to the door. I hurried to the freight yards. I was fortunate enough to find an empty boxcar. I sat in a corner and tried to sleep, but Claro's words kept coming back to me. He wanted me to go back to fight for our people when I was ready. I knew I would go back, but how soon I did not know. I would go back to Claro and his town. His food had warmed me and I felt good.

CHAPTER XVI

I BEGAN to be afraid, riding alone in the freight train. I wanted suddenly to go back to Stockton and look for a job in the tomato fields, but the train was already traveling fast. I was in flight again, away from an unknown terror that seemed to follow me everywhere. Dark flight into another place, toward other enemies. But there was a clear sky and the night was ablaze with stars. I could still see the faint haze of Stockton's lights in the distance, a halo arching above it and fading into a backdrop of darkness.

In the early morning the train stopped a few miles from Niles, in the midst of a wide grape field. The grapes had been harvested and the bare vines were falling to the ground. The apricot trees were leafless. Three railroad detectives jumped out of a car and ran toward the boxcars. I ran to the vineyard and hid behind a smudge pot, waiting for the next train from Stockton. A few bunches of grapes still hung on the vines, so I filled my pockets and ran for the tracks when the train came. It was a freight and it stopped to pick up carloads of grapes; when it started moving again the empties were full of men.

I crawled to a corner of a car and fell asleep. When I awakened the train was already in San Jose. I jumped outside and found another freight going south. I swung aboard and found several hoboes drinking cans of beer. I sat and watched them sitting solemnly, as though there were no more life left in the world. They talked as though there were no more happiness left, as though life had died and would not live again. I could not converse with them, and this barrier made me a stranger. I wanted to know them and to be a part of their life. I wondered what I had in common with them beside the fact that we were all on the road rolling to unknown destinations.

When I reached Salinas, I walked to town and went to a Mexican restaurant on Soledad Street. I was drinking coffee when I saw the same young girl who had disappeared in the night. She was passing by with an old man. I ran to the door and called to her, but she did not hear me. I went back to my coffee wondering what would become of her.

I avoided the Chinese gambling houses, remembering the tragedy in Stockton. Walking on the dark side of the street as though I were hunted, I returned eagerly to the freight yards. I found the hoboes sitting gloomily in the dark. I tried a few times to jump into the boxcars, but the detectives chased me away. When the freights had gone the detectives left.

Then an express from San Francisco came and stopped to pick up a few passengers. The hoboes darted out from the dark and ran to the rods. When I realized that I was the only one left, I grabbed the rod between the coal car and the car behind it. Then the express started, gathering speed as it nosed its way through the night.

I almost fell several times. The strong, cold wind lashed sharply at my face. I put the crook of my arm securely about the rod, pinching myself when I feared that I was going to sleep. It was not yet autumn and the sky was clear, but the wind was bitter and sharp and cut across my face like a knife. When my arm went to sleep, I beat it to life with my fist. It was the only way I could save myself from falling to my death.

I was so exhausted and stiff with the cold when I reached San Luis Obispo that I could scarcely climb down. I stumbled when I reached the ground, rolling over on my stomach as though I were headless. Then I walked to town, where I found a Filipino who took me in his car to Pismo Beach. The Filipino community was a small block near the sea—a block of poolrooms, gambling houses, and little green cottages where prostitutes were doing business. At first I did not know what the cottages were, but I saw many Filipinos going into them from the gambling houses near by. Then I guessed what they were, because cottages such as these were found in every Filipino community.

I went into one of the cottages and sat in the warm little parlor where the Filipinos were waiting their turn to go upstairs. Some of the prostitutes were sitting awkwardly in the men's laps, wheedling them. Others were dancing cheek to cheek, swaying their hips suggestively. The Filipinos stood around whispering lustily in their dialects. The girls were scantily dressed, and one of them was nude. The nude girl put her arms around me and started cooing lasciviously.

I was extricated from her by the same Filipino who had taken me into his car in San Luis Obispo. He came into the house and immediately took the girl upstairs. In ten minutes he was down again and asked me if I would like to ride with him to Lompoc. I had heard of the place when I was in Seattle, so naturally I was interested. We started immediately and in about two hours had passed through Santa Maria.

Beyond the town, at a railroad crossing, highway patrolmen stopped our car. Speaking to me in our dialect, Doro, my companion, said:

"These bastards probably want to see if we have a white woman in the car."

"Why?" I asked him, becoming frightened.

"They think every Filipino is a pimp," he said. "But there are more pimps among them than among all the Filipinos in the world put together. I will kill one of these bastards someday!"

They questioned Doro curtly, peered into the car, and told us to go on.

I came to know afterward that in many ways it was a crime to be a Filipino in California. I came to know that the public streets were not free to my people: we were stopped each time these vigilant patrolmen saw us driving a car. We were suspect each time we were seen with a white woman. And perhaps it was this narrowing of our life into an island, into a filthy segment of American society, that had driven Filipinos like Doro inward, hating everyone and despising all positive urgencies toward freedom.

When we reached the mountains to the right of the highway, we turned toward them and started climbing slowly, following the road that winds around them like a taut ribbon. We had been driving for an hour when we reached the summit, and suddenly the town of Lompoc shone like a constellation of stars in the deep valley below. We started downward, hearing the strong wind from the sea beating against the car. Then we came to the edge of the town, and church bells began ringing somewhere near a forest.

It was the end of the flower season, so the Filipino workers were all in town. They stood on the sidewalks and in front of Japanese stores showing their fat rolls of money to the girls. Gambling was going on in one of the old buildings, in the Mexican district, and in a café across the street Mexican girls and Filipinos were dancing. I went inside the café and sat near the counter, watching the plump girls dancing drunkenly.

I noticed a small Filipino sitting forlornly at one of the tables. He was smoking a cigar and spitting like a big man into an empty cigar box on the floor. When the juke box stopped playing he jumped to the counterman for some change. He put the nickels in the slot, waving graciously to the dancers although he never danced himself. Now and then a Filipino would go into the back room where the gamblers were playing cards and cursing loudly.

The forlorn Filipino went to the counter again and asked for change. He put all the nickels in the slot and bought several packages of cigarettes. He threw the cigarettes on the table near the juke box and then called to the old Mexican men who were sitting around the place. The Mexicans rushed for the table, grabbing the cigarettes. The Filipino went out lighting another big cigar.

I followed him immediately. He walked slowly and stopped now and then to see if I was following him. There was some mysterious force in him that attracted me. When he came to a large neon sign which said Landstrom Café, he stopped and peered through the wide front window. Then he entered a side door and climbed the long stairs.

I opened the door quietly and entered. I heard him talking to a man in one of the rooms upstairs. When I reached the land-ing a hard blow fell on my head. I rolled on the floor. Then I saw him with a gun in his hand, poised to strike at my head again. Standing behind him was my brother Amado, holding a long-bladed knife.

I scrambled to my feet screaming: "Brother, it is me! It is Allos! Remember?"

My brother told his friend to stop. He came near me, walking around me suspiciously. He stepped back and folded the blade of the knife. There was some doubt in his face.

"I am your brother," I said again, holding back the tears in my eyes. "I am Allos! Remember the village of Mangusmana? Remember when you beat our *carabao* in the rain? When you touched my head and then ran to Binalonan? Remember, Amado?" I was not only fighting for my life, but also for a childhood bond that was breaking. Frantically I searched in my mind for other remembrances of the past which might remind him of me, and re-establish a bridge between him and my childhood.

"Remember when I fell from the coconut tree and you were a janitor in the *presidencia*?" I said. "And you brought some magazines for me to read? Then you went away to work in the sugar plantations of Bulacan?"

"If you are really my brother tell me the name of our mother," he said casually.

"Our mother's name is Meteria," I said. "That is what the people call her. But her real name is Autilia Sampayan. We used to sell salted fish and salt in the villages. Remember?"

My brother grabbed me affectionately and for a long time he could not say a word. I knew, then, that he had loved my mother although he had had no chance to show it to her. Yes, to him, and to me afterward, to know my mother's name was to know the password into the secrets of the past, into childhood and pleasant memories; but it was also a guiding star, a talisman, a charm that lights us to manhood and decency.

"It has been so long, Allos," Amado said at last. "I had almost forgotten you. Please forgive me, brother. . . ."

"My name is Alfredo," said his friend. "I nearly killed you!"

He laughed guiltily, putting the gun in his pocket. "Yes, I almost killed you, Allos!"

My brother opened the door of their room. It was a small room, with one broken chair and a small window facing the street. Their clothes were hanging on a short rope that was strung between the door and a cracked mirror. I sat on the edge of the bed, waiting for my brother to speak. Alfredo started playing solitaire on the table, laughing whenever he cheated himself.

"Go out in the hall and wash your hands," said my brother. "Then we will go downstairs for something to eat. Where is your suitcase?"

"I don't have any—now," I said. "I lost it when I was in Seattle."

"Have you been in Seattle?" he asked.

"I have been in Alaska, too," I said. "And other places."

"You should have written to me," he said. "You shouldn't have come to America. But you can't go back now. You can never go back, Allos."

I could hear men shouting in a bar two blocks down the street. Then church bells started ringing again, and the wind from the sea carried their message to the farmhouses in the canyon near the river. I knew that as long as there was a hope for the future somewhere I would not stop trying to reach it. I looked at my brother and Alfredo and knew that I would never stay with them, to rot and perish in their world of brutality and despair. I knew that I wanted something which would ease my fear and stop my flight from dawn to dawn.

"Life is tough, Carlos," said my brother. "I had a good job for some time, but the depression came. I had to do something. I had to live, Carlos!"

I did not know what he was trying to tell me. But I noticed that he had started using my Christian name. I noticed, too, that he spoke to me in English. His English was perfect. Alfredo's English was perfect also, but his accent was still strong. Alfredo tried to speak the way my brother spoke, but his uncultured tongue twisted ridiculously about in his mouth and the words did not come out right.

"We are in the bootleg racket," said my brother. "Alfredo and I will make plenty of money. But it is dangerous."

"I like money," Alfredo said. "It is everything."

They spoke with cynicism, but there was a grain of wisdom in their words. We were driving a borrowed car toward a farmhouse, away from the flower fields that made Lompoc famous. We drove across a dry river and into a wide orchard, then Alfredo knocked on the door. An Italian came to the door and told us to follow him into the back yard.

"How many bottles do you want?" he asked my brother, starting to dig under a eucalyptus tree.

"I think I can sell two dozen," said Amado.

"The big size?" asked the Italian.

"The big size," Alfredo said.

The Italian looked at me suspiciously. When he had all the bottles ready, Amado paid him, and the Italian opened a small bottle and passed it around to us. I refused to drink, and Alfredo laughed. Then we went to the car and drove carefully to town.

They disappeared with the bottles, peddling their bootleg whisky in gambling houses and places of questionable reputation. They were boisterous when they entered the room, throwing their money on the bed and talking excitedly. They were disappointed when I told them that I wanted to go to Los Angeles.

"Don't you want to go into business with us?" Alfredo asked me.

"Maybe I will come back someday," I said.

"Well, I was hoping you would want to begin early," he said. There was a note of genuine disappointment in his voice. He put some money in my pocket. "Here is something for you to remember me by."

"If you would like to go to school," said my brother in parting, "just let me know. But whatever you do, Carlos, don't lose your head. Good-bye!"

I sat in the bus and watched them walking toward the Mexican district. I wanted to cry because my brother was no longer the person I had known in Binalonan. He was no longer the gentle, hard-working janitor in the *presidencia*. I remembered the time when he had gone to Lingayen to cook for my brother Macario! Now he had changed, and I could not understand him any more.

"Please, God, don't change me in America!" I said to myself, looking the other way so that I would not cry.

CHAPTER XVII

I REACHED Los Angeles in the evening. An early autumn rain was falling. I waited in the station, looking among the passengers for Filipino faces. Then I went out and turned northward on Los Angeles Street, and suddenly familiar signs on barber shops and restaurants came to view. I felt as though I had discovered a new world. I entered a restaurant and heard the lonely sound of my dialect, the soft staccato sound of home. I knew at once that I would meet some people I had known in the Philippines.

I sat on one of the stools and waited. I saw three American girls come in with three Filipinos. I thought I knew one of the Filipinos, so I approached him and spoke in Ilocano. But he did not understand me; even when I spoke in Pangasinan, he did not understand me. He was of another tribe, possibly a Visayan.

"If you are looking for your brother," said the proprietor to me, "go to the dance hall. That is where you always find them."

I asked him to direct me. It was still early, but the girls were already arriving. They went hastily up the stairs and their perfume lingered after them. I stood outside for a long time watching through the door until the guard closed it.

Filipinos started going inside, putting their hands high above their heads so that the guard could search them for concealed weapons. The guard was a white man and he was very rough with them. I went to Main Street, turned to the north, and found the Mexican district. The sound of Spanish made me feel at home, and I mingled with the drunks and the jobless men. In the old plaza some men were debating a political issue; a shaggy old man was preaching to a motley crowd. And farther down the street, near Olvera Market, I saw little Mexican boys carrying shoeshine boxes. They were eating sunflower seeds and throwing the empty shells into each other's faces.

It was now getting late. The crowd in the street was dispersing. The bells in the church tower began to ring. I looked up and saw devotees coming out of the door. It was already ten o'clock and the night services were over. The haggard preacher in the plaza leaped from his perch and disappeared in the crowd. I sat on a wooden bench and put my cap over my face so that I could sleep in the glare of the street lamps.

Toward midnight a drunk came to my bench and lay down to sleep. I moved away from him, giving him enough space to be comfortable. Then a young Mexican whose voice sounded like a girl's sat beside me. He put his hand on my knee and started telling me about a place where we could get something to eat. I was hungry and cold, but I was afraid of him.

I walked away from him, watching the church across the street. When I was sure no one was looking, I rushed to the door and entered. The church was empty. I went to a comfortable corner and lay on the floor. I saw on old man with a white beard coming in the door, and I thought he saw me. But he went to the candles and blew them out one by one, then disappeared through a side door. It was like heaven, it was so warm and quiet and comfortable. I closed my eyes and went to sleep.

I was awakened in the morning by the merry peals of tiny bells. I ran across the room and through the door, bumping into many people who were arriving for the morning services. I walked in the crowded street toward the Filipino district. I felt as though a beast were tearing at the walls of my stomach. The pain nauseated me: I was hungry again.

I thought I saw my brother Macario in a streetcar. I jumped on with all the power of my legs, but I was wrong. I got out on the next block and started walking aimlessly. I began to wonder if my life would always be one long flight from fear. When had I landed in America? It seemed so long ago. I crossed the green lawn of the new City Hall.

✦

I walked from Main Street to Vermont Avenue, three miles
away. I returned to town by streetcar and went to First Street
again. A Filipino poolroom was crowded, and I went inside to
sit on a bench. The players were betting and once in a while
they would give the table boy a dime. I waited until the men
started coming in groups, because their day's work was done.

I was talking to a gambler when two police detectives darted
into the place and shot a little Filipino in the back. The boy fell
on his knees, face up, and expired. The players stopped for a
moment, agitated, then resumed playing, their faces coloring
with fear and revolt. The detectives called an ambulance, dumped
the dead Filipino into the street, and left when an interne and
his assistant arrived. They left hurriedly, untouched by their
act, as though killing were a part of their day's work.

All at once I heard many tongues speaking excitedly. They
did not know why the Filipino was shot. It seemed that the
victim was new in the city. I was bewildered.

"Why was he shot?" I asked a man near me.

"They often shoot Pinoys like that," he said. "Without provocation. Sometimes when they have been drinking and they want
to have fun, they come to our district and kick or beat the first
Filipino they meet."

"Why don't you complain?" I asked.

"*Complain?*" he said. "Are you kidding? Why, when we complain it always turns out that *we* attacked them! And they become more vicious, I am telling you! That is why once in a
while a Pinoy shoots a detective. You will see it one of these
days."

"If they beat me I will kill them," I said.

The Filipino looked at me and walked away. As the crowd
was beginning to disperse, I saw the familiar head of my brother
Macario. He was entering the poolroom with a friend. I rushed
to him and touched his hand. He could not believe that I was
in America.

"Why didn't you write that you were coming?" he asked.

"I did not know I was coming, brother," I said. "Besides, I

did not know your address. I knew that I would not stop traveling until I found you. You have grown older."

"I guess I have, all right," he said. Then suddenly he became
quiet, as though he were remembering something. He looked
at me and said, "Let's go to my hotel."

I noticed that he did not speak English the way he used to
speak it in the Philippines. He spoke more rapidly now. As I
walked beside him, I felt that he was afraid I would discover
some horror that was crushing his life. He was undecided what
to do when we reached Broadway Street, and stopped several
times in deep thought. He had changed in many ways. He
seemed in constant agitation, and he smoked one cigarette after
another. His agitation became more frightening each minute.

"Why was the Filipino shot?" I asked, pretending not to notice
his mental anguish.

"Someday you will understand, Carlos," he said.

Carlos! He had changed my name, too! Everything was changing. Why? And why all this secrecy about the death of one
Filipino? Were the American people conspiring against us? I
looked at my brother sidelong but said nothing. Suddenly I felt
hungry and lonely and tired.

We turned to the north and came to a hotel near the Hall of
Justice building. We took the slow elevator to the fifth floor.
My brother knocked on a door and looked at me. There was
a hunted look in his face. I heard many voices inside. A patter of
feet, then the door opened. The strong smell of whisky brought
tears to my eyes. It was so strong it almost choked me. I knew
at once that there was a party. I saw three American girls in
evening gowns and ten Filipinos. I was amazed at their immaculate suits and shoes.

"Friends," my brother announced, "this is my kid brother—
Carlos! He has just arrived from the Philippines."

"More than six months ago," I corrected him. "I went to
Alaska first, then came down to Los Angeles. I think I like it
here. I will buy a house here someday."

"Buy a house?" a man near me said, his face breaking into a
smile. But when he noticed that my brother was looking hard

at him, he suddenly changed his tone and offered me a glass. "Good, good!" he said. "Buy all the houses you want. And if you need a janitor—" He turned around to hide the cynical twist of his mouth.

Then they rushed to me. All at once several cocktail glasses were offered to me. The girls pulled me to the table, tilting a glass in my mouth. The Filipinos shouted to me to drink.

I looked at my brother, ashamed. "I don't drink," I said.

"Go on—drink!" a curly-haired boy prodded me. "Drink like hell. This is America. We all drink like hell. Go on, boy!"

He was only a boy, but he drank like a man. I watched him empty three glasses, one after the other. My brother came to me.

"This is a wedding party," he whispered.

"Who got married?" I asked, looking around.

"I think that one," he said, pointing to a woman. "That is the man. I think he is twenty years old."

"She is old enough to be his mother," I said.

"What is the difference?" the curly-haired boy said to me. "They know what they want, don't they?" He winked at me foolishly and emptied another glass.

I gripped the glass in my hand so hard that it nearly broke.

It was past midnight when the party was over. I thought some of the men would go home, but it was only Leon who announced that he was leaving. The bridal couple started undressing in the other room, and the other men came to the outer room with the two girls. The curly-haired boy switched off the lights and the men started grabbing the girls.

I could see the red glow of their cigarettes moving in the dark. The girls would protest for a while, cursing the men. Then they would quiet down and go to bed, laughing yolkily when they threw their gowns on the floor. My brother took my arm and told me to follow him. We walked silently through the hall and down the stairs. I heard the married woman squealing and laughing, and I was bewildered and afraid. I wanted my brother to explain everything to me.

The sky was overcast and the lights in the streets were out.

Newsboys were shouting the morning papers. We walked for hours because it was hard to talk. We had not seen each other for years, and it was difficult to begin. We could only pick up fragments of our lives and handle them fearfully, as though the years had made us afraid to know ourselves. I was suddenly ashamed that I could not express the gentle feeling I had for my brother. Was this brutality changing me, too?

At dawn we walked back to the hotel. What I saw in the room would come back to me again and again. One of the girls was in the bed with two men. The other girl was on the couch with two other men. They were all nude. Six men were sleeping on the floor and three others were sprawled under the bed.

My brother motioned to me to undress, switching off the lights. I found a space near the closet, and I lay down hoping to sleep. My heart was pounding very fast. Leon came into the room with another girl. He cursed the sleeping forms and took the girl to the other room. They went to bed with the married couple.

I wanted to talk to my brother in the dark. But when I put my ear close to his mouth, I knew that he was already asleep. I could not sleep any more; my mind was wandering. I rolled over on my other side and tried to remember a prayer I used to recite when I was a little boy in Mangusmana.

A man named Nick was the first to wake up. He was making coffee in a big pot when I went to the kitchen. The girls were still in bed. My brother woke up suddenly and went to the bathroom. He was fully dressed when he came out.

"I'll look for a job today," he said.

"There is no use," Nick said. "I have been looking for a job for three months."

"I'll try, anyway," said my brother.

"Well, I hope some worker dies today," Nick said.

My brother looked at me. The girls woke up. They walked unashamedly in the room. The other men came to the kitchen and began drinking whisky again.

It was then that I learned their names. José, the curly-haired boy, was Nick's brother. They had both been going to college some months before, but the depression had deprived them of their jobs. Mariano, with the well-trimmed mustache, had been an agent for a clothing company that had failed. Victor and Manuel had worked in an apartment house in Hollywood. Luz, long out of a job, had come from the farm to live in the city. Gazamen was the life of the party: he was always singing and playing his portable phonograph. Leon was selling tickets in a dance hall: he was the only one who had a job. Alonzo was a college student, and had never worked as far as the other men knew. Ben was doing house work in Beverly Hills, but he seldom came home with money.

I found my brother Macario in a strange world. I could stand the poverty and hunger, but this desperate cynicism disturbed me. Were these Filipinos revolting against American society in this debased form? Was there no hope for them?

One night Leon, who was the sole mainstay of our company, came home with a bottle of bootleg whisky. He brought a girl with him. She was small and dark. Suddenly, in the middle of the night, the girl started screaming. We rushed to the other room, but it was too late. Leon was dead and cold. The girl cried loudly and hysterically. Mariano struck her with his fist, felling her. The blow was so hard it stunned her. It was not that he hated her; it was that this was the sad end of a little world that had revolved around a man who sold tickets in a dance hall.

CHAPTER XVIII

WHEN Leon died the proprietor gave us notice. Mariano's girl went away with him to Santa Barbara where, for reasons I did not know at the time, they were driven out by the police. They went to Lompoc, and Mariano, hoping to make a fresh start, started working in the pea fields. The girl stayed in the house where several other Filipino farmhands were living; then she ran away with one of them to Delano, where she became a professional prostitute. Mariano, disgusted and bitter, left the farm and went to town, entering a career of crime that drove him to the very edge of insanity.

Nick's girl, Rolla, graduated from college and took up teaching, and after a while she refused to see him. Nick moved with my brother Macario and me to Hope Street, in the red light district, where pimps and prostitutes were as numerous as the stars in the sky. It was a noisy and tragic street, where suicides and murders were a daily occurrence, but it was the only place in the city where we could find a room. There was no other district where we were allowed to reside, and even when we tried to escape from it, we were always driven back to this narrow island of despair. I often wondered if I would be able to survive it, if I would be able to escape from it unscathed, and if the horrors in it would not shadow my whole life.

Manuel married a white girl from Oklahoma, who had been married at twelve and had had two children. Her mother, two older sisters, and a brother came to live with them. Manuel was a janitor in a big apartment house in Hollywood, but his sixty dollars a month was not enough to support a large family. He was doing the work of two men and slowly his health gave way and he went to a hospital with tuberculosis. His wife gave birth to a baby girl and lived with Victor, running away from him in Salinas to live with a farm-labor contractor. Afterward she was stabbed to death by a Filipino gambler, and her children, fatherless and without support, were put in a state orphanage.

Luz found a Mexican woman in the street one cold night and took her to our room. José and my brother Macario were sleeping in a small bed, but Nick and I were together on a couch near the door. When Luz and his woman came into the room, Nick spread a blanket on the floor and told me to sleep with him. I cursed the cold night and the hard floor.

Luz and his woman made love all night. The woman was very drunk, and she screamed and laughed alternately, depending on what they were doing. Now and then José, who was constantly cursing, threw something at them. Once Luz went to the bathroom in the hall, leaving the door open. José, seizing his opportunity, jumped into the couch where Luz's woman was waiting. I got up hurriedly and bolted the door, hoping to avoid a scene. Luz started pounding on the door, shouting threats to the woman. The tenants came out into the hall and shouted to him to stop. Nick jumped to his feet and opened the door. But José was already back in his bed, feigning innocence when Luz switched on the lights to see which one among us had gone to his woman.

I almost died within myself. I died many deaths in these surroundings, where man was indistinguishable from beast. It was only when I had died a hundred times that I acquired a certain degree of immunity to sickening scenes such as took place this night, that I began to look at our life with Nick's cold cynicism. Yet I knew that our decadence was imposed by a society alien to our character and inclination, alien to our heritage and history. It took me a long time, then, to erase the outward scars of these years, but the deep, invisible scars inside me are not wholly healed and forgotten. They jarred my equilibrium now and then, and always, when I came face to face with brutality, I was afraid of what I would do to myself and to others. I was terribly afraid of myself, for it was the beast, the monster, the murderer of love and kindness that would raise its dark head to defy all that was good and beautiful in life. It was then that I would cry out for the resurrection of my childhood.

Not long afterward Luz died in a gambling house. He was playing at a card table when suddenly he collapsed, clutching desperately at the man near him. Then he tore at his tongue and died. His woman, the Mexican, went into prostitution on Central Avenue, in the Negro district, and died of syphilis. Luz's death was one of the many tragedies that hardened me, and drove me into a world of corruption that almost wrecked my whole life.

Alonzo, the student, met a divorcée who sent him to college. But one night, when they were living together (they could not marry in the state), detectives broke into their apartment and took Alonzo to jail.

"You can't do this to me," he kept saying. "I know my rights. I haven't committed any crime."

"Listen to the brown monkey talk," said one of the detectives, slapping Alonzo in the face. "He thinks he has the right to be educated. Listen to the bastard talk English. He thinks he is a *white* man. How do you make this white woman stick with you, googoo?" Another sharp slap across the face, and Alonzo, staggering from the blow, fell on the floor. Blood came out of his mouth, dripping on the threadbare carpet. He rolled away from the detective when he saw that a kick was coming, jumped to his feet and ran outside where two others felled him with blackjacks. He was carried downstairs to a car that took him to jail.

It was the turning point of Alonzo's life. The divorcée was driven out of town, warned never to see Filipinos again. And Alonzo, when he came out, went back to college with a great determination, majoring in languages and international law. Years afterward, in the Philippines, he became a bitter exponent of an anti-American campaign, fighting his crusade through the nation's press. He was another who conditioned my thinking, who affected my social attitudes. I thought there was no hope for Filipino unity in the United States, so I fought the way Alonzo fought against injustice and intolerance.

But our lease on the small room on Hope Street was about to

expire. My brother Macario had pawned his only suit, so that he walked in the streets in a torn jacket. Nick sold all his books and an overcoat. But José still had his suitcase and a typewriter. When we had sold everything and were still unemployed, I knew that we would soon separate. I knew that I must again hurl myself against a wall of destruction.

One day my brother and I walked to a splendid street near Wilshire Boulevard, asking the apartment managers for work for us to do. My brother walked on one side of the street, while I walked on the other. But it was futile, and we were tired from walking so long. We jumped into a waiting bus, and two Negro laborers followed us. We did not drop any money in the slot; the Negroes took the blame. I felt ashamed. But it was another lesson: the persecuted were always the first victims of misunderstanding.

We got off on a street of many new houses. My brother walked on one side of the street again, and I walked on the other. I asked the people in the beautiful houses if they had rugs to be cleaned. I was about to give up when my brother came running out of an alley and told me that he found something for us to do.

We walked into the backyard of a large house and a servant told us to pick up all the rugs. My brother took off his jacket and rolled up his trousers, beating the rugs vigorously with a broom. When we had beaten the rugs and had put them in their proper places, the woman of the house came down and gave us fifty cents each.

"Fifty cents for eight hours' work?" Macario said.

"What more do you want?" said the lady, slamming the door.

The days of hunger and loneliness came. Aching hunger and stifling loneliness. Every dawn was the opening of a cavern of starvation and exile: from the touch of friendly hands, of friendly voices. And every hour was a blow against the senses, dulling all impulses toward decency.

"You must be strong in America," said my brother to me one day. He was frying chopped oxtails he had bought at the Central

Market for ten cents. "I'll get a job and go back to school. In two years I'll be able to return to the Philippines. Wait and see!"

I did not understand him, but I knew that I could not wait for those two years to pass. I was afraid to wait for another day. I wanted to be strong because he was my brother, but it was like our life in Binalonan again. I went to the employment agencies, but every job in the list was taken. The agencies sold jobs to the highest bidder. I did not have the money to compete with them.

Then the manager of the hotel closed our room, locking our few remaining belongings inside. Macario and I slept in the five-cent theaters on Main Street, where the jobless and other denizens of the city slept. I could hardly stand the stifling filth of the men and the monstrous rats that ran over our feet when the lights went out. But it was cold outside and there was no place to go, and no food to appease the hunger that was gnawing at my vitals as viciously as the rats in the theater.

One day Nick found some money in the street. He happened to be following a woman when he saw her purse fall. He ran for it and grabbed the money. When the woman claimed that it was her money, Nick argued that he had found it and ran off defiantly. It was a beastly struggle for existence in a cold city.

Gazamen, who had come back from his "foxhole," found a cheap rooming house on Wall Street, in the Mexican district. He was always disappearing and when he appeared again we had music. He was our song of praise. It was only when melancholia attacked him that he went away, leaving us to wonder what would happen to him.

The room was small: no bathroom, no closet, no window. The washroom was outside in the hall, where the other tenants hung their washing. One tenant, an old man, had a small icebox in his room. José climbed through the window and pried open the icebox, which was padlocked on both doors. He found only a rotten piece of barracuda, but the old man raved as if he had lost a thousand dollars. José ate the fish but he could not sleep for the pain in his stomach.

One evening my brother came to our room with a sickly

Filipino, who looked as though he had not eaten for weeks. His name was Estevan, and when he saw the food on the table, he fell upon it like a dog. It was only when he had emptied all the plates that he began to talk, banging on the table with his fist when he wished to emphasize a point.

"I haven't become a writer in America in vain," he shouted. "Someday, my friends, I will write a great book about the Ilocano peasants in northern Luzon."

"When are you going to write it?" José interrupted him.

Estevan looked at José silently; then ignoring him, he continued: "The man of our generation, the person who shall direct the course of our history for the next fifty years, will come from the peasantry. And this I know—" he looked defiantly at José— "will be the turning point of my life. I will be the greatest writer of my time!"

"Has he written anything?" I asked my brother.

"He has written stories and essays, but has not published anything," said Macario. "The poor fellow. He is starving."

Poor Estevan! He was the first writer I knew. But the fire was dying in him, eating away at his vitals. Two days afterward he jumped out of the window of his room. I rushed to the hotel with my brother and found stacks of unpublished manuscripts in an old suitcase. I took one story which was titled "Morning in Narvacan," a poetic recitation describing a peasant town in northern Luzon. I carried it with me for years, reading it again a decade after, when I was intellectually equipped to understand the significance of Estevan's tragic death and the merit of the story. Thus it was that I began to rediscover my native land, and the cultural roots there that had nourished me, and I felt a great urge to identify myself with the social awakening of my people.

Nick paid our whole month's rent, which was ten dollars for the five of us in the small room. But one night José came to our room with a Mexican girl and asked for the rest of Nick's money.

"I would like to have twenty-five dollars," José said to his brother, looking at the girl morosely.

"What for?" Nick asked.

"Lupe wants an abortion," José said.

"Why don't you be careful?" Nick shouted. But he knew that it was useless, that he would give the money. He handed it to José and looked down when the girl took it.

That was the end of our money. But José was saved from marrying a girl he did not love. We were thrown into the streets again. Days of hunger and pain followed. And loneliness that clouded the mind, plunged the consciousness into an impenetrable darkness. And the nameless urge to seize something warm and tangible, to clutch it to me that this void inside of me might be filled.

My brother and I were sitting in a barber shop when a friend told us about a job. Macario borrowed twenty cents from the barber and rushed to the place. Then he came back to tell me that he had been hired.

Every Saturday night he came to town with two dollars for me. He was working at the house of a movie director who paid him twenty-five dollars a month for cooking and doing the general housework. The place was large and magnificent, and I asked myself why my brother was paid only that much for doing all the work in that great household.

When I saw the lady of the house with her jewelry and perfume, sitting in the house all day drinking expensive liquors, and her fat husband smoking fifty-cent cigars, I hated myself for accepting a part of my brother's hard-earned money. On the first night that I went with him to try to help him, he cooked something special and told me to wait on the table. He instructed me carefully. He was very patient. When the dinner was over the guests went to the library. My brother came out of the kitchen and started serving their drinks.

"Boy," said one of the men to my brother, "I enjoyed the dinner."

"Thank you, sir," Macario said, smiled, bowed, and withdrew into the kitchen.

"He is an educated servant," said the lady of the house. "He was a schoolteacher in the Philippines. And he went to college here."

"You can hire these natives for almost nothing," said her husband. "They are only too glad to work for white folks."

"You said it," one of the men said. "But I would rather have niggers and Chinamen. *They* don't have a college education, but they know their places."

"And I won't have a Filipino in my house, when my daughter is around," said one of the women.

"Is it true that they are sex-crazy?" the man next to her asked. "I understand that they go crazy when they see a white woman."

"Same as the niggers," said the man who did not like Filipino servants. "Same as the Chinamen, with their opium."

"They are all sex-starved," said the man of the house with finality.

"What is this country coming to?" one of the women said.

I withdrew into the kitchen, where I found my brother silently cleaning glasses. I walked outdoors to the end of the road, returned to the house, and helped him put the house in order. It was past midnight when we finished the work. It seemed I had hardly slept two hours when the bell rang for breakfast.

Macario rubbed his eyes sleepily and looked at the clock. Then he rushed to the kitchen and started preparing coffee and toast. He came back to the room and told me to carry the tray upstairs.

The lady of the house was still in bed. She got up and went to the bathroom when she heard me knock on the door. She came back to the room without clothes, the red hair on her body gleaming with tiny drops of water. It was the first time I had seen the onionlike whiteness of a white woman's body. I stared at her, naturally, but looked away as fast as I could when she turned in my direction. She had caught a glimpse of my ecstasy in the tall mirror, where she was nakedly admiring herself.

"What are you staring at?" she said.

"Your body, madam," I said, and immediately regretted it.

"Get out!" She pushed me into the hall and slammed the door.

I did not forget her for a long time.

Macario came to town the following week end and tried to give me another two dollars, my weekly allowance for room rent, food, and other necessities. I refused. I knew that I had to go away. I was angered at Marcario's subservience to these people. What had happened to him? What happened to the young man who had opened such a treasure house of knowledge for me?

José came to my room and confided to me that he had to run away. It was another girl. My opportunity to escape the city presented itself.

"I am going to Imperial Valley where there is plenty of farm work," I said to my brother on the phone. "I will see you again when the season is over."

"Be strong, Carlos," he said.

I wanted to cry out to him. I could not tell him why I was running away. Not now. I could not bear to see him working for people who were less human and decent than he, and who believed, because they were in the position to command, that they could treat him as though he were a domestic animal. . . .

José and I went to the freight yards. I heard something shouting at the edge of my mind:

"I will never let them touch me with their filthy hands! I will never let them make a domestic animal out of me!"

"What are you crying about?" José asked me, the cold wind lashing his words away.

CHAPTER XIX

I T WAS now the year of the great hatred: the lives of Filipinos were cheaper than those of dogs. They were forcibly shoved off the streets when they showed resistance. The sentiment against them was accelerated by the marriage of a Filipino and a girl of the Caucasian race in Pasadena. The case was tried in court and many technicalities were brought in with it to degrade the lineage and character of the Filipino people.

Prior to the *Roldan vs. The United States* case, Filipinos were considered Mongolians. Since there is a law which forbids the marriage between members of the Mongolian and Caucasian races, those who hated Fipilinos wanted them to be included in this discriminatory legislation. Anthropologists and other experts maintained that the Filipinos are not Mongolians, but members of the Malayan race. It was then a simple thing for the state legislature to pass a law forbidding marriage between members of the Malayan and Caucasian races. This action was followed by neighboring states until, when the war with Japan broke out in 1941, New Mexico was the nearest place to the Pacific Coast where Filipino soldiers could marry Caucasian women.

This was the condition in California when José and I arrived in San Diego. I was still unaware of the vast social implications of the discrimination against Filipinos, and my ignorance had innocently brought me to the attention of white Americans. In San Diego, where I tried to get a job, I was beaten upon several occasions by restaurant and hotel proprietors. I put the blame on certain Filipinos who had behaved badly in America, who had instigated hate and discontent among their friends and followers. This misconception was generated by a confused personal re-action to dynamic social forces, but my hunger for the truth had inevitably led me to take an historical attitude. I was to understand and interpret this chaos from a collective point of view, because it was pervasive and universal.

From San Diego, José and I traveled by freight train to the south. We were told, when we reached the little desert town of Calipatria, that local whites were hunting Filipinos at night with shotguns. A countryman offered to take us in his loading truck to Brawley, but we decided it was too dangerous. We walked to Holtville where we found a Japanese farmer who hired us to pick winter peas.

It was cold at night and when morning came the fog was so thick it was tangible. But it was a safe place and it was far from the surveillance of vigilantes. Then from nearby El Centro, the center of Filipino population in the Imperial Valley, news came that a Filipino labor organizer had been found dead in a ditch.

I wanted to leave Holtville, but José insisted that we work through the season. I worked but made myself inconspicuous. At night I slept with a long knife under my pillow. My ears became sensitive to sounds and even my sense of smell was sharpened. I knew when rabbits were mating between the rows of peas. I knew when night birds were feasting in the melon patches.

One day a Filipino came to Holtville with his American wife and their child. It was blazing noon and the child was hungry. The strangers went to a little restaurant and sat down at a table. When they were refused service, they stayed on, hoping for some consideration. But it was no use. Bewildered, they walked outside; suddenly the child began to cry with hunger. The Filipino went back to the restaurant and asked if he could buy a bottle of milk for his child.

"It is only for my baby," he said humbly.

The proprietor came out from behind the counter. "For *your* baby?" he shouted.

"Yes, sir," said the Filipino.

The proprietor pushed him violently outside. "If you say *that* again in my place, I'll bash in your head!" he shouted aloud so that he would attract attention. "You goddamn brown monkeys have your nerve, marrying our women. Now get out of this town!"

"I love my wife and my child," said the Filipino desperately.

"*Goddamn* you!" The white man struck the Filipino viciously between the eyes with his fist.

Years of degradation came into the Filipino's face. All the fears of his life were here—in the white hand against his face. Was there no place where he could escape? Crouching like a leopard, he hurled his whole weight upon the white man, knocking him down instantly. He seized a stone the size of his fist and began smashing it into the man's face. Then the white men in the restaurant seized the small Filipino, beating him unconscious with pieces of wood and with their fists.

He lay inert on the road. When two deputy sheriffs came to take him away, he looked tearfully back at his wife and child.

I was about to go to bed when I heard unfamiliar noises outside. Quickly I reached for José's hand and whispered to him to dress. José followed me through the back door and down a narrow irrigation ditch. We crept on our bellies until we reached a wide field of tall peas, then we began running away from the town. We had not gone far when we saw our bunkhouse burning.

We walked all the cold, dark night toward Calexico. The next morning we met a Filipino driving a jalopy.

"Hop in, Pinoys!" he said. "I'm going to Bakersfield. I'm on my way to the vineyards."

I ran for the car, my heart singing with relief. In the car, José went to sleep at once.

"My name is Frank," said the driver. "It is getting hot in Imperial Valley, so I'm running away. I hope to find work in the grape fields."

It was the end of spring. Soon the grapevines would be loaded with fruit. The jalopy squeaked and groaned, and once when we were entering Los Angeles, it stalled for hours. Frank tinkered and cooed over it, as though the machine were a baby.

I wanted to find my brother Macario, but my companions

were in a hurry. In Riverside the jalopy stalled again. José ran to the nearest orange grove. In San Bernardino, where we had stopped to eat pears, José took the wheel and drove all through the night to Bakersfield.

We found a place on a large farm owned by a man named Arakelian. Hundreds of Filipinos were arriving from Salinas and Santa Maria, so we improvised makeshift beds under the trees. Japanese workers were also arriving from San Francisco, but they were housed in another section of the farm. I did not discover until some years afterward that this tactic was the only way in which the farmers could forestall any possible alliance between the Filipinos and the Japanese.

Some weeks after our work had begun rumors of trouble reached our camp. Then, on the other side of town, a Filipino labor camp was burned. My fellow workers could not explain it to me. I understood it to be a racial issue, because everywhere I went I saw white men attacking Filipinos. It was but natural for me to hate and fear the white man.

I was nailing some boards on a broken crate when Frank came running into the vineyard.

"Our camp is attacked by white men!" he said. "Let's run for our lives!"

"I'm going back to Los Angeles," José said.

"Let's go to Fresno," I insisted.

We jumped into Frank's jalopy and started down the dirt road toward the highway. In Fresno the old car skidded into a ditch, and when we had lifted it back to the highway, it would not run any more. Frank went to a garage and sold it. I told my companions that we could take the freight train to Stockton. I knew that the figs were about ready to be picked in Lodi.

We ran to the freight yards, only to discover that all the boxcars were loaded. I climbed to the top of a car that was full of crates and my companions followed me. The train was already moving when I saw four detectives with blackjacks climbing up the cars. I shouted to my companions to hide. I ran to the trap door of an icebox, watching where the detectives were going.

José was running when they spotted him. He jumped to the other car and hid behind a trap door, but two more detectives came from the other end and grabbed him. José struggled violently and freed himself, rolling on his stomach away from his captors. On his feet again, he tried to jump to the car ahead, but his feet slipped and he fell, shouting to us for help. I saw his hands clawing frantically in the air before he disappeared.

I jumped out first. Frank followed me, falling upon the cinders almost simultaneously. Then we were running to José. I thought at first he was dead. One foot was cut off cleanly, but half of the other was still hanging. Frank lifted José and told him to tie my handkerchief around his foot. We carried him to the ditch.

"Hold his leg," Frank said, opening a knife.

"Right." I gripped the bleeding leg with all my might, but when Frank put the sharp blade on it, I turned my face away.

José jerked and moaned, then passed out. Frank chewed some tobacco and spread it on the stump to keep the blood from flowing. Then we ran to the highway and tried to hail a car, but the motorists looked at us with scorn and spat into the wind. Then an old man came along in a Ford truck and drove us to the county hospital, where a kind doctor and two nurses assured us that they would do their best for him.

Walking down the marble stairway of the hospital, I began to wonder at the paradox of America. José's tragedy was brought about by railroad detectives, yet he had done no harm of any consequence to the company. On the highway, again, motorists had refused to take a dying man. And yet in this hospital, among white people—Americans like those who had denied us— we had found refuge and tolerance. Why was America so kind and yet so cruel? Was there no way to simplifying things in this continent so that suffering would be minimized? Was there no common denominator on which we could all meet? I was angry and confused, and wondered if I would ever understand this paradox.

We went to the hospital the following morning. José was pale but gay.

"I guess this is the end of my journey with you fellows," he said.

"For a while," Frank said. "You will be well again. We will meet you again somewhere. You will see!"

"I sent a telegram to your brother," I said. "He will be here tomorrow."

"We've got to go now," Frank said.

"We have a long way to go," I said.

"You are right," José said.

"Good-bye till we meet again," Frank said, taking José's hand affectionately.

I looked back sadly. It was another farewell. How many others had I met in my journey? Where were they now? It was like going to war with other soldiers; some survived death but could not survive life. Could I forget all the horror and pain? Could I survive life?

I walked silently beside Frank to the highway. I was tired and exhausted and hungry. Frank and I had given all our money to José. We walked several miles out of town and took the first freight train going north. I did not care where we were going so long as it was away from Bakersfield. I shrank from tragedy, and I was afraid of death. My fear of death made me love life dearly.

We jumped off in Fresno where Filipinos told us that trouble was brewing. Frank wanted to proceed to Alaska for the fishing season, but I told him that conditions there were intolerable. The east was still an unexplored world, so we agreed to take a freight train to Chicago.

When we arrived in Idaho, I changed my plans. The pea fields decided me. Why go to an unknown city where there was no work? Here in this little town of Moscow were peas waiting and ready to be picked. So Frank and I worked for three weeks picking peas. But his heart was already in Chicago. He could not work any more.

I took him to the bus station and gave him a little of my

money. I hate slow partings. I patted him on the back and left. I met some Mexican families on their way to the beet fields in Wyoming. I rode on a truck with them as far as Cheyenne, where they stopped off to work for a month.

I went to town and walked around the premises of the Plains Hotel, hoping to see some workers there who might have come from Binalonan. I tried to locate them by peering through the windows, but gave up when some women looked at me suspiciously. I was too dirty to go inside. And I was afraid. My fear was the product of my early poverty, but it was also the nebulous force that drove me fanatically toward my goal.

I caught a freight train that landed me in Billings, Montana. The beet season was in full swing. Mexicans from Texas and New Mexico were everywhere; their jalopies and makeshift tents dotted the highways. There were also Filipinos from California and Washington. Some of them had just come back from the fish canneries in Alaska.

I went to Helena and found a camp of Filipino migratory workers. I decided to live and work with them, hoping to put my life in order. I had been fleeing from state to state, but now I hoped to gather the threads of my life together. Was there no end to this flight? I sharpened my cutting knife and joined my crew. I did not know that I was becoming a part of another tragedy.

The leader of our crew was a small Filipino called Pete. He walked lightly like a ball. When he was thinking, which he seldom did, he moved his head from side to side like a cat. He had a common-law wife, a young Mexican girl who was always flirting with the other men. I do not know what tribe he came from in the Philippines because he spoke several dialects fluently.

Every Saturday night the men rushed to town and came home at dawn, filling the house with the smell of whisky and strong soap. Once I went with them and found out that they played pool in a Mexican place and bought cheap whisky in a whorehouse where they went when the poolroom closed at midnight.

I was distracted by Myra, Pete's wife. She was careless with herself, in a house where she was the only girl. I noticed that she was always going to town with Poco, a tubercular Filipino who loved nice clothes and dancing. One afternoon when it was my turn to cook, I saw Myra come to the kitchen with her suitcase.

"I'm going now," she said to Pete, looking at the other men who were eating at the table.

Pete was at the far end of the table, his bare feet curling around the legs of the chair. He stopped the hand with the ball of rice in mid-air and leaped to the floor. Then he placed the rice carefully on the edge of his plate.

"Are you going with Poco?" Pete asked.

"Yes," Myra said.

"You can't go with him," he said.

"You are not married to me," she said, picking up her suitcase.

Pete grabbed her with one hand and struck her with the other. Then he dragged her to the parlor like a sack of beets, beating her with his fists when she screamed for Poco. Myra's lover was waiting in a car in the yard. Pete pulled off Myra's shoes and started beating the soles of her feet with a baseball bat, shouting curses at her and calling her obscene names.

I could not stand it any longer. I stopped washing the dishes, grabbed a butcher knife and ran into the parlor where they were. But Alfred, Poco's cousin, leaped from the table and grabbed me. I struggled violently with him, but he was much stronger than I. He struck me at the base of my skull and the knife went flying across the room. It struck a pot in the sink.

When I regained consciousness, I heard Myra moaning. Pete was still beating her.

"So you want to run away!" he kept saying. "I will show you who is going to run away!"

I got up on my knees and crawled to a bench. Pete threw Myra on the floor and went back to his plate. Alfred grabbed Pete's neck and hit him on the bridge of his nose with brass knuckles. Pete fell on the floor like a log and did not get up for minutes. When he regained consciousness, Alfred was sitting in the car with Poco. Pete resumed eating silently, but the blood kept coming out of his nose. He stopped eating and bathed his nose in the sink. Then he went to the parlor and began washing and bandaging Myra's feet.

I gathered the plates and continued washing. I heard Myra laughing and giggling softly. She was in bed with Pete.

"I won't do it again, honey," she kept saying.

"Will you be good now?" Pete asked her.

"I love you, darling," she said, laughing. "I love you! I love you!"

I cursed her under my breath. What kind of a girl was she? I cursed him, too. Pete bounced suddenly into the kitchen, rolling from side to side. I did not look at him. He was preparing something for Myra to eat. Then he carried the plates to her bed, walking lightly like a cat. I looked up from the sink. He was feeding her with a spoon, holding her head with one hand. Myra reached for Pete's neck and kissed him.

Suddenly Poco came into the house and started shooting at them. I ran out of the house terrified, shouting to Alfred. But he opened the door and told me to jump into the car. Poco showed his face at the door.

"Run away, Alfred!" he shouted to his cousin. "Run away and don't come back! I will kill them! Go now!"

Alfred hesitated for a moment; carefully he put the key in the lock and shifted the gear. Then we were driving furiously down the dirt road.

"The damn fool," Alfred wept. "That damn fool is going to be hanged—and all for a prostitute!"

I grabbed the front seat for fear I would fall out when we turned a corner. I could tell by the stars in the wheeling sky that we were driving west. I was going back to the beginning of my life in America. I was going back to start all over again.

CHAPTER XX

IT WAS not easy to understand why the Filipinos were brutal yet tender, nor was it easy to believe that they had been made this way by the reality of America. I still lacked the knowledge to synthesize the heart-breaking tragedies I had seen, and to project myself into their core so that I would be able to interpret them objectively. There were times when I found myself inextricably involved, not because I was drawn to this life by its swiftness and violence, but because I was a part and a product of the world in which it was born. I was swept by its tragic whirlpool, violently and inevitably; and it was only when I had become immune to violence and pain that I was able to project myself out of it. It was only then that I was able to integrate my experiences so that I could really find out what had happened to me in those tragic years.

While I was fleeing from the barbarity of the two Filipinos in Montana, I was also trying to escape from the barbarian that was myself. It took me a little lifetime to fight against the death of myself, to fight the slow decay that devoured me like a cancer.

I tried to get a freight train in Spokane for Seattle, but the railroad men drove me away. I took a bus and sat in the back seat, hiding myself from the white passengers. And once again, in the night, I saw Bremerton shining by the lake. When had it been that this bright city had softened the sadness in my heart? It seemed so long ago! A few more hours of slow driving, and I was at the station. I left the bus and walked around the block, watching for Oriental signs on the buildings and stores. I found the hotel where I had stayed when I had arrived in Seattle from the Philippines, but it was now under new management. I took a room for twenty-five cents and sneaked away with the sheets the next morning. I sold them in a Negro store down the block.

That was my first deliberately dishonest act. How did I feel? Did my conscience bother me? I was surprised to discover that I looked upon it merely as a part of my daily life. I did not feel guilty. I even thought of doing it again. With the money, I went to a Japanese restaurant where I ate broiled fish and fish-bone soup for ten cents. Then I walked lazily in the sun, standing on street corners for hours, waiting for nothing.

Not far from King Street laundry workers were on strike; there was a picket line around the building. I stood on the bridge watching them, then climbed down the embankment to a shack where a man was running a mimeograph machine. He stopped when he saw me; then seizing a placard from a table, he placed it in my hands and dropped twenty-five cents in my pocket. I could not understand it. I was being paid to walk around a building with a sign. I went again the following morning, but the strike was called off and the workers went back to their machines.

I mingled with the cannery workers who were still in Seattle. They gambled away their earnings in the Chinese gambling houses and stayed on in the city, waiting for the apple season in Yakima Valley. I was fortunate to find a man with a car. He took me as far as Portland, where he found a job washing dishes at the bus station. I walked idly about the business district, then to the residential section, finally along the river where I stopped, remembering the young American girl who had walked with me in the night, years before.

It was still summer. There was a freshness in the air, something new and vibrant. I walked under the trees for hours. Then I went to the bus station and slept on a bench, sitting up when a policeman came to drive me away. I was terrified of being sent to jail. Toward dawn a Filipino, who was a busboy at the station cafeteria, told me that I could go to a certain address for something to eat and a place to sleep.

"Is it free?" I asked.

"Yes," he said. "I hope there is still room for you. If not, there is always something to eat."

"I am hungry," I said. "I don't care about the room. I can walk in the streets. Food is what I need."

"Here is the address," he said, giving me a piece of paper.

I thanked him and left, my stomach aching for food. I found the place near Chinatown. I went up the stairs and gave the piece of paper to the man in the little office. He registered my name in a big ledger and gave me a ticket.

"Give this ticket to the night clerk and he will give you a place to sleep," he said kindly. "Now you can go to the café downstairs and show this ticket. You will get something to eat. You can get two meals a day with it."

"Thank you, sir," I said, going down the stairs in a hurry.

The place was full of unemployed men, standing by the wall and waiting their turn. The men at the tables and the counter were eating hungrily, wiping their mouths and beards with dirty handkerchiefs. I found a chair and sat down, forcing the scorched soup into my mouth. I wanted to eat it all, but my stomach roared. I put plenty of salt and pepper to kill the taste. It was another way of saving food that I had inherited from the peasants of Luzon who, because meat was almost impossible to preserve properly, spread strong vinegar and sprinkled salt over it.

I gave the ticket to the clerk when night came. He gave me a blanket and took me to a large hall where he chalked a space on the floor.

"This is your bed," he said.

"Yes, sir," I said, spreading the blanket on the floor. When he was gone, I saw my number on the wall.

I could not sleep because of the musty smell of my blanket and the stench of the unwashed bodies of the men. They snored noisily. I put my hands on my nose and mouth, turning over on my stomach. I was the first to awaken. I rolled up my blanket and gave my number to the clerk. He gave back my ticket and told me to eat in the café under the building. I went downstairs so that the daytime man could sleep in my place by the wall.

The men were not allowed to bring women, but they could easily sidetrack the old night clerk. The women sneaked into the building in men's clothes. They were not prostitutes, but homeless women on the road. Once, on my second night, a prostitute came into the hall with the other women and tried to solicit business, but she was brutally knocked down by a man and dragged into the washroom. I saw her again the next morning staggering like a drunken sailor on the sidewalk across from the building. I felt impelled to guide her through the busy city, for she reminded me of a woman I had once seen in Binalonan who had lost her mind.

I was terrified in this building of lost men. I tried to exclude myself from them, to shut myself off into a room of my own, away from their obscenities. But one daybreak, when I was suffering from stomach pains because of the food I had eaten that afternoon, I heard an old man creeping slowly toward me. I thought he was looking for his place on the floor, but when he reached me and started caressing my legs, I sprang to my feet and flung him away. I ran desperately in the dark, stumbling over the sleeping men, and down the stairway and into the street, where the sudden rush of fresh air brought tears to my eyes.

I went to the freight yards and waited for a train to California. I jumped into an empty boxcar and found there two Filipino cannery workers who had lost their money on the boat to Seattle. The train was slow, but the night was cool. The wind was soothing and the sky was clear. I was asleep when we passed through Eugene, but in my sleep I breathed the air freshened by its trees.

When I woke up my companions were gone. I crept to the door and opened it. I looked up and saw the sky burning with millions of stars. It was as bright as a clear summer day. The moon was large and brilliant, but its light was mild. I wanted to shout with joy, but could not open my mouth, so awestruck I was by the moonlight. I looked into the bright night sky. I looked without saying a word. I heard the metallic cry of the freight train, and I knew that heaven could not be far from the earth.

✦

I got off the train in Klamath Falls. I was eating in a small restaurant when two policemen entered and grabbed me. It was so sudden and so unexpected that the spoon in my hand went flying across the room. A million things rushed into my mind at once: Were Pete and Myra killed by Poco? Did Frank commit a crime somewhere and implicate me? Had my brother Amado robbed a bank? I did not know what to say. I obediently followed my captors to the jailhouse.

I was hiding two dollars in my shoes when one of the policemen came into the cell. I knew from experience that money was important and the men in my world hungered and died for it. I watched him stand boldly before me, his strong legs spread wide apart, his hands on his hips, showing the menacing gun.

"Where did you come from?" he asked.

I played dumb, pantomiming that I did not speak the language.

"Are you Filipino?" He was trying another angle.

"Yes."

Crack!

It was that quick and simple. His right fist landed on my jaw, felling me instantly. Seeing his shoes approaching, I quickly rolled over on my stomach and jumped to my feet; then retreating to a corner of the cell, I put up my hands to cover my face.

"You goddamn bastard!"

He hit me again.

I fell on the floor. I rolled over, face down, covering my head with my hands. He kicked me twice in rapid succession, rocking my body and plunging me into a dark ocean that drowned me in sleep. . . . Then from far away, I heard voices.

"Is the son-of-a-bitch dead?"

"I don't think so."

"Did you find any money on him?"

"Only two dollars in his shoes."

"We could have a round of bourbon on it."

"We might be able to bypass another brown monkey in town."

"Yeah!"

They left. I heard them laughing outside, their car gliding softly down the street. I opened my eyes. It was dark! It could not be night. It was only a moment ago that I had been eating in a restaurant, and it had been bright morning. Slowly rising to a sitting position, I raised my right hand to my forehead. I was aware of the acrid smell of blood, but could not feel anything. I looked at my hand. It was smashed! I rubbed my face with my left hand, feeling the lacerations where the man's fist had struck. I tore a piece off my shirt and wrapped my hand in it, blowing upon it to ease the pain.

The next morning the policemen dragged me from my cell. Their breaths were strong with whisky. I knew they were through with me. They told me to walk to the border of California, while they followed me in their car. When I stopped to remove the pebbles from my shoes, they drove the car a little faster so that the bumper kept hitting me. My feet were bleeding when I reached California soil.

They came out of the car. The policeman who had terrorized me the previous night struck me sharply across the face, laughing when he saw the blood coming out of my nose.

"That will teach you not to come to this town again," he shouted.

I fell on my knees. I heard them laughing. There was a sadistic note in their voices. Was it possible that these men enjoyed cruelty? The brutality in the gambling houses was over money; it was over women among Filipinos. But the brutality of these policemen—what was it?

I started walking across a wide forest land toward the coast highway, some two hundred miles away. It seemed an endless journey. After two days and three nights, I came to a railroad town and caught a freight train for San Francisco. I sat on top of an empty boxcar and watched the beautiful land passing by. I saw places where I thought I would someday like to build a home.

My hand was swollen when I arrived in San Francisco. The city was windswept at night, but in the daytime the sun was tropic hot. The streetcars were clanging everywhere and the people were walking up and down the streets. It was like Seattle

—the streets going upward and downward, the dark alleys curving suddenly to Chinatown, and the women coming into the light on their short, sturdy legs.

I took a freight train that carried me to Guadalupe, a small Oriental town off the coast highway. The streets were lined with gambling houses. It was Sunday and the Filipino farm workers were riotously spending their wages. I found an empty shack under the bridge that connected Guadalupe and Oceano's rich farm land. I nursed my wounds in this shack. At night I went to the gambling houses. I could not work yet. So I begged from the lucky gamblers. Then I met a man who claimed that he had come from Binalonan. His name was Cortez, and he had a crew of farm workers in Santa Maria. When I was well enough to work I joined his crew.

It was autumn, the season for planting cauliflower. I went to the field at six in the morning and worked until six in the afternoon. It was tiresome, back-breaking work. I followed a wagon that carried cauliflower seedlings. The driver stopped now and then to drop a handful of the seedlings between the long furrows. I picked up the seedlings with one hand and dug into the ground with the other; then, putting a seedling into the hole, I moved on and dug another hole. I could hardly move when six o'clock came. I climbed into the wagon that took me slowly to the town.

The bunkhouse was made of old pieces of wood, and was crowded with men. There was no sewage disposal. When I ate swarms of flies fought over my plate. My bed was a makeshift tent under a huge water tank, away from the bunkhouse. I slept on a dirty cot: the blanket was never washed. The dining room was a pigsty. The cook had a harelip and his eyes were always bloodshot and watery.

I became acquainted with Benigno, one of the men in the camp. He was big and husky, but a sinus infection in early life had ruined his voice. One Sunday night, when I was already asleep, he came to my tent and woke me up.

"There is fun going on in the bunkhouse," he said.

"I am tired," I said.

"Come on." He flung the blanket away from me and jerked me out of the cot. "Come on!"

I followed Benigno into the bunkhouse where thirty workers were quartered. Their cots were arranged in two rows, fifteen in each row, running from wall to wall. There was only a foot of free space between them. I noticed four men holding up some bedsheets around a cot. A fifth man was standing by, holding a basin of water. A hand came out of the sheets and took the basin. Benigno winked suggestively to me.

A young Filipino, half-dressed, came out of the sheets. Then an old man entered the wall of sheets, and the man who was holding the basin ran to the stove in the far end of the bunkhouse and poured warm water from a pot, then returned to the place where he was standing, waiting for the mysterious hand to reach for the basin. I looked around at the other men: they were sitting on their cots playing cards and musical instruments; writing letters; reading movie magazines. Others were smoking and staring into space; some were walking up and down, looking toward the wall of sheets when the basin of water disappeared. I knew at once that I had to run away. Was it possible that they were not horrified?

I was backing to the door when Benigno and two other men grabbed me. I struggled desperately. I knew what they would do to me. They carried me toward the wall of sheets, and the men who were holding them made way for me. I trembled violently, because what I saw was a naked Mexican woman waiting to receive me. The men pinned me down on the cot, face upward, while Benigno hurriedly fumbled for my belt. The woman bent over me, running her hands over my warming face. The men released me, withdrawing sheepishly from the wall of sheets. Then, as though from far away, I felt the tempestuous flow of blood in my veins.

It was like spring in an unknown land. There were roses everywhere, opening to a kind sun. I heard the sudden beating of waves upon rocks, the gentle fall of rain among palm leaves. Was this eternity? Was this the source of creation? Then I heard a thunderclap—and suddenly the sound and stench of

humanity permeated the air, crushing the dream. And I heard
the woman saying:

"There, now. It's all over."

I leaped to my feet, hiding myself from her.

"Did you like it?" she said.

I plunged through the wall of sheets and started running between the cots to the door. Benigno and the other men laughed,
shouting my name. I could still hear their voices when I entered
my tent, trembling with a nameless shame. . . .

CHAPTER XXI

WHEN the cauliflower season was over my crew moved to Nipomo to work in the lettuce fields. I went to Lompoc and found the town infested by small-time gangsters and penny racketeers. My brother Amado was still with Alfredo, but they had given up bootlegging. Now they were partners in gambling, cheating the Filipino farm workers of their hard-earned money. I could not live with them.

I found a crew of lettuce workers on J Street and joined them. It was cold in Lompoc, for the winter wind was beginning to invade the valley from Surf. The lettuce heads were heavy with frost. I worked with thick cotton gloves and a short knife. When the lettuce season was over the winter peas came next. I squatted between the long rows of peas and picked with both hands, putting the pods in a large petroleum can that I dragged with me. When the can was full I poured the pods into a sack, then returned to my place between the long rows of unpicked peas.

Then the pea season was over in Lompoc, although farther down the valley some farmers were in need of workers to pick Seattle peas. I went to town and found that Amado and Alfredo had given up their gambling establishment, a large green table at the back of a Mexican poolroom. Amado told me that he wanted to go into the restaurant business, so he borrowed my money to start it. But as soon as he had my money he entered a dice game and lost all of it in a few throws. I was not angry. I felt that it was my obligation to help him. I still believed in certain codes that I had brought with me from the Philippines.

I learned that the Filipino dishwasher in a local restaurant called the Opal Café had died of poisonous mushrooms which he had picked somewhere in the valley. I took his place. I knew that I must help my brother. The place was notorious for its

Saturday night crowd. Some two hundred school boys and girls came for refreshments and sandwiches after the dance at the public auditorium. Because they came only when the cook was gone, I did all the work in the kitchen. It was a job that took me seventeen hours to finish.

It was a new experience. When I was rushing the orders some of the boys brought their girls into the dark side of the kitchen and made love to them. I saw them and I was shocked by their wanton behavior. I cursed them under my breath, preparing their sandwiches and spitting on the bread when my understanding of their morality became confused, and a personal issue. They were always drunk, and careless with foul words, shoving a bottle of whisky into my mouth, and laughing when the choking tears came out of my eyes.

After work, at daybreak, I put slices of ham or chicken in a box and covered it with newspapers, as though it were garbage ready for the big can in the alley. While the manager was eating, I went to my room through the back door, picking up the box of sandwiches on my way. Up in the room, sitting morosely on my bed, was my brother, waiting for the food. He was going to pieces fast, because he had started drinking, too; and a chasm was opening between us, widening each time he committed a crime.

I was transferred to the bakery department of the Opal Café, at fourteen dollars a week, an increase of four dollars from my former salary. Men of influence came now and then to the back room where I was scrubbing pans, and cast malicious glances at me. Once a local businessman came into the back room with a bottle of whisky. He sarcastically said to me:

"Mr. Opal tells me that you are reading books. Is it true?"

"Yes, sir." But realizing that my tone had a challenging note in it, I said immediately: "Well, sir, there is nothing else to do after working hours. I hate to go to the Mexican quarters because, as you know, gambling and prostitution are going on there all the time. And I'm a little tired of the phonograph in my room, playing the same records over and over. I find escape in books, and also discovery of a world I had not known before. . . ."

I had not been looking at him, because my words came in a rush.

"Well, you bring it upon yourself," he said tonelessly. "I mean prostitution and gambling."

"I don't know what you really mean," I said. "But the gambling and the prostitution are operated by three of this town's most *respectable* citizens. As a matter of fact, I can tell you their names—"

"Watch your yellow tongue, googoo!" he shouted at me, hurling the half-filled bottle in his hands.

I ducked too late, and the bottle hit the back of my head. I fell on the floor on all fours. When I saw him rushing at me with an empty pan, I jumped to my feet and grabbed a butcher knife which was lying on a table and met him. Slowly he backed away, escaped through the door to the dining room, and came back with the manager.

"What is this?" Mr. Opal asked.

"This barbarian wants to murder me," the man said.

Something snapped inside of me, and my whole vision darkened. I lunged at the man with the knife in my hand, wanting to murder him. He ran behind Mr. Opal, shouting to the waitresses in the dining room to call for the police.

"You are fired!" he shouted, crossing his hands in front of his face, as though he could ward me off with them.

You are fired! How many times did I hear these words? Why did they pursue me down the years, across oceans and continents? A nameless anger filled me, and before I knew it I was screaming:

"I'll kill you, you white men!"

There was a crash, as though lightning had struck the building. Then silence. I looked up. I was hiding in the alley where I had hidden my box of sandwiches many times before. I groped my way in the dark, feeling the warm blood on my face.

I had struck at the white world, at last; and I felt free. Was my complete freedom to be fought for violently? Was murder necessary? And hate? God forbid! My distrust of white men grew, and drove me blindly into the midst of my own people; together we hid cynically behind our mounting fears, hating the broad white universe at our door. A movement of the hand, and it was there—yet it could not be touched, could not be attained ever. I tried to find a justification for my sudden rebellion—why it was so *sudden*, and black, and hateful. Was it possible that, coming to America with certain illusions of equality, I had slowly succumbed to the hypnotic effects of racial fear?

It was about this time that I received a letter from the Philippines, from my cousin Panfilo, telling me of my father's death. It seemed that he had gone back to Mangusmana to plant rice in a strip of land belonging to one of our relatives. He was better then—much better than when I saw him for the last time in San Manuel harvesting *mongo* with my mother and sisters. But he did not realize that he was sick, that he was dying. And he died a lonely death; he had been dead for five days when his neighbors found him. My cousin wrote that he must have been eating when he died because there was still rice in his mouth and untouched plates were scattered around him. He died alone in the place where he had been born.

My father's death was the turning point of my life. I had tried to keep my faith in America, but now I could no longer. It was broken, trampled upon, driving me out into the dark nights with a gun in my hand. In the senseless days, in the tragic hours, I held tightly to the gun and stared at the world, hating it with all my power. And hating made me lonely, lonely for love, love that could resuscitate beauty and goodness. For it was life I aspired for, a life of goodness and beauty.

But I found only violence and hate, living in a corrupt corner of America. I found it in a small Filipino who appeared in town from nowhere and, strangely enough, called himself Max Smith. Max pretended to be bold and fearless, but his bravado was only a shield to protect himself, to keep the secret of his cowardice.

"Have you a gun?" Max asked me one night.

"Yes," I said.

"Give it to me," he said.

"Go to hell!" I told him.

"Give it to me!" He was trembling, not with anger but excitement.

I gave him the gun.

"Follow me," Max said, ducking into an alley.

I followed him down the block. He stopped near a small truck and told me to hide behind a tree. A Japanese appeared in the alley, walking toward the truck as though he were dancing. He wobbled a little and his breath was heavy with liquor. Max leaped from the darkness and hit him on the head with the butt of the gun, felling him instantly. Waving the gun at me, Max began searching the victim's pockets. I jumped from behind the tree and bent over the Japanese, my legs shaking. Max jumped to his feet, motioned to me to follow him, and ran up the alley toward the town jail.

Robbery? It was something I had never done before—but it was a desperate year. Anything could happen, even in Lompoc. Max procured another gun somewhere, and I got back mine. I roamed the streets at night, following Max, banging at the doors of prostitutes when he wanted whisky. Then a tremendous idea came to my mind, driving me like a marijuana addict when it seized my imagination.

"What is it?" Max asked.

"The bank," I whispered. "Let's rob the bank."

He seized my hand, thought deeply for a moment. "It could be done!"

"Yes!" I said. "Now here is what we will do. Remember there is only one night watchman. We will stop him in the street and force him to go to the house of the president of the bank. Then we will take them to the bank and—presto!—the large safe where all the bills are kept." I stopped to catch my breath, so great was the idea, so breathtaking and courageous! "Then, Max, we will drive them to the mountain. We will tie them to the car, set fire to the car, and plunge it into the deep ravine below the highway. There will be no trace of them! And perhaps the fire will turn the mountain and this town into ashes! Let's do it tonight!"

Max held my hand tightly, looking from side to side. "We'll make it our last act in this damned town!"

It was settled. We would rob the bank and run away. I was standing in front of the Chinese gambling house when Max went inside and came out running, ducking into the dark alley with a bag of money. The excited proprietor came out with a gun, followed by other Chinese, chattering in singsong voices. I pointed in the other direction when they asked where Max went, cursing them in my dialect so that the Filipino gamblers would understand, and go away.

I knew where Max was hiding: the local jail. It was the safest place to hide because it was always empty, and the sheriff never bothered to investigate it. When the streets were clear, I went to the jailhouse. Max was waiting with my share of the loot.

"Let's go to San Luis Obispo and have fun," he said. "We will come back tomorrow for the bank. The grand finale!"

"Okay, Max," I said.

"Wait for me at the bus station," he said.

"Right." I went to the station and bought our tickets. Then Max came back with a bottle of whisky, his hand on the pocket where the gun was hidden. He jumped into the bus and took his seat beside me.

He began to get drunk. I watched him close his eyes and go sound asleep. I looked out the window. Night was gathering fast. The sky was dark and boundless.

In San Luis Obispo, walking in Chinatown, Max pointed to a house in a corner. "This is where my wife lives," he said.

"Your wife?" I did not know he was married.

"Yeah," he murmured. "The bitch!"

I walked silently. Then I *knew!* Max was trembling. He looked tranced, like a gamecock before it is thrown into the arena. He put his hand where the gun was hidden.

"Wait for me here," he said.

I saw him cross the street toward the house. In a little while he came running out, the gun still hot in his hand. I rushed to meet him.

"What happened?" I asked.

"I shot him!" he said. "I killed the white bastard who lives with my wife!" He shoved some money into my pockets. "Go away! Now!"

"How about you, Max?" I could not leave him alone.

He pointed the gun at me. "Go!" he screamed.

I leaped to my feet and ran down the street. I stopped at a corner and looked back. Max was crossing the street toward the house again. There was no time to lose. I ran to the bus station and bought a ticket for Los Angeles. I tried to reach my brother Macario by phone, but he was busy in the garden. He was still working in the big house in the hills above Hollywood.

I took a train to New Mexico. But the farther I went away, the more the thought of the crime possessed me.

CHAPTER XXII

THE PRIMITIVE beauty of Santa Fe reminded me of the calm and isolation of Baguio, the mountain city in Luzon where I had worked for Miss Mary Strandon. Morning was like a rose cupping its trembling dews, shattering and delicate, small but potent with miracles. But the nights were tranquil with millions of stars.

When I looked out the window of my room, I felt as though I were thrown back into a familiar scene of childhood. Far away, in the desert, I could see buzzards circling in the sky, waiting for the carcass of a dying coyote. And frightened little birds ran into the bushes to hide, and came out when the danger was over and the sky was clear again.

But I did not know what to do, away from my people. When I was alone, sitting in my room, I would think of going back to California, to the violent life I knew. Then I received a letter from my brother Amado, who was serving a jail sentence in Santa Barbara. It was my opportunity to run away from the solitude and loneliness that wrapped me and stifled my desire to live.

I took a bus to California. I stopped in Los Angeles for a lawyer. I was disappointed when I found that there were no Filipino lawyers. I called my brother Macario, but he informed me that Filipinos could not practice law in the state. I was angry and bewildered, but I left immediately for Santa Barbara.

I found an American lawyer who promised to reopen my brother's case, paid him two hundred fifty dollars, and looked for a job. The lawyer, of course, did his best, but Amado stayed in jail for six months. It seemed that he had been implicated in a robbery in Lompoc, but he swore he had had nothing to do with it.

I felt that I should stay near Amado. I found work at an ice plant, but it was too strenuous for me. I lifted a block of ice almost twice my weight into a wheelbarrow and pushed it to a truck outside the plant. My hands became brittle and dead with the cold. But I stayed on for five weeks. On week ends, when I visited my brother, I bought chop suey and Filipino dishes with the money I earned at the ice plant.

I still do not understand why I almost killed myself working for Amado when he had free board and room. In reality he was enjoying life, for outside where I was living there were cold and hunger. But perhaps it was because of my belief that it was dishonorable to be in jail. Amado might come out, but the stigma would cling to him and ruin his life. Yet, looking back now, I can see that his life was already ruined, and I know that all my efforts to rehabilitate him were futile.

Sometime afterward, when Amado came out of jail, I found work in a milk company. It was lighter work because the cans weighed only twenty-five pounds, and it was easy for me to carry them into the trucks. But it was night work, and it was cold when I started washing and filling the cans at one o'clock in the morning. When the truck drivers came at about four, I washed the floor and put the empty cans in order. I went to my room about seven, after I had cleaned the cans, when the drivers came back to take over the plant.

I thought I had lost interest in everything. But here I was again, working industriously as before, hoping to survive another winter. It was a planless life, hopeless, and without direction. I was merely living from day to day: *yesterday* seemed long ago and *tomorrow* was too far away. It was *today* that I lived for aimlessly, this hour—this moment. It gave me an acute sense of time that has remained with me.

When Amado came out of jail, I told him that he should go to work, and he did. He was an excellent cook: it was the only trade he learned in America. I noticed, some months afterward, that he was losing interest in his work. I gave him my money to start a business. He bought a restaurant down the block near where I was working and renovated it. I helped him when I was not working at the milk factory, and when he needed money for additional equipment, I gave it to him. I felt confident that he would succeed in this new life.

The restaurant prospered and Amado, exhilarated by his new prosperity, leased the building above the restaurant. It was an old, two-story building that belonged to an Italian woman. In a little while Amado's old friends, who had scattered when he was in jail, began coming to his place. They helped him in the kitchen and at the counter, but they also slept in the hotel. Slowly and gradually they came and soon the place was full of them, depriving the farm workers of hotel accommodations when they were in town.

But I was learning something vital from Amado. What mattered to him was the pleasure he had with his friends. There was something urgent in their friendship, probably a defense against their environment. They created a wall around themselves in their little world, and what they did behind it was theirs alone. Their secrecy bordered on insanity. It was something I did not want to be a part of, but was not strong enough to escape from.

Then Amado was forced to close the restaurant and to give up the hotel. The milk factory discharged me. It was a dark year. There were many unemployed men in the streets, ready to work for almost nothing. I gave up my room and went to the Mexican district. Amado went to Chinatown. One night, after several weeks of isolation, I went to a Chinese gambling house on Cañon Perdido Street. I was asking the gamblers about my brother when I saw Alfredo coming through the door with a wide smile.

"You look hungry, Carlos," he said.

"Yes, I am hungry," I said.

"Well, you won't be in a few minutes," he said, taking my arm. I followed him to a chop suey house across the street, where he ordered enough food to feed four hungry men. I ate silently, watching the widening grin in his face.

"Open your eyes, Carlos," he said, showing me the fat roll of bills in his hand. "This is a country of survival of the fittest.

Quit sleeping on top of pool tables. There is plenty of money around. Here. . . ."

I reached for the money in his hand. "Where did you get it?" I asked, not understanding what he was driving at. "You have enough to feed this town."

"Where did I get it?" He laughed. "I found a Mexican girl picking peas in Arroyo Grande. Then, my friend, I bought some nice clothes for her. When I was convinced that I *had* her, I borrowed a car and took her to the Pinoy camps in Santa Maria Valley. She was beautiful. The boys were crazy about her."

I wanted to stab him with the fork in my hand. But I was hungry and there was no place to stay. I was beginning to cough at night.

"I am sick, Alfredo," I said. "Please leave me alone. Now!"

"I'll be seeing you around," he said.

But I did not see him again. He disappeared with another girl and never came back. It was only some years afterward that I began to have some understanding of his life, but he had already been deported to the Philippines. He became a playboy among the rich women in Manila, a gambler among the politicians, and a gangster in the provinces.

When Alfredo disappeared from Santa Barbara, Amado became restless and unhappy. He left for Los Angeles where, he told me, he would look for a job. He found one in a downtown hotel, cooking for visiting businessmen and retired gamblers. Happy for the first time, he told me that he would save his money and start another business.

I stayed on in Santa Barbara, hoping the farmers in Goleta, a town ten miles to the north, would need hands for the carrot season. But there was no price and the farmers plowed their crops under. The gambling houses closed because most of the Filipinos were out of work, and the Chinese who operated them gambled among themselves.

Later I found work in Solvang, farther north, picking flowers and seeds for a big company that supplied these to the nation. But the pay was only ten cents an hour, and what I earned in a week's time was scarcely enough to pay for the gloves I used to keep my hands from the cold. I was enchanted by these flower fields and the kind, tall, blue-eyed Danish farmers in the valley, so that I felt like crying when I left for Buelton.

Here, in this highway town, I washed dishes in a large hotel where rich tourists stopped for a rest. I slept under the peach trees in the yard when my work was over. Once the proprietor, a Frenchman who spent more time drinking than attending to his business, sat beside me and began crying.

"It's the sound of home, boy," he sobbed. "I'm lonely for the sound of home."

"This is your home, sir," I said.

"No, my boy," he said. "Home is where my heart lives. Home is in the blue hills of Normandy."

"*This man*," I said to myself, "*who came to America as a young boy and made a fortune and married a beautiful white woman is lonely for the blue hills of his childhood*."

"Go home, my boy," he said. "Home to your islands before it's too late." Then he started talking rapidly in French, gesticulating and laughing. He jumped to his feet and began dancing what must have been a folk dance of the farmers in those blue hills in Normandy. There were tears of joy in his eyes. Then he stopped and went into the hotel.

The sound of home! Would I also someday yearn for the sound of home? Would I also cry for the sad songs of the peasants in Mangusmana? And before I realized it, I began talking in our dialect: "*Ama! Ina! Manong! Ading! Sicayo!*" The sound of home! Home among the peasants in Mangusmana!

Across the street, working in a grocery store, was a young girl who fascinated me. She was my size, with brown hair and blue eyes. I would go to the store pretending to buy something, but I wanted only to look at her. The way she moved around the room, the grace of her arms, the smile on her face. . . . But when she asked me what I wanted, I felt embarrassed and fumbled for something to say.

"Oh, you don't understand English well?" she asked.

"No, ma'am," I said.

"Oh, don't ma'am me," she said kindly. "I'm just a young girl. See? My name is Judith. I have some books. You'd like to read, perhaps?"

"Yes, Judith," I said.

"Follow me," she said, smiling.

I followed her through the back door and up into a house. I followed her slowly, drinking in her grace, the lovely way she moved her body. In the living room, piled along the wall, were books of many sizes and colors. Books! I was enchanted when I saw them. They drew me irresistibly to them.

"Maybe you would like this one," Judith said. "It's called *The Light That Failed.*"

"What is it about?" I asked.

"Well, it is the story of a painter who went blind," she said. "And there is a beautiful girl in it, too. Shall I read something to you?"

"All right," I said.

And she started reading the story of a painter in another land who went blind. When my dishes were done, working faster, I ran to the store so that Judith could read to me. Oh, the sound of her voice! But one day, when a Filipino and a white woman came to the restaurant to eat and were refused, I flung my apron away and attacked the headwaiter with my fists. The son of the proprietor, who had come home from a university for vacation, came running with words of anger.

"You are fired!"

These same stabbing words that followed me everywhere. *You are fired!* All right. I packed my things and went to the grocery store to say good-bye to Judith.

"If only you could stay on in this town," she said.

"I'll come back someday," I said.

"Good-bye." There was something lost and faraway in her voice. She raised her arm and turned away.

I went to the door and out into the sunlight.

CHAPTER XXIII

I TRIED hard to remain aloof from the destruction and decay around me. I wanted to remain pure within myself. But in Pismo Beach, where I found Mariano, I could not fight any more. He and I slept on the floor of a small cottage, where two others were living. It was used by prostitutes when summer came and the farm workers were in town with money. When our companions woke up in the morning, Mariano and I rushed to the small bed and slept all day, waking up only at night when the gambling houses opened. I would walk among the gamblers hoping they would give me a few coins when they won.

Throughout the winter and far into spring, I lived in this cabin with my companions. When I was hungry I went to the chop suey house in our block. I would sit with gamblers and when the waiter came with a pot of hot tea and rice cakes, I would drink four or five cups and put the cakes in my pockets. Then my hunger was appeased, and I could talk again. I almost lost my power of speech, because when I was hungry the words would not come; when I tried to speak only tears flowed from my eyes.

One night, when the Korean woman who owned the restaurant saw me looking hungrily at some half-emptied plates left by white customers, she said: "When you are hungry, come here and eat. This is your home."

When I went to the kitchen to wash dishes to pay for my food, the woman threw her hands up and said: "That is enough! Go home! Come again!"

I went again and again. But I had no home that winter. One of my companions died of tuberculosis, so Mariano burned the cabin and left town. The nights were cold. Once in a while I could hear church bells ringing, and I would say to myself: "If you can listen long enough to those bells you will be safe. Try to listen again and be patient." They were my only consolation, those bells. And I listened patiently, and that spring came with a green hope.

I went to Seattle to wait for the fishing season in Alaska. There seemed no other place in this wide land to go; there seemed to be tragedy and horror everywhere I went. Where would I go from here? What year was it when I had landed in Seattle with a bright dream? I was walking on Jackson Street when I suddenly came upon Julio, who had disappeared in Sunnyside after the riot in Moxee City.

I went with Julio to a Japanese gambling house on King Street, where he taught me how to play a game called Pi-Q. I watched him play, learning his tricks. Before the gambling houses opened, we sat in his room for hours playing Pi-Q. Julio was very patient and kind.

"Gambling is an art," he said to me. "Some people gamble because they think there is money in it. Yes, there is money in it when you are lucky. But then the meaning of gambling is distorted, no longer an art. You could win ten dollars a day all your life, and make an art of gambling, if you would only try. I am an artist."

When Julio had perfected the art of gambling, he turned to picking pockets. I watched him practicing for hours. He would put a silver dollar on the edge of the table and walk toward it, snatching the dollar swiftly as he passed. Then he would use a fifty-cent piece, a quarter, and finally a dime. When he could snatch a ten-cent piece without dropping it, he mingled among the people in the streets and practiced a new art.

I followed him. How swift and nimble he was! Once, in a department store, he was almost caught. I hurried past him whispering in my dialect that he was being watched. His room was filled with inexpensive trinkets.

"Why don't you sell it and use the money for something good?" I said.

"You are distorting the art of picking pockets again," he said.

"My 'pickings' are works of art. I use them for artistic expression only."

His "pickings" were neatly arranged on the table, on the floor; and some of the cheap wrist watches were hanging on the bed posts. I thought I had understood Julio when we walked across the Rattlesnake Mountains. But I was wrong. He was again a new personality, shaped by a new environment. I felt that I should leave him. I was angry that the old Julio was lost, for he had given me something, a kind of philosophy, which had sustained me for a long time.

"I'm going away," I said. "I want to work—anything but gambling. Or picking pockets."

"You are a damn fool!" he shouted. Then suddenly, realizing that he had made a mistake, he said: "There is no work anywhere. Why don't you go to the gambling houses and wait for the hop-picking in Spokane?"

It seemed a good idea. I went to a Chinese gambling house and started playing at a Pi-Q table. At night, when the place was crowded, I stopped playing and sat by a table. I noticed a Filipino farm worker, an elderly man, who was playing heavily at one of the tables. He left when he had lost all his money. Then he came back with a gun and began shooting at the Chinese dealers.

There was a general scramble, and I ducked behind a table that had fallen on the floor. I was terrified but managed to gather a handful of bills, crept to the back door, and rolled down the stairs. I ran frantically to the street, in front of the gambling house.

The Filipino had gone completely crazy. He was running up and down the sidewalk with a long knife, stabbing everyone in his way. The people ran for their lives. But for some it was too late. He had killed eight and wounded sixteen before the policemen caught him.

I lost track of Julio. But I was glad, when I took the freight train for Portland, of the things he had taught me before he disappeared. Word of the incident in Seattle had reached Portland before I arrived, and all the gambling houses were closed. I took another train to Sacramento where a Filipino mass meeting was being held. I skirted the crowd and took a bus for San Bernardino, where Chinese gambling houses were open to Filipinos.

I lost almost all my money. I stayed on for another day, but on the fourth day I gave up hope. I had only fifteen cents left. At night, when the gambling houses closed, I went to a Filipino poolroom and slept on a pool table, which was warmer and softer than the hard benches along the walls. But it was not the first time, for I had slept on pool tables in Santa Barbara, before Alfredo had appeared with plenty of money.

The next morning, desperate and hungry, I sat in front of a gambling house hoping to try my luck with my fifteen cents when the place opened. I did not go in right away, but killed time talking to the other gamblers. Three hours before closing time, I started playing and went on until the place was closed. I was jubilant. I had won nearly five hundred dollars!

"*Now*," I said to myself, "this is the life for me in America."

I took the bus for Los Angeles. No more freight trains for me. They were only for hoboes. I called up my brother Macario from the station, but he had left his job. I did not know where Amado lived, so I took a train for San Diego hoping to gamble there for a week.

It was twilight when I arrived in San Diego. I rented a room at the U. S. Grant Hotel. It was a new life. No more sleeping in poolrooms and going hungry. No more fear of want.

It was Sunday and the gambling houses were closed until Monday. I took a ferry boat to Coronado, a small island off the bay. When I returned to the ferry station the boats had stopped running for the night. I walked back to town and tried to get a room, but all the hotels refused me.

I went to the ferry station and slept on a bench. The following morning I took a streetcar to Coronado where, in a drugstore fountain, I was refused service. One young girl, who was a student, told me that there was a Filipino clubhouse on the island.

I went to the clubhouse. Frank opened the door, and it was a happy reunion. I thought that he had gone to Chicago when we parted in Utah. He was now a photographer. He was living with fifteen other Filipinos, mostly hotel and restaurant helpers. He took me to the kitchen where some of the men were playing Pi-Q.

I took my place by the table, pulling my hat down over my face. I wanted to win their money: it did not matter to me whether they were laboring men or not. I had to play with them, and cheat them, when I had the chance. Cheating was an imperative of the game.

The men went to work reluctantly, one at a time, and came hurrying back to the table, throwing their wages on it. I cheated them flagrantly because they were poor players, laughing aloud and kidding them while I won. But I was afraid of this bunch of work-worn, fear-stricken men. I knew that they were capable of violence, unlike professional gamblers who, upon discovering that you are one of them, lose a few more dollars and leave the table. I had discovered that there was fraternity among professional gamblers; when one was destitute, others are ready to give him a hand.

In the afternoon, when all the men came back, I won all their money. They became quarrelsome. Frank told me that one of the men had a wife who was in a hospital. But the man was shy and full of pride, and I knew I could not do anything for him. Why did he gamble his money when his wife needed it? Did he think he had the right to marry when he was scrubbing floors for thirty-five dollars a month? To hell with him!

So I was becoming hard, and brutal too: and careless with my talk. I went to San Diego and played in Chinatown. But I could not forget the man whose wife was in a hospital. I kept seeing his face on the gaming table, forlorn and pitiful. I played without direction, angry with myself. And I began to lose.

The next morning I went to Coronado. On my way to the Filipino clubhouse, I bought fifty dollars' worth of groceries for the men. They were all in when I arrived; some were dancing with their girls, and a man was playing a guitar. I gave the groceries to Frank and went out to buy some whisky. When I returned Frank was cooking a meal.

The men started playing Pi-Q in the kitchen. I sat at the table and purposely lost one hundred dollars, the remainder of the money I had won from them. I stopped playing and joined the dancers in the living room. A young Mexican girl dragged me to the floor. I began dancing with her, feeling the warmth of her body close to mine.

"My name is Carmen," she said. "What is yours?"

I told her.

"Let's go to my room," she whispered.

"All right." The blood was pounding in my temple. "I will follow you."

Her lips were hot upon mine when Frank came into the room, stopped at the door, then sat weakly on the bed.

"This is my room," he said. "We have very little memories in America," he said, looking at the girl with sad eyes. He crossed the room and opened a drawer, bringing out a girl's diaphanous gown. "I got this for a girl years ago. I promised to keep it for her always. But she said that if I ever found one I could like—" he looked at Carmen sadly—"it would be all right with her. Will you try it on, Carmen?"

Gentle and loving he was, helping Carmen on with the gown, kneeling on the floor around her and smoothing it to her body. Then it came to me that I would never again hurt Frank, or Carmen; that if I felt like hurting someone, it would be those men and women who had driven Frank to the floor, kneeling by an unfaithful girl.

I left the room quietly. I stayed on in San Diego and gambled. When I had a stroke of luck, I transferred to the El Cortes Hotel. I sent a postal money order to myself and went to San Francisco, but the city was dead. The gambling houses were closed. I stayed in Chinatown, and walked up and down Market Street. Once, in a cheap rooming house, I met a Filipino who was struggling to become an artist. I gave him some money, and left for Stockton.

It was again the asparagus season and the farm workers were itching to lose their money. But I hated to gamble in the Chinese houses. I went to Walnut Grove, thirty miles away, where the

Japanese controlled the gambling. I stopped playing when I had only five dollars left.

At noon the following day, I played again and made twenty-five dollars. I went to Stockton hoping to find Claro, but his restaurant was closed. I became restless and went to the bus station and bought a ticket to San Luis Obispo.

I felt that it was the end of another period of my life. I could see it in my reaction to the passing landscape, in my compassion for the workers in the fields. It was the end of a strange flight.

I bought a bottle of wine when I arrived in San Luis Obispo. I rented a room in a Japanese hotel and started a letter to my brother Macario, whose address had been given to me by a friend. Then it came to me, like a revelation, that I could actually write understandable English. I was seized with happiness. I wrote slowly and boldly, drinking the wine when I stopped, laughing silently and crying. When the long letter was finished, a letter which was actually a story of my life, I jumped to my feet and shouted through my tears:

"They can't silence me any more! I'll tell the world what they have done to me!"

CHAPTER XXIV

I WENT to bed resolved to change the whole course of my life forever. Where was I to begin? Where did rootless men begin their lives? Who were the men that contributed something positive to society? Show me the books about them! I would read them all! I would educate myself to be like them!

In the morning, rising to the clouds with my dream, I walked out of the hotel a new man. My first impulse was to walk past the house where Max's wife lived. I had seen it only once years ago, and I had a difficult time locating it. I remembered Max running toward me with the gun in his hand. I stopped when the memory of that day became too vivid in my imagination.

At last I found the house. It was a small house, with a wide yard. I went to the door and knocked, not really knowing why. The door opened and a tall, thin, white woman with gray hair showed her face.

"Good morning, ma'am," I said wondering if she were Max's wife.

"Come on in," she said quickly.

I followed her into the living room, sat on a couch, and fumbled for my hat. This was a new experience. Who was she? I saw a bedroom door. *That must be the place where Max shot the white man*, I thought. I edged toward the door. My life of fear and flight had taught me to seek the nearest exit.

The woman came back to the living room with a tall glass of port wine. "Do you drink in the morning?" she asked.

"Yes, ma'am," I said.

She gave me the glass and filled another for herself. A man stirred in one of the bedrooms.

"Who is that, honey?" he asked.

"We have a visitor," she said. "It's a little Pinoy who looks like a rabbit." She looked at me, smiling. "My husband is a Filipino. We edit a small newspaper. We have two other Pinoys with us. Where did you come from and what is your name?"

"My real name is Allos," I said. "But my friends call me Carlos."

"Now we will call you Carl," she said, pouring more wine into my glass. "You don't look like a farm worker. What have you been doing?"

"I have been at many things," I answered. "I am a gambler now; that is, I was yesterday."

The bedroom door opened and her husband came into the living room. He limped badly as he came toward me.

"My name is Pascual," he said. "I hope my wife didn't get you drunk at this time of day."

The woman laughed. "Now, honey," she said, "I was only trying to entertain him. Don't you like to drink with me, Carl?"

Suddenly José and Gazamen came into the living room.

"Carlos! Carlos!" They reached for my hand.

"It has been a long time," José said. "I thought I would never see you again after the accident in Bakersfield!"

"Do you know this little rabbit?" the woman asked.

"He saved my life," José said, reaching for the bottle of wine on the table. "Here's to a new life, Carlos!"

Pascual said: "Good! That's good! We can all work together! Do you know how to write your name?"

"Sure," I said.

Pascual produced his brief case and gave it to me. "From now on don't part with it, unless you part with your life."

I could not find words to express my joy. Here was the answer to my confusion. Pascual was a socialist. He was a lawyer by profession, but his talent had found a fuller expression in writing. He was small and semi-paralytic, but versatile and fiery. He had brought his American wife from Chicago to California—a woman almost twice as tall as he. Together they had started a newspaper in Stockton, appealed to the farm workers, prospered, until a rival newspaper drove them to the Santa Maria Valley. Then they had gone to San Luis Obispo where, at that time, the Filipino agricultural workers were voiceless and treated like peons. The agricultural workers were beginning to ask for unity, but had been barred from established unions. The Filipino workers started an independent union, and José was one of its organizers. I was happy to work with him, too. And happy also to know that in this feudalistic town the social awakening of Filipinos in California was taking shape.

I carried Pascual's brief case from store to store, listening to him talk to the storekeepers. The responsibilities of a Filipino editor were enormous: besides editing and soliciting advertisements, he also distributed the paper and campaigned for subscriptions. I was learning fast, and remembering, and soon I tried writing news items. Pascual recast what I wrote but urged me to write more.

"You have the idea," he said. "But you need practice. You have the chance to practice on this paper."

I wrote more—but the news items became lengthly articles, mostly expressing my personal reactions.

"That's it, Carl," Pascual would shout, storming around the room. "Write your guts out! Write with thunder and blood!"

I wrote about blood and conspiracies in the pea fields. Once, when urged to write a headline story, I sat down and composed this title:

MURDER OVER CALIFORNIA!

Pascual danced with glee around the room, drinking wine, shouting. "Let's fight them with our bare fists, Carl! Five against the world!"

I knew that something fatal was happening to him, making him hysterical and irrational. Then one day he suffered a stroke and his legs became completely paralyzed. It was the end of his thunder and blood.

José and I took over the editorial work. Gazamen and Pascual's wife were the business managers. It was a difficult job. I did not really know how to write. I stammered when I tried to solicit advertisements. I was starving again. But my determination to write was indomitable. I pounded my head with my fists when I found that I could not write what was in my mind!

I knew, even then, that it was not natural for a man to hate himself, or to be afraid of himself. It was not natural, indeed, to run from goodness and beauty, which I had done so many times. It was not natural for him to be cruel and without compassion.

I had come to the crossroads of my life. But there was yet time to find my way. I was fortunate to find in José something that I called dignity—and in Pascual, at least in part, a passion for abstract, universal ideas.

One day José and I went to Pismo Beach to solicit advertisements. He started on one side of the street and I on the other. It was a bad season; only a few vacationists had come to the town and the storekeepers could not afford to pay for a space in our paper. The gamblers and prostitutes on the other side of town patronized only the Japanese stores.

I sold space to a man who kept a liquor store and for pay received a quart bottle of whisky. I was coming out of his place when José whistled to me. I looked across the street and saw him with a Japanese girl. He was smiling. I crossed the street hurriedly.

"Meet Chiye, Carl," he said, putting his arm around her.

"Who is she?" I asked in Filipino.

"She is a waitress at that café across the street," José said. "But she is *ours* now. Let's go, Chiye!"

"We don't have any money," I said in English.

"I have money," Chiye said. "I have a car, too."

"You have?" José said. "Go get it, Chiye!"

She crossed the street and disappeared in an alley. She came out driving a car, and we jumped in, laughing and drinking from my bottle. We drove toward San Luis Obispo, looking at the blue sea and the heavy peas on the hills on both sides of the highway. José threw the empty bottle on the highway: it made a tinkling noise on the hard shoulder of the road. Suddenly Chiye turned to the left and drove madly toward Avila Beach where, she said, we could buy more whisky.

I bought three bottles, and Chiye rented some fishing tackle. We sat on a rock near the water. I threw the line into the water. Chiye leaned on my shoulder and went to sleep. I looked at José: he, too, was sleeping, the empty bottle rolling near his head. When they woke up we improvised a stove and broiled the fish I had caught. Then, in the evening, we rented a cabin under the trees.

The night was warm, and a breeze came into the room. The stars shone between the trees. It was like a long time ago in a land far away. Was it in Mangusmana that I had seen this same sky? And that lone star—had I seen it among the pine trees in Baguio? Chiye slept warmly between us, her legs bare and white. Shadows were moving on her body. I knelt beside her, feeling the world sinking slowly under me. . . .

After a while she got up and began crying.

"What are you moaning about?" José asked.

"I've got to go back to Pismo Beach," Chiye said. "My husband is waiting for me."

"You told me you had no husband," I said.

"Oh, hell!" José said.

I went to the car. Chiye was laughing when we reached the highway. José and I jumped out and walked to San Luis Obispo.

It was morning when we arrived at the house. Pascual's wife met us at the door.

"The pea pickers are striking in Pismo Beach," she said.

I went to the kitchen where Gazamen was finishing a placard for the strikers. José told him to hurry and went out to the car. Pascual's wife, Lucille, sat at the wheel. I jumped in after Gazamen.

There were about a hundred workers who had refused to strike. In Pismo Beach, while the meeting was going on with José as chairman, I went to the back room of a poolroom and started preparing a leaflet. I sent Gazamen to an American farmer, a sympathizer, to borrow his mimeograph machine. Then Lucille came and made the stencil, leaving with Gazamen when the meeting was over.

José entered the room with several strikers. He gave them a few sheets of the leaflet to distribute to the men. Then he took the handle of the mimeograph machine and told me to go out and ask the gambling proprietors to close their businesses for the duration of the strike.

When I returned to the poolroom a man told me that José had been arrested and taken away. I borrowed a car and drove back to San Luis Obispo. I told Pascual of José's arrest.

"There is only one thing to do," he said. "Contact Santa Barbara."

Lucille called an organization in Santa Barbara and explained the strike and José's arrest. In the morning a man came, and when he went to the county jail, José was released. I was sitting in the courtyard when he came out. The man from Santa Barbara shook hands with him and left.

José sat beside me on the green lawn. "I know what is in your mind, Carl," he said. "It's hard for me to explain to you. It is a long story. This is a war between labor and capital. To our people, however, it is something else. It is an assertion of our right to be human beings again, Carl. But in order for you to understand what this struggle means to me, I'll begin from the beginning of my life in the United States. . . ."

He began to tell me the story of his life, which was similar to mine.

CHAPTER XXV

Pascual's condition was getting worse each day. His only desire now was to go back to the Philippines. His legs were paralyzed, but he could still move his hands. I knew that it was the end for him. But he had served his purpose. He belonged to yesterday. And although his socialistic ideas were vague and fumbling, I gained something vital from him. I was to add something new to it: a new significance and meaning.

As Pascual's days came to a close, I went to the Filipino camps and asked for contributions. Some of the agricultural workers came to town and sat around Pascual. He was dying, and he wanted to say something. He turned his face toward me and began to speak.

"It is for the workers that we must write," he said weakly. "We must interpret their hopes as a people desiring the fullest fulfillment of their potentialities. We must be strong of voice, objective of criticism, protest and challenge. There is no other way to combat any attempts to suppress individual liberty. . . ."

It was Pascual's last message. When he died his wife went to San Francisco with the newspaper and resumed its publication there with the co-operation of a farm worker who had become an editor. I never saw her again.

When the house was closed, I took a bus for Los Angeles. I found that my brother Macario and Nick, José's brother, were living together. They had started a literary magazine with a man named Felix Razon. To my amazement, he was the same peasant boy who had warned me to leave the rice fields in Tayug, before the Colorum revolted against the landlords.

I was becoming aware of the dynamic social struggle in America. We talked all night in my brother's room, planning how to spread progressive ideas among the Filipinos in California.

Macario had become more serious. When he talked, I noticed his old gentleness and the kind voice that had rung with sincerity at my sickbed in Binalonan. His words seized my imagination, so that years afterward I am able to write them almost word for word:

"It has fallen upon us to inspire a united front among our people," he said. "We must win the backward elements over to our camp; but we must also destroy that which is corrupt among ourselves. These are the fundamentals of our time; but these are also the realities that we must grasp in full.

"We must achieve articulation of social ideas, not only for some kind of economic security but also to help culture bloom as it should in our time. We are approaching what will be the greatest achievement of our generation: the discovery of a new vista of literature, that is, to speak to the people and to be understood by them.

"We must look for the mainspring of democracy, but we must also destroy false ideals. We must discover the origin of our freedom and write of it in broad national terms. We must interpret history in terms of liberty. We must advocate democratic ideas, and fight all forces that would abort our culture.

"This is the greatest responsibility of literature: to find in our struggle that which has a future. Literature is a living and growing thing. We must destroy that which is dying, because it does not die by itself.

"We in America understand the many imperfections of democracy and the malignant disease corroding its very heart. We must be united in the effort to make an America in which our people can find happiness. It is a great wrong that anyone in America, whether he be brown or white, should be illiterate or hungry or miserable.

"We must live in America where there is freedom for all regardless of color, station and beliefs. Great Americans worked with unselfish devotion toward one goal, that is, to use the power of the myriad peoples in the service of America's freedom. They made it their guiding principle. In this we are the same; we must also fight for an America where a man should be given unconditional opportunities to cultivate his potentialities and to restore him to his rightful dignity.

"It is but fair to say that America is not a land of one race or one class of men. We are all Americans that have toiled and suffered and known oppression and defeat, from the first Indian that offered peace in Manhattan to the last Filipino pea pickers. America is not bound by geographical latitudes. America is not merely a land or an institution. America is in the hearts of men that died for freedom; it is also in the eyes of men that are building a new world. America is a prophecy of a new society of men: of a system that knows no sorrow or strife or suffering. America is a warning to those who would try to falsify the ideals of freemen.

"America is also the nameless foreigner, the homeless refugee, the hungry boy begging for a job and the black body dangling on a tree. America is the illiterate immigrant who is ashamed that the world of books and intellectual opportunities is closed to him. We are all that nameless foreigner, that homeless refugee, that hungry boy, that illiterate immigrant and that lynched black body. All of us, from the first Adams to the last Filipino, native born or alien, educated or illiterate—*We are America!*

"The old world is dying, but a new world is being born. It generates inspiration from the chaos that beats upon us all. The false grandeur and security, the unfulfilled promises and illusory power, the number of the dead and those about to die, will charge the forces of our courage and determination. The old world will die so that the new world will be born with less sacrifice and agony on the living. . . ."

PART THREE

CHAPTER XXVI

The old world will die. . . .

This was the new dictum of my life. I did not exactly know what it meant, but it was enough that my brother Macario had expressed it. It was a stirring law that governed my life and thoughts. And it did not matter who was going to die; it was enough that something horrible was to perish from the earth.

The simple beginning of my intellectual awakening—the tragic death of Pascual and the imprisonment of José, the sudden change of Macario into a personality passionately reaching out for understanding, and my second encounter with Felix Razon —all these influences were enough to make my last few months of freedom useful and significant.

The first issue of *The New Tide* was with the printers; when it came out, José and I took a hundred copies and distributed them to some of the more literate farm workers. It did not create a sensation, but we did not expect anything spectacular. It was the first of its kind to be published by Filipinos in the United States, and it was fumbling and immature, but it promised to grow into something important in the history of Filipino social awakening.

The magazine was one of several publications that had arisen all over the nation, and had tried to grasp the social realities and to interpret them in terms of the needs of the decade. It sustained our lives, drowned our despair, and gave us hope. It broadened our scope and vision.

Then it went out of existence. Its founders tried to revive it. But like the other publications born overnight to rally behind a new social idea, it died a natural death. It was like a world that died. Felix Razon wanted to save it; he went to work in a hotel in Hollywood and lived in the basement in order to save it. Nick found an apartment house in Beverly Hills; he worked seven days a week for twenty-five dollars a month. Macario went to work in a restaurant but, upon my advice—since there was no hope for the magazine—he went to New Mexico hoping to attend the University there.

However, the magnificent spirit behind it did not die. It was born again, in a more dynamic form, when I acquired enough knowledge to revive the high idealism behind it. But what awed me, in those early days, were the sacrifices of the founders. I would ask myself why three starving men were willing to give up their hard-earned money to make an obscure magazine live, denying themselves the simple necessities of food and shelter. They had surrounded the publication as though it were a little life about to die, or dying, or dead—and breathed life into it one after the other, looking desperate and lost when they realized that their efforts were futile. But it was an inspiring experience, watching these young men breathing life into a dead thing. Their efforts came to me again and again in the course of my struggle toward an intellectual clarification and a positive social attitude.

An old world literally died with the magazine. An old generation of writers died with it, too. A new generation was born with the same ideals, perhaps, but re-envigorated with new social attitudes. The labor movement was the paramount issue; it was winning the support of intellectuals and the advanced sections of the proletariat. Listening and watching attentively, I knew that it was the dawn of a new morning. I did not have to wait for the birth of a new world, because what I had been told to fight for was here with its brilliant promises.

How was I to understand it? Could I help? I knew that the most forlorn man, in those rootless years, was he who knew that love was growing inside him but had no object on which to bestow it.

Upon my return to the Santa Maria Valley, I found that the Filipino Workers' Association, an independent union, was disintegrating. I rushed to join José in Lompoc, where he had gone with Gazamen to see if there was a possibility of establishing a workers' newspaper. The three of us decided to form a branch there and to make it the center of Filipino union activities in Central California.

Salinas was still the general headquarters of the Association, but it was fast losing its authority and prestige. There was a mad scramble for power in the Association among the national officers, and their bitter rivalries wrecked our chance toward the establishment of a more cogent labor organization. Actually, however, it was the birth of progressive leadership in the Filipino labor movement.

The membership of the Filipino Workers' Association was tremendous, considering the myriad difficulties it met in the campaign to spread throughout the agricultural areas of California. The vigilant Filipino workers—their whole-hearted support of the trade union movement, their hatred of low wages and other labor discriminations—were the direct causes that instigated the persecutions against them, sporadic at first and then concerted, but destructive to the nation's welfare.

In Salinas, for instance, the general headquarters were burned after a successful strike of lettuce workers, and the president of the association was thrown in jail. Upon his release, he moved to Guadalupe, in the south, and campaigned for the purchase of a new building. Always alert, the Filipino agricultural workers throughout the valley rallied behind the proposal, and after a few months a new national office was established. Again, striking for better wages, the Filipino lettuce cutters and packers succeeded, but lost the building and their right to build another in Guadalupe.

Finally, José and I made the office in Lompoc the temporary general headquarters. It was unconstitutional, of course, but the moment called for drastic action. Our move was without precedent, but we hoped to accomplish something, and we did.

It was during our membership campaign that I came in contact with fascism in California. The sugar beet season was in full swing in Oxnard, but the Mexican and Filipino workers were split. The companies would not recognize their separate demands, and although there were cultural and economic ties between them, they had not recognized one important point: that the beet companies conspired against their unity.

I contacted a Filipino farm-labor contractor and a prominent Mexican, and José, who joined us later, planned a meeting in the town park. I felt a little elated; harmony was in the offing. But in the evening, when we were starting the program, deputy sheriffs came to the park and told us that our right to hold a meeting had been revoked. I did not know what to do. I was still a novice. An elderly Mexican told us that we could hold a meeting outside the city limit.

There was a large empty barn somewhere in the south end of Oxnard. A truck came and carried some of the men, but most of them walked with us on the highway. They were very serious. I glanced at José who was talking to three Filipinos ahead of me, and felt something powerful growing inside me. It was a new heroism: a feeling of growing with a huge life. I walked silently with the men, listening to their angry voices and to the magic of their marching feet.

I was frightened. But I felt brave, too. The Mexicans wanted a more inclusive union, but that would take time. We were debating the issue when I heard several cars drive into the yard. I signaled to the men to put out the lights and to take cover. They fanned out and broke through the four walls, escaping into the wide beet fields.

I rushed upon the improvised stage and grabbed José, whose wooden leg had become entangled in some ropes and wires.

"This is it!"

"Yeah!"

"Follow me!"

"Right!"

I jumped off the stage, José following me. Then there was the sudden patter of many feet outside, and shooting. I found a pile of dry horse manure in a corner of the barn. I told José to lie down; then I covered him with it, exposing only his nose. I lay beside him and covered myself with it, too. When I tried to talk, the manure went into my mouth and choked me. I lay still, waiting for the noise outside to subside.

A man with a flashlight came inside and stabbed the darkness with the steely light, cutting swiftly from corner to corner. He came near the pile of manure, spat on it, and searched the ceiling. A piece of manure tickled my throat, and I held my breath, bringing tears to my eyes. The man went outside, joined his companions, and drove off to town.

I pushed the dung away and jumped to my feet.

"Did you see his face?"

"No!"

"I saw it. He is a white man, all right."

"Let's run. There is still time."

I crept to the wall and crouched in the darkness. I wanted to be sure that every man had gone. The way was clear. José followed me outside. Then we were running across a beet field, our feet slapping against the broad leaves that got in our way. The moon came up and shone brightly in the night. As I ran, I looked up to see it sailing across the sky.

Then my fear was gone. I stopped running and sat down among the tall beets. José sat beside me. There were no words to describe the feeling in our minds and hearts. There was only our closeness and the dark years ahead. There was only the dark future.

We walked across the beet fields to Camarillo, five miles south. The town was quiet and dark. It was surrounded by orange groves. We went into the local school building and slept on the floor. A teacher found us there in the morning. She threatened to call the police, and we rushed outside. We walked in the morning sun, smelling the orange blossoms and the clean air. I looked at the tall mountains on our right and stopped, remembering the mountains in my village.

"You like the landscape?" José asked.

"It's like my village," I said.

"Tell me about it."

"Well, it is hard to describe it to you. But the farther I go from it, the more vivid it becomes to me. Perhaps I am sentimental. But my village is not like any other village. There are mountains on one side, and there is the wide river on the other. A tongue of land extends into the river and on this land are hills that are covered with guava trees. Now is the time for the guavas to bloom. I used to go there when I was a child and the smell of the blossoms followed me down into the valley. Between the mountains and the river, in the center of the valley, is a papaya grove. Papayas are in bloom now. Did you ever smell papaya blossoms? There is nothing like it. Someday I will go back and climb these guavas again. Someday I will make a crown of papaya blossoms. Do you think I am sentimental?"

"No," José said. "I know what you mean. We will go back someday. I will climb those guavas with you. We will swim in the river. The papayas are in bloom now, you say?"

The journey to Ventura was shortened. We were following the state highway when a police patrol stopped us and took us to the city jail and held us on charges of vagrancy. When we were released, three days afterward, we took a bus to Lompoc.

But another strike was in progress there. The lettuce workers had walked out three days before. I was informed that some of the men did not approve of the strike, but a white woman from Fresno had agitated them. Gazamen told me that she was staying at a local hotel. I asked José to go with me.

It was already one in the afternoon, but the hotel was very quiet. I knocked on the door. A short, stocky, ordinary-looking woman with dark hair stood before me.

"My name is Helen," she said, coming out with her overnight bag. "How is the strike this morning?"

"My name is José," José said. "We came to you to talk about it. I hope you don't mind our bothering you."

"José!" Helen was beaming. "You are the person I've been looking for in Lompoc. Mr. Magna in San Francisco recommended you—"

José's doubts vanished immediately. He knew Magna intimately. I walked eagerly with them to the office. But why did Helen talk as though this strike were a business? I was filled with doubts and premonitions.

CHAPTER XXVII

HELEN, realizing the importance of time, suggested that we proceed with the strike. Fired with a new impetus, José worked night and day. The strike spread to Solvang and Las Cruces, where the Lompoc farmers controlled the agricultural products. The strikers organized reconnaissance squads and guarded the highway and other exits from the valley.

It was exactly what Helen wanted. The trucks that carried the lettuce were driven by Japanese and white men to Las Cruces, where they were inspected by government officials before proceeding to Los Angeles. Helen wanted the hauling stopped. It was a dangerous move, because the job of taking out the crates from the fields was done by Japanese and Mexican workers under the surveillance of highway patrolmen.

I tried to argue with Helen against the use of firearms and violence in general, but gave up when some of the strikers became hysterical. The leaders of the squads wanted to install me as the new secretary of the local. I accepted it, not because I wanted it, but because the strike called for quick decision. Besides, I was beginning to understand the organized conspiracy against the agricultural workers in California.

The strike taught me that I was definitely a part of the labor movement. On the third day, the reconnaissance squads rushed to the main highway where the loaded trucks would pass. The men spread out and waited on both sides of the road, becoming tense when the trucks appeared in the distance. But the drivers were guarded by motorcycle patrolmen, three on either side, releasing their sirens whenever they approached the strikers.

When the first truck appeared in the bend of the road, the strikers came out and signaled to the driver to stop. The patrolmen rushed forward, clubbing the men who tried to climb into the trucks. About a dozen men turned over a truck, fighting their way out when the patrolmen turned around to beat them. The drivers leaped out and stayed away from the fight.

In a few minutes, finding resistance impossible, the strikers rushed to their cars and drove madly to the office. Three strikers were arrested on the spot, brought to town, and thrown in jail. In the afternoon a newspaper reporter from Santa Barbara came to our headquarters and reported that the strike was inspired by Communists. The next day, believing the newspaper story, some of the townspeople joined the Mexican and Japanese laborers in the fields.

The strike was completely broken. Great damage was done to organized Filipino labor. I was reluctant to believe that Helen had betrayed us, but when she disappeared at the termination of the strike, I suspected that she might be a professional strike-breaker.

Helen had shown me a subtle way of winning the rank and file. But she had also shown me a way of winning the leaders. In fact, she had shown me another way of abusing the trust and confidence of honest working men.

When the strike was broken in Lompoc, José followed Helen to Salinas, where she had gone to spread calamity. I knew that they were living together as husband and wife, in the Mexican section, and I intimated to José my suspicion. But he ignored my warning. Because he was the ablest organizer among Filipinos in California, Helen got her man. She was paid to curtail the trend of agricultural workers toward the labor movement.

Then I heard that the Salinas strike had been defeated, or betrayed, and again Helen disappeared. A ranch house was burned by unidentified persons, and the blame was put on the strikers. It was the same old tactic, but still workable. José was arrested; but Helen, who was also arrested, was released immediately. It was evident that she was paid to create disunity among the strikers and to turn public opinion against them. When José was released by the International Labor Defense, which handled such cases, he went to San Francisco where he attended a workers' conference.

I went to Los Angeles hoping to persuade my brother Macario to go to Santa Maria with me, where the two of us could work together, because he was proficient in languages and was a forceful speaker. But he already had a job. He was more interested in the theoretical approach. I discovered with disappointment that his desire to go to college was fading. He was, however, reading extensively and acquiring books about world politics.

I wanted Macario to complete his education because, at that time, I still believed that it was the only course for him. I remembered how our family had sacrificed everything for him, and when I saw him losing interest, I thought of the years when I had been with my father on the farm in Mangusmana. I recalled that my most wonderful days were those centered around Macario—when he was away from Binalonan, when he was studying in Lingayen, and when he came back one vacation time to cut my hair.

I wrote to my brother Amado, in Phoenix, but when he received my letter he was already in San Francisco. He was living at the St. Francis Hotel with the man for whom he was working —a big-time racketeer lawyer from Los Angeles. I went to San Diego, where the Filipino pea pickers were on strike. When I returned to Los Angeles a letter from Amado was waiting for me. He was in Hollywood.

I went to see him immediately. He was staying in a luxurious room. But it was actually rented by the lawyer; they always lived together when they were traveling.

"In fact," Amado said proudly, "we sometimes sleep with the same woman."

I did not believe him. How was it that a successful lawyer would share a room with his servant? But Amado disappointed me: he was in a position to help Macario go to college but would not. It was the beginning of a long estrangement between Amado and me.

"I'm going into a new world, Carlos," Amado said. "Away from our people. I'm sorry it's this way."

I knew that he had deserted us—even his speech was rapidly becoming Americanized.

"I'm sorry, too," I said.

"Good-bye."

I walked out of his room and his life forever.

I lived with Macario in his little room on Flower Street, hoping to read some of his books and magazines. I went to the public library, fumbling for knowledge in the enormous building. One day Macario took a civil service examination, although he knew that he could not get the job.

"Why?" I asked.

"California doesn't employ Filipinos in civil service jobs," he said.

"Is there a law about it?"

"None. But it is a matter of personal interpretation of our status in the United States."

"Citizenship, then, is the basis of all this misunderstanding?"

"You can put it that way."

I was discovering things. Where should I begin? It was then that Helen came to Los Angeles. She saw me at a meeting of the Labor Relations Board and the workers' representatives at the post office. She grabbed me, pretending excitement and joy. I played my part, wanting to know what she was doing.

We went outside and walked in the autumn shower: the sky was dark and there was a cold wind. I took Helen with me to my brother's room; there was no other place for us to go. Because my brother was beginning to integrate his beliefs, I warned him against Helen. But it was useless. She had found her next victim, but her method was more subtle. She was dealing with an intellectual, and used a different strategy.

She succeeded, living with Macario and despising me. I was dejected and lost. I could not believe it: the gods of yesterday were falling to pieces. They were made of clay. I had to make my own gods, create my own symbols, and worship in my own fashion. Yes, this is what I would do, now that all of yesterday was dying.

I was about to leave Los Angeles when José arrived. He had heard that Helen was in town. He wanted to stop her doing any more damage to the Filipinos. She was not only involved with powerful agricultural groups, but was also connected with certain self-styled patriotic organizations that considered it their duty to terrify the lives of minorities in the state.

Helen's suspicion that Macario was what she called a "professional agitator" revealed her stupidity. There was nothing in my brother's activities that would indicate his political connections; he was simply a man who had been awakened by a dynamic social idea. How to realize it was beyond him. Although he wanted a course of action, he was incapable of working it out to the end. He was by inclination an intellectual, a visionary, a dreamer. The turmoil in the agricultural areas of California were but reverberations of a greater social catastrophe.

When José, infuriated by Helen's lack of integrity, accused her of being an agent of anti-union interests, she retorted savagely:

"I hate the Filipinos as deeply as I hate unions! You are all savages and you have no right to stay in this country!"

I struck her in the face with a telephone receiver. Something fell from her mouth. Now let her speak arrogantly about the Filipinos! When José saw that I was going to hit her again, he charged suddenly and knocked me down. When I scrambled to my feet Helen was already running down the alley toward the street.

It was the end of Helen among Filipinos. But she had done enough damage. I had often wondered what became of her. I later heard unconfirmed reports that she had been beaten to death in Visalia.

CHAPTER XXVIII

THE DISAPPEARANCE of Helen marked the end of the Filipino Workers' Association. Terrorism was loosed upon the agricultural workers and special committees were formed to lobby in the state legislature and in Congress to bring about the regimentation of migratory workers. The big farmers had gone so far as to curtail all civil liberties for farm laborers. They also designed to wreck unionism by instigating lurid campaigns among the urban population to teach them to fight union activities.

In this open conspiracy to undermine a democratic government, the farmers had miscalculated the reaction of the workers who led an urban life; for they succeeded only in epitomizing the fact that both urban and rural workers depend on each other's labor in the struggle for security and the right to organize and bargain collectively.

But not realizing that we were facing a powerful enemy, José and I and other labor leaders met in the house of a newspaper reporter, Millar, in San Francisco, and mapped out a plan to start a unified statewide union campaign. When we adjourned Ganzo, who was working with Pascual's wife on a new newspaper in San Francisco, went to Santa Maria where he was familiar with the workers. José and I wanted to work together in Central California, embracing, of course, all the agricultural towns in San Luis Obispo and Santa Barbara counties.

Felix Razon, toughened by the years, enthusiastically went to Imperial Valley, where the fascist elements worked more openly than in other parts of the state. Nick went to Los Angeles, where he could work with my brother Macario among the city laborers, but the orange counties and San Diego were also his territories. Millar remained in San Francisco, to work closely with a Filipino Communist in Sacramento, who went to Stockton afterward to help me organize a political steering committee.

Conrado Torres, who had worked with me in the fish canneries in Alaska several years before, went to Seattle and from there proceeded to Yakima Valley, leaving Mauro Perez to consolidate what he had started to organize. Gazamen went to Portland, where they were joined by Mariano—and the three started an aggressive, militant, and progressive committee. Jim Luna and I were the only members of our group who had had no college education. But Jim had served in the navy for many years and had gained experience.

When we parted we were conscious of the tremendous task before us, that if we failed in ourselves we would also fail in its realization. From this day onward my life became one long conspiracy, working in the daytime and meeting other conspirators at night. I was so intensely fired by this dream of a better America that I had completely forgotten myself; but when I discovered myself again, I found that I was still a young man though broken in health. I was suffering from a disease that changed the whole course of my life, that halted my pursuit of the dream in a corner of the terrible years.

In Santa Maria, where I was working with José, I received a disturbing communication from Millar. Trouble was brewing in San Jose, forty miles south of San Francisco. José and I took the first bus, stopping a few hours in San Luis Obispo to see how Ganzo was progressing. In the early morning, after a lengthy deliberation with Ganzo in his cabin, we rushed to the station and slept in the bus until Salinas.

I still do not know why José and I never discussed unionism and politics when we were alone. It was only when we were with others, when we were in action, that we spoke aloud and acted according to our judgment. But I knew that I was coming to a way of thinking that would govern my life in the coming years. I surmised that the same evolution was taking place in José. But there was still no term for it. I believed then that agitating the agricultural workers was enough, but the next five years showed me that a definite political program was also needed.

Millar was not at our rendezvous in San Jose. I went to the lettuce fields and talked to the workers. The companies had drastically cut the wage scale: the year before it had been thirty cents an hour, but now it had been reduced to twenty cents. The Filipino workers struck, but the companies imported Mexican laborers.

"There should be a law against the importation of labor," I said. "It should be included in the interstate laws."

"The time will come," José said.

"Without it the workers will always be at the mercy of the employers."

"You are absolutely right, Carl," José said. "But we have a good president in Washington, so we will probably win some of our demands—if we use enough pressure."

I was not satisfied, but there was some hope. I went to the Mexican district and gathered together some of the Mexicans who had quit the fields that day. José, who spoke fluent Spanish, came and explained to them the importance of the strike. They were enthusiastic. A runner was sent to the fields to stop the Mexicans who were still working, and he came back to tell us that only fifty remained.

But we wanted an all-out strike, although we doubted that it would be possible. That night, when José and I were in the back room of a restaurant, preparing a leaflet to be circulated, five white men came suddenly into the room. I started to run to the door, but it was too late. Two big men, one wearing dark glasses, carried off José. The other man suddenly turned around and shot out the light bulbs.

I was kicked into the back seat of a big car. José was in the front seat, between the driver and the man with dark glasses. When the car started to move, I looked down and saw Millar bleeding on the floor. He looked up at me with frightened eyes, pleading, wanting to tell me that he had nothing to do with our arrest. I turned the other way, aching to hit him in the face.

I looked through the window hoping to find some escape. I was sure that if the car turned a corner, I could jump out. If I succeeded in jumping out—could I escape their guns? My heart almost stopped beating. It was better to die trying to escape than to wait for death.

But when the car came to a deserted country road, I knew that flight was impossible. I lost all hope. I glanced quickly at the wide, clear fields, catching a fleeting glimpse of the sky. Looking swiftly to the east, I saw the big moon and below it, soon to move away, a mass of clouds that looked like a mountain of cotton balls. Suddenly I remembered that as a child I used to watch snow-white clouds sailing in the bright summer skies of Mangusmana. The memory of my village made my mind whirl, longing for flight and freedom again.

I was helpless now. I watched my companions: they seemed to have given up all hope. There was only death at the end of the road. The white men were silent. Millar touched my legs when we passed in the shadows of trees. The driver turned off the road and crossed a wide beet field, heading for the woods not far away.

We entered the woods and in five minutes the car stopped. One of the men in front jumped out and came to our door.

"You have the rope, Jake?"

"Yeah!"

The man on my right got out and pulled me violently after him, hitting me on the jaw. I fell on my knees but got up at once, trembling with rage. If only I had a gun! Or a knife! I could cut these bastards into little pieces! Blood came out of my mouth. I raised my hand to wipe it off, but my attacker hit me again. I staggered, fell on my face, and rolled on the grass.

"Up! Goddamn you! Up!"

Painfully I crawled to my feet, knelt on the grass, and got up slowly. I saw them kicking Millar in the grass. When they were through with him, they tore off José's clothes and tied him to a tree. One of them went to the car and came back with a can of tar and a sack of feathers. The man with the dark glasses ripped the sack open and white feathers fell out and sailed in the thin light that filtered between the trees.

Then I saw them pouring the tar on José's body. One of them lit a match and burned the delicate hair between his legs.

"Jesus, he's a well-hung son-of-a-bitch!"

"Yeah!"

"No wonder whores stick to them!"

"The other monkey ain't so hot!"

They looked in my direction. The man with the dark glasses started beating Millar. Then he came to me and kicked my left knee so violently that I fell on the grass, blinded with pain. Hardening my body, I wished I were strong enough to reach him. He spat in my face and left.

Another man, the one called Jake, tied me to a tree. Then he started beating me with his fists. Why were these men so brutal, so sadistic? A tooth fell out of my mouth, and blood trickled down my shirt. The man called Lester grabbed my testicles with his left hand and smashed them with his right fist. The pain was so swift and searing that it was as if there were no pain at all. There was only a stabbing heat that leaped into my head and stayed there for a moment.

"Shall we burn this yellow belly?"

"He's gone."

"I'd like a souvenir."

"Scalp him!"

"What about the other bastard?"

"He's gone, too."

They left me. One of them went to the car and took out a bottle of whisky. They started drinking, passing the bottle from hand to hand. Once in a while, when a bottle was emptied, one of them would come over and beat me. When they were drunk enough, I feared that they would burn José. Millar crawled painfully over to where I was lying.

"Knife in my left shoe," he whispered.

"Quiet." I rolled over and reached for the knife. Now I could cut the ropes that tied my legs. My hands were free! Then I was ready to run! I handed the knife back and whispered to

Millar to roll away. I crawled in the grass slowly; when I reached the edge of the woods, I got up and tried to run. But I had almost no use of my left leg, so that most of the time I hopped through the beet fields like a kangaroo.

The night was clear and quiet. I was afraid they would see me. I heard their voices on the wind. Once a flashlight beamed from the edge of the woods. I lay flat on my stomach and watched it disappear among the trees. Then I got up and staggered toward San Jose.

I stopped when I came to the lighted areas to avoid suspicion. I turned away from the business district and headed for the Oriental section. A police car came by. I turned in at a side door and opened it. I found myself in a little room, with dolls on the bed and a portable radio on a small table. On the dresser was the picture of a woman who might have been twenty-five. Someone was in the bathroom for I could hear a noise there. I was reaching for the doorknob when a white woman came out.

She stopped short in surprise, letting the towel fall from her hands.

"Please don't be afraid," I said. "Some men are after me."

She came forward. "Have you killed somebody?"

"No."

"Did you steal some money?"

"No. I—well, I—work with the unions."

She ran to a little room and brought me a clean shirt. She brought a basin of warm water and began washing my face gently. Then she took me to the kitchen, where she prepared something for me to eat. I watched her. She might inform the police. Could I trust her?

"When did you eat last?" she asked.

"I don't remember," I said.

"Poor boy." She got up. "Eat everything and go to sleep."

I almost cried. What was the matter with this land? Just a moment ago I was being beaten by white men. But here was another white person, a woman, giving me food and a place to rest. And her warmth! I sat on the couch and started talking. I wanted to explain what happened to me.

"Poor boy." There was kindness in her face, some urge to reach me, to understand what I was telling her. And sometimes when she was touched by my description, I could feel her kind hand on my face. There was tenderness in her touch.

"Thank you so much," I said.

"Go to sleep now." She switched off the lights and went to her bed. I watched her in the darkness of the room, because by now I was used to darkness. I could see in the dark almost as clearly as in a room flooded with lights. "Good night," she said.

I lay quietly on the couch; then tears began to come to my eyes. What would happen to José and Millar? Had I the right to run away? Had I? *The fight must go on*, José used to say. All right. I would go on with the fight. I would show them. The silence outside was deepening. Not far away, in a nearby farmhouse, I could hear a rooster crowing.

The woman was still awake. She sat up. She heard me crying. She got up and came to my couch.

"What is your name?" she asked.

"Carl," I said. "Remember me only as Carl, that's all."

"Mine is Marian," she said. "Go to sleep now."

She woke me early in the morning. I was surprised to find that she had packed her things.

"Wait for me here," she said. "I'll get my car."

In five minutes she was back. I carried the suitcases into the car. She sat at the wheel and put the key in the lock. Then she looked back to the town, as though she were committing it to memory. I knew her look because I had done the same thing a hundred times. It was a farewell look—forever. The car started to move.

"We'll go to Los Angeles," she said.

I looked out of the window. The sun was rising.

CHAPTER XXIX

WHEN we were a few miles from San Jose, Marian began talking. I discovered that she had lived in Oregon as a child. The town was Tigard, she said, where the ground was covered with snow all winter.

"I washed dishes in Portland while I was going to college," she said.

"I have also washed dishes—all over California." I knew that there were girl dishwashers in Portland. Most of them were employed in little restaurants, but they were poorly paid. I looked at Marian's hands: it was obvious that she had done manual work. Her hands were rough; the fingers were stubby and flattened at the top. My heart ached, for this woman was like my little sisters in Binalonan. I turned away from her, remembering how I had walked familiar roads with my mother.

"I went to Reed College for two years," Marian went on, "hoping to escape from the narrowing island that was Tigard. When summer came, I picked hops with Mexican families. But some gypsies came to the fields too. When winter came I went to Portland, and there I met a man. I thought it was love, you know. We women always think that it is love, although we may feel that perhaps it is not. We are more emotional, I suppose. I lived with him for a while, working and planning for the future. Then I found out that he was married, had three children, and was a gambler. It was the beginning of my life of bitterness."

She stopped and offered me a cigarette. I told her that I did not smoke.

She continued: "I tried to make a new life. Without illusions, I went on my way. I worked here and there, living a new life, beginning to be strong inside again. I even thought of going back to college. I wanted to teach, you know. Then I met another man who took me to Los Angeles, and there he died in an automobile accident. My whole world died with him, and I died too."

I saw tears falling from her eyes. She blinked them away. I looked straight ahead, feeling an ache inside me. Now she was crying.

"I wanted to go to school, too," I said. "But that was a long time ago. In the Philippines."

"You are still young," she said. "There is plenty of time."

"I don't know."

"I'll help you. I'll work for you. You will have no obligations. What I would like is to have someone to care for, and it should be you who are young. I would be happier if I had something to care for—even if it were only a dog or a cat. But it doesn't really matter which it is: a dog or a cat. What matters is the affection, the relationship, between you and the object. Even a radio becomes almost human, and the voice that comes from it is something close to you, and then there grows a bond between you. For a long time now I've wanted to care for someone. And you are the one. Please don't make me unhappy. . . ."

We arrived in Salinas in the late afternoon. Marian sent me to a hotel. She told me that she had relatives in town whom she wanted to see. I sat in my room and told the clerk to send a bellboy. I was hungry and I wanted something to eat. I did not want to be seen. I paced endlessly, waiting for Marian. I tried to contact Mariano, who had come to Salinas with Ganzo.

I waited for Marian until one o'clock in the morning. When I woke up at seven, I saw her smiling near my bed. She had brought some peaches and a bottle of milk. She was very tired and sleepy.

"Where have you been?" I asked, and there was excitement in my voice.

"With friends," she said, trying to be gay. "I'm sorry if I have worried you. But you must get used to it, Carl. Now I need a few hours of sleep."

I sat around watching her. She woke up a little after noon and told me that we would proceed to Los Angeles.

"I would like you to go to school there," she said. She was very gay. She kept tossing her brown hair back to the nape of her neck. She hummed a sweet tune that was new to me.

I began telling her about my life, from my Island village up to that time. She looked at me with surprise when I said something incredible. She opened the window of the car on her side and strong, fresh air flooded in, blowing her hair upon my face. I smelled the sweetness of her, like delicious wine.

I was not afraid any more. I felt free now, and inspired, and my defenses were down. I was weakening. This Marian: she was small, quiet, and lovely with long brown hair. Her hair—where had I seen it before? The girl on the freight train! Could it be the same person? I glanced at Marian's face. I was not sure—it was so long ago. She was sweet and near. But I could not touch her. Even when she was close to me, even when all her thoughts were leaning toward me and her heart was in my heart.

We stopped in San Luis Obispo. Marian left me in a chop suey house. I walked to the house where Pascual had lived, in the Chinese district. I knocked on the door and Ganzo opened it. He was silent and mysterious. I did not understand why.

"I thought you were in Sacramento," he said.

"I didn't go there."

He reached for a bottle of wine and poured some into a large glass. I knew that something was bothering him.

"How is the work in San Luis Obispo?" I asked.

"*They* are coming closer," he said weakly. "I don't think we will succeed. We are outnumbered."

I noticed that his hands were not steady.

"We will be crushed to the last man," he said. "But we will show them that we are not afraid. I guess that's it: heroism of the spirit."

"We have it, all right," I said.

Ganzo got up to reach for the bottle and suddenly crashed to the floor. I rushed to pick him up. Then I saw the horrible lacerations on his back! He, too, had been beaten! He looked helplessly at me.

"Gazamen has been caught," he whispered. "Try to do something, Carl."

I could not do anything for Gazamen. I stayed with Ganzo until the following morning. I was drinking coffee when I heard Marian's horn. How she knew where I was, I have never found out. I told Ganzo that I was leaving for Los Angeles.

"Are you quitting?" he asked.

"No. But I would like to have a few days of rest."

"Don't desert us, Carl. No matter what becomes of you. No matter where you are. Good-bye!"

I ran to the car feeling like a traitor. Marian was silent for a long time while we were among the hills and the wide fields, the verdant valleys and forests. It was only when we were entering Santa Barbara that she began to talk.

We stopped on Cañon Perdido Street, where Marian told me to wait. But when she drove off, I walked to the Chinese district. There I met Florencio Garcia, a busboy in a local hotel, who took me to his room over a garage. In the narrow space between his bed and a pile of books, Garcia sat down and started reading his manuscripts to me. He was writing, he said, but could not sell his stories. He jumped to his feet when he wanted to emphasize some point, stabbing the air with his fists.

"I'll be the greatest Filipino novelist in my time!" he screamed, his hungry eyes popping in their sockets.

"You will, Florencio," I said.

"I'll not be a busboy for long. I'll show them!"

His urge to write was spurred by hate. I recalled another lonely Filipino writer who had committed suicide, and I felt sorry for Florencio. I knew that he would destroy himself like Estevan, who had jumped from the window of his hotel when starvation had reached his mind. When I made a motion to leave, Florencio started to cry.

"Don't leave me, Carl!" he wept. "I'm lonely. I have not

found a human being for twelve years. Don't ever leave me, my friend!"

I walked down the creaking stairs, looking up at his window when I reached the ground. I saw his ugly face, breaking into tears. I walked back to Cañon Perdido Street and slapped my own face so that I would not cry.

Marian was waiting for me. "Hello, Carl," she said, leaning over to touch my face. Then she started the car, driving faster and faster as we sped toward Los Angeles.

It was only when we reached Santa Monica that my tension died. I got out in the business district of Los Angeles and told Marian to meet me at a downtown hotel. She was gone for three days. I stayed in my room most of the time. I tried to contact Macario, but failed. I knew that Amado was in Phoenix with the lawyer.

I communicated with Conrado in Seattle about the progress of the work there. He wrote that there had been a clash between the union and the company. I felt helpless and torn. I stayed in my room without food, thinking, fighting against myself, and waiting for Marian. When she appeared, singing and laughing, I was disarmed. I could not run away from her.

"Now you can go to the university," she said, tossing a roll of money on the bed. "Nearly three hundred dollars. All for you—from Marian." She laughed. "I have deposited some more for you, Carl. Now I'll go to bed, but wake me up if I over-sleep."

She flung herself upon the bed and in a few minutes she was sound asleep. I stood watching her face. I took off her shoes and dress and tucked her inside the bed. It was like a fairy tale. Here I was with a white woman who had completely surrendered herself to me. "*The human heart is bigger than the world,*" I said to myself.

Marian woke up at ten in the evening. "Let's have a *capitalist* dinner," she said.

I had no idea of what she was driving at. But I said: "All right, Marian."

"Thank you," she said.

"For what?"

"For mentioning my name. I like the sound of it. The feel of it, too. Thank you again!"

"It's love, I guess."

She put her face up like a white rose and wept. Then she pushed me gently away and said, "Turn away now. I'll change my dress."

I turned away, amused. She was dancing and humming. When I looked at her, I was startled by her beauty. She seemed an entirely new person. She was wearing a dark suit: there was a red hat in her left hand and a pair of white gloves in the other. She was tall and straight and lovely. She was the song of my dark hour.

We took a taxi and went to a famous night club in Hollywood. I was afraid to go inside, but did not want to show my fear to Marian. I followed her slowly, hardening myself. But I found that the people were more tolerant there than in any other place. They looked toward our table now and then, but it was merely curiosity.

I looked at Marian's animated face. It was unbelievable that I could sit with a *white* girl in a famous place. I began remembering my years in the freight trains. Marian touched my hand. Oh, she was happy! She wanted to dance. I had never danced in a place like this, but I would do anything for Marian. I knew that if a man insulted me, I would jump at him with my knife. But the people were very tolerant. We danced twice; then, having swept the dining room with a beaming face, Marian told me that she was tired.

It was when we were crossing the street toward my hotel that she fainted. I gathered her in my arms, put her on my bed, and called a doctor.

"She is very sick," he said. "I'll have to transfer her to my office."

"It is the only way?"

"It is."

I could not sleep when Marian was gone. I went to the doctor's office early the next morning. Marian was sitting up in bed.

"It was foolish of me to faint last night," she said apologetically. "It was such a lovely evening."

"I'll always remember it," I said. "How do you feel?"

She turned away. She looked at me again when I touched her hand.

"Listen carefully, Carl," she said. "When I'm gone remember me once in a while. And if you meet someone that you could like, take her with you and remember my face in hers."

"Don't talk like that, Marian."

"I'm dying—didn't the doctor tell you? Look at those trees on the hills! Isn't this land of ours a paradise!" Silence. Then she said, "Promise me something, Carl."

I nodded.

"Promise me not to hate. But love—love everything good and clean. There is something in you that radiates like an inner light, and it affects others. Promise me to let it grow. . . ."

I wanted to ask her what I would do with her money, but she had turned toward the hills again. Her eyes were lost and faraway. Slowly she closed them; then she was sound asleep. I got up and walked away, committing her face to memory.

I went to see her again the following morning. She was delirious. The doctor told me to leave. I went to a bar and started drinking heavily. I staggered aimlessly along the street; then my mind collapsed into darkness. It is, I believe, called toxic amnesia. I found myself walking in Alhambra, ten miles away from Los Angeles.

I rushed to a public phone and called the doctor.

"You'd better hurry," he said. "It is only a matter of minutes."

I dashed down the street shouting for a taxi. When I arrived the doctor met me.

"It is too late," he said kindly. "She is gone now."

I was stunned. I groped blindly into the room and looked at her still face. Her brown hair was like a nest around her head. A nurse came in and slowly rolled her away. The world stood still. I walked outside and the doctor stopped me.

"What was it, doctor?" I asked.

"Syphilis," he said. "But it was more than that. Complications. She gave up without a struggle. I'm sorry I couldn't do anything for her."

Slowly I walked down the suddenly darkened street.

CHAPTER XXX

THE DEATH of Marian marked one of the darkest periods of my life. I bought a one-way ticket to Seattle. But I drank a pint of whisky in Bakersfield and lost consciousness until I reached Stockton, where I stopped because it was familiar to me. I wandered aimlessly on El Dorado Street, entering bars and drinking quantities of whisky. I did not know why I had suddenly turned to drinking; why I was driven into it by the death of a strange woman. Yet, looking back, perhaps it was because there was no other place for me to go, and because I met there only drunkards and other denizens of lost worlds who were as hopeless as I.

I went to a Chinese restaurant and tried to eat. I went to a Japanese place and waited for hours for it to open. When I could wait no longer, I went to a liquor store and bought a bottle of port wine. I met a Filipino farm worker who helped me finish it. Then I lost consciousness; when I came to myself again, I was sprawling on a chair at the Lincoln Hotel. It was already morning, but the lobby was still dark.

Then I walked blindly to the station; luckily, there was a bus waiting. I climbed aboard and tried to sleep. Two girls were singing in the back seat. I dozed off now and then, but at Roseville I began to feel better.

A girl with a red ribbon in her hair, who was called Rosaline, suggested that I sing with them. We sang several popular tunes and ended with *America*, which affected an elderly lady on the first row. The other girl, Lily, was more talkative than her companion. It seemed that they had left their town without telling their parents. They had gone to San Diego, married sailors, and were now on their way home to break the news to their families.

In Redding, where the air smelled of pine trees, I stepped out and went to the cocktail bar in the station. I had a few drinks, and when I came out the bus had already gone. I told my predicament to the driver of another bus, which had just arrived, and we were off in pursuit, speeding up and down the mountain highway until we caught up with the first bus forty miles away.

We were now entering the forest country. Lily and Rosaline were sleeping, their heads close to each other, their mouths open in calm repose. I woke them up and gave them the sandwiches I had bought for them, and they thanked me very prettily. I looked out the window and saw a little girl milking a cow. She looked in the direction of the bus and waved her hand.

It was a familiar land. How many times had I passed through it? The air was clean. The trees were tall and straight. I could see little streams in the deep canyons below. Now we were nearing the place where I had been humiliated by two highway patrolmen.

"Why don't you stop in Medford?" Lily asked when we were crossing the Oregon border. "We have a nice lake and a big dancing pavilion."

"You could stay at our house," Rosaline said.

"I invited him first," Lily said.

"I'll accept your invitation to stop in Medford," I said. "But I'll stay at a hotel. All right?"

It was the best solution, they agreed. The girls' mothers came to meet them. I was embarrassed, but they gave me their hands. Lily explained how they had met me, my nationality and a little of the history of the Philippines, which she seemed to know. I felt at home with these people who had never seen Filipinos, and I wept a little in my room when they took me to a hotel, while they were waiting in the lobby for me.

When the dinner at Lily's house was over, I was suddenly lonely for Marian. Rosaline, noting my introspection, suggested that we go to the lake. They invited some of their friends. We rode in two jalopies, singing in the bright moonlight and the soft wind that sighed through the pine trees. The night was like an arrested dream: so calm it was almost unreal.

Then the lake came into view; like a piece of polished glass, it lay in the palm of a dark hand. The jalopies stopped; the girls and boys jumped out and undressed hastily, plunging naked into the waiting water. I watched their agile bodies glide through the phosphorescent water.

I laughed and swam among them, trying to forget my own tragedy. Now and then I stood up in the water remembering the time when my father and I had gone to the mountains. I remembered the clear, deep pool where we had bathed. Lily suddenly pushed me vigorously and swam away, turning back to see if I would follow her. I dived and swam swiftly under the water. I caught her and for a moment was tempted to hold her tightly; but I merely splashed water into her face and swam away.

It was already midnight when we returned to Medford, and they all accompanied me to my hotel. Rosaline sent one of the girls to get her radio, and we started dancing in my room and the clerk, a man about forty, came up and danced with Lily. Then they all left and waved good-bye to me when they reached the street. I watched them disappear with a great loneliness.

I called the clerk for something to drink. He came up with a bottle of bourbon and we sat drinking and talking for hours. When he left, I went to bed, trying to forget Marian. I awakened in time for the first bus. I wrote a note to Lily and Rosaline and their friends, and gave it to the morning clerk.

I was full of premonition when I arrived in Seattle. Walking on King Street, I came accidentally upon Conrado Torres. We went to a Japanese restaurant and sat in a corner.

"Something big will break soon," he said. "The Japanese contractors have hired some thugs and they are running around with guns."

"Who do you think is the victim?" I asked.

"It's a fellow named Dagohoy. He started the union in the fish canneries; that is, he is the first president. Now the Japanese contractors, and perhaps Filipinos also, are after him."

"Is it a conspiracy of the Japanese contractors?"

"Well, in a way. Actually, however, the friction arose because a powerful Japanese contractor feared he would be deprived of his income when the cannery workers were organized. He was making a fortune from his double-dealings with the companies and with the workers. But when a progressive union was born . . ."

I suddenly discovered that I was sitting in the same corner where I had sat years before. The place was unchanged. There was even my name and the date of my arrival in the United States where I had carved it on the table. I kept remembering the shooting in the street outside; and the policemen spreading out to catch the crazed Filipino gambler, trapping him in the basement of a hotel. Then Marcelo came to my mind also, and the tall blonde who had screamed when the lights had gone out in the dance hall. Wherever I went memories crowded my mind, and sometimes my heart was heavy. But I could run away or forget. I was pursued by my own life.

Then something happened so swiftly that I could scarcely believe it. Dagohoy and two other Filipinos, also officers of the newly established cannery workers' union, came into the restaurant while we were leaving. Conrado and I were talking outside when we heard shooting inside; then suddenly people started running into the restaurant.

We followed them. Dagohoy was profusely bleeding from bullet wounds, crumbling over one of his dead comrades. The other Filipino was sagging on his knees. They had no chance to defend themselves against their assailants.

All of them died. It was believed that a Japanese labor contractor in the fish canneries in Alaska had hired assassins to eliminate the leaders of the union.

I *knew*—now. This violence had a broad social meaning; the one I had known earlier was a blind rebellion. It was perpetrated by men who had no place in the scheme of life. I felt a deep responsibility for Dagohoy's death. But I left Seattle immediately when he was buried. I went to San Francisco where a meeting of Filipino trade unionists was scheduled.

But I did not stay long in San Francisco. When I had seen

José, who was still nursing his wounds received in the San Jose incident, I left word for Ganzo, who was also in San Francisco, to go to the meeting. I was still tracing a maze and it seemed impossible for me to stay in one place without feeling persecuted and hunted.

I left for Salinas, where I found Mariano. I was in Pismo Beach when I received word that the United Cannery, Agricultural, Packing and Allied Workers of America (UCAPAWA) had been formed and had adopted a broad democratic program. Now we really had something around which to rally our forces.

I waited for José, and when he came, I left him in Santa Maria where he planned an intensive campaign. The UCAPAWA had assigned him to Central California, a fascist country, where he had failed before with Helen, the strike-breaker and professional agitator for the powerful farmers. I told José that I was leaving for Los Angeles, where I expected to pick up some of my clothes, but would return to work with him.

I agreed to meet José in Lompoc, but did not go there. I did not go back to active duty, because before long I went to a county hospital and stayed there for two years. I was lying in a sickbed when war was going on in Spain, a civil war to stop the tide of fascism from spreading throughout the world.

I found my brother Macario in Los Angeles. He was again staying with Victor. I was writing in their room when a girl knocked at the door. She came in unannounced and told me that she knew my brother and Nick, who was now working in a night club in Hollywood. Dora Travers, for that was her name, waited until nine in the evening for my brother. Then she asked me to take a walk with her, because she was becoming restless in the room.

"Are you a member of the YCL?" Dora asked when we were eating in a Mexican place on Main Street.

"What is that?" I said.

"Don't pretend that you don't know what it is!" There was genuine arrogance in her voice.

"I don't know what it is—really," I said, feeling foolish.

She said proudly: "It's the Young Communist League."

"What makes you think that I would be useful to the organization?" I said. "I don't know anything about it. You see, I have been on the move since I was a little kid. . . ."

"Don't be silly, Carl!"

I wanted to leave her then, because I was angry. Yet I needed her company, her nearness, her assurance. My lonely life had made me sensitive to words and sounds, and when one of these touched my inner feelings, I became drunk with it as on wine.

So it was with Dora. I was intrigued by her sweeping generalizations. She walked beside me silently to my brother's hotel, but Macario was still out. We climbed the narrow passageway to the top of the hotel. There was a light breeze. The beacon lights on the city hall were stabbing the sky.

Dora sat in a corner, her back to the wall. In a little while she fell sound asleep. I felt a slight tug at my heart. I watched her still face. She was no longer arrogant. She even looked lonely in repose. I turned away from her, looking over the city in the night.

The next morning I sat in my brother's room and started to write a poem, remembering Dora Travers and how she slept.

I read the poem to Dora when she came again.

"Write more poems, Carl," she said. "I don't care if you are a Communist or not. I like your music. I think you will be a good *American* poet."

I was glad. I felt inspired. Yes, there was music in me, and it was stirring to be born. I wrote far into the night, subsisting on coffee and bread. I did not stop to analyze why my thoughts and feelings found expression in poetry. It was enough that I was creating. I was like a little boy who had suddenly come upon a treasure of gold. I felt the words come to my mind effortlessly. I wrote ten or fifteen poems in one sitting.

Then I knew surely that I had become a new man. I could fight the world now with my mind, not merely with my hands. My weapon could not be taken away from me any more. I had an even chance to survive the brutalities around me. But I was beginning to cough, and I could not sleep at night. I was sick: the years of hunger had found me at last.

I was reading some new poems to Dora when I began to cough violently and could not stop. I rushed to the bathroom and bent over the washbowl, coughing out blood and bringing tears to my eyes. Dora came and held my head, rubbing my throat and forehead. When Macario arrived he called a doctor.

"What is it, doctor?" he asked.

"I'm afraid it is TB," he said. "Advanced stage. I'm sorry."

"Oh, Carl!" Dora said.

There was great shock in Macario's face. He knew what it meant then: that I, too, would have to wait for slow death. How did my brother Luciano die? He had gone to Binalonan and waited ten years; when he died, finally, there was nothing left of his body. Macario stood by my bed for a long time. The gentleness came back to his face, as though I were a little boy again.

"Don't worry, Carlos," he said kindly. "I'll find a job and stay in it until you get well. I'll do anything until you are well again."

CHAPTER XXXI

A<small>T FIRST</small> I did not realize the extent of the disease. I did not know that it would incapacitate me for years. But during the first days of anxiety, lying in bed alone and thinking of my interrupted work, I had only one desire: to get well as soon as possible and go back to the labor movement. It was an exhilarating feeling—this belonging to something vitally alive in America. But when three months passed and my condition seemed to get worse, I began to doubt that I would get well. I became intensely aware of the room: the four gray walls that seemed to fall upon me, the antiquated furniture, ugly and dark, and the utter dullness of everything around me. And I became aware of the presence of other things that had seemed inconsequential before: why Macario—why all of us were constantly hounded by the terrible threat of unemployment and disease.

Macario found work in a restaurant on North Broadway. He would come home at noon with sandwiches and soup, and leave in the early afternoon to resume his work. It was not easy to make salads and pastries in an Italian restaurant that fed nearly five thousand customers a day.

I wanted to run away so that Macario could pursue his own career. I wanted to lose myself somewhere in the world so that he would be free to live his own life. But I crumpled on the floor when I tried to get up, crawling and moaning until Macario arrived from work.

"You shouldn't get up, Carlos," he said lovingly. "Just stay in bed and wait for me. I'll get you some books tomorrow."

I felt angry with myself. Why did I have to be sick? I disliked pity and sentiment, yet I was sentimental and always pitying some unfortunate creature. If I could only get up on my feet and run in the sun again!

Once in a while Dora came to read my poems, weeping silently when the lines touched her. I was unhappy when she did not appear for a week. But when she came again there was sadness in her face.

"What is it, Dora?" I asked.

"I'm going to the Soviet Union, Carl," she said. "I'm going home."

"Home?" I did not understand her. "What do you mean *home?*"

"I was born there. I came to the United States with my parents when I was two years old. I'm going back to have my child born in a land without racial oppression."

"I didn't know you were going to have a child."

"It's Nick's child. I have always wanted a Filipino child. It wouldn't have a chance in America, just as Nick has never had a chance."

How could she again condemn America in one sweeping generalization? Dora Travers went to New York and from there she disappeared from my life.

I was writing poetry in bed, trying to forget the monotony of my life. Then several of my poems appeared in *Poetry: A Magazine of Verse*. I felt it was a great triumph for me, and also a definite identification with an intellectual tradition. Now I could lie in bed and write down all my thoughts.

I received a letter from the editor of the magazine, Harriet Monroe, telling me that she would like to arrange with a university to give me some kind of scholarship. I was overjoyed, but did not tell her about my confinement. I did not explain to her that I did not have the necessary requirements to enter college.

Soon afterward Harriet Monroe went to South America to attend an international convention of the P. E. N. Club, and from there she wrote again that she would pass through Los Angeles and hoped to see me. I was greatly excited. Here was a famous editor who wanted to help me, one who had discovered most of America's leading poets and writers. I read her magazine and the work of her discoveries. There was something definitely American, something positively vital, in all of them—but more visible in Hart Crane, Malcolm Cowley, William Faulkner, and also in their older contemporaries, Carl Sandburg, John Gould Fletcher, Vachel Lindsay. I could follow the path of these poets, continue their tradition, and if, at the end of my career, I could arrive at a positive understanding of America, then I could go back to the Philippines with a torch of enlightenment. And perhaps, if given a chance, I could help liberate the peasantry from ignorance and poverty.

It was a bold dream—so big it tore one apart. But shortly afterward, on her way back to the United States, Harriet Monroe died somewhere in the Andes Mountains. It was the death of a dream which did not come to life again for several years.

Before Harriet Monroe left the United States she wrote about me to Jean Doyle, a contributor to *Poetry*. She came with a young man who was a versatile poet, and reminded me of the time when I had visited her house some years before—when I had been a migratory worker. But she did not remind me of the three hard-boiled eggs and the sandwiches that she had shoved into my pockets when I left, because she knew that I was hungry. I had walked on the dark side of the street then and eaten the sandwiches, and once again the stars had sung in the sky. I had been looking for this side of America; surely this was the real side of living America. . . .

It was at this time that a young woman in Hollywood, a writer of promise, saw my poems and wrote to me. Her name was Alice Odell—a familiar name, because I had seen it under the titles of some fine proletarian short stories. But now, she wrote, she was writing a novel about her starved childhood in Utah, and she would like to show me what she had written.

I was in a quandary. I could not ask her to come to my room, because the landlady would not allow *white* women in the building. I wrote back telling her that I was leaving town indefinitely. I did not know how I could meet her. But back of it all, I think, was what I thought of as social position. I knew from the way she wrote that she was a person of intelligence and of a more privileged life than the women I had known, and because of this barrier between us I was reluctant to meet her. This fear of the middle classes was deep-rooted: it had sprung from the humiliations of my mother and I suffered when we were selling beans in Binalonan and neighboring towns. It followed me down the years until I became brave enough to fight it.

But Alice Odell was a persistent woman. She had warmth and a genius for arousing warmth. So finally I agreed to meet her at the Los Angeles Public Library. I was too weak to walk. I had been in bed for months, and normal activity was almost impossible. I staggered like an old man into the library, leaning against the brick wall when my knee bothered me. It had never mended and it was the unforgettable souvenir of the vigilantes in San Jose, who had tortured me that night in the woods.

I sat at a table in the Literature Department and watched the clock. At exactly three o'clock an attractive woman with dark brown hair came to the door and swept the room in one fleeting glance. I knew at once that she was Alice Odell and I was not mistaken.

I got up to greet her. But touching her hand, I became self-conscious. I wrote what I wanted to say on a piece of paper, and she also wrote what she wanted to say, so we wrote notes to each other as though we were mutes. She was very kind: she thought I was ashamed to talk to her. But I was only afraid she could not understand me, because my accent was still thick and difficult. I wrote again that we could go out in the sun, so she took my hand and helped me down the stone steps of the library.

I sat beside her on a stone bench. There were little dark birds among the trees, and we looked blankly at them. Where should I begin? Could I tell her about my years of flight? The brutalities and horrors? Maybe we could discuss poetry and current prose writing. Perhaps I could tell her about my family and my childhood in the Philippines. How would I approach a *decent* white woman? How was I to begin?

Alice was understanding. She was sensitive and lonely. She started talking of herself, revealing the background of an American life. When I showed concern for the development of this life into what it had become—into Alice Odell—she described the terror that had haunted her childhood. Then it came to me that her life and mine were the same, terrified by the same forces; they had only happened in two different countries and to two people.

Alice had been born in a small farming town, but her father's farm had been ruined by tornadoes. Once, in a desperate year, her father and grandfather planted broom wheat, but a tornado had swept it all away. It was her family's last attempt to hold onto the land. They moved to Iowa, and Alice watched her father become a gambler.

"My father taught me a trick," she said softly. "When the gamblers came to our house, I would stand by the table and watch them. Then my father would say, 'Alice, show the men something cute!' I would catch the hem of my dress, give a wide grin, and pull it up to my chest. And the men would howl and stamp on the floor, throwing coins into the fold of my dress. I was four—maybe five. But my mother was always away when the gamblers came; she would be working somewhere or visiting friends. My mother—"

She stopped, wiping the tears from her eyes.

"I have a mother, too," I said, remembering, running down the years to my mother, fighting wildly through the mud of Binalonan to reach her as she picked up the scattered beans in the public market of Puzzorobio. "My mother is poor. We are poor peasants in Luzon."

Alice had been born poor too. But she grew up rapidly and had sent herself through school.

"Then I was a reporter on a small-town paper," she said. "I helped Eileen, my sister, who was going to high school."

When Alice talked of her sister it was as though Eileen were her own daughter. But Iowa was becoming smaller every day, driving Alice into a corner until she could no longer breathe. Finally she went to Hollywood and found a job as secretary to a man who had gone bankrupt. And once again Alice was thrown into the world, without work, young and lonely. Then she met a Puerto Rican—a fine man, she said—whom she wanted to love. She went with him to Puerto Rico and lived with him on a large plantation. What happened between them she did not tell me.

But she came back to the United States, to Hollywood, and after a year of working at odd jobs, met a wealthy man who became her lover.

She could send for Eileen now, and she did. Eileen was teaching in a little Nebraska town. But Hollywood was more glamorous, and the splendor of Alice's new life was tempting.

"Eileen had two pupils last year," Alice said. "But this year she has only one—a boy."

I laughed. Only one pupil!

Shortly after Eileen had arrived in Hollywood, Alice's lover had left her. Left with nothing, she sold a diamond ring and rented an apartment for them. When winter came, Eileen fell ill with tuberculosis. It was a bad year for them, for Alice was attacked by pneumonia.

She had wanted to begin from the beginning: her early responses to life, the influences of various environments. She wanted to say that she had been made stronger and more courageous; that she was not like other women who are afraid to break through the walls of prejudice. But although she felt that way about other women, Alice believed in their essential dignity, because she herself had it, so simply, so strongly.

This, I believe now, was what she actually wanted to say.

The following week, when I was alone in the room, Alice came unannounced, and I wondered how she had escaped the ever-vigilant landlady. She found me in bed, coughing and sweating miserably. When I told her about the progress of my disease, she sat by the bed and comforted me. Then sitting near me, she began to read Thomas Wolfe's *Look Homeward, Angel*.

"This is about a boy who had a great hunger for life," she told me. "He was a big boy—so big he wanted to acquire all knowledge, see the whole world, embrace all humanity. He was a very unhappy boy. He grew up into manhood and loneliness."

"I like that passage," I said when she had finished reading of the mountains in this big boy's childhood. "We also have mountains in Mangusmana. But no trains."

Once, fragrant with violets, Alice came with food and fed me. She felt that I had been confined too long. She put my black hat on my head and told me that I needed fresh air. We went out and walked in the late summer afternoon.

We went to the Japanese section and walked in San Pedro Street, stopping in the dark alleys near the factories.

There was a thorn in my heart. I stumbled to a dark little house and sat on the broken wooden steps. Alice followed me, and sat beside me in the gathering dusk. But the occupants of the house, an old man and his wife, came home and told us to leave.

We walked back to the hotel. I was tired and weak, and went eagerly to bed.

I stayed in bed. On the fourth of June, when Victor was coming home from the movie studio where he was working as an extra, an ambulance came to take me to the Los Angeles County Hospital.

I watched the buildings, committing them to memory. I knew that I would not see them for a long time.

My ward was above the hospital jail. It was dark and overflowing with dying men. The building was old and all the patients had contagious diseases. But I felt happy when Alice Odell came to see me, bringing her youth and vitality.

"I'm leaving tomorrow, Carl," she said one day.

"Where are you going?" I asked, feeling a weight in my heart.

"East. I have a job in New York. I hope you will get well soon, Carlos."

From Chicago, she sent me Herbert Gorman's *Herman Melville*. Later she sent me Marcel Proust's *Remembrance of Things Past*. And again a pamphlet edition of Frederic Prokosch's *The Asiatics*. She was directing my education, I felt, and I read everything she sent me.

I wrote a series of poems and called it, "For the Builders of

Cities." I sent them to Alice. As I was being prepared for the operating table, Alice phoned me from New York and said that she liked my poems. The operation was successful, and I wrote her about it. But when I heard from her again she told me she was on her way to the Soviet Union.

CHAPTER XXXII

WHEN Alice Odell had left California she had asked her sister to visit me. One day Eileen came with several books and a large paper sack full of delicacies. When I saw her emerge from the long hallway, I was surprised to see that she was almost crystalline. She was the exact opposite of her sister: there was no disturbing sensuousness about her. She was tall, erect, and smiling, and, I found later, derided sentimentality. Her objectivity perhaps stemmed from the poverty of her childhood—the same influences that had made Alice rebellious.

I did not know then that I would see Eileen almost every week for three years. I did not know that we would share each other's thoughts, live each other's lives. What had been begun by Alice was finding continuance in Eileen, in her intellectual honesty, her almost maternal solicitude.

I was shy when Eileen was near me. But when she had gone, I opened the little bundles of roast meat, celery, tomatoes, and apples. I noticed that each item was carefully wrapped in wax paper. I noticed also that she always gave me many varieties of fruits and vegetables. I discovered later that her affinity for these was the aftermath of their absence in her childhood. And so at last in California, with its abundance, she had developed a taste for vegetables and fruits that was almost animalistic.

I created for myself an illusion of understanding with Eileen, and in consequence, I yearned for her and the world she represented. The grass in the hospital yard spoke of her, and when it rained, the water rushed down the eaves calling her name. I told her these things in poems, and my mind became afire: could I get well for Eileen? Could I walk with her in the street without being ashamed because of my race? Could I see her always without fear?

But she talked but little when she came to see me. When she left, leaving some books, I imagined I read the words she would have spoken. And so from week to week, Eileen came and sat quietly near me, leaving just as quietly. We found intimate conversations in the books she gave me. When I became restless, I wrote to her. Every day the words poured out of my pen. I began to cultivate a taste for words, not so much their meanings as their sounds and shapes, so that afterward I tried to depend only on the music of words to express my ideas. This procedure, of course, was destructive to my grammar, but I can say that writing fumbling, vehement letters to Eileen was actually my course in English. What came after this apprenticeship—the structural presentation of ideas in pertinence to the composition and the anarchy between man's experience and ideals—was merely my formal search.

One of the numerous books that Eileen gave me, *World Politics* by R. Palme Dutt, was a revelation of great significance. It gave me a realistic approach to history, for here before my eyes human civilization unfolded in one continuous procession of struggle against tyranny. To go back farther, she gave me Lewis Morgan's *Ancient History*, Robert Briffault's *Rational Evolution*, and Frederic Engels's *Origin of the Family*.

I trembled with excitement and a feeling of superiority. Here within my grasp was one of the great discoveries in the life of man. Why was it kept from the world? Perhaps Eileen knew the reason. But when she came the words died in my mouth, for there was only a flow of appreciation. As the months passed a feeling of understanding was cemented between us, and she wept silently when I suffered pain and loneliness.

Eileen's frugality was also conditioned by the past. She dreaded the approach of winter, the horrors of poverty in Hollywood, where the economic pitch was sky-blown. Yet she managed to send me flowers occasionally, on important holidays. She was undeniably the *America* I had wanted to find in those frantic days of fear and flight, in those acute hours of hunger and loneliness. This America was human, good, and real.

When I found Eileen I found the god of my youth. I can say that my insatiable hunger for knowledge and human affection were the two vital forces that made my days of great loneliness and starvation a frantic determination to live. In the back of my mind was the parting request of my sister Francisca—that I would go to school in America and return to the Philippines to teach both my sisters to read because they had had no chance in the village. But now it had changed, for I was beginning to think that if I returned to my native land, I would spread a new enlightenment to my whole village—perhaps throughout the Philippines.

And my hunger for affection, because of the lack of it in America, had driven me blindly to Eileen, and my long-denied urge to feel a part of the life about me burst forth like a blazon of burning stars. This force annihilated all personal motives, and again I began to feel stirrings inside me, coming out in torrents of poetry.

My knee began to interfere with my nights of rest and days of study. The doctor put it in a cast hoping that the shooting pain would cease. I lay immobile, because the slightest movement of any part of my body would arouse the pain in my knee and spread it to all parts of my frame. I read ceaselessly, suffering, trying to forget that I was dying.

I could scarcely eat any more. When I ate my soup, because I could take no solid food, the nurse put a glass siphon in my mouth. There seemed to be no hope for me. From the open porch, where the convalescing patients were kept, I was transferred to a dark little room where three other patients lay waiting to die. There was a young man whose throat was stuffed with rubber tubes. I watched him die clawing for breath, gasping desperately for the air that could not enter his lungs.

I knew it was hard to die. It was hard to live I had discovered, but it was even harder to die. Why did some men live thoughtlessly? Why did they think life was something they could borrow from other men?

The other two men, old and lonely, also died gasping for the last bit of air. They stared blankly into the ceiling, waiting for the final heartbeat. When death came to them, and it came slowly, they closed their eyes and put their hands over their flat chests. Then they were dead. I could see the deep yellow lines in their still faces.

The cast on my leg only provoked the pain. At last the doctor told me that he would attempt an operation. I was wheeled through the long tunnel between the TB buildings and the new hospital. I waited in the hall near the operating room for what seemed hours before two nurses came and prepared me for the table. An interne injected a local anesthetic into my spine. When the drug began to take effect, I saw the doctor come into the room. He patted my leg and spoke to his assistants. Then I was swallowed by a deep sinking darkness that carried me into eternities.

Three hours afterward I began to hear faint whispers around me. It was like waking from a dream. The doctor had done his job and was gone. The internes were putting on a new cast. I could see filmy white shadows in the gallery, where medical students were watching and taking notes. Then I was swallowed by the impenetrable darkness again.

When I awakened it was morning. I could hear a slight rain falling. Eagerly I looked about the clean, well-lighted room. My leg was suspended from a small rack strapped across my bed. Everything smelled fresh and new; evidently I was in the new building.

Eileen came the following Sunday. She was anxious to know what the doctor had done to my leg. I told her that the doctor had cut off two inches of bone and put the knee together with four sharp steel spikes. I was to wear the cast until the muscles had grown together and were strong enough to encase the bones.

"My leg will be stiff from now on," I said.

"Oh." She started to cry.

When she had gone I discovered that she had left a copy of Rainer Marie Rilke's *Journal of My Other Self*, a book which later led me to other writers: Franz Kafka, Ernst Toller, Federico Garcia Lorca, and Heinrich Heine. These writers collectively represented to me a heroism of the spirit, so immeasurably had they suffered the narrowness of the world in which they lived, so gloriously had they succeeded in inspiring a universal brotherhood among men.

When I became better a nurse pushed my bed into a larger room, where two patients were recuperating from operations. One was a boy of ten whose arms had been amputated; the other was a young man who had had three operations. The boy's courage made me feel at once brave and ashamed.

I was wheeled back to my ward in the old building across the tunnel. It was Christmas Eve. Eileen came with pieces of roast chicken and fruits. She was soaked through from the rain. I noticed that she was unhappy, but tried to conceal it. She had not heard from Alice since the war had started in Spain.

"The Loyalist Government is denied help from all the capitalist countries," she said. "Now it is desperately fighting a death struggle."

"But Soviet Russia is sending men," I said.

"It's not enough. Mussolini and Hitler are sending planes and tanks."

That was the way Eileen always talked. She took it for granted that I knew the world situation, that I understood her political views. I wanted to—yes. But it actually took me several years to really achieve a literate understanding of fascism.

When Eileen left I wrote a poem for her.

Eileen came again and again, bringing books and magazines, writing paper and stamps and envelopes. She wanted to be sure that I would read and then write to her. Sometimes she brought friends—one of them, Laura Clarendorn, was a young woman who had just written a proletarian novel about the Northwest. This book, the first of its genre to appear in the early thirties, had won a national contest. It had the defects and crudities of a form that was taking shape out of the sterility of American writing: the racialism of Margaret Mitchell, the opportunism of Ben Hecht, the decadence of Joseph Hergesheimer, and other literary barbarians of that period.

But what attracted me to the book was its Filipino protagonist.

Hitherto Filipinos had been only stockpile characters in entertaining stories such as those by Peter B. Kyne or Rupert Hughes. When Laura Clarendorn came again with her husband, a composer and professor of music, I urged her to go deeper into Filipino life in America.

I felt she would write it. She was still in her middle twenties and had plenty of time. But she never wrote another book, and I never heard from her again. About the time she disappeared from American literature, I witnessed the emergence of a new writing. It was, however, a direct product of the form such as Laura Clarendorn had helped to shape, not a counterpart of it as some reactionary critics would have people believe.

When some of my Filipino friends came to visit while Eileen was with me, I would tell them to wait in the dark hallway. I felt ashamed. But I understood them. One such friend, Felix Razon, the rebel peasant from Tayug, understood me. He waited patiently; when Eileen was gone he sat near me.

"The UCAPAWA is now well on its way," he began. "But there is a bigger task calling me."

"Are you thinking of leaving this country?" I asked.

He became serious. "Over in Spain an historical conflict is going on. The Italian-German fascists are sending tanks and planes to Franco. What is the rest of the democratic world doing for the Spanish peasants and workers? Spain is significant in our fight for democracy: the Loyalists are holding the destiny of the world. Do not laugh. You will see someday that I am right. If Republican Spain is crushed, fascism will spread, not only in Europe but throughout the world. I am afraid, Carl, of the world to come. I am tired now. But I have to fight on, Carl." He stopped and looked down, remembering, searching his past for some hope. And in a fleeting moment, I caught the startling image of the rebel peasant boy in the rice fields. "Spain is blockaded. The embargo law has been passed. We can't even send volunteers to Spain. But I'm going anyway, Carl. I'm going with twelve of our friends to Mexico. Your brother Macario and Nick will go with me."

I was startled. "I didn't know my brother was going with you. He didn't mention it to me last Sunday."

"He will see you tonight," Felix said.

Felix Razon went away. I never heard from him again. Whether he was killed in Spain I have never found out. He was one of those who gave meaning to the futilities of other men's lives—and one who, because he came from the peasantry, had planted in my heart the seed of black hatred against the landlords in the Philippines.

"All right, Felix Razon," I wrote in my diary when he went away. "You found no peace. The wise men lied to us. All right, go fight a war on another continent, like my brother Leon. But if I live I will go back to our country and fight the enemy there, because *he* is also among our people. . . ."

CHAPTER XXXIII

W HEN my brother Macario came to tell me that he was leaving for Spain, I realized that the Loyalist cause symbolized what he had been fighting for in California.

"Maybe dying under a fascist bomb doesn't necessarily mean that Filipinos would have the right to become naturalized American citizens," he said. "But it means that there are men of good will all over the world, in every race, in all classes. It means that the forces of democracy are found in all times, ready to rally behind a cause of worldwide significance."

My brother always talked as though he did not exist. He was working in a restaurant as a pantryman, but his ideas were so universal and his ideals so lofty I knew he meant everything that he said. There was something in the way he talked—the impeccable movements of his hands, for instance—that dispelled all doubts. Slowly he was giving form to my dream, showing me a coherence of thought and action. When he talked about a land far away that needed him, I knew that his idealism was so great that it moved his whole life.

I said: "It's much easier for us who have no roots to integrate ourselves in a universal ideal. Were we not exiles, were we not socially strangled in America, we would never have understood the significance of the Civil War in Spain."

"I hope you will not think that I'm running away from you, Carl," he said. He was looking at his rough hands, picking at them absent-mindedly.

I had not noticed his hands before. They were hard and calloused, like my mother's. They were ugly and twisted. I wanted to shout with anger at the whole world. Macario's cracked and bleeding hands. I wanted to grab and kiss them. Now, now that I was a grown man I knew the meaning of my father's struggles

to hold his land, my mother's sacrifices in order that her family
might survive.

I wanted to educate myself as fast as possible, and the fury
of my desire was so tumultuous, I could not rest. I was drawn
closer to Eileen Odell, and now, significantly enough, we were
beginning to discuss some of the books she gave me to read.

About William Faulkner I asked: "Why is he so concerned
with decay?"

Eileen said: "He writes about the South, where he lives. It
is a dying world; it is decayed; so he wants us to know that it
is futile to prop it up with a false foundation. The South was
built on human slavery, but the slaves are stirring. They will be
free and the South will collapse with its decadent institutions."

These would have been my own words. Were we thinking the
same thoughts? When Eileen was gone, I returned to some of
William Faulkner's books. I wanted to be confirmed. Strange that
I remembered many things! I could even remember a cousin who
used to scare the girls when they bathed in the creek near our
village. He would hide in the bushes and then spring from them
with a growl. The girls would run in all directions, their hands
flying to their naked legs and bouncing brown breasts. My
cousin was playful: he screamed with joy when he saw the girls
hopping about in the field.

When I was in Montana, during the beet season, I met a Jewish
girl in a drugstore. I remembered what she had said: "It is hard
to be a Jew!"

I also remembered a man in Binalonan who had killed another
man when he had tried to steal water from his irrigation ditch.
He sent his son to the town police to inform them of his crime.
A policeman came to his house while the man was eating.

They conversed in this fashion:

Policeman: "Señor Juan, are you ready to go to town with
me?"

Juan: "Could you wait for three hours? I have not had my
siesta yet."

Policeman: "I will wait, Mr. Juan. But don't sleep too long. I would like to attend the late cockfights."

So while the criminal was sleeping pleasantly the policeman sat under the house waiting for him. Now and then the policeman would climb up the ladder and look through the door to see if he was still asleep. When the man woke up he walked complacently with the policeman, stopping now and then at a wine store for a glass and to inform the loafers of his crime. But in the *presidencia*, free to wander about like the non-prisoners, he played chess with the policemen and hangers-on. Sometimes he played baseball with the schoolboys in the yard. He was also free to eat at home, and the policemen would sling him across a horse when he had too much wine.

I laughed when I remembered the prisoner in Binalonan. I did not know, however, that I would someday write a book about my town's characters; that because I wrote about them as human beings, I would invoke the philistinism of educated Filipinos and the petty bourgeoisie, and the arrogance of officials of the Philippine government in Washington.

CHAPTER XXXIV

I was psychologically unprepared when the doctor started operating on me. Two other experiments by another doctor —phrenic operation and a treatment called pneumothorax—failed to assuage the widening lesion in my right lung. The contagion was rapidly spreading to my left lung, and thoracoplasty, or a rib operation, was the last possible way to arrest its advance.

My first operation came in June; in three weeks I had another. Finally in the middle of August, when the wound had healed, I had the third and last. The last was easy and the wound healed faster than the other two. I saw the doctor before he left the hospital.

He said, "You have no more ribs on your right side, young man. But you will live for a while. *Mabuhay!*"

For a while! All right, then. I lay on my right side so that my weight would press my body down, one way of finding relief from the pain. I was transferred to a small ward where another patient, a tall Mexican, was waiting for his operation. His left lung was gone. There was a wide hole in his back, where two small rubber tubes were inserted to drain out the fluid. He could not speak English, but we understood each other.

One Sunday night, during the visiting hours, the Mexican told me to watch for the door when his wife came. The wife, a gaudy woman, gathered her dress about her and went into the bed with her husband.

I woke up the next morning to see a nurse rolling the Mexican away. He was dead. Maybe he knew that he would die. I had seen men die before, but not the way this Mexican died.

I returned to the old building. I went to my place on the porch, facing the lawn where WPA workers were digging a wide hole. There were three: a supervisor, who was always lying under a

tree, a man with a shovel, and another man who took the shovel
from him when he was not reading a newspaper. When the hole
was about five feet deep the two men would fill it up with the
earth that they had dug from it. Then they would move about
ten feet from it and start digging another hole. For six months
they dug holes in the lawn and filled them up. I wondered what
they were doing. But when they were gone some of the patients
said that it was one way of keeping unemployed men out of
trouble.

Once a week, on Sundays, amateur musicians and singers came
to the hospital. I was still on my back, so the attendants propped
me up. Their voices cracked, but I enjoyed the hula-hula dancers.
Some of the patients who could afford it threw dimes and quarters on the floor. The entertainers went from ward to ward,
dancing and singing, but six months afterward they stopped
coming. It was then that the WPA was vehemently assailed by
reactionary politicians in Congress.

But I had my books. Throughout that year I read one book
a day including Sundays. I could obtain all the books I wanted
from Eileen Odell. I discovered a world of music, of light and
immortal things. I trembled with delight when I came upon a
brilliant phrase or a novel idea. While the other patients were
worrying and complaining, I explored the worlds of great men's
living minds.

One of these men was an American poet, Hart Crane, who
wrote *The Bridge*. His intense frenzy of words captivated my
imagination. I leaped with him across the magnificent steel arc
over the river, flew into the dizzy heights of fire, plunged into
the sea and peace. Here was a writer in the tradition of Whitman
and Melville: he tried to find a faith strong enough to challenge
modern chaos. The bridge, the symbol of his faith in America,
an ecstatic conjuration against false gods and legends, was also
a myth that he tried to create out of the turmoil of modern
industrialism.

And another book, Mikhail Sholokhov's *And Quiet Flows the
Don*, gave me a panorama of the historic birth of a socialist country. But it also gave me an insight into the collective faith of a

people, its growth and flowering. I knew that it was good literature, that it was honest and written with a *purpose*. It was an introduction to other Russian writers: Maxim Gorki, Alexander Pushkin, Nikoli Gogol, Leo Tolstoi, Ivan Turgenev, Fyodor Dostoevski, and Anton Chekhov. But it was Gorki, the vagabond and tramp, the tubercular outcast, who most attracted me. Perhaps it was because I identified myself with him in his lowly birth, his wanderings in the vast Russian land, his sufferings and the nameless people who had suffered with him.

Gorki made me aware of his counterparts in America: Jack London, Mark Twain, and the youngest of them all—William Saroyan. Although these Americans did not stir my social conscience, their struggles and successes fired me with ambition. Now I could understand and appreciate the appearance of a Chinese writer named Lu-sin, whose stories were compared with Maxim Gorki's: not in style, but in dignity and humanity.

I discovered that one writer led to another: that they were all moved by the same social force. While Federico Garcia Lorca was writing passionately about the folklore of the peasants in Granada, Nicolas Guillen was chanting verses of social equality for the Negro people in Puerto Rico. While André Malraux was dramatizing the heroism of the Chinese Communists, a Filipino, Manuel E. Arguilla, was writing of the peasantry on the island of Luzon.

So from day to day I read, and reading widened my mental horizon, creating a spiritual kinship with other men who had pondered over the miseries of their countries. Then it came to me that the place did not matter: these sensitive writers reacted to the social dynamics of their time. I, too, reacted to my time. I promised myself that I would read ten thousand books when I got well. I plunged into books, boring through the earth's core, leveling all seas and oceans, swimming in the constellations.

CHAPTER XXXV

I HAD cultivated a friendship with a young boy named John Custer, a patient in another ward. He came to our ward one morning and looked at me for a long time, as though he were afraid to talk.

"Will you do something for me?" he said finally. He fumbled in his pockets for a piece of writing paper. "It's for my ma in Arkansas."

I took the paper from him.

"You just say I'm okay."

I started writing to an American mother in Arkansas. She had never heard of me, and I had never seen her, but her son was a common bond between us. I was writing to her what I had had in my mind and heart for years. The words came effortlessly. I was no longer writing about this lonely sick boy, but about myself and my friends in America. I told her about the lean, the lonely and miserable years. I mentioned places and names. I was not writing to an unknown mother any more. I was writing to my own mother plowing in the muddy fields of Mangusmana: it was the one letter I should have written before. I was telling her about America. Actually, I was writing to all the unhappy mothers whose sons left and did not return. There were years to remember, but they came and went away. I was telling them about those years. Then it was finished.

I read the letter slowly. When I finished reading it, he was crying.

"I have never learned to write," he said. "I had no time for learning in Arkansas."

I realized that this poor American boy had worked all his life. I could have told him then that I had worked all my life, too. I could have told him that I came from that part of my country where there were very few schools. I could have told him that for a long time the world of books was closed to me. I could have told him that I had been denied the little things in life that were denied to him. I could have told him that I had acquired my education by working hard. *Yes*, I could have told him, because when I looked at him I knew he would understand.

When he left the hospital, I said to him: "Rediscover America. You are still young. Someday I will hear from you."

"I will remember what you said," he said.

"Yes, John," I said, "it's only in giving the best we have that we can become a part of America."

"Thanks." And he left.

Years passed and the war came. Then one day I received a letter from him. He wrote in part:

"I doubt if you remember me. I met you in the Los Angeles County Hospital years ago and you wrote a letter for me. I returned to Arkansas and followed your suggestion. I found a job and educated myself when I was not working. I have studied American history, which was your suggestion. Learning to read and write is knowing America, my country. Knowing America is actually knowing myself. Knowing myself is also knowing how to serve my country. Now I'm serving her. . . ."

When summer came I was free to go outside the building. I would take the elevator and go down and sit on the sunlit grass beyond our porch. My brother Macario came back to Los Angeles.

"I couldn't get a visa," he said. "Nick couldn't get one, either. But Felix is now in Spain."

But the war in Spain was about to end; the Republican Government was about to be crushed. Macario knew that the fight would be over in a few months. He had found work in a downtown restaurant and rented a house in Echo Park.

Nick, who had come back with my brother from Mexico, went to Alaska to work in the fish canneries. When he returned to the mainland he proceeded to Portland where UCAPAWA, Local 226, an affiliate of the CIO, had fallen into the hands of reactionary leaders because of the departure of Jim Luna for the Philippines. Nick seized his opportunity, and offering a progressive program, was elected secretary-treasurer.

Now the local in Seattle was also in the hands of our group. The leadership in San Francisco was held by Americans and Chinese. But José tried vainly to break into it because the Filipino membership was large. He gave up in failure and went to San Pedro, where the cannery workers had been organized into the AFL by a dynamic Mexican woman unionist. Again José's attempt to put the workers into the CIO failed, so he went to Alaska to observe the situation there. When I heard from him again he was in Portland fighting against the element that was trying to break the local which had been re-envigorated by Nick's progressivism.

So while I was waiting for a possible improvement in the hospital, my companions were fighting in the trade union movement and for the propagation of progressive ideas. I wanted to work with them again.

CHAPTER XXXVI

Toward the end of May the sun came close to the earth; the heat was stifling and the patients were alarmed. Those in the ward seemed to die as fast as the flies that came into the hospital through the wide squares of the screens. Now in the summer there were more deaths than in the winter, when the cold gravely affected the patients. But the porch where I was had become a luxury and a symbol of my attachment to life, for there was a soothing coolness under the large tree near it. There was no other tree near the building, and as the number of deaths in the ward piled higher, the tree began to indicate recovery and survival to me.

I believed in the potency of the tree. I who had grappled with the forces of evil also believed in its power. Perhaps it was because I wanted to live so urgently that I ascribed a mystical power to the tree, and in this urgent need to live, I worshiped it like a pagan. I knew that no man in our ward died, or in the other wards that were near the tree.

I was not alone in this superstitious attachment to the tree. Other patients felt the same faith: we felt we were alive because of it. When the slight breeze rustled its leave we got up from our beds and stood near it. I held onto my faith although the doctors disputed it. Let them. I held onto the tree, as though its leaves protected me from death.

When one of the patients went to a rest home or sanitarium, a lucky patient in the ward would take his place on the porch. Most of us on the porch were "walking patients," and we helped the attendants with the racks of food. We also helped them change the beds of the other patients. Perhaps from this psychological basis we created an immunization.

I noticed that when a bed patient was transferred to the porch

he recovered rapidly and helped the attendants with the trays
or other patients. I was allowed to do minor chores for the nurses,
and all of us were free to play cards. Panagos, the Greek, was
very adept at sweeping the floor: he woke up early in the morning, before the nurses came out with the charts, and started
pushing the laundry rack so that he could clean the floor before
the attendants came with the trays of food. But Sobel, the Jew
from Poland, could not be outdone: he would stand in the hall-
ways waiting for the racks of food, and when the attendants
came with them, Sobel would push them into the porch and
ward, singing peasant songs as he carried the trays of those who
were too weak to get out of their beds.

I liked this part of my life on the porch. I promised myself
that if I got out I would go back to visit those who would be
left. I had something to eat. I had books. I had Eileen Odell. I
had many friends—now. I had had none of these on the outside;
I had had only violence. I was afraid, even if I were well again,
to go out and live in such a world.

The hot days of summer came and went. The war in Spain
was nearly over. I read Barbusse's *Under Fire*, and then, at the
insistence of Eileen Odell, Erich Maria Remarque's *All Quiet on
the Western Front*: passionate war books, intensely written with
a message for a tottering world. Then Romain Rolland's *Jean-
Christophe*, Thomas Mann's *Magic Mountain*; the stories of
Liam O'Flaherty, the plays of Sean O'Casey, and the poetry of
the proletarians in the United States.

I felt that I was at home with the young American writers
and poets. Reading them drove me back to the roots of American
literature—to Walt Whitman and the tumult of his time. And
from him, from his passionate dream of an America of equality
for all races, a tremendous idea burned my consciousness. Would
it be possible for an immigrant like me to become a part of the
American dream? Would I be able to make a positive contribu-
tion toward the realization of this dream?

I was enchanted by this dream, and the hospital, dismal as it
was, became a world of hope. I discovered the other democratic

writers and poets, who in their diverse ways contributed toward the enlargement of the American dream.

My sudden discovery of America made me a lost man in the hospital. I felt I could not converse with the other patients because of their intellectual sterility. I acquired a mask of pretense that became a weapon I was to take out with me into the violent world again—a mask of pretense at ignorance and illiteracy, because I felt that if they knew that I had intellectual depths they would reject my presence. I remembered Robinson Crusoe, and compared him with my fate. But my lostness was deeper because I was lonely among men. This loneliness was to encircle my life, to close around it, marring my vision, so that my thoughts were filled with melancholia.

I wanted to go away from the hospital; perhaps a new environment would give me a fresh outlook. In fact, I had been in the hospital two years now—long enough to be transferred to a sanitarium for complete recovery. I told my doctor of my desire to be moved away. He told me that it was beyond his jurisdiction.

I asked the Social Service Department to look into my case. A woman came to interview me. She wanted to know when I had come to the United States; my brothers' names and occupations, and the names of their wives and children; and also, which I thought ridiculous, the names and education of my parents and their immediate relatives. Could I tell her about my labors in Mangusmana and Binalonan? Could I tell her how I started working as a herd boy at five? Could I tell her about my starvation in Baguio? And my early years in America—could I tell her some of the violence and of my fears, my flights?

It was the simplest way of eliminating certain patients from relief care for technical reasons. My plea for a transfer was shelved. I could not go to a sanitarium. I should have known, but I had illusions, and was immersed in my studies. This was one of the realities that I had overlooked in the brilliance of my gigantic dream to know all America.

I revealed my predicament to the doctor when he came to

see me. He took it up with the Social Service Department, and another woman came to see me.

"There is nothing I can do for you," she said. "You are ineligible to go to a sanitarium for technical reasons."

"I didn't commit any crime," I said.

"You were a minor when you came to the United States," she explained kindly. "If you had any relatives who had taken care of you when you came, it would be a different story. As it stands, you were a minor and, as far as I know, you need a guardian to sign all these papers."

"It is very foolish," the doctor said. "We doctors try our best to help these patients toward recovery, but their future is dependent upon stupid restrictions."

"I'm sorry," said the woman. "There is nothing I can do. This is a big institution and I'm just a worker here."

"You are actually hanging him on a tree," the doctor said.

The woman left. All right, that was it. I began to feel like the Mexicans who thought the doctors were killing them off because there were too many of them. I was angry and afraid at the same time. Slowly I reviewed my life: it had always been chaotic. I became truly afraid to face America.

I brought my case before the Social Service Department again. The first woman came, not to help me but to tell me that there was racism even in the Los Angeles County Hospital.

"You Filipinos," she said calmly, "ought to be shipped back to your jungle homes!"

I felt consoled when I realized that this Social Service woman was only voicing a personal opinion, an individual hate against Filipinos. I had read enough books now to know the roots of racism: I had had experience with it when I was still on the outside.

I was crushed. I wanted to be brave, but there was no hope. And once again, as when I landed in the United States, I felt a rising tide of fear and revolt. Fear always worked this way with me. I had seen so much prejudice that I reacted murderously when confronted by it.

When my brother Macario came to see me, I told him about the whole affair.

"I'll get you out of this hole, Carl," he said. "I have a job now and I'll take care of you until you are well again."

"I don't know if we should take this step," I said. "I need medical attention and care."

"I'll take care of that, too," he said. "Don't worry now. I'll come next week."

I knew that I would be a burden to Macario. But it seemed the only way. I packed all my books and magazines. Eileen Odell came with a new brief case with my name on it and arranged my poems and some scattered chapters of my autobiography. Then Victor, who was living with my brother in a Japanese hotel downtown, came to take my things away.

One June morning, exactly two years after I went to the hospital, I said good-bye to my companions and the personnel on our floor.

CHAPTER XXXVII

I WAS afraid to leave the hospital. I knew that a perilous life awaited me outside, that I would be inevitably caught in its whirlpools. I had never known peace, except in the hospital, where there was always something to eat and a place to sleep on the cold nights. There were also genuine friends, who had sat with me in the hopeless hours, the black days of my operations. On the outside life was alien and unfriendly, and the summer days were long and the winter nights were sharp with cold. I was determined to face it again, but now with an unswerving intellectual weapon. Maybe I would win this time, and if I did—would I not create a legend of courage and valor that other poor young men could emulate?

My brother was not yet in the hotel when I arrived. I waited in the lobby. Victor came first. We climbed the winding stairs into their little room. Then my brother came with sandwiches, and Victor went downstairs for a bottle of milk. It was good to be with them again.

On Sundays they awoke at noon and walked to First Street, talked to the Pinoys, ate Filipino food, and went to a movie when night came. Their friends also lived the same humdrum life. They met in a dingy restaurant or a dark poolroom to exchange news; then they scattered for another week of endless drudgery. It was the same life that had filled me with fear when I had arrived in America. It was the same life that led me to the labor movement. Now I must decide what to do with my remaining years.

I slept with Victor in the bed, while Macario slept on the floor. It was the same routine all over again—only now Leon was long dead and other members of our group were in jail or wandering somewhere. Then my brother decided that we had to move from the hotel, because climbing up and down the four flights of stairs with my stiff knee was dangerous to my health.

Victor suggested that we find a place around Vermont Avenue. We packed our belongings. I was surprised to know that after eight years in the United States I had only one old blue suit, a cheap suitcase, and three shirts. Victor and my brother were a little better off because they had worked more steadily.

Macario and I boarded a streetcar and went to the Vermont Avenue district. What we encountered almost broke my heart. We saw a nice little apartment house near Commonwealth Avenue and when we approached the landlady took away the "For Rent" sign. She went inside the house and peered furtively through a window. When sure that we would not go back, she went out to the yard again and put up the sign.

The next woman was more discreet. She stood by the sign as we approached.

"This house is not for rent," she said awkwardly. "The sign is nailed to the wall and it's hard to pull out. Maybe you can find one next block."

But the next woman faced the issue squarely. She said: "We don't take Filipinos!"

My brother was persistent. He interviewed every apartment manager in the whole area. I have often wondered why he seemed so blind to the open prejudice of the people. Perhaps his good education and correct upbringing in the Philippines and his association with educated and well-meaning Americans made him forgiving. I do not know what made him tolerant, because even now, when he is once more in the Philippines, he writes to tell me how much he has missed America.

I was different. Where there was prejudice, I challenged it with prejudice. But where there was goodness, I reacted with goodness. This attitude, too, was conditioned by my experiences. In the years before I went to the hospital, when I was growing up in a world of horror, I fought against the perpetuation of brutal memories. Maybe I succeeded in erasing the sores, but the scars remained to remind me, in moments of spiritual vicissitudes, of the tragic days of those years. And even now, when I can look back without the black fury of hate that I had, I still double my fists.

I gave up looking for a better place to live. The only section where we were allowed to stay was notorious for criminals, pimps, gamblers, and prostitutes. We could not find a place even in Boyle Heights, the Jewish section, nor in the Mexican district.

I was washing our clothes when José, who had suddenly appeared in Los Angeles, knocked on the door.

"I'm married now, Carl," he said. "And I have a little boy. I named him after you. I hope he will grow up to carry on the tradition!"

"I know he will, José," I said. I knew that he hated to be tied down. José knew that it was the end, that the happy yet violent days in the labor movement were over. I saw it in his face, and seeing its unmistakable presence, I was more determined to live and to study harder. I felt that I must vindicate José and our other companions, who had either given up the fight or left for the Philippines. I knew that I must acquire all the knowledge that would have been theirs had they fought on; that I must succeed for them all, now that they had given up.

"Would you like to see my wife and son?" José asked.

"All right." I followed him into the street. He was driving a car. We arrived at the bungalow where his wife was still sleeping.

"My wife can't read," he whispered when we entered the living room. "But how she can love!"

In the kitchen, standing and sitting on the floor, dark and light, were José's wife's numerous sisters.

"Which one among my sisters-in-law would you like, Carl?" José asked, winking suggestively. "They are all single except Teresa." He pointed to the married woman.

"I would take Teresa any time," I said.

"Let's celebrate, then," José said, producing a bottle of port wine.

In the evening, filled with wine, I stumbled into the hotel room with Teresa's help. I sat for an hour on a chair waiting for the effects of the wine to subside. When I was a little better, I jumped to my feet and touched Teresa's face. She pushed me away and flung herself upon the bed, weeping bitterly when I moved to touch her again.

Why were the women in my world always crying? Was there too much frustration in their lives? Were they hungry for compassion? I remembered my sisters: they, too, were always weeping. What was it that made all of them cry? I remember my mother crying when my sister Irene died with the unfinished polka dot dress in her little hands.

I was to run from crying women, because I was afraid they would evoke emotion in me. I was afraid of such emotions because they emanated from pity. I hardened myself against pity. And so in later years, after I had successfully persevered through a spiritual crisis, I hurled contempt at women who tried to arouse deep emotions in me. I flung against them the tides of my hate, and when they started to weep, I only increased my bitterness. I thought it was the only way for me to live: to stand free, to walk unhindered across the land.

"Well, there is nothing else to do but go back to *our* world," said my brother.

"I saw an apartment on Temple Street," I said.

Victor's face darkened with disapproval. Teresa came with her car and drove us to the place. It was known as a house of prostitution, but there was no other house for rent. The street was filled with pimps and prostitutes, drug addicts and marijuana peddlers, cutthroats and murderers, ex-convicts and pickpockets. It was the rendezvous of social outcasts: known for its wide-open red-light district.

What would happen to Eileen if she were to try to visit me here? What would I say if the police broke into our apartment? Was there a place in this vast continent where Filipinos were allowed to live in peace?

There were two bedrooms and a bath upstairs; downstairs, a living room, a kitchen, and a storeroom. The back door faced a vacant lot brown with tall dead grass. Grass! Oh, the years of green grass and the earth! In the center were three old houses, toppling slowly but inevitably to the ground, where several Mexican families lived. At night I could see them in their beds: they were careless and primitive.

One night the apartment on our left was raided and three prostitutes were caught with their customers. I heard them run out of the apartments and hide in the dead grass. The policemen found them with their strong flashlights and dragged them to their car in the street. One of the prostitutes had jumped from the window and broke her leg. She was groaning with pain when two policemen carried her away.

One time a Filipino in the apartment across from ours shot his American wife in the abdomen. I was reading Gustavus Myers's *Ending of Hereditary American Fortunes* when I saw the man come home from work. He arrived too soon. His wife was entertaining another Filipino—a gambler. A quarrel between the Filipino and his wife ensued, during which the gambler walked out unnoticed. There was silence for an hour; then I saw the wife coming out with her suitcase. The husband stopped her at the door. They wrestled for the suitcase. The woman disappeared for a moment and there was silence. Then she appeared at the door again, and the Filipino reappeared with a gun and shot her in the abdomen. He fired another shot into his own chest.

They lay side by side in the living room. In a little while the Filipino stirred, then rolled over on his side and crawled to the door for support. Holding his chest tightly, he stumbled into the pathway. He staggered to the landlady's apartment and told her to call the police. Then he walked blindly to his wife and tried to carry her upstairs. He fell three times. Then there was silence, and I thought they were dead. When the police came they were lying side by side on a blood-soaked bed, but still breathing and alive.

In another apartment a husband took poison because he discovered that his son belonged to another man. His wife, thinking that he was dead, took poison and died. But he came out alive and took care of the child, as though it were his own.

One night I found Teresa sleeping on the cement steps near our apartment. I carried her inside and watched her sleep until she woke up. Then she told me that she was unhappy with her Italian husband.

"He is a gambler," she confessed. "One day I came home from work and found that he had sold our stove. I had some food with me and I wanted to cook it. But the stove was gone."

Was there a happy situation in the world outside of books? My despair led me to fairy tales: *Arabian Nights*, Grimm's *Fairy Tales*, Andersen's *Tales*, Aesop's *Fables*, Lewis Carroll's *Alice in Wonderland*. These books stimulated me to go back to the folklore of my own country. I discovered with amazement that Philippine folklore was uncollected, that native writers had not assimilated it into their writings. This discovery gave me an impetus to study the common roots of our folklore, and upon finding it in the tales and legends of the. pagan Igorots in the mountains of Luzon, near my native province, I blazed with delight at this new treasure. Now I must live and integrate Philippine folklore in our struggle for liberty!

My interest in folklore led me to the lives of Filipino heroes. Knowing them led me to the mainsprings of our history—to José Rizal whose story had been told to me years ago by my brother Macario when I had been sick in Binalonan. Why I had forgotten him until now, I did not know.

This was the world into which I was thrown when I left the hospital. I wanted to run away from it, but did not know where to go. I could take the freight train again—but was I strong enough? I could no longer work with my hands; the right was partially paralyzed. My left leg was shrunken and stiff. I had never learned a trade.

One day the doctor from the hospital came to see me. "I think I should tell you, Carl," he said. "You haven't many years to live."

"How many do you think?" I asked.

"It's hard to say. Your lungs are greatly impaired. The perforation in the right one is the size of a silver dollar. And the way you live—" He looked around the bare room and outside to the tenement houses. "If you go on this way you are lucky if you live another five years."

Five years! I was terrified. I loved life so much. But now I knew that I would be deprived of it. All right, I knew what to do. I would show those who had driven me to this corner of death that I would not be cheated of these last five years. All right. I would show them. All right. . . .

"I don't want to die yet," I told Macario. "I cannot believe that I have only a few years left. There are so many things I would like to do."

"There is nothing we can do, Carl," he said. "But we will stick together until the end."

"I would like to do something positive," I said.

"I will work for both of us," he said gently. "You stay home." He was so kind, so gentle. "Maybe you will find something to do."

"I would like to write," I said. "But maybe I was not meant to be a writer. I would like to tell the story of our life in America. I remember vividly how you described our fate: 'It's a great wrong that a man should be hungry and illiterate and miserable in America.' Yes, yes, it is a great wrong. Maybe I could write it down for all the world to see!"

"I'll sacrifice my life and future for whatever you think is right, Allos," he said.

I felt vast and immortal. Now he had used my native name again. I looked at him and knew that he meant it. I knew that he would help me live for a while so that I could write about our anguish and our hopes for a better America. I knew that if he died somewhere in pursuit of what he had wanted to be, he would live again in me and in all the words that seized my mind.

PART FOUR

CHAPTER XXXVIII

I FELT that I was nearing the end, and every day created a havoc in me. I wanted to do something but I did not know where to begin. I had a vague desire to write, my mind was teeming with ideas, but I was not sure of myself. I yearned to know someone who was a successful writer, but the men around me were violent and crude. I needed some kind of order to guide me in the confusion that reigned over my life.

I had only one escape—the Los Angeles Public Library. I planned to read ten thousand books on all subjects, but reading only made me live the acute pain of the past. When I came upon a scene that recalled my own experiences I could not go on. But mostly I felt that other writers lied about life, that they were afraid to depict it as it really was in their environment.

I returned to the writers of my time for strength. And I found Younghill Kang, a Korean who had immigrated to the United States as a boy and worked his way up until he had become a professor at an American university. His autobiography, *The Grass Roof*, gave me an enlightening insight into the history of the Korean revolutionary movement. But it was his indomitable courage that rekindled in me a fire of hope.

Why could not I succeed as Younghill Kang had? He had come from a family of scholars and had gone to an American university—but was he not an Oriental like myself? Was there an Oriental without education who had become a writer in America? If there was one, maybe I could do it too! I ransacked the library, read biographies omnivorously, tried to study other languages. Then I came upon the very man—Yone Noguchi! A Japanese houseboy in the home of Joaquin Miller, the poet, who became the first poet of his race to write in the English language.

Here at last was an ideal. Noguchi led me to other writers:

Louis Adamic, Carey McWilliams, and John Fante. Adamic, because of his phenomenal success, overshadowed the others. But McWilliams's interest in the agricultural workers in California, including some 35,000 Filipinos, eventually drove him into the progressive movement, where we met and worked for civil liberties for the Filipinos and other minorities. On the other hand, Fante's obscure background and racial origin aroused in me a sense of kinship. I considered his imperturbability as merely a defense against an alien world, for his Italian pride and prejudice were similar to my Filipino pride and prejudice. But at the same time I feared that, because he lacked a positive intellectual weapon with which to cope with his environment, he might eventually lose the vigor of his peasant heritage.

These, then, were the writers who acted as my intellectual guides through the swamp of a culture based on property.

Now I had the urge to write about my experiences, but still lacked the intellectual preparation to undertake such a tremendous task. One day I met an American poet in the Los Angeles Public Library. Ronald Patterson invited me to his little room, and in a corner, piled to the ceiling, were magazines of all sorts—*New Masses, Partisan Review, The New Republic, Left Front, Dynamo, Anvil,* and other Leftist publications, many of which sprung up and died in that one decade.

I took some copies of the magazines with me. Here was something that intrigued me. Here was a new pattern of ideas. I looked back to the abortive *The New Tide,* and its full significance came to me. I asked my brother to read every magazine as fast as I could get them from Ronald, and when José came to our apartment, I asked him to read them too. Although the defeat of Republican Spain and the rise of Hitler were reflected in these publications, the magazines died with the setback of democratic forces all over the world. The course of international politics was changed, and new social ideas emerged and affected the literary movements in all countries.

One evening Ronald came to our apartment with a young Jewish girl. They took me to a meeting on Spring Street where, to my surprise, I met a girl who claimed she was Dora Travers's sister. The audience was composed of many nationalities. Current issues were discussed passionately; but every argument was directed toward one purpose—the unification of the minorities so that they might work effectively with the progressive organizations and the trade unions toward a national program of peace and democracy.

I felt that Filipinos could participate in this program. I said so to Ronald and he referred me to a certain Anna Dozier, who in turn referred me to a Filipino in Boyle Heights. It seemed a great opportunity to rally Filipinos toward unity behind a vast democratic program.

I asked José to go with me to Boyle Heights, hoping it would help him regain his early enthusiasm. He was no longer sure of his decisions. But I took a chance, because I felt that if he had the making of a good labor leader he should also have an instinctual direction for sound politics.

I found the Filipino working in a restaurant on Brooklyn Avenue, a wizened little fellow who could hardly speak English. It was very difficult to converse with him. I tried some of the principal Philippine dialects, but he knew only his obscure island patois.

"Yes, comrades," he said in effect, "I'm the first Filipino Communist in Los Angeles. That is why the Party refers to me when a Filipino wants to join us. Are you ready to sign up?"

I was surprised. I had thought that he would explain the circumstances. Was he not referred to us by the Communist Party? I had not expected to sign up with the organization, but if it was the *only* way by which I could get the support of organized groups in Southern California, I would do just that without considering the consequences.

"I didn't come to join the Party," I said apologetically. "I mentioned the difficult situation of our people in the state at a meeting the other day, and I was referred to you. I am in favor of unity. Perhaps we could have a statewide conference somewhere and plan a strategy."

. "First," he said, "you got to join the Party. You can't plan intelligently without Party direction. I tell you, comrades, you got to work with me as Communists."

"There must be some other way," José interposed.

"There is no way other than the Party," he said with finality. I asked him to give us more time, and left.

"There is something in what he said," I told José.

"I don't know," he said.

I wanted José to reconsider the proposal of the Filipino Communist, because I could have his confidence and he could have mine. I took up the matter with my brother.

"We are familiar with Filipino problems," he explained. "But we must sound out their sentiments and feelings. Would they like to work under the direction of the Communist Party?"

It was a logical question. But I said: "They wouldn't have to know it."

"The truth always comes out," José said.

"Perhaps the formation of a separate Filipino unit of the Party is the answer," I said. "I understand that there are several members in California. Why couldn't we put these members in a group of our own?"

"It seems logical," José argued. "But there must be a broader, more democratic, all-inclusive organization around which we could rally our forces."

"We must have a mass meeting next Sunday," my brother said.

I prepared a leaflet and distributed copies to the Filipinos in the county. When Sunday came a crowd gathered in the Workers' Hall on Main Street. José presided and I acted as secretary. The meeting was very simple and orderly.

"How come we Filipinos in California can't buy or lease real estate?" a man asked.

"Why are we denied civil service jobs?" asked another.

"Why can't we marry women of the Caucasian race? And why are we not allowed to marry in this state?"

"Why can't we practice law?"

"Why are we denied the right of becoming naturalized American citizens?"

"Why are we discriminated against in relief agencies?"

"Why are we denied better housing conditions?"

"Why can't we stop the police from handling us like criminals?"

"Why are we denied recreational facilities in public parks and other such places?"

Ten important points—a broad generalization of our difficulties in California. It was comforting to know that these men too were stirred by the social strangulation of our people. But it was our plan to listen to the community, not to propose a program of action. The meeting was only a sampling of ideas—although, I found out later, it was also the beginning of a state-wide campaign for the recognition of Filipino rights and privileges.

Still José and I could not agree. My brother suggested that we take separate trips along the coast. I was reluctant to pursue this suggestion. But it was my opportunity to get away from my brother for a while, because I was oppressed by the drudgery of his everyday life. Perhaps my return to the land and working people would give me a better understanding of our problems. I had not seen the familiar California coast for two years, and perhaps I had lost my perspective. Historic events had taken place while I was in the hospital, and one of the most significant was the emergence of the CIO: several of its locals were dominated by Filipino cannery and agricultural workers.

I was about to leave when the Filipino Communist and Anna Dozier came to our apartment.

"You can't establish a separate Filipino unit of the Party," she said. "Why, it is a divisionist tactic!"

"It is complete disobedience of the Party's rules," the Filipino said. "Every action regarding the Party must come from me."

"But I'm not a member," I countered.

Anna was hesitant. Then she said, "Nevertheless."

"The Party is a democratic organization," the Filipino said.

"I didn't say it was undemocratic," I answered. "And if it's communism our countrymen want, let them have it. I think that is democracy."

"You talk like an intellectual," Anna said.

"You know well enough that I have washed dishes for a living," I said. "You know well enough that I have never made any pretensions to intellectualism."

"I don't trust him," the Filipino said to Anna as he turned to leave the apartment.

I was naïve. I wanted to be sure that communism was what Filipinos needed. I felt somehow that I needed it too. What was the nemesis of communism? Was it Trotskyism? Whatever it was that seemed relevant to the needs of the Filipinos in California, I knew that I must assimilate it.

I left for the north in confusion. I knew that I would battle with myself for a decision. I rode in the bus and watched familiar scenes that evoked poetry in me. When was it that I had first seen this broad land?

I trembled with joy passing the familiar scenes. It was where I belonged—here in the color of green, the bitter taste of lemon peels, the yellow of ripe peas; in the pleasure, the beauty, the fragrance.

CHAPTER XXXIX

I STOPPED in San Fernando, a citrus town twenty-five miles north of Los Angeles. I walked to a big Filipino agricultural laborers' camp, in the center of a wide lemon farm. It was Sunday and there was a light rain in the sky. I found the lemon pickers crowded in a large garage, where they were playing cards and washing clothes. I asked one of the men where I could find the leader of the crew. I was courteously guided to a little house under two tall eucalyptus trees.

I knocked softly on the door and a young Filipino woman opened it. I said that I would like to see her husband, but she answered that he had gone to town. She invited me into the house. I could wait for her husband. I knew from the way she spoke English that she was an educated woman.

"That is my husband," she said, pointing to a picture of a man about forty-five on the table. "I met him in Manila when I was going to college there. He was in the Philippines for ten months. I found out later that he went there to look for a wife."

"I have seen your husband around," I said. "But I don't know him. I understand that he has been managing this camp for fifteen years."

"Yes," she said. "But I have been here only two years. I went to Stanford University for three years, then came here for good. I can't use my education." She stared at me and said: "The Pinoys can't use their education, either. That is why Pinoys have only one objective—to marry someone with economic security. But the parents are partly to blame: they teach their daughters to be greedy. So Pinoys in general are arrogant and stupid and lacking in humor."

I nodded silently.

"I didn't get your name," she said.

I told her.

"Don't you write for the Filipino press?" she asked.

"Now and then," I said. "I'm just learning. . . ."

"I like your poems," she said finally.

A car came into the yard. She went to the door and opened it. It was her husband. He climbed up the stairs and stomped onto the porch, shouting at the children there. Then he burst into the house with his arms full of packages.

I jumped to my feet to help him, introducing myself. He acknowledged the introduction with a swift jerk of his head, as though he had heard of me somewhere. When we had piled the packages on a table, he invited me outside. We sat on the porch steps, throwing pebbles into the tall grass. He talked easily though with visible restraint. I could see that he had been lonely —that the apparent happiness of his marriage could not make him forget the loneliness which had shadowed him during his fifteen years in this lemon grove.

"When I first came to this camp," he said, "these lemon trees were only a foot high. The land on the west side of my camp was still a desert. I went to the town and recruited Mexican laborers. Afterward I went to Los Angeles and carted off Filipinos who had just arrived from the sugar plantations of Hawaii and from the peasant country of the Philippines."

He looked affectionately toward the lemon groves east of the camp, then at the orange groves on the west.

"I have made this valley fruitful and famous," he said quietly. "Some ten years ago I wanted to go into farming myself, so close I was to the soil, so familiar with the touch of clay and loam. But I found that I couldn't buy land in California. I had served in the United States navy in World War I, so I thought I had the privilege. But after the war I was on the ocean most of the time, because I didn't resign when the armistice was signed. I didn't know that three years after the armistice I could no longer file my citizenship papers. I could no longer become an American citizen. I wanted to become an American citizen for many reasons, but at that time my most urgent desire was to buy a piece of land so that I could farm. I guess I'm a sucker for the land."

He had the gentleness and the passion of my father when he spoke about the land. Perhaps he had come from the peasantry in the Philippines. I also felt attached to the land, but it was now a different attachment. In the years long gone it was merely a desire to possess a plot of earth and to draw nourishment from it. But now this desire to possess, after long years of flight and disease and want, had become an encompassing desire to *belong* to the land—perhaps to the whole world.

I felt this way when I talked to him. It was a discovery. I found myself in him, in the strange melody of his attachment to the land that did not belong to him, in his almost mystical belief in the fertility of the earth. I talked for a while to some of the laborers and then walked to the dirt road that led to town. I had not gone very far when I heard a car approaching from behind. I stopped and waited. The car came slowly and stopped. The woman at the camp called me. I jumped in, sure now that I could catch the first bus to Bakersfield.

I was wordless with gratitude. I had cultivated silence early in life, and there were times when I felt I would burst into tears if I spoke.

"Come back to see us again," she said at the bus station. "Come back next year! Maybe the year after! Come back, *Mr.* Bulosan!"

I boarded the bus and left San Fernando. But in the night, passing through blooming orange groves, I could hear the woman's lonely voice: "*Come back, Mr. Bulosan!*" It was the first time that anyone had addressed me that way.

I arrived in Bakersfield and walked from poolrooms to gambling houses. The season for picking grapes was still far off. The vines were just pruned. There was no work for the cold months of winter. From the gambling houses I went to the whorehouses, hoping to find someone I knew. There were no other places where Filipinos could go. I sat in the living room and watched lonely Filipinos paw at the semi-nude girls. I felt angry and lost.

Where in this wide country could I go? I felt the way other Filipinos felt. I rushed out and cursed the cold night.

I discovered that three Filipino farm labor contractors controlled the grape industry. Nearly three thousand Filipino workers depended on them. They lived in crowded bunkhouses operated by these men. It was exploitation everywhere, even among ourselves. It was the same thing I had known years before.

I wanted to see one of the contractors. I was introduced to Cabao, who had nearly eight hundred Filipinos under him. He was younger than most contractors, but I was skeptical. He drove me to his ranch. His house was large and gaudy. I saw a college diploma on the wall above his writing desk.

I was looking at it when a car drove into the yard. Cabao rushed to the window and looked out.

"My wife," he said.

She burst into the house and came to the study with a bottle of whisky. I was shocked when I saw her face. Where had I seen her before? I stumbled to my feet when Cabao introduced me to her. But she did not stay long. I heard her drive out of the yard. Then I remembered where I had seen her! I looked at Cabao sadly.

"I'm sure you have seen my wife before," he said apologetically. "Everybody knows what she was before I married her. She worked in every important town in California. That is why everybody knows her. She followed the seasons, the way Filipinos follow the crops."

I wanted to find out why he married her. He had almost everything he wanted. He had had a good education.

"I saw your wife once some years ago," I said carefully. "But I didn't mean to ask you about her life history."

"It's all right," he said. "When I talk about it I feel free. Do you think it's money she wants? I give her enough. But she still is eager for the attention of men. I guess they are all the same."

"Why did you marry her?" I asked.

"She was young when I saw her in Watsonville," he said. "I was young, too. I had gone there to work for the summer, because I wanted to earn enough money to pay my college fees that year. I was taking Sociology at the University of California. I took her with me and worked for her. There were years of desperation. But when I came here and made a little money, I bought this house for her. I thought she would settle down. I was wrong. Do you know where she is going tonight?"

I did not want to know. But I could guess. I got up and started moving to the door.

"I'll drive you to town," Cabao said.

At the station, when Cabao had left, I discovered that he had put some money in my coat pocket. I took the bus and sat silently in a corner.

I was on my way north again. Familiar towns. But I could not erase Cabao from my mind. I recalled his gentle, educated voice, his delicate hands. There was something lost and futile, something utterly defeated in him.

"It's all right for me to suffer," I said to myself. "I'm stronger than he is. He has no right to suffer. . . ."

I arrived in Stockton during a strike. Filipino asparagus workers were in the midst of a general walkout. A long parade was moving down El Dorado Street, but the strikers were orderly and quiet. I stood on a corner reading the pennants and placards carried by some of the men. I noticed that all the stores and other buildings were closed on either side of the street. Even the gambling houses and liquor stores were closed.

I saw Claro leading a section of strikers. He was boldly carrying a sign which said:

PAISANOS! DON'T PATRONIZE JAP STORES!
IT MEANS HUNGER!

His chin was up, his face animated. There was a grin on his mouth. Suddenly I felt an urge in me to run to him. When was it that I first saw him? It seemed so long ago! I shouted to him and pointed to the sign. He looked in my direction but did not recognize me. I ran to him and shouted into his ear.

"Don't you remember me?"

For a moment he stopped, his eyes wandering wildly into the

past, and then he flung his arms about me. There was genuine affection in his voice. The gesture of Claro, similar to the moving salutation of the French, was to spread to the members of our circle—to the Filipinos in the labor and progressive movements. It was to become a sign of affinity and affection.

"You have changed, Carlos!" he said.

I ignored him. But I said, "I don't understand some of your placards. I thought this was a general walkout of asparagus workers."

"Yes, it is!" he shouted with anger. "But a Japanese woman is breaking it. She is supplying laborers." He walked on, looking from side to side, shouting greetings to friends watching from doorways. When he saw a Japanese face he became furious.

Where had I met a similar character? Was it in Gorki's *Decadence?* In this novel, in one of the crowded streets, a revolutionist was walking with a surging crowd, anonymously. There was a powerful secret in his heart, and as he moved with the crowd remembering comrades who had fallen and thinking of the promise of the future, his eyes glowed with happiness and his whole face became animated with sudden joy.

I tugged at his sleeve. Could I tell him that I had come back to fight? Would he remember that he had sent me away long ago but advised me to return when I was ready to fight for our people? Would he remember that autumn day when I ate hungrily in his restaurant?

"This strike means more than dollars and cents in the asparagus fields," Claro said. "This very day the trade union movement and other progressive groups in Manila are demanding that the government boycott Japanese products. But it is deeper than you think. Tons and tons of scrap iron are going to Japan from the United States. These are made into bombs that are being dropped upon the peaceful Chinese people."

"I thought you didn't like the Chinese people," I said.

"There are good and bad men in every people," he said. "For instance, I didn't like the Chinese vice lords in Stockton. I still don't like them, but they are co-operating in this strike."

"What do you mean?" I asked.

"They have closed all their gambling houses. Do you see what this means? The Pinoys will keep their money and spend it only on food. The strike will last longer, and the farmers will lose two million dollars this season. Of course, the Chinese will also lose—but they figure that they will win in the end."

"There is no sense to it," I said. "If you win from one side, you lose to the other. Is there no way of winning from both sides? Isn't there, Claro?"

The parade moved eastward to Main Street and into the huge auditorium where local leaders were assembled to address the strikers.

"The UCAPAWA is now in power in the agricultural areas of the coast," Claro said. "But we have a strong independent union here."

I went to the back room and sent a dispatch to a labor paper in San Francisco about the strike. A representative from the Philippine government in Washington went to the rostrum and offered his support. This man was a spectacular figure in Filipino life. A labor commissioner in Hawaii as a young man, he was also a writer and an editor. He was multilingual. He was a leader for the common man, and he tried, in his brief career among Filipinos in California, to bring their predicament to the attention of the home government. Unfortunately he died before he could accomplish his mission.

CHAPTER XL

AFTER the meeting I found Percy Toribio, the secretary-treasurer of the striking union. He was also editor of the union's organ. He was young and unsure of himself, a graduate of the University of Washington and a foreign correspondent for one of the weeklies in Manila.

"I'm more interested in writing," he confided. "I started a novel some years ago, upon the insistence of my professor, but it is still unfinished. Family life and labor problems—"

There was something about the way he talked that disturbed me. I was skeptical, remembering other college-bred Filipino leaders. But I envied Toribio's education and writing ability.

"I read some of your stories in the pages of *Graphic*," I said. "I liked some of them—especially those pieces about cannery workers in Alaska."

"I haven't written a story since I left the university," he said sadly.

I said, suddenly changing the subject, "Have you thought of affiliating your organization with either the CIO or the AFL?"

He leaped to his feet. "No!" he shouted emphatically. Suddenly he said, "That is not what I mean. If the members wanted to affiliate with the big organizations, it's probable they would join with the AFL."

"But the CIO seems more democratic," I said. "Besides, it has some of its most militant organizers in this valley."

"I don't think it is feasible," he said impulsively. "The farmers might think we were a bunch of radicals. It doesn't work here."

I began to boil with anger. "Are you afraid of losing your job?" I said coldly.

"I wish you hadn't said that, Carl!" He turned and walked silently away.

I knew it was impossible to talk with him. I had never trusted college-bred leaders because, in my experience, when the crucial moment came, they were not to be found.

I walked down El Dorado Street thinking of Toribio. I felt that if I met him again he would be against me. Was there no common ground? He was a representative of the Filipino intelligentsia, while I represented the peasants and workers. I was also a revolutionist. And because of my firm conviction that Filipino workers should be educated politically in order to contribute effectively to the general upsurge of democratic forces in the United States, Toribio and I would oppose each other if we met again.

I was eating in a restaurant when Claro came in with a morning paper. He spread it in front of me, his face beaming. I read the headline:

FILIPINO COMMUNIST LEADS STRIKE!

Swiftly I read the article, filled with premonition. It did not mention my name, but the description was almost exact. Who could have done it? José, perhaps? Perhaps the Filipino Communist in Boyle Heights? I could not understand it.

Claro was smiling mysteriously.

"Why didn't you tell me, comrade?" he said, raising a clenched fist. "I could have saved you all this trouble."

"You are greatly mistaken," I protested.

"It's all right to be cautious," he whispered. "I understand your position. How is it down there? Are we strong enough to start something big?"

I saw Steve Laso come in hurriedly. A foreman for one of the big farmers, he was one of the first to withdraw from the fields. A folded copy of the morning paper was in his pocket. He looked very tired.

"You'd better leave this town right away!" he said. "They are looking for you."

Claro interrupted. "Let him stay, Steve!"

"It's impractical," Steve argued. "He will mess up everything if he stays. You must go at once, Carl!"

I walked to the back door. Claro's face darkened; there was grim determination in his eyes. He raised his hand in the Communist salute.

"I'll be back, Claro," I said.

"I'll drive you out of town," Steve said. "The patrolmen are watching the highways. But we will take a chance."

We ran to Steve's car and started driving on the highway to Oakland. What was happening to all of us? What was going on among Filipinos? Was everybody moving toward a faith strong enough to blast away the walls that imprisoned our life in America? I yearned to talk to Steve, but he was driving madly down the road. I would go back to Stockton after the strike and talk to Claro.

Several miles out of town, near the hills, we saw the shiny motorcycles of patrolmen guarding the highway. They were searching every car. Steve told me to take off my coat and muss up my hair. He shoved a big cigar into my mouth and told me to light it. I lit it when the patrolmen stopped us. They looked at me suspiciously for a moment, opened the rumble seat, came back to the wheel to look at me again. Then they let us go. I sighed with relief.

"I don't like to run away, Steve," I said. "But if it's for the good of the strike, I will go."

"It's better this way," he said. "But I will be waiting for your return. You fooled them with your youthful looks. You must take good care of that face and those hands. Your youth is a weapon. Good-bye!"

I stopped the bus when it came to the bend of the road. I jumped on and settled myself comfortably. I was tired and sleep came at once, with troubled dreams.

In one dream I saw my mother serving my brothers and sisters. When my father told her to eat she answered that she was not hungry. But I knew that she was hungry, because I had been with her all day. We had gone to the villages together selling salt and salted fish; we did not eat anything except a few stalks of young rice that we snatched from the fields. The dream shifted to another evening, and my mother was serving again. She would not eat. Then I knew why. There was not enough food in the house. She was starving herself so that her children would have something to eat. I knew now, because I had been with her all day.

I stopped eating and announced that I was feeling faint. My mother looked up at me and a flash of understanding crossed her face. I walked to the ladder and went out into the yard. It was a dark night and the coconut trees stood like ghosts among the grass houses. I climbed an acacia tree in the front yard and looked through a window into our house. I could see my brothers and sisters eating; even my mother was eating now. I was happy then, seeing my mother eating, and laughing too when one of my brothers told a joke. I looked up and prayed that my mother might live long under those skies.

I was awakened by my tears of remembrance. I looked out the window and saw the water shimmering with lights. San Francisco was glowing, and behind us Oakland was fading. I could hear foghorns in the bay. They sounded like *carabaos* lost in a wide meadow. I felt like going to a land far away. Then I went to sleep again and dreamed about my father!

I was up in the acacia tree again. I was watching my mother cooking a few kernels of corn. I could see them shining golden in the lamplight. There was a worried look in my mother's face. What was it? She came to the front window and called for me, looking up and down the twilight road. I did not answer; she returned to the kitchen.

I climbed down the tree and started running away from our house. I wanted to run away from all that poverty. I did not want to, because there was affection in our family—but I hated the aching misery. I did not know where to go now. I seemed to hear someone shouting to me in the coming darkness.

"Run! Don't go back! Run!"

I lifted my shirt and wiped the blinding tears out of my eyes. I ran swiftly in the dark. I was running away from love, from all that was good and true. I was afraid to know that we were poor. I could not bear to see my mother starving herself. Wait for me, star of night. . . . Days and nights I walked until a policeman found me sleeping in the public market of a strange town. When I refused to reveal my name, he took me to the town jail. The chief of police, a kind young man, came into my cell with bananas. I ate some of them while he watched me.

"You like them?" he asked.

"Yes, sir," I said.

"You looked hungry so I thought maybe you would like to try our bananas in this town. I raised them myself. Would you care to see the trees?"

He lifted me off the bench and took me to the low window that overlooked the backyard of the *presidencia*. There in the wide yard, tall and fragrant and full of fruit, bananas stood under the sun like village girls on their way to church.

"You planted them, sir?" I asked.

"Sure!" he said.

"We have bananas too," I said. "My father and I are farmers. I wish you could see our banana grove. And our coconuts! Sir, that is something to see!"

"I would like to see your farm now," he said.

"Let's go!"

He took my hand and went outside where an old Ford was waiting. He jumped behind the wheel and started the motor.

"Where to, partner?" he asked.

"Binalonan," I said.

"*Binalonan!*" There was sudden recognition in his face. He smiled at me and drove on. "I used to have a friend from your town. He became a maker of songs in America. . . ."

I looked at him with great yearning. When he saw that I was curious, he patted my head as if I were his own son.

"America is a land far away," he said.

It was the first time I had heard about America. I was going back to my family from a town that seemed hundreds of miles away. When the man drove into our yard, my father came down and carried me lovingly into the house.

"You mustn't run away again, Allos," he said.

He took me to the kitchen where my brothers and sisters were waiting. My mother was spreading food on a low table, but when she saw me in my father's arms, she dropped the ladle in her hand and reached for me.

"We have *enough* food now, son," she said.

I sat on the floor and started to eat; then suddenly I remembered the man who had driven me in his old car. I ran to the window and looked into the yard. But he was already gone— he who was so kind, gentle, and good. Would I see him again somewhere? Would I? Were all people *from* America like him? Were all people *in* America like him?

"He is gone," I said, rushing to the ladder. . . .

I woke up when the man next to me shook me vigorously.

"You were crying in your sleep," he said.

"It was just a dream," I said apologetically.

"We are in San Francisco now," he said, walking to the door of the bus and into the station's waiting room.

I followed him slowly. Suddenly it came to me: it was not a dream. It had actually happened to me when I was a little boy in Binalonan. It had come back to me in a dream, because I had forgotten it. How could I forget one of the most significant events in my childhood? How could I have forgotten a tragedy that was to condition so much of my future life?

CHAPTER XLI

I RETURNED to Los Angeles where I found José waiting for me. He had gone only as far north as San Jose. We prepared a form letter and sent copies to well-known Filipino labor leaders on the Pacific coast. We invited them to a conference in Los Angeles with the idea of organizing a committee on which we could work together irrespective of affiliations.

Ganzo, who had been publishing the *Philippine Commonwealth Times*, was the first to arrive. Three delegates came from Seattle, two from Portland, one from San Francisco, five from Central California, and one from San Diego. There were twenty-one delegates when we finally assembled in the house of the Filipino Communist in Boyle Heights.

I knew most of the delegates because some were members of our old group: the same men who had fought for unionism when it was still illegal to organize workers in California. But the unions had come to stay, and the progressive movement had come too; and some of the Filipinos were joining the ranks of the Communists. All of us wanted to create a working committee from which we could form the nucleus of a broad organization for Filipinos on the Pacific coast.

I did not know that the Los Angeles delegation was controlled by two parvenus, Roman Rios and Javier Lacson, who came to the conference with a red-headed girl from New York. But a nucleus had already been formed in San Francisco, where José, Nick, and Conrado Torres met before they joined us in Los Angeles. When they arrived with the other delegates, I was sure that they would propose a plan for a broad organization. And I was not wrong: on the first day of the conference the Committee for the Protection of Filipino Rights (CPFR) was created.

I was new to two delegates from Seattle, Joe Lozano and

284

Marc Dorion, who came with Torres to represent the state of Washington. These two were active in the labor movement in the north, and officers of the UCAPAWA, Local 7. They were to become the most active supporters of the progressive movement in the Northwest.

On the second day of the conference, the CPFR took up as its major task the campaign for the right of Filipinos to become naturalized American citizens. The new organization had vitality and direction at a time when intelligent leadership among Filipinos was sorely needed. It became, in a way, the most effective weapon of the Filipinos on the West Coast.

I had found something to occupy my time, for in the CPFR I had a channel through which I could release my creative energies. I wrote articles and special news items about our work in the organization. With the intermittent help of José, we published Ganzo's paper. It was the only publication interested in the struggle for a definite social security for Filipinos in the United States. But it lacked the strong financial support that publications of its kind required. My brother Macario, who was never idle for a moment, put up his own money when an issue was withheld by the printers due to unpaid bills.

I believe my inclinations are toward conspiracy. I became restless working on the paper: there was not enough drama in it. I asked myself in moments of agitation what it was that made me react to violence with all my fury. Was violence the only force that could stir me intellectually?

In my sickroom, following the activities of the members of our committee, I became frantic and lonely. I wanted to live their lives, suffer their sufferings. Even when Representative Vito Marcantonio introduced a bill in Congress proposing Filipino citizenship, even then I looked out the window of my room like a prisoner on some isolated island.

I knew, however, that the Marcantonio bill gave us a chance to campaign nationally. I kept in close touch with the branches of the CPFR, which had been established in every important city on the West Coast. I corresponded with the American Committee for the Protection of the Foreign Born, an organization in New York whose program was similar to that of the CPFR. Thus our work was centralized.

Upon the approval of the central committee of the CPFR, I began speaking before American audiences in Southern California. The Hollywood Democratic Committee was very active, so, much as I distrusted the middle class, I embarked upon this new phase of my life with great enthusiasm.

Once, when I spoke in the meeting hall of the Hollywood Chamber of Commerce, where I discussed the predicament of the Filipinos in the United States, I met an American woman who invited me to her house. We rode in her car down Sunset Boulevard until we stopped in front of a white house.

The rug in the living room was as white as the clouds in the skies of Mangusmana. When she went to the icebox, I bent over and felt the soft strands of white hair that were woven into the rug. How luxuriously this woman lived! Was this the reason that made me hate her class? Was my lack of comfort the mainspring of my dark fear?

I sat on a chair deeply agitated. She sat down and we talked about the CPFR. I patiently traced its origin: how it had sprung from the need of Filipinos for a broad organization. It was when she was mixing drinks that the doorbell rang. She looked uncertainly at me, then at the door. Finally she hurried me into the kitchen and ran to the front door.

I heard a man come into the house. But I could not hear what they were talking about. I was burning with indignation. Was I right in my fear after all? Was there no way to cure this land? Why did she push me into hiding when a friend of hers came into the house? Was she ashamed because of my race? What was the real reason? I could not understand it. I did not notice the time. When she came to the kitchen again the man had gone.

"I'll give a party for your organization in my house," she said. "Will you be my guest?"

"Yes, thank you," I said.

"Next week?"

I nodded. My personal pride was hurt. But I was working for

something big. This I knew: Filipinos worked and lived in national terms, so that when they were maligned they thought their whole race was maligned. And so it was with me—with this slight difference: my deepening understanding of socialism was destroying my chauvinism.

But it was strange that when I emerged from the house, I thought of the white rug in the living room with yearning. There was a comforting, delicious feeling in me. As I walked farther from it, I was possessed by a strong desire to buy a rug like it someday.

I had one important job to do: the campaign for the Marcantonio bill. But the race-haters in California were also busy lobbying against it. Headed by a Congressman, with the backing of big farmers and allied interests, they fought the bill and killed it. And there were other groups against Filipinos: Liberty League of California, Daughters of the Golden West, Daughters of the American Revolution, and the Parent-Teacher Association. These, with the Associated Farmers of California as the sharp spearhead, were instrumental in killing every bill favorable to Filipinos in Congress and in the state Legislature. They worked as one group to deprive Filipinos of the right to live as free men in a country founded upon this very principle.

My brother's spirit was broken. His savings had gone into our campaign. One afternoon he came home sick and tired. He went to bed, hoping to gather strength to go back to work the next day. In the morning a man from his place of work came to our apartment.

"You'd better come to work, Macario," he shouted to my brother, "if you want to keep your job."

I was preparing some soup for Macario when I heard him moving about upstairs. I knew he would go. He was searching for his working shoes now. Was he thinking of me? Was he afraid for me if he had no job? Suddenly I seized a butcher knife from the table and rushed madly up the stairway. My brother saw me first, and he leaped for my arm before I could raise it.

"No, Carlos!" he shouted, hanging on the arm with the butcher knife. "No! Let him alone!"

"I'll kill you!" I shouted to the man.

He ran into the other room. When my brother had taken the weapon from me, he went to the room where the man was hiding.

"You must go now," I heard him say.

"I didn't do anything to him," the man protested. "What is the matter with him? Is he crazy?"

"Please go now," Macario said.

I heard them go out together. I closed the door and burst into tears. Why hadn't I killed him? I heard Macario coming back to the house. He went to his room and lay weakly on the bed. I went to the door and peered through the little opening. His hands were neatly folded on his chest. I felt like a little boy whose god has been struck down by evil winds.

I wanted to work now that my brother was ill, but I was too frail to do anything that demanded much physical exertion. Was there no one among our friends who had money to lend? But we were all in the same predicament: we were cornered beyond rescue and the only escape was death.

I walked in the streets at night hoping to meet someone with money. Would I go back to the violence of the old days—with Max and Julio? I felt the gun in my pocket and the desire to kill for money seized my mind. Was not this weapon a symbol of my past? Max had killed a white man with it. I had smashed the head of a Japanese farmer with it. Maybe I could use it again! Why not?

I ran down the street and stopped to look up at the State Building. There was a light in Carey McWilliams's office. I calmed down. I sat on the cement stairway. Maybe I could borrow money from him. I looked up again with anticipation. But when the light went out of his office, I could not face him. I got up quickly and ran home.

I was climbing the cement stairway that went up to our court when I noticed that one of the houses was open. Stealthily I went to the door and peered inside. I heard a woman taking a bath upstairs. On a portable radio, shining like a firefly, was a diamond ring. I slid inside the door and grabbed it. I ran outside and down the stairs into the street, where the sudden warm wind calmed my nerves.

I remembered a place that was a rendezvous of gamblers down the block. It was crowded with the outcasts of Temple Street. I stood patiently behind a lucky gambler; when he had counted his money, I showed him the diamond ring. His dull eyes sparkled. I sold the ring to him with the understanding that I would redeem it when I had the money to pay him back. I knew I could trust a gambler because I had been one of them.

When I arrived at our apartment, I sent for a doctor to examine my brother. In the morning I bought enough groceries to last him for three months, paid the rent, and gave the rest of the money to my brother. I knew that I had to go away for my own sake, because if I did not escape now, I would probably steal again. I had come to the end of the road; in spite of my reading and my association with educated people, I had only become more confused and desperate.

One night, deep in meditation, I was aroused by my brother's sudden stillness. I was seized with panic. I switched on the lights. He was sleeping soundly. How old he had grown! My brother who had never worked in the Philippines! I switched off the lights and went downstairs. Oh, my brother who gave me light in the dark of night!

I sat at the bare table in the kitchen and began piecing together the mosaic of our lives in America. Full of loneliness and love, I began to write.

CHAPTER XLII

WHEN our campaign for Filipino citizenship was broken up, Rios and Lacson tried to convert the CPFR into a separate unit of the Communist Party. Anna Dozier was indefatigable: she sought the different members of our committee. Then she and Lacson drove to San Francisco where, after converting our members there, they proceeded to Portland. But from there Lacson came back to Los Angeles alone, silent about Anna Dozier, secretive about his activities.

A week afterward an attractive middle-aged American woman, Lucia Simpson, began appearing at our meetings with Lacson. Almost at the same time another woman from San Diego came to see me. She had an amazing intuition. Sometimes, when it was raining, we sat in the apartment and discoursed for hours. I would stop in the middle of a sentence to listen to the gentle patter of rain on the roof (how it reminded me of years long gone!) and resume our conversation unperturbed. And Jean Lawson, for that was her name, would discuss mankind, smiling, so that every building, stone, face—yes, even a blade of grass loomed large with a new meaning.

Why were there so many strange women all of a sudden? Was there something going on among Filipinos that I did not know about? But my unflagging interest in people drew me close to Jean Lawson. While I was interested in the fundamentals of abstract ideas, I was not blind to the emotional urgencies. It seemed that Jean had been married to a man prominent in the labor movement in Seattle.

"But that was when I was young," she said. "I went to the Philippines and taught at the University of Manila. But my participation in the boycott against the entry of Japanese products aroused the anger of some native fascists. I was forced to resign.

I was too naïve at first. I didn't know that Philippine capitalists were closely tied up with the Falangist movement in Spain."

"I think the Falange gets its orders direct from Berlin," I said.

She looked up at me, curling up like a little doll on the couch. "I went to the peasant provinces of Luzon," she continued. "I worked with the people there, taught their children, and helped some of their women. But I was chased out by the vanguards of absentee landlordism, the enemy of the peasantry. I went to Manila and helped in the formation of the Philippine Writers' League, an organization of artists and writers with progressive ideas. Then my health began to give way; so I came back to the United States."

Jean's interlude among Filipinos in California touched me more deeply than the others. I later discovered that she had been sent by an educational director of the Communist Party to guide me. But by then she had gone. She died later in New Mexico.

Lucia Simpson took it upon herself to put new life into the dying CPFR. She rented a house and persuaded Lacson and Rios to live with her; but some time later Rios, jealous of Lacson, stabbed Lucia in the arm. Rios fled, and Lacson took possession of Lucia's household. But when Mariano was introduced in our group, Lucia asked him to take the place of Rios. When she had an argument with Lacson and Mariano, she drove them off and took an innocent Filipino newspaperman into her house.

I was disgusted and broken-hearted. José proposed that we should affiliate the CPFR with the American League for Peace and Democracy. It seemed to me that it would have been a good move, but I was losing interest. I was tired. At night when I came home from work, I sat by my brother's sickbed and read to him. There was one book that he wanted me to read over and over—Thomas Wolfe's *Of Time and the River*. I read the beautiful passages about October and death, and Macario turned away from me, deep in thought, his gaze far away.

When I was reading Michael Gold's *Jews Without Money*, Macario stopped me.

"It's not impossible for a man with very little education to become a writer," he said. "You can do it, Carlos."

"I'll do it," I told him.

"I'll wait, Carlos," he said.

Macario was growing worse. I wanted to locate Amado; although he had gone out of my life, I felt that he must conciliate with Macario. I wanted him to know that in the face of death, in this alien land, we could hold onto each other. I tried all my resources, but he had vanished completely. Then, as a last recourse, I made contacts with the Filipino underworld. It was from this attempt to locate Amado that I uncovered the most sinister influence of Filipino gangland upon the Filipino people.

I was frightened. There was Eileen Odell—she would understand my thoughts and feelings. But I did not realize, until she told me, that I had not seen her for one whole year. I did not realize that my work in the organization had kept me away from her.

I also discovered that Lucia Simpson was now in full control of the CPFR. She was again living with Lacson and receiving money from unknown sources. Was her interest in Filipino problems a blind for her emotional demands? I was amazed at her insatiable thirst for the company of men.

I deliberated with myself. I felt that Lucia's participation in our cause was merely a front. I was convinced of it when she ran off to Honolulu with Lacson. It was the last time I saw her. But Lacson came back to the United States after two years, bitter toward the Communist Party which was, according to him, the embodiment of all that was evil in Lucia Simpson.

But Lacson was diabolical; he had the characteristics of a primitive who might run berserk, upon slight provocation. And Rios, one of Lucia's disciples, practiced tribalism. I could not understand their "proletarian feeling of superiority." They sneered at me because I was now showing signs of being an "intellectual"—this was the word they used contemptuously behind my back. I tried to explain that my fraternity with them was genuine and rooted in a common ground, that what they termed the "rapid liberalization of my radicalism" was not necessarily a sure sign that I would ultimately betray the working class.

I felt that their distrust would draw them away from me. I felt that we could work harmoniously together if only they would discard their mask of "proletarian pretense"—a phrase I used to describe their working class arrogance. And they hated me more for it. I knew, then, that I must rise above them: that I must consolidate our gains in my own way.

Lacson and Rios were immature, stupid, ignorant, and useless. They paraded as members of the Communist Party although they had no actual membership in it. The Party had little use for the Filipinos as a group because they were too few. But the time came, later, when a better type of Filipino took up their people's cause and thereby contributed positively to the prestige of the Party.

I can say now that communism among Filipinos had a false start. It was propagated by stupid little men, anti-Filipino. The principles for which the Party stood were nebulous and inspiring. If they were subscribed to by little men like Rios and Lacson, the unavoidable result would be confusion and misunderstanding. And confusion it was: the educated Filipino understood the Party, but the ordinary working man was afraid of it.

But the Communist Party had contributed something definite toward the awakening of Filipinos on the West Coast. Even when it had entirely forsaken them, a few of the more enlightened members gathered the carcass of their hope in socialism and tried to breathe a new life into it. I felt that I belonged to this second phase of the Communist movement among Filipinos, that I would draw inspiration and courage from it to withstand the confusion and utter futility of my own life.

With this last hope, I looked toward the north once again. I wanted to run away from the stifling narrowness of Temple Street. There in the broad fields, under the wide skies, there in the wide world of grass, trees, and stars my mind would stir and radiate with a new light. I was obsessed with looking across vast lands and staring into the sky. In vast spaces I found a nameless relief from the smallness of my world in America.

I had saved enough money for my brother to last him two months. I bade him good-bye, but I was afraid to shake his hand. I wanted him to understand that my farewell was like his farewell, years ago. I was not running away from him because he was sick and helpless. I was running away from myself, because I was afraid myself. I was afraid of all that was despairing in that swamp of filth—that dark dungeon of inquisitional terror and fear.

CHAPTER XLIII

O N A cold winter day I went to the freight yard and boarded a boxcar to Bakersfield. I coughed violently. I remembered bitterly my years of flight across the continent. I had been young and strong then. Now I felt tired and old. There were no hoboes any more. The unemployed men of another decade had gone. I felt my whole youth slipping away from me.

I sat in the dark corner of the boxcar and reviewed my life. The cold could not touch me any more. It came to me that poverty was the thread of my life, that it gave it a rounded meaning. It was toward midnight when I arrived in Bakersfield. I went to Chinatown hoping to find someone I knew. The gambling houses were closing and the farm workers were returning to their camps.

I was cold and hungry. I went to a Mexican beer joint. I sat in an empty booth, close to a gas heater. I must have dozed off, because when I looked up a man in a large overcoat stood near me. I was startled when I saw him. It was my brother Amado! My heart sank, not because of his sudden appearance, but because of his condition. He had grown old and haggard. There was a long scar on his left hand. He looked as though he had been roughly handled.

"Amado!" I said.

He looked down at me. "What are you doing here, Carlos?"

"I just arrived by freight from Los Angeles," I said.

"I thought you were dead," he said tonelessly. "I heard that you had died at the hospital."

"It was a false alarm," I said. "I'm not dead yet. Not yet. I'll let you know when the time comes."

"I was in Los Angeles at the time of your last operation," he said. "I gave a pint of my blood and left."

"Why didn't you tell me?" I asked. "I knew that some man gave his blood for me."

"I told the doctor not to tell you. I wanted to see you when you were better, but later I heard that you were dead. So I left Los Angeles and wandered here and there."

"You should have told me," I said.

"It's all right now," he said. "Let's go to my room."

We walked three blocks to an old building, and climbed up the dark stairway. It was the smallest room I had ever seen, probably six feet by five. We sat on the cot. When I mentioned that I had not yet eaten, Amado looked down at his hands and fell silent. I saw the length of scar on the back of his hand.

As though he wanted to justify himself, Amado looked at me pleadingly. He said: "This room is only fifteen cents. I have to have a place to sleep. I can't stand the cold any more, Carlos! I've been away in a cold, hard place—" His voice trailed off in a whisper.

"You shouldn't have sent me the money when you were in Arizona," I said.

"Did you send it to mother as I told you?" he asked.

"I did. But it was too late. Luciano was already buried when the money reached Binalonan. Mother gave it to his children."

"I'm glad," Amado said. And then: "I cough at night. There is something tight in my chest when it is cold."

I was angry with myself again. I wished I had not come upon him. When I fell suddenly asleep on the cot, Amado covered me with an old army blanket. He slept in his ragged overcoat on the floor. In the morning we agreed to meet at a gambling house. I went to several Filipino camps near by. When I met him at our rendezvous, Amado was jubilant. He had two dollars. We rushed to a chop suey house and ordered enough food to last us for two days.

When the feast was over we sat in the sun. At three in the afternoon, when the gambling houses opened, I took his last twenty-five cents. I almost lost it, but after two hours of careful playing, I made one dollar. Amado pulled my arm vigorously. He wanted me to stop. But I played on until I had five dollars.

I began to believe that if I took up gambling as a profession, I could probably be a great success.

In the evening, on my way to the freight yard, I told Amado about Macario.

"I'll look for a job, Carlos," Amado said seriously. "If you say Macario is ill, I'll go to Los Angeles and look for a job."

"I'm glad you feel that way," I said. "Here is the rest of the money. Go to Los Angeles now."

He grabbed the money and looked at me as though he wanted to cry. His mouth trembled.

"Thank you, Carlos," he said. "Thank you for being my brother."

I saw him in the pale light waving his hand with the long scar. He was weeping—not because I was going away from him, but because of the swift, frightening years. His eyes, when he looked at me for pity and understanding, were haunted with the terror of those years. They were the same eyes that had looked at me kindly in the heavy rain of Mangusmana. They were the same eyes that had looked startled when my father had struck him sharply across the face—the same eyes that cried with a deep brotherly love when he shouted to me in the heavy rain, "Good-bye, Allos!"

It seemed so long ago that Amado had waved his hand to say good-bye. When I remembered him waving at me with his mud-caked hand, I was startled when I discovered that it was now scarred. All my hate and bitterness had turned to pity for him. When I told myself that I had gone out of his life entirely in Hollywood, when I asked him to help Macario go to college, I was angered only by my own inability to help either of them. But now I knew that in a strange way we were together again—that no terror could ever make us hate each other.

When I arrived in Portland snow was falling. I phoned Nick at the office of the UCAPAWA, where he was still secretary-treasurer. He came immediately and drove me in his car. We went to his room. I was eager to know about his work, but he was very quiet. Finally, when I had pressed him, he confessed that the CPFR had completely disintegrated in Portland.

"It's dead, Carl," he said.

"There is no hope then?" I asked.

"We need new men to work with us," he said. "Our forces are deeply entangled in the labor movement. We need new men, that's all."

I felt that it was true. But I stayed on in Portland hoping to proceed to Seattle. One night, on our way back to Nick's room from a meeting of John Reed College students, who were members of the Young Communist League, an avalanche of snow fell upon the car. It took us hours to dig it out, but it was not damaged. We cursed the dark sky and drove on, feeling desolate with cold.

When I woke up in the morning to put some wood in the stove, I was stricken by a fit of coughing and began to hemorrhage. My chest ached. My eyes were bloodshot. Nick was alarmed: he walked ten blocks to get me something to eat. Then he rushed to his office, coming back again in the afternoon to give me what I needed.

Was this *it?* The doctor had told me it would be five years. Was this to be the end of my life? I was not afraid to die, but there were so many things to do. Every day for a month Nick ran back and forth between his office and the room. I thought I should never live to see California again.

CHAPTER XLIV

THIS was the third time Nick had come to my rescue. He knew that wine would irritate the lesions in my lungs. But he knew too that it was not only the disease that was weakening me, but also the black frustration that wrapped my life. Nick brought a bottle of wine one evening and drank with me. The wine dulled the edges of my pain, and my loneliness was temporarily forgotten. I put my head against the wall and wept, so deep was my hunger, so great my loneliness.

I decided that I would live under any compromise with death. To laugh and shout and sing in the world, facing ultimate death, was dramatic and violent. I had what I wanted at last: a physical violence that evoked the cruelest mental violence. From now on, death or life, I would squeeze every minute to the last drop of activity, rushing toward millions of moments of death in the world.

I cried and drank wine with Nick while the snow fell upon the city and melted in the street, while the sky darkened and clouds massed together above Portland, while the winter slowly slipped away and gave flashes of the momentary light of spring. After a month I felt strong again, and the thought of California sunshine consoled me. Nick drove me to the bus station, shook my hand in grave parting, then rushed back to the union office where a charge of mismanagement of funds was awaiting him.

I transferred to another bus in San Francisco, and sat at the back with a girl of about nineteen. Her hair was light brown, her skin milk-white. But her eyes were deep blue and frightened. Her name was Mary.

"I'm on my way to Los Angeles," she said. "But I don't know anybody there.

"I was born in a small town in Pennsylvania," she told me. "It's a miserable mining town, full of Irish and dark Europeans. But at the age of twelve, when my mother died, I went to live with relatives in Philadelphia. I had a disagreement with my relatives when I finished college. The depression had already begun. I left then with a college friend, a boy of some wealth from a midwest city. . . ."

She lighted a cigarette and fell silent, staring out of the bus window. It was raining when we arrived in Los Angeles. I got a taxi and asked her if she would like to ride with me. When I got out at my street, Mary got out too and followed me with hesitant steps up the cement stairway that led to our apartment.

I almost stepped on Victor and my brother Amado, who were sleeping on the floor in the living room. José was sprawled on the couch—he had left his wife, I was told later. On the floor of the kitchen, wrapped in blankets, was Ganzo's hulking form. He was snoring: he filled the house with the smell of liquor.

I woke up José and told him to go upstairs. He opened his eyes with a start, reached for his artificial leg, and hopped up the stairway holding the stump in his hands. I went to the kitchen and pulled a blanket from Ganzo. I gave it to Mary and told her to sleep on the couch. I lay down on the floor near her.

But I could not sleep. It was the same life all over again. None of us was employed. But we were together, and out of this fraternity something binding might come, to give us some sort of a foothold in America. Quietly I got up and lighted a match. I watched Mary's face. She woke with a start.

"It's all right," I said.

"I was frightened," she said.

"You can go to sleep now," I told her.

"Good night."

Sometime afterward, in answer to my inquiry regarding the charges against him, Nick told me that he had been ousted from the union. I remembered what Nick had told me in confidence when I was in Portland: that during the last two years of his administration unemployed union members had borrowed money from him to sustain themselves. Nick's salary was negligible. His enemies had accused him of taking money from the union treasury, and of covering it with his salary. Waiting to trap him, when they were sure that Nick was unable to produce the money, they brought him before the members. Despite his good intentions he was tried and discharged, but his defeat was also the defeat of progressive unionism among Filipinos in Oregon.

Nick tried to regain his prestige in Alaska, where he had gone the following season to work, but even there the protagonists of the contract system were also gaining ground. This was the same method used when I had worked in Rose Inlet. I also received a letter from Conrado Torres in Seattle. Thus one by one, upon the disintegration of the CPFR, the UCAPAWA locals fell into the hands of opportunists. It was the beginning of a new reactionary leadership. This was significant because fascism had spread rapidly in Europe, giving way to a general confusion in all the civilized countries.

But I had Mary, and she was very understanding. She was ready to listen when I had something to say. I talked only when I was lonely and melancholy. She had become a symbol of goodness. My companions felt the same toward her. She became the delicate object of our affections. She was an angel molded into purity by the cleanliness of our thoughts. When a stranger came into our household and looked at her longingly, I could see some of my companions doubling their fists. This platonic relationship among us was healthy and clean, and in a way it gave me a new faith in myself.

Then from Seattle, tired of the confusion there, Conrado Torres came to stay with us. He and José, who were forever drinking, filled the apartment with the smell of whisky and sour wine. Every morning the Mexican children in the neighborhood came with their dirty juke sacks and collected the empty bottles in the backyard and sold them in a grocery store down the block; then, running to a bakery shop farther down the street, they bought loaves of bread and retired to their squalid houses.

Sometimes, however, emboldened by our camaraderie, they came into the kitchen and tasted the white rice that Mary

cooked. They crowed with delight when the plates were filled
with Filipino food and set before them. One time a boy of five
came into the kitchen unannounced. José and Ganzo were preparing an edition of the *Philippine Commonwealth Times*. I did
not see the boy grab the tall glass of wine on the table. When
I looked for it the boy was already rolling on the floor. The
glass was empty; the boy's mouth was dripping with red wine.
He was already drunk.

I was frightened. But José got up from the table and filled
another glass with wine. He knelt by the boy and offered the
wine again, laughing idiotically when the child emptied the
glass. Then the boy lay flat on his stomach, speechless, as though
he were dead. José carried him to the couch where he slept off
his drunkenness.

But every day afterward the boy came into the kitchen looking eagerly for the bottle of wine. He had learned to enjoy
drinking. I was ashamed of his debauchery. I could not look at
him. But I knew that he had to drink, that he would drink. He
would look at me with his beady, watery eyes when I hid the
bottle, his mouth hanging loose, his hands jerking with nervous-
ness. I filled the glass and placed it on the table, close within his
reach. I would look in the other direction when he grabbed it.

Mary came home one afternoon and saw the Mexican boy
with the bottle of wine. She took it away and slapped him
sharply. Then she pushed him outside the house. He did not
resist. He waited patiently in the backyard. When he was sure
that Mary had gone, he threw pebbles at the window. José went
out with the bottle. They drank the wine standing, passing the
bottle back and forth. When it was empty they started cursing
each other; then José smashed the bottle against the wall of the
house.

I was ashamed. But we were in a poverty-stricken neighborhood. I knew that the Mexican boy was starving. The wine gave
him release, and soothed his hunger. I thought of myself when
I was his age. Would he grow up to revolt against his environment? Would he strike at his world? Would he escape? I knew
that he would grow up to destroy this planless life around him,

or it would destroy him. I knew that he would make a great
noise before he was through with it.

Those were dark days. A black melancholy filled me. And
then my brother Amado, who had not worked as he had promised when I saw him in Bakersfield, began bringing suspicious
characters into the apartment. Mary was still with us, but she
withdrew into her room. Then one day she disappeared without
a word of farewell. When I came upon her months later, in a
music store where she was a salesgirl, she clutched me and wept.
The whole world could not contain my thoughts and emotions,
losing one so delicate and molded into purity out of our hope
for a better America.

Mary would not come to our apartment any more; she would
go out into the cities; she would disappear forever. She would
not want to see us any more. She would be lost to us forever.
I wanted to shake humanity out of its insensibility. I wanted to
crush all life into tiny fragments of hate. The tears that fell upon
my coat were heavier than the whole world. I never saw Mary
again. Conrado ran off to Alaska and stayed there for three
years, coming back to the mainland only when he joined the
war that had come upon the world.

Ganzo also retreated to Pismo Beach, in a shack by the sea.
Victor went away to live with an eighteen-year-old girl with two
children. He came back when the girl left him. I became acutely
aware of my brother Macario. How old and work-scarred he
had become! He dragged himself into the house at night, fell
into bed like a log; when morning came he rushed off to work
again, his steps becoming shorter and slower as the months
passed.

I was ready for violence again, ready to lash out at anything.
And I was afraid—afraid that I might kill.

I was reading a story I had written when Macario and Amado
started arguing in the kitchen about Amado's suspicious-looking
friends. They were eating when suddenly I heard the table crash
to the floor. I ran to the kitchen and found them grappling on
the floor, rice still in their hands. I stood watching them, not

knowing what to do. They were both my brothers. I did not
want to take sides. But this fight was to decide on which side I
would be, because as I watched them with mixed emotions, I
knew that it was like the other incidents in my life. I had come
at last to the turning point in my relationship with my brothers.

Suddenly Macario shouted to me. "Go away, Carlos!"

Amado was reaching for a butcher knife. I jumped to grab
it away. But I was too late. It was already in his hand. Then
doing what seemed to me the only thing to do, I grabbed a frying pan and struck Amado's head with all my force. He fell
backward and rolled over on his stomach. I snatched the knife
from his weakening hand. Macario looked at me with surprised
eyes, then went upstairs to wash the blood from his face and
hands.

I watched Amado stir. Slowly he opened his eyes; when he
saw me and memory returned, he got slowly to his feet and went
to the living room. He sat on the couch and began to cry.

"You shouldn't have done it, Carlos," he said bitterly.

"I had to do it," I tried to explain. "You were going to kill
Macario. It was the only way I could take the knife away from
you. I had to strike you into unconsciousness."

"You shouldn't have done it," he said again. He went upstairs. He came down with his suitcase and stopped at the door.
"You shouldn't have done it," he said almost in a whisper and
left.

I ran to the door to ask for forgiveness, but he was gone. It
was not only the physical pain that had hurt him; there were
many things involved. I had no right to strike an older brother.
It was a bad omen; I would never be happy again. I had not only
transgressed against a family tradition; I had also struck down
one of the gods of my childhood.

CHAPTER XLV

I was afraid to plunge into the life of violence on Temple Street. But I was driven to its very edge, since there was no intellectual preoccupation to hold me. Several times I found myself falling into it. I went back to books and tried to pick up where I left off. I became fascinated by three young American writers: Howard Fast, Jesse Stuart, Irwin Shaw. Fast had just written an historical novel, Stuart a volume of sonnets, and Shaw a collection of bitter short stories.

I was irresistibly drawn by their contemporaneousness, their realism and youth. In Fast, for instance, I caught a glimpse of the mainsprings of American democracy in the armies of George Washington; but in Stuart, I felt the quality and depth of men's lives in their attachment to each other and to the common earth that sustains them. I felt a kinship with Shaw, whose bitterness and oblique humor are traceable to a feeling of isolation in a society where he is an unwilling heir to bourgeois taste and prejudice.

I was intellectually stimulated again—and I wanted to discuss problems which had been bothering me. But when I came home to our apartment, sitting alone in the midst of drab walls and ugly furniture, I felt like striking at my invisible foe. Then I began to write.

I began writing brief sketches of a time in my life long shrouded by the years. I wrote stories and sketches about my early life in America. It was easy to write: the words came swiftly and ideas shaped effortlessly out of them. I was in everything I wrote—in poetry, stories, and autobiographical pieces. Then some magazines in Manila began publishing me; in a little while small checks arrived to give me new hope. I wrote

305

every day and the past began to come back to me in one sweeping flood of memories.

The time had come, I felt, for me to utilize my experiences in written form. I had something to live for now, and to fight the world with; and I was no longer afraid of the past. I felt that I would not run away from myself again.

Meanwhile our landlady died of an heart attack and another took her place, a young blonde woman new to the district. Not realizing that it was a notorious neighborhood, she wanted to make the apartment houses as respectable as possible. She threw out tenants one after the other until, eventually, we were all requested to move.

I knew the impossibility of finding a *decent* house. I suggested to Macario that a hotel room would be just as comfortable as an apartment. I found a hotel on Third Street that was tenanted by dark Europeans. It was managed by an elderly woman who, when I asked if Orientals were accepted, explained that it was *not* an American establishment. She meant that Filipinos were allowed to stay so long as they abided by the rules. In other places I had felt like a criminal, running up to my room in fear and closing the door suspiciously, as though the whole world were conspiring against me.

One evening, when Macario was well enough to work again, I was invited to attend a private party for a Filipino educator who had just arrived from the Philippines to study phases of the modern educational system in the United States. The party was held at the back of a restaurant on First Street; only men were invited because it would be *primitive*. When we were seated at the table, I noticed that there was no silverware. Then I understood what was meant by *primitive*, which was, of course, to eat with bare hands—the way I used to eat as a peasant in Luzon.

The prominent educator put on his ribboned glasses and began balling the steaming rice with his hand. He told brilliant anecdotes when his mouth was not full, recalling his youth with the poor peasants of northern Luzon where, it seemed, he had learned to eat rice with bare hands.

We were in the middle of dinner when two police detectives broke into the back room and shouted:

"Put up your hands and don't move!"

I raised my hands out of habit, but I felt the old panic and indignation in me. My companions also submissively raised their hands—some even jumped to their feet and held their hands high above their heads. I resented raising my hands, but what could I do? The detectives pointed their guns at us, shouting for absolute silence. All of us raised our hands except our guest, who was innocent of the attitude of the police toward the Filipinos.

I saw one of the detectives staring at our guest; then, infuriated because he had not been obeyed, he jumped at him. The beribboned glasses fell on the floor and broke into pieces. The educator unwillingly raised his hands, the hot rice still neatly balled in his small palm.

I felt violated and outraged. I looked at my companions, old-timers like myself and familiar with this kind of treatment. I thought of my gun lying on the table in my room. If only I had it with me! I turned around to look for a side door. But there was no way to escape.

When the detectives had searched our pockets for concealed weapons, they went their arrogant way and gave warning to the proprietor not to let white women into the place. The educator lowered his hands slowly and blinked at us. I thought for a moment he would break down and cry, but he bit his lips and gathered his dignity about him.

"My countrymen," he said, "is there no way to make the American people respect us in the way that we respect them?"

I felt the old anger inside me. I jumped to my feet and rushed outside, running blindly toward my hotel. I wanted my gun. With it I could challenge our common enemy bullet for bullet. It seemed my only friend and comfort in this alien country— this smooth little bit of metal. As I ran through the crowd, hopping like a frog because of my stiff leg, I thought of Max Smith who had killed a white man with my gun. If he were only here! I knew he would have faced the two detectives with it. I knew he would rather die than witness the humiliation of a respected countryman.

But in my room Macario grabbed the gun from me, unloading it so that I could not use it. For a moment I looked at him with hatred, then I turned, went to my bed, and lay face down, holding my chest against the wild beating of my heart.

I felt numb for days. When I regained my composure, I sensed the futility of my writing. I wanted action—and violence. The monotony of my existence led me into the Filipino underworld, into the tangle of Oriental gangland, where I came upon Julio of the Moxee City days. He had become a Robin Hood among Filipinos, because he swindled only Chinese and white men. He had a partner, a young, handsome Filipino named Rommy, who had just stolen nearly three hundred Federal Social Security checks.

"This is nothing," he boasted. "I have already cashed about ten thousand dollars."

"Do you call that excitement, Rommy?" Julio asked him jokingly.

"But there is money in it," Rommy said.

"How do you get the checks?" I asked.

"It's simple, pal," Rommy said. "In the morning when the mailman comes around, I follow him with a bundle of shopping papers. I pretend to deliver the papers to the houses, but the moment the mailman turns his back, I grab the letters in the box and follow him to the next house. It is easy. I could follow him for blocks, and he wouldn't suspect anything. Nobody suspects anything until after the checks fail to arrive."

"Rommy can't write his name," Julio whispered to me.

"How do you cash the checks?" I asked Rommy.

"I cash them at the racetracks and in gambling houses," he said.

"Tell him how you got into the racket, Rommy," Julio said.

"I was tired of washing dishes," Rommy said. "I was tired of democracy. Phooey!" He screwed up his eyes, twisted his mouth, and sneered.

One afternoon Ganzo found me wandering, walking aimlessly in Golden Gate Park. He took me to his room and gave me a bath. Then he put me in bed and locked the door. At midnight, when I awakened, he came in with sandwiches and a bottle of milk.

"What happened to me?" I asked him.

"You have been on a bender," he said.

"Where am I?"

"San Francisco. I was told you were here, so I stayed on, hoping to bump into you. I still have the paper and I need a good writer. Drink this milk and eat these sandwiches. We will go back to Los Angeles together."

I told Ganzo that I was ready. We rushed to the station. In the bus, warm with the thought of seeing my brother again, I told Ganzo humorous stories of my childhood in Mangusmana.

"You should write those stories," he said.

"I will, Ganzo," I said.

"Why not practice on my paper?"

It seemed a brilliant idea. "Why not?"

"You shouldn't get drunk again," he said almost paternally. "You are the only one left in our crowd. Now, those stories. When you arrive in Los Angeles, get a job and start writing again."

"It will be the last pull, Ganzo," I said. "I have tried it several times. If I fail again, it will be horrible. I could become the most vicious Filipino criminal in America."

"That is why you must not fail this time, Carl," he said. "You've got to succeed for all our sakes."

"I'm afraid," I said.

And I was really afraid. . . .

CHAPTER XLVI

I TRIED to find a job in Los Angeles, but the only thing I could get was manual labor too heavy for me. I even had the temerity to apply at the offices of the large daily newspapers. I knew without doubt that I could not get a job from them, but I thought I would try. I helped Ganzo put out an edition of his paper and went to San Pedro, where the fish canneries were just opening for the season. On my second day of work, when I was walking along the waterfront, I met Nick on his way to one of the canneries. I did not know that he had left Portland when he had been discharged from the union.

One day standing in the slight rain, waiting for the cannery to open, I wrote a short, reminiscent story entitled "The Laughter of my Father." I stuck it in my hat and forgot all about it; when I came upon it nearly two years afterward, I found the literary opportunity for which I had been working so hard. But in San Pedro, when Ganzo came back from his monthly tour around California for advertisements, I wrote for his newspaper without a byline. I was not paid for my work, but it was something I knew. The variety of my writings in Ganzo's paper was to become a valuable asset in later years.

I found out that Nick was trying a new territory, now that he was through with the canneries in Alaska. One night he invited me to go to a house not far from my hotel, and in the living room, discussing in whispers, were several cannery workers: Japanese, Mexicans, Filipinos, and white Americans. The woman of the house, a big Yugoslav, was possessed of a dynamic personality. She dominated the group, but her gentleness was unmistakable. Sometimes her husband, a longshoreman, came late at night and joined our discussion.

I felt something growing inside me again. There was the same thing in each of them that possessed me: their common faith in the working man. I sat with them and listened eagerly. Sometimes I participated in the discussions. Then it came to me that we were all fighting against one enemy: *Fascism.* It was in every word and gesture, every thought.

My brother Macario was also awakening to a new decade's demands. When I went to Los Angeles to see him, I met strange people in his room. They talked wisely and sometimes exuberantly. But always they were honest, eager, gentle. They were ordinary laborers, but none of them was conscious of the kind of work the other did. It seemed to me that they were bound by a common understanding that shone in the room.

I was slowly becoming a part of their thoughts and hopes. Here at last was the configuration of my labors and aspirations. In San Pedro, among the cannery workers, the old men started attending our meetings. They spoke out their minds in broken English, but always with sincerity and passion. I was amazed to find that they were politically informed. Then it came to me how absolutely *necessary* it was to acquaint the Filipinos with the state of the nation.

When the fishing season in San Pedro was over, I left for a small agricultural town called Nipomo. I worked with a crew of pea pickers. I found a new release. The land had always been important to me. I felt my old peasant heritage returning with fresh nourishment. I knew that my future was linked with these tillers of the soil, from whose common source I had sprung.

I started a little workers' school and invited the pea pickers. They were shy at first, but as the days went by, they became more natural and then bold. They were interested in American history. I quoted from memory, remembering the hundreds of books that I had read in the hospital. I traced the growth of democracy in the United States, illustrating the achievements of each epoch with the contributions of its dominant personality.

Then the old men who spoke little English began to participate in the discussions. When I pointed out that the advance of democracy was related to the working man's struggle for better wages and living conditions, I felt a warm feeling of humanity growing inside me. It was easy for them to understand me, and I understood their bold, broken thoughts. I understood the simplicity of their hearts, the eagerness of their faces.

I left Nipomo before the season was over, giving my place to a young man who was the most alert among them. I knew that he would finish my pioneering work among the pea pickers. I went to Betteravia, a town fifteen miles away. In this little town, nestling like dried mushrooms, were Filipino and Mexican sugar beet workers. I worked with them and started another class. But unlike the Filipinos in Nipomo, these men were religious and wanted their discussions salted with biblical parables.

I went to Santa Maria and bought a Bible. I started my lectures on American history, but always went back to the Bible for historical analogies. I talked about the flight of Moses and his tribe; the sorrows of Ruth among an alien people; the enduring patience of a grand old man named Job. As I spoke to them, and beyond them, I thought of an earlier time in Binalonan when my brother Macario was explaining the message of Moses in the Old Testament. Now, here among common laborers, I understood the full significance of Moses's flight from the enemy of his people.

"All these persecutions happened a long time ago in an ancient land," I told them. "But they are significant to us because we are undergoing similar persecutions. We who came to the United States as immigrants are Americans too. All of us were immigrants—all the way down the line. We are Americans all who have toiled for this land, who have made it rich and free. But we must not demand from America, because she is still our unfinished dream. Instead we must sacrifice for her: let her grow into bright maturity through our labors. If necessary we must give up our lives that she might grow unencumbered."

Their eyes glowed with a new faith. They nodded with deep reverence. This was what I had been looking for in America! To make my own kind understand this vast land from our own experiences. When I was sure that I had implanted the seed of my message, I gave my place to a Mexican. I felt that I had done my job well in Betteravia.

I went to Pescadero, among the brown hills of Central California. I went from town to town, forming workers' classes and working in the fields. I knew that I was also educating myself. I was learning from the men. I was rediscovering myself in their lives. They had been exiled from me for years. But now we were together again. I felt my faith extending toward a future that shone with a new hope.

When I went to Monterey I again found José. I had been separated from him for a whole year, and I was eager to know what he was doing. He took me to a little wooden house not far from the sea. When I sat on a bench to look at the pile of political magazines on a table, José disappeared for a moment and came back with a bottle of wine. He gave me a glass and started telling me about his work.

"I have been teaching the history of unionism," he said.

"It's strange!" I exclaimed.

"You have been doing the same, Carl?" he asked.

"Yes," I said. "But we are not alone. Your brother Nick is doing it too. And my brother Macario, in his own way, among the city workers. It seems so long ago that we started the education of our people."

"You remember that night in Oxnard? And in San Jose? I thought I would never live to see you again."

"The revolution is not far off," I said, laughing. "I will live to see it."

"Then the real work will begin!" José shouted.

I was sure now that we were at last beginning to play our own role in the turbulent drama of history. I did not understand it then, did not realize that this was the one and only common thread that bound us together, white and black and brown, in America. I felt a great surge of happiness inside me!

I jumped to my feet and walked around to stop the tears of joy that were appearing at the edges of my eyes. Our awakening was spontaneous: it grew from our experiences and our responses to them. A long time ago in Los Angeles, when we had been less articulate, my brother Macario had spoken of *America in the hearts of men*. Now I understood what he meant, for it was this small yet vast heart of mine that had kept me steering toward the stars.

I had not noticed that several men and women had come into the house. Some of the men were hanging electric bulbs in the yard. When everybody had arrived, a Mexican girl distributed the gifts. Where had I seen this fraternity before? Was it in Mangusmana among the peasants?

I saw a Chinese farmer coming toward me with a sack of rice. He dumped it laughingly in front of me and said:

"You! You! You!"

I laughed, too, because I knew that it was for me. I touched his rough hand.

"Thank you," I said.

He laughed and the sincere ring of his laughter filled the house. Then he turned around and disappeared in the crowd. I went outside and two Filipinos followed me. I walked down the block and stopped under a pepper tree. A Mexican came running to me with a jug of wine. He uncorked it. I took it from him.

"Good *vino*, no?" he said.

"First class," I shouted in the wind.

"It's first class *vino*, all right," he said, tilting the jug above his mouth.

I took it from him again. Then the orchestra in the yard began to play. The men and women started dancing. I could see the glow of their shiny heads in the pale light.

The Mexican was listening eagerly to the music. "*Vamos—* dance!" he said suddenly.

I ran toward the house, the half-filled jug gurgling under my arm. The Mexican was running beside me and slapping the cob-webs of drunkenness from his face.

CHAPTER XLVII

O NE SUNDAY afternoon as I sat in a bar, the radio suddenly blared into my consciousness:

JAPAN BOMBS PEARL HARBOR!

My first thought was for my brother Macario. I ran to his hotel, past the people in the lobby, and up to his room. Joe Tauro was there, listening attentively to my brother's portable radio.

"It has come, Carlos!" he shouted.

Macario came out of the bathroom and stood behind Joe. I stood facing them, our thoughts running back to the Philippines. Suddenly Joe slumped to the floor and burst into tears, beating the chair with his fists. My brother lifted him to his feet and motioned to me to follow them. We went out of the hotel and walked aimlessly in the streets. Somewhere on Broadway Street we came upon José, who had just arrived from Monterey with his son.

"The end has come, Carl," he said sorrowfully.

I could not say anything: it was impossible to think now. I took his son's hand and walked on with them, thinking of the time when I was a little boy and Macario had come home from Lingayen for a visit. I had been José's son's age then, and the day had been like this one; I had walked comfortably between my father and Macario toward our house. I looked at the boy with sadness.

I thought, "Will another war wreck your life? Will you be another lost person on the earth?"

Silently we walked to Joe's apartment, on Sunset Boulevard, where he lived alone. Joe went into the kitchen and came out with a quart bottle of bourbon. He and my brother did not drink, but the time had come for them to try it. José drank a whole glass: soon he started shouting drunkenly and kicking at his wooden leg. Joe jumped to his feet and ripped off the wall a portrait of our national hero and began slashing it savagely with a knife.

My brother was sitting stupidly on the couch. He was trying to drink like José. Why were we confused by the war? Was there nothing we could do? I realized that we had been but little boys when we had left the Philippines, and what childhood memories we cherished were enhanced by the frustration and bitterness of our life in America.

I felt deeply sad that my brother Luciano was dead. He was a good soldier: he could have fought in defense of his country. But where was my brother Leon? He should know about war because he had fought in Europe. I had not heard from him since he had left our village. My father was also a soldier—but he, too, was dead. And my mother! What would happen to her and my two sisters? Suddenly I felt an acute remorse. Why hadn't I written to them when there was plenty of time?

I drank and remembered other years. When evening came more friends dropped in at Joe's apartment, and we talked excitedly, remembered childhood names, got drunk, and shouted angry words at each other without provocation. The war rekindled our loneliness with a queer poignancy.

I left first, wanting fresh air. They followed me, falling on the hedges along the dark passageway and rolling down the cement pavement. Macario and José were holding each other, singing the *Internationale* and weeping like two children. Around the next block, on Temple Street, a Mexican night club was in full swing. I followed my companions down the dark stairway and we spread out in the cocktail room.

A semi-nude girl entertainer was singing *White Christmas*, but she stopped suddenly and crumpled to the floor. Another entertainer appeared from somewhere, straightened up the microphone and began dancing, peeling off her scanty garments one after the other until she leaped into the middle of the dance floor completely nude. The drunken men screamed, throwing coins, hats and shoes at her. Then a man extricated himself from the crowd and, staggering toward her, grabbed her in his arms and swung her about in drunken ecstasy.

I saw it too late. Three men sprang from their tables and jumped on the man holding the entertainer. There was an uproar, men pushing chairs and tables, women running and screaming. I grabbed José and pulled him beneath the table. I saw my brother struggling toward the stairway. He ducked under a table and crept slowly to the door. I saw him climbing up the cement steps like a baby too weak to use his legs. He was swallowed by the darkness in the street.

I heard sirens screaming, coming toward the place; then, when I was about to run to the door, I saw a special police patrol rush into the bar. The disorder was stopped immediately. Tables and chairs were smashed. But the bottles were untouched. The manager came forward and explained to the peace officers that he would not press charges against anyone.

I left, beckoning to José to follow me to the restaurant across the street. My brother Amado, who had disappeared a year before, was sitting at a table with Conrado Torres. I did not know that Conrado was in town either, because he had returned to Seattle when Mary had left our apartment.

"The delegates arrived today," José said to me.

"What delegates?" I asked.

"Don't you remember our conversation in Monterey?" José said.

I sat on a stool, remembering. Then it came to me: I had suggested to José a conference of labor and social leaders in Los Angeles. Inspired by my educational experiment among the agricultural workers, I had considered the possibility of co-ordinating our work and of creating a flexible educational system for Filipino laborers in California.

"Where are the others, Conrado?" I asked.

"They are all damned," he said.

Amado reached for his necktie. "Don't talk like that in front of a gentleman!" he shouted, shaking Conrado vigorously.

"Who is a gentleman in this stinking whorehouse?" Conrado asked, slapping away Amado's hand.

They punched each other in the face. They got up and pulled themselves into a narrow corner. The men moved away. Conrado grabbed my brother around the neck, but Amado wound his leg around Conrado, and they crashed to the floor. Suddenly two girls came in and sat at a table. Conrado and Amado looked up tentatively, stopped punching each other, jumped to their feet and joined the girls.

"Beer!" Conrado shouted.

"You are cute," one of the girls said.

My brother started laughing with the other girl. I was angry. I hated all of them, and I despised their weaknesses. I could not understand what was happening to them. Was the war breaking them? I wanted to run away from them. I looked at José sadly and left the restaurant.

"Please, God, make me strong," I said to myself.

But the confusion that created havoc in the lives of my friends lasted only a few days. We rushed to the recruiting offices when they were opened, and volunteered for service. We were refused, since we were classified as aliens in the National Selective Service Act. Our fight to become naturalized American citizens some years before, which had been opposed by the officials of the Philippine government in Washington, now became important and significant. I felt a personal bitterness toward a past Philippine Commissioner to the United States, whose arrogance when I had presented the subject of citizenship to him revealed his incompetence and opportunism, for he later readily collaborated with the Japanese enemy during the occupation.

When Binalonan was crushed by a special tank detachment that rushed from Tayug toward Manila, I went to the nearest recruiting office. As I stood in line waiting for my turn, I thought of a one-legged American Revolutionary patriot of whom I had read. But Filipinos were not being accepted. I ran to José's room and told him to contact the remnants of the delegates.

The meeting was successful; a resolution was sent to Washington asking for the inclusion of Filipinos in the armed forces of the United States. Copies of the resolutions were sent to all

Filipino organizations for endorsement; members of the delegation returned to their communities and campaigned. For once we were all working together; even those who had opposed our fight for citizenship were now wholeheartedly co-operating.

I was waiting for this very moment; it was a signal of triumph. But it took a war and a great calamity in our country to bring us together. President Roosevelt signed a special proclamation giving Filipinos the right to join the armed forces of the United States. Filipino regiments were formed in the United States; similar units were also formed in Hawaii.

CHAPTER XLVIII

A WEEK after the fall of Bataan a letter came from a small publisher. He wanted to publish an edition of my poems. Was it possible that I would have a book at last? Not quite sure if it was time for me to assemble my poems, I arranged and revised them in restaurants at night. I had stopped working because my right hand, the one smashed by the police patrol in Klamath Falls, was rapidly becoming paralyzed. I wrapped my hand tightly with a towel and wrote slowly, painfully, until the cold outside air came into the restaurant and stopped me.

When the manuscript was finished, I sent it to the publisher. I began another assignment, a small anthology of contemporary Philippine poetry. My anxiety about my relatives in the Philippines dampened the excitement I would have felt at this notice of my literary work. Here was something I had been working for with great sacrifice, but the war had come to frustrate all feelings of fulfillment.

When the bound copies of my first book of poems, *Letter From America*, arrived, I felt like shouting to the world. How long ago had it been that I had drunk a bottle of wine because I had discovered that I could write English?

The book was a rush job and the binding was simple, but it was something that had grown out of my heart. I knew that I would not write the same way again. I had put certain things of myself in it: the days of pain and anguish, of starvation and fear; my hopes, desires, aspirations. All of myself in this little volume of poems—and I would never be like that self again.

I put a copy of the book under my coat to keep it from the rain that had begun to fall, and went to Amado's hotel. I hoped I would be able to thaw his anger, for ever since I had struck his face, I had been feeling a deep emptiness. But Amado was not in. I went to several places. I could not find him. I walked silently in the rain.

I had written a book, but I had no one to share my happiness. The aching emptiness of our life in America came to me, and I was angry and sad and tragic. I was deep in memories. I could not feel the heavy rain any more. I walked to Temple Street slowly, scarcely knowing that my steps were moving in that direction. There I had always found companions. There on that narrowing island of despair was a ready crowd that I could reject or accept.

My brother Amado was drinking beer with two girls. I went up to him, touched his hand and opened my mouth to speak, but I could say nothing. The girls looked up and offered me a glass. I sat with them, feeling the sharp corner of my book rubbing against my chest. I wanted to show it to my brother, but his silence came between us. Then one of the girls, thinking perhaps that I had a bottle of whisky under my coat, pulled at my arm. When she saw that it was only a book, her joyous anticipation vanished.

"It's a damned book," she said.

"Yes, it's my book," I said.

"Ha-*ha!*" she laughed. "Poetry!" She began tearing out the pages and throwing them at my face.

"Don't do that, please!" I said, rising to take the book away from her.

It was like tearing my heart apart. Amado suddenly grabbed the book from her and gave it to me. Then he got up and started beating her with his fists, cursing her.

"Let my brother alone!" He struck her again. "Let him keep his poetry, you goddamned whore!"

The girl fell on the floor. The other girl looked dully at her. I picked her up and gave her a glass of beer. She looked at me and began crying brokenly.

"I just felt bad, that's all," she said. "I just felt bad. If you stay on in this lousy street you'll be ruined. See what happened to me? I wanted to be an actress. I came from a nice family, a nice family in Baltimore. . . ."

I put the remnants of the book under my coat and walked to the door. Amado got up to say something, but stopped and looked down in defeat. I thought his unforgettable left hand would be raised as in other times, in Mangusmana, Lompoc, and Bakersfield—but he filled a glass and gulped down the beer, closing his eyes. I saw only the long scar that wound to his wrist.

A few days later, Amado came to my room with all his belongings.

"I'm joining the navy, Carlos," he said.

"You are too sick to go," I protested.

"There is always the transport service," he said.

I took him to breakfast. Then we went to the station and waited for his train. I kept remembering when he had run away from our village. I kept remembering his last words. Now this was another parting, and perhaps there would be no return. He kept twirling his large thumbs. I looked at his thumbs again: flat on the top like a spatula, hard and cracked with toil. I doubled my fists inside my pocket.

"I'm sorry that I was not able to help you," I whispered to myself.

"Did you say something, Carlos?" he said suddenly.

"I think your train is ready," I said.

He got up and took my hand. He put something in it and ran to his bus. It was a little envelope that contained twenty-five dollars and a note. He had written:

"I'm not as well-read as you are, but I know that a little volume of poetry can give something to the world. I could have striven to raise myself as you have done, but I came upon a crowd of men that destroyed all those possibilities. However, I'm glad that I remained what I am, because it will give you the chance to see your own brother in darkness; in fact, it will give you another chance to look at yourself when you were like me. My lostness in America will give you a reason to work harder for your ideals, because they are my ideals too.

"I did not have a rich and easy life, but it was my own. I would like to live it over again. I'm sorry that there are people who hate and destroy in our time. I'm sorry that they kill. There is so much to do—if not for each other, for the world. I know this is not the last good-bye. But if I'll not come back, I know that you will make me live again in your words.

"I'm sorry that I can't understand all that you are doing in America. But I'm sure that it's for the good of us all. You are my brother, and that is why I know. Good-bye till we meet again, Carlos. . . ."

At last in this war that had come upon us, we had found a release for our desires. One by one my friends left for the armed forces. When Amado had gone, Macario stopped working and walked the streets aimlessly for weeks, then joined the army the day Corregidor fell to the Japanese. We sat in his room the day he enlisted, remembering the Philippines. I reminded him of the time when he had read primers at the side of my sickbed, and he laughed when he recalled the story of *Robinson Crusoe*.

"The world is an island," he said again, remembering. "We are cast upon the sea of life hoping to land somewhere in the world. *But there is only one island, and it is in the heart.*"

I felt again the same seriousness that I had seen in him years ago, when he and Felix and Nick had been trying to revive the publication of a little magazine. I was shy; even now that I had amassed a fair English vocabulary, I was still held down by the old awe and respect for my brother.

I reminded him of the time when he was still a student in Lingayen and had come home for a visit. There was nothing to eat, so in the darkness of night we had gathered snails in the mud under the house.

"We were poor," he said.

We walked to the station and waited for his bus.

"Keep all my books intact because I'd like to come back," he said. "I'm not going on a worldwide crusade to save democracy. I don't want to talk about going away. I'm just doing my job, but however small it is, I'll try to do my best. I think this is really the meaning of life: the extension of little things into the future so that they might be useful to other people."

I kept remembering the past. He was the last to go away from me, while I was the last to go away from our family.

"Don't fail to tell Nick to follow me soon," he continued. "And say good-bye for me." He got up suddenly and took my hand, pressing it affectionately. I could feel the roughness of his toilworn hand; the toughness of his palm revealed more of himself than his words. I was ashamed of my little soft hand in his. Then, as though he remembered something of great importance, he gave me ten cents. "Don't forget to give this to the Negro bootblack across from my hotel," he said. "I forgot to pay him today."

He ran to the bus and climbed in quickly. I saw his face smiling in the window, before the bus drove away.

I knew it was the end of our lives in America. I knew it was the end of our family. If I met him again, I would not be the same. He would not be the same, either. Our world was this one, but a new one was being born. We belonged to the old world of confusion; but in this other world—new, bright, promising— we would be unable to meet its demands.

I walked toward my hotel. In my room, standing against the mirror, Macario had left a large envelope. I found two hundred dollars in it, a Social Security card, and a photograph of himself. I hurried to his hotel and packed his books. Then I went to the Negro bootblack across the street.

"Is your name Larkin?" I asked.

"Yes, that's my name," he said.

"My brother owes you ten cents for a shoeshine," I explained. "He asked me to give it to you. He went to the army this morning."

He took the ten cents and looked at me.

"Would you like to have a glass of beer with me?" he said.

"All right." I had felt a ring of sincerity in his voice. "There is a small place down the block."

He bought a glass of draught beer with the ten cents. He offered it to me when he had drunk half of it. I took the glass and drank the rest of the beer.

"Well, I think I'm going now," he said, giving me his hand. His hand, too, was like my brother's—tough, large, toil-scarred. "I'm joining the navy tomorrow, so I guess this is good-bye. I know I'll meet your brother again somewhere, because I got my dime without asking him. But if I don't see him again, I'll remember him every time I see the face of an American dime. Good-bye, friend!"

I watched him go down the block. He stopped in a corner and looked around slowly and then skyward, as though he were committing it all to memory. He raised his hand and disappeared. I walked to my hotel filled with great loneliness.

CHAPTER XLIX

THE NEXT morning I put my brother Macario's money in the bank, in his name, and went to the bus station. I wanted to catch the last crew of cannery workers in Portland.

I looked out of the bus window. I wanted to shout good-bye to the Filipino pea pickers in the fields who stopped working when the bus came into view. How many times in the past had I done just that? They looked toward the highway and raised their hands. One of them, who looked like my brother Amado, took off his hat. The wind played in his hair. There was a sweet fragrance in the air.

Then I heard bells ringing from the hills—like the bells that had tolled in the church tower when I had left Binalonan. I glanced out of the window again to look at the broad land I had dreamed so much about, only to discover with astonishment that the American earth was like a huge heart unfolding warmly to receive me. I felt it spreading through my being, warming me with its glowing reality. It came to me that no man—no one at all—could destroy my faith in America again. It was something that had grown out of my defeats and successes, something shaped by my struggles for a place in this vast land, digging my hands into the rich soil here and there, catching a freight to the north and to the south, seeking free meals in dingy gambling houses, reading a book that opened up worlds of heroic thoughts. It was something that grew out of the sacrifices and loneliness of my friends, of my brothers in America and my family in the Philippines—something that grew out of our desire to know America, and to become a part of her great tradition, and to contribute something toward her final fulfillment. I knew that no man could destroy my faith in America that had sprung from all our hopes and aspirations, *ever*.

CLASSICS OF ASIAN AMERICAN LITERATURE

America Is in the Heart: A Personal History, by Carlos Bulosan,
with a new introduction by Marilyn C. Alquizola and
Lane Ryo Hirabayashi

No-No Boy: A Novel, by John Okada,
with a new foreword by Ruth Ozeki

Citizen 13660, drawings and text by Miné Okubo,
with a new introduction by Christine Hong

Nisei Daughter, by Monica Sone,
with a new introduction by Marie Rose Wong